Broken Council

Book 10 of the System Apocalypse

By

Tao Wong

License Notes

Broken Council

A Starlit Publishing Book
Published by Starlit Publishing
69 Teslin Rd
Whitehorse, YT
Y1A 3M5
Canada

www.starlitpublishing.com

Ebook ISBN: 9781989994450
Print ISBN: 9781989994467
Hardcover ISBN: 9781989994474

Contents

Books in the

System Apocalypse Universe

Main Storyline

Life in the North

Redeemer of the Dead

The Cost of Survival

Cities in Chains

Coast on Fire

World Unbound

Stars Awoken

Rebel Star

Stars Asunder

Broken Council

The Forbidden Zone

System Finale

Anthologies

System Apocalypse Short Story Anthology Volume 1

Comic Series

The System Apocalypse Comics

What Has Gone Before

John Lee has come a long way from his mountain campsite in the Yukon when the System first initiated on Earth. He's helped stabilize Earth's politics, travelled across the galaxy and, in his latest adventure, helped the Erethran Empire choose its next Empress.

Along the way, he's continued his search for an answer to the first Quest he ever received – What is the System.

At the end of his recent adventure, he achieved a new height of power, a Heroic Class. Except, unknown to most, is the fact that his Heroic Class shown to all – Grand Paladin – is but a ruse, a lie for what he truly gained. For John found a Hidden Class, that of a Junior Administrator of the System.

It's a secret with dire implications and those who would keep it hidden have already acted, attacking Earth's embassy on Irvina, the capital of the Galaxy.

Chapter 1

The Portal opens five hundred sixty meters in the air. When I step through it, I free-fall. Beneath me, the herd of L'liest CaTues cover the ground like the bison herds of yore, their mottled brown and green skin hiding the trampled earth beneath.

The L'liest are six-legged scaled behemoths whose bellows reach me high above, as does the never-ceasing pounding of their feet. They're tiny figures to my eyes, belying their actual size tens of meters tall and half as wide. Spirals of razor-sharp spikes, dripping with poison, jut from their bodies in a vicious pattern. From their six-eyed, conical faces, roars of dissatisfaction and grunts of anger erupt in rhythmic regularity as they search for prey.

In the distance, the earth shakes and rocks dance on cracked, sun-baked pale-yellow clay. The desolate vista is broken by the occasional glimpse of purple cacti. Around me, as I plummet, the sky is lit with the pale-yellow light of the dying sun, a massive thing in the last couple of million years of its life.

A surge of will and I call forth their Status information.

L'liest CaTues (Level 187)
HP: 18,736/18752*
MP: 2457/2457
Conditions: Hardened Skin, Scaled Protection, Poisonous Fog, Acoustic Beat, Power of the Herd*

* Health is shared among all members of the herd, as is damage.

Beside me, as I fall, Ali hovers, cross-legged. My tiny, six-inch-tall Spirit companion is clad in his usual orange jumpsuit. Skin the color of tanned wood, with a sculpted goatee, his fingers play across invisible screens as we plummet.

"You know, I'm sure you've done dumber things in the past. But I am forgetting them…"

"It's the pressure. I've done a lot dumber things," I reassure Ali. Even as I speak, I've split my attention enough to begin the process of calling forth my Skills. I start with the simple ones.

Soul Shield for protection.

A Thousand Blades to give me access to copies of my Soulbound sword.

Aura of Chivalry for the damage bonus and intimidation effect.

Eye of the Storm to concentrate their focus on me.

The Evolved Penetration Skill to give me a secondary shield defense.

Then I kick on my Hoverboots and float. The creatures below are trumpeting their disatisfaction, my Soul Shield shimmering as their audio attacks slam into it. I'm not in my Hod right now, the power armor stored away. Replacing it would be expensive, and between my evolved Penetration Skill shielding and Soul Shield, I should be safe enough.

Lastly, to add shielding points to my Penetration Skill, I call forth a Beacon of the Angels. The ritual glyph forms in the air, a circular oval of light showering the herd with pure, unadulterated energy.

L'liest CaTueses crisp beneath the azure glow of formed energy, scales cracking, poison mists burning away. They thrash and scream as a damage counter in the corner of my vision ticks up.

Beacon of the Angels is an area effect Skill, a near-perfect Skill for dealing with the horde. Near perfect since the radius of damage is insufficient as portions of the damage dealt are split between the entirety of the herd. Those caught outside see a small blip down, tens of hit points before their natural regeneration pops them back up.

Individual L'liest caught within the attack take more damage as only a portion of the damage is transferred. But their resistances, their Levels are high enough that I'd have to keep spamming the Skill to take out a single L'liest.

All this takes place in fractions of a second.

I hover, watching the effects of my attack—or the lack of them—and end up shaking my head. There's a reason the L'liest have managed to survive this long and overrun an entire planet. Built up to this level, Power of the Herd is an insane Skill to overcome. You either have to get a whole army hammering at them in multiple assault locations to drive down the hit points of the entire herd or…

Well.

Me.

But for now, I take my time. Spell buffs are cast, just the basics. Health and Mana Regeneration, some physical damage resistance. An Elemental damage spell boost to add a little punch. And that's about it.

There are other buffs that might work and wouldn't directly conflict with the buffs I already have. I could even have asked for them from the fleet hanging around in space above. But then I'd have to share the XP. And it wouldn't be a proper test of what I can do alone.

So.

Me, by myself, to start. Until I tear down enough of the monster herd's health that it makes sense for the fleet to get involved. I watch the living carpet of scales and furious six-legged monsters, a writhing, heaving mass of anger, and find myself grinning.

There were other options. Other ways of doing this.

Considering everything over the last few months, everything that happened since Katherine's call, letting loose feels right. That I gain the support of the Erethran Empire as a by-product is a nice bonus.

"You know, cackling madly to yourself isn't normally considered normal, boy-o," Ali says.

"Bite me."

To punctuate my point, I raise my hand and call forth the first of my untested Skills.

Immovable Object / Unstoppable Force (Level 1)

A Paladin cannot be stopped. A Paladin cannot be moved. A Paladin is a force of the Erethran Empire on the battlefield. This Skill exemplifies this simple concept. Let all who doubt the strength of the Paladin tremble!

Use: User must select to be an Immovable Object or Unstoppable Force. Effect varies depending on choice. Skill combines with Aura of Chivalry to provide a smaller (10% of base effect) bonus to all friendlies within range.

Effect 1 (Immovable Object): Constitution, Health, and Damage Resistance (All) increased by 200% of User's current total. All knockback effects are mitigated (including environmental knockback effects).

Effect 2 (Unstoppable Force): Agility, Movement Speed, Momentum, and Damage Calculations based off Momentum increased by 200% of User's current total. Damage from other attacks increased by 100%. Only active while user is moving.

Cost: 5MP/s

I only put a single point in this because I wanted to reach Domain. I'd even gone so far as to spend my Credits—okay, the Empire's Credits—to get this Skill level.

Now, I'm curious how it would affect things. A surge of energy sent a simple Firestorm spell down into the midst of the monsters, in the same area where I'd launched my initial attack.

"So?" I ask Ali. I'd rather do that than run the math myself.

"Nowhere near enough."

"I was hoping for a little more detail," I mutter.

"Really? You really want to know the math? Fine. The L'liest have a base fire resistance of 287% with their Power of the Herd Skill boosting that by another 63%. However, you've got a 90% Penetration Skill, allowing you to disregard all but 46.781% of that damage resistance. Now, your Firestorm does approximately a thousand points of base damage, which means you are dealing on average 532.19 points of fire damage," Ali lectures me. "But that's if you land a head-on strike, which excludes mitigating maneuvers, dodges, et cetera.

"Which, luckily for us, the L'liest are too dumb to do. So, 532.19 points of fire damage is applied to their hit points, which is doubled by Unstoppable Force. However, you have to include critical damage strikes to those that didn't blink, minus those that did, add in the base regeneration levels they all have, take away crowding effects—"

"Enough, I get it," I say, waving. "We're doing around a thousand plus points of damage to the L'liest or so, but they've got eighteen thousand points just base. And that's not including them shaving off a chunk for the rest of the herd."

"Exactly," Ali says. "You aren't doing enough."

"That figures," I say.

It's one of the reasons why I bought the damn Skill direct from the System. It's not good enough for a lone fighter like me. If combined with the Aura Skill in the front of an army, that ten percent boost would be amazing. Split across thousands, and if those thousands were elites?

Either way, not my problem. I call forth the next Skill. It forms around me, seeming to twist the atmosphere by its very presence. I feel the Mana around me warp, change as my Skill takes it in-hand and make reality bend to its will. Immediately, I feel the Domain Skill working on me.

Domain (Level 1)

With chains that bind, and threads that extend from one to another, a Paladin is the center of events. In his Domain, enemies will break and allies will bend knee. Let the enemies of the Empire tremble before a Paladin with his Domain.

Effect 1: All enemy combatants receive -10% attribute decreases, a +10% increase in Mana cost, and lose 25 HP per second while within range of the Domain.

Effect 2: All allies receive a +10% increase in health regeneration, a 10% increase in attribues, and a reduction of -10% in Mana cost (semi-stackable) while within range of the Domain.

Range: 10 Meters

Cost: 500 Mana + 5 Mana per Second

One of the biggest aspects of Domain is its significantly lower upkeep cost. For example, my Eye of the Storm costs me a ridiculous 20 Mana per second, which leaves me using it only occasionally to draw attention and keep the focus of enemies on me for a short period. As a taunt Skill, it's incredibly wasteful, other than its ability to affect multiple individuals at a time. Then again, it costs so much because it is a taunt Skill, since direct affect Skills on emotional and mental states are more expensive than physical effect Skills.

Whereas Domain, I could theoretically keep running constantly. Its upkeep is low enough that my natural regeneration leaves me able to keep it active, though obviously, I have fewer options if I do so.

Unfortunately, its range is pretty short, and it doesn't stack damage effects. While it increases my base attributes, it doesn't increase my Mana regeneration at all.

"All right, let's try this again anyway," I mutter.

Another Beacon of the Angels hammers the angry herd below. Ali watches the damage logs while I wait for my Mana to regenerate. I idly throw a Firestorm too when Ali bitches about messing with test results.

Now, you might be thinking, that's great and all, but why isn't the giant fleet in orbit showering kinetic weapons and beam attacks down onto the herd below? My Beacon of the Angels is pretty powerful, but it's hard to compete with orbit-launched kinetic weaponry. Even with the penalties that the System places upon pure tech, there's still something to be said about a gravity-drawn half-ton of mass.

There are a few reasons, as always. There's the issue of lost XP. Launching orbital bombardments on monsters is damn safe, so it means that the System reduces the XP gain quite a lot. In a world where everyone wants more experience to go up in Levels, no one wants to waste it.

But more importantly, the System doesn't let it happen. Oh, you can still drop giant rocks, and if you've got the Skills, you can do damage. But the farther away you are from entering a planet's boundary, the greater the mass of Mana you have to push through. The greater the amount of Mana— and Mana generally is denser the closer you get to the surface—the greater the damage reduction.

Again, tossing planet killers or other orbital strikes around is still possible, but the cost and time taken in many cases is incredibly high.

As importantly, you need to have backup options—individuals on the ground to deal with the sudden increase in spawning as the attacks and subsequent deaths release a bunch of unruly System Mana. Without sapients on the ground to soak up the Mana, you have a different problem—unchecked Mana mutations. And those mutations often result in some truly scary monsters—the kind that can fire back at orbiting spaceships.

It wasn't always like this. At one point, it was possible to unleash a ton of nukes and kinetic strikes and then mop up a little. But thousands of years ago, so far back that most people don't even realize it, that changed. It was one of the first major changes in the way the System worked.

M: …this change in damage done via technology makes no sense. The Council should not be choosing to do this, not when we need to keep our planets from being overrun.

J: Agreed. This can't be the Council's doing.

K: Then who? The Council controls the System.

M: I think that's why we have the System Quest. To find out who controls the System, really.

J: I disagree. If it meant that, it should have said so. Not ask what the System and Mana itself is.

…

The memory from the library surfaces, detailed correspondence from a time so long ago, humanity was still beating each other with sticks and huddling around a fire. It sweeps me away for a second before I wrestle the memory under control.

I'm getting better at controlling the uncontrolled release of information into my brain. The Corrupt Questor's library, the entire damn repository of their knowledge squeezed into my brain and then encrypted. The encryption has been breaking down, and with it, additional secrets are coming to the fore.

"Are you done yet? Some of us are getting impatient here," Bolo's voice cackles over the communicator.

I grunt, almost imagining the seven-foot-tall alien with his ram-horns glowering at my image. "Soon. Hold your… dragons."

"Why would I hold my dragons? Do you think we do not take good care of them?" Bolo growls. "That's a lie! Any dragon the Knights take control of are well cared for. Who told you—"

I kill the communicator, focusing on my next Skill. This is the big one from the Master Class that I wanted to try. It's a pity I failed to Evolve it, but that's the risk you run.

Judgment of All (Level 6)

An Emperor might sit in judgment of those who defy them, but a Paladin sits in judgment of all who fall before his gaze. Desire bends and debases itself. Duty shatters under the weight of ever-greater burdens. Morality shifts under the winds of circumstance. In the eyes of those he serves, a Paladin's judgment must be impeccable. Under his gaze, those underserving will fall. So long as his honor holds true, judgment will follow.

Effect: Skill inflicts (Erethran Reputation*$HonSysCal*1.5 = 442) points of on-going Mana damage to all judged unworthy within perception range of user.

Duration: 65 seconds

Cost: 1000 MP

I've never used the Skill before, but this seems to be the perfect place to try. I tap the portion of my mind that hosts the Skill, that slotted bundle of calculations that the System has imparted to me. I reach within, feeling the connection to the System, the portion it has dedicated to me and this Skill.

I trigger it, feeling Mana gush through my body, into the System to set the system running as Judgment of All activates. The world twists and bucks, turning grey and black, figures beneath me, above me, through my communicator and through the very threads that bind me to others activating.

And I know, with just a gentle push, I could make the Skill affect them all. Anyone I perceive, that I can sense, I can injure with this Skill. No matter the range, no matter the distance. I could kill with naught but a thought.

The people who are after my friends, the Council, the bounty hunters and the fighters who have attacked us, the merchants and petty criminals who cheated us. The fools in their corporations and Guilds who blocked us. I could kill them all just by letting the System know they are unworthy. Kill them with an activation of the Skill.

And a twist of the System.

I shut down that line of thought.

Hard.

I let the Skill run as it is meant to. Taking my physical senses, my hearing, my sight, the targets that the System and Ali have marked within range of me. And it shoves power down through the very same connection the System has formed with each of them.

Weaponizing itself.

For those without my Skill, without my Class, the show is just as spectacular. I glow as I float high above, like a wrathful god come down to lay his petty grievances upon the unworthy. All caught within the effect find themselves irradiated, glowing from within and without.

Skin, scale, and flesh crack, light spilling out from within. System-regeneration wars with the damage the Skill provides. L'liest burn from within, and even the herd's Skill can't shunt the damage aside fast enough. Hundreds of monsters fall, bellowing as they die. Experience notifications roll in without end, and I ignore them all.

Deep within, I stare as the System itself strains to deal with all the deaths. Mana, released from the dead monsters, gushes into the atmosphere. Some—a small portion—slides into the System itself, disappearing to places I cannot follow.

The rest escapes into the world while the System struggles to calculate and divvy damage, life and death, to all those within range. The planet itself bends and twists as the System struggles, released Mana searching for a place to deposit itself.

Some finds its target in me as experience, though the way it enters me and boosts me feels... different. Other streams of Mana find creatures too small for me to have noticed before. Forcing mutations, forcing growth. Cacti twist and expand, insects balloon in size, and leylines draw the rest away to dungeons throughout the planet.

In the corner of my mind, I note friends and allies curse and exclaim. A Paladin's ultimate combat Skill is something that has not been seen in hundreds of years. And though the Erethrans might not hold me in the highest regard, I still hold some place in their culture, in their litany of legends.

And I've yet to call forth the best Skills.

***

It takes a while for the L'liest herd to resume their journey. Even as I fly to the nearest unharmed portion, the herd is disquieted, concerned by the first attack that has managed to harm them in decades. I've killed a noticeable percentage of the L'liest and they are wary now, in the way prey are when they know they're being hunted. But they have to move or be crushed by those behind, so they eventually resume their never-ending journey away from the dungeon that first created them.

Beneath my feet, Ali flickers from point to point, his form split into multiple tiny copies. He scoops up the loot, dumping it in my storage, shunting it via Portals into a pile when we run out of space. His latest trick is amusing and potentially useful.

Even if he's only used it to spy on sapients while they're showering thus far.

"Are all final Master Class Skills that powerful?" Mikito asks over the comms, sounding intrigued rather than scared like many who shouted in my ear before. The Advanced Samurai is my most loyal supporter, though I doubt she understands the full extent of what happened. Hell, I don't either. That sudden surge of megalomania... now that I'm not riding the high, I'm certain it's not as easy as I thought to abuse my Skill. "Or is that just..."

"The Paladins'?" I shrug. "In a way. This is based off Reputation in the Empire. Before I came here, if I had picked this up, it would have done maybe a couple hundred points. Now..."

"Now, it's an army killer," Bolo rumbles. "Yes. The Lords of the Flight have a similar Skill. Beast Lords do too, though some draw from the power of their pack. A double-edged Skill." I hear a pounding sound, and I imagine Bolo thumping himself in the Chest. "A true Dragon Lord does not require such base Skills. Strength comes from within the individual."

"What he means is that Dragon Lords are geared toward individual strength rather than army-destroying Skills," Brerdain says. The Chief of Staff for the Erethran Navy is with us, a courtesy addition to keep us out of trouble. Well, that and run the fleet we've brought along. I imagine the portly Admiral sneering at Bolo when he isn't looking.

"Then my Master Class Skill…" Mikito says.

"Probably closer to Bolo's than mine." Then I frown, remembering aspects of her Skill. "Though I don't know. The Samurai Skillset is…"

"Different. A servant-Class based off their lord's potential, rather than their own," Harry says. The smooth, dulcet tones of the British War Reporter's voice slides into the conversation. "Not unique, but uncommon for sure. Few care to tie themselves in so tightly. Potentially extremely powerful, but like yours, also circumstantial."

"Bah. Let me down and I shall show you true strength!" Bolo says. I imagine him drumming his fingers on his hammer, though I doubt he's taken it out on the bridge they've been watching me from. That would be too rude, even for him.

"Calm yourself, Dragon Lord. The Paladin desires to test his Skills," Brerdain says.

"I would like some experience too," Mikito says.

"Crazy combat monkeys," Harry mutters.

Bolo growls. "We cannot gain experience by standing around recording the Paladin's actions, unlike some."

"Maybe, but I know patience."

"Patience! I have shown much patience, all these weeks!"

"Enough, you two," I say. I'm over another large herd. Big enough, among the rolling hills that look like tiny bumps beneath my feet, for the following Skill to work. More than sufficient. "One more only."

Two. But they don't need to know the second. In fact, they're better off not knowing the second. At least for now.

"Last Skill. Grand Cross," I announce.

I reach within, touching the bundle of information, and let it flow. Only a single point… but the effects are as spectacular as my Judgment of All.

***

The crater that lies before me is impressive in a truly disturbing way. I'd let the Skill expand to its maximum limit, though I know I could also compress it so that it becomes a single-person attack too. One of the advantages of a Heroic Class Skill is that it's a lot more flexible by design.

The crater is tens of kilometers wide and at least a couple of kilometers deep. The earth is compressed, minor hills flattened as though a titan had pushed a seal upon the earth and all those beneath it. Once again, another rush of experience. Again, that feeling of wrongness, of unsettlement as that experience resides… somewhere. Somewhere wrong.

Beneath me, dead L'liest and a scorched earth. Around me, Portals open, landing craft screaming down to the ground as Erethran soldiers deploy, feet touching upon the new planet, the first sapients in decades since its abandonment.

They pour out, weapons out, taking position and setting up moving shield walls. Specialized ships land and transform, artillery ships transforming as they hide behind the shield generators, already receiving instructions from orbital spotters. Mana flows as specialized buffing units throw out spells, catching me as an afterthought while the Erethran army gets to work.

In another corner of the planet, I sense my friends stepping onto the planet. Party chat flickers to life, connections firming, and then fade as they stride into the bowels of hell itself to suppress the former capital city's dungeon. The source of all the trouble.

I consider joining them. Briefly.

But I can offer them just as much, if not better, aid out here. I get moving, taking the fight to the L'liest CaTues herd. With troops on the ground, I drop everything but my shields and utilize Judgment of All again and again. Ali's confirmed it's the most Mana efficient Skill, at least against the L'liest.

I get to work, and if I'm paying attention to something else, to a Skill that has been humming along in the background, one that almost begs me to make use of it. No one but Ali and myself need know.

Or should.

After all, its very existence and my hidden Class pit us against the Galactic Council itself.

System Edit

A core Skill for System Administrators.

Effect: Make trivial to minor amendments to System processes

Cost: Variable (HP & MP)

Chapter 2

Clean up of the planet Gurrant took just under an Earth week. Of course, that worked out to about eleven days with the faster rotation on Gurrant and a tiny fraction of its year. The L'liest herd had grown unchecked for over a decade, spreading across the super-continent that made up the overly dry landmass of the planet.

"We could have beaten the Dungeon," Bolo says, arms crossed as he glares at me. The seven-foot-tall, ripped Dragon Lord is complaining—again—as we stand around the remnants of the dungeon entrance. Over his shoulder is the over-sized hammer he uses, the emerald scalemail glinting in the light with every breath.

All around us, drones and Erethran army personnel work to clear out the remains of the monsters. It's rather intimidating, when you think about it, how much has been destroyed. One of the first things to land was the Quartermaster Station, which has an abbreviated System Shop that allows people to funnel in entire corpses to be sold off.

At the same time, a growing manufactured city has sprung up, where automated factories and Artisan butchers and leatherworkers are tearing apart the L'liest. They extract scales, organs, meat, and bones with gusto. Everything is being used, with even the most damaged parts being stored for composting. It's a massive undertaking, but it all goes off without a major hitch.

System communications, extremely organized personnel, and Classes help provide a level of efficiency that no pre-System human army could ever hope to achieve. Not that I'd ever expected to see an abattoir on a battlefield.

"I'm sure you could have," I say, "but hogging all the experience was getting a little much."

"Hogging?" Bolo frowns, cocking his head to the side. "There were no pigs involved."

"Seriously. Buy a new English pack." I can't help but shake my head, always amused when the cultural assimilation portion breaks down. I'm not exactly sure who Bolo downloaded, but there are very strange gaps in his understanding at times.

"Or you could speak Galactic, and stop being rude to our hosts," Bolo says with a finality that makes it sound as if he's won this fight.

Ali chuckles as he continues to multitask, paying attention to what is being taken apart by the army and making sure we're getting our share of the earnings while also watching a Monty Python sketch.

"There's no one else here, not even Mikito," I point out.

That's true enough, since the Samurai was teleported off for another arena battle. This time she has acquired a sponsor, someone willing to pay for the expensive teleportations to ensure she is included in a number of such fights around the galaxy. Truth be told, she probably could have taken part in a lot more battles if it wasn't for the fact that she spends most of her time hanging out with me.

A galaxy is a big place, and arena fights are extremely common. In fact, Mikito's collected a wide array of championship Titles. The fact that most of those Titles don't provide much of a boost to her is offset by the occasional one that does. Add the fact that Titles can conflict—and might not stack— and chasing after them is a select and expensive sport.

Still, according to Mikito, with enough Titles, they could consolidate, providing her another boost to attributes, damage, and if she's really lucky, a Skill. Heck, some of the more famous championships have Titles that come with their own Skill.

"Maybe, but we're not on your backward planet at the moment. It's polite to use Galactic," Bolo says in Galactic.

I switch as well, sniffing then regretting doing so. The charnel house smell of thousands of dead animals has not disappeared, making me gag. "Doesn't really matter anyway. They needed to take out that dungeon to begin the settlement process for the capital. Without stabilizing the Mana flows, we'd never be able to retake this planet."

"True, though one wonders about the Dungeon Master. Must have been insane to focus the entirety of the capital's Mana overflows into a single dungeon, especially when the capital was as extensive as it was." Bolo shakes his head. "Even I know better than to do that."

I shrug. Whatever the Dungeon Master's sins or hubris, he has paid the final price. As did most of the population that didn't manage to find a method off planet. Luckily, in a System world, that is relatively easy, especially in a state of emergency. Bindings like serf contracts, System regulated teleportations, and the high cost of interplanetary ships are relaxed.

Of course, to some extent, that just shifts the emergency from the surface of the planet to near space. Hundreds of ships overloaded with sapient passengers launched to escape the L'liest. And then, many found themselves stranded, unable to reach the next habitable planet.

Finally, the Empire stepped in, scooping them up and throwing the vast majority of them into serf contracts to pay out the costs of the rescue. Still, between forced servitude for a number of years and certain death, most chose correctly. The few that hadn't, died.

For the most part.

A coral-eared man strides up to me, barely five feet tall, with blond hair and an angry look. He skips over dead corpses without a care, giving them as much regard as I do, too focused on his objective. Once he arrives, he plants his feet, tilting his head up as he stares at me in his rolled up, castoff Erethran Army uniform.

"I understand you're the one to thank for saving us," Ito Karan, the tiny man, says.

I'm not entirely sure how to react, so I nod. He's the self-selected leader of the survivors, many of whom made their way underground, finding places to hide from the L'liest in the far corners of the continent and beneath it.

They've existed below the surface of the planet in holdout rooms and small complexes. Occasionally they popped up long enough to make sure that nothing had changed before returning to their underground prisons. Total survivors are in the thousands, less than one percent of those who chose to stay. Most had not expected to be below ground for so long.

"What took you so long? We expected a rescue mission within months, not decades!" Ito Karan says.

"You'll have to ask someone else." I shrug. "I wasn't around for your initial disaster."

"But you're a Grand Paladin, correct?" Ito snaps at me.

"Yes."

"Then you're the one in charge. We expect compensation!"

I consider smacking him, I seriously do. This really has nothing to do with me, and I have other, better things to do. Greater worries occupy my mind. But a small part of me is curious to see what he wants. It's the same part that used to poke at open wounds, or that disturbed ant nests when I was younger. Curious to see what lay below the sand.

So I ask him.

"Credits to start. Enchanted weaponry and privileged access to the dungeons as they are created. In addition, because we've lost so many years, we will need trained guides to help us progress." Ito shows no hesitation as he rattles demands.

He keeps going, but I cut in. "You need my thirdborn son as well?"

"What?" Ito falters, apparently confused.

"All right, all right. You drive a hard bargain. My apprentice has my firstborn, so I can only give you my secondborn. I won't go any higher."

"I don't want your children. What kind of backward society do you come from that you think I want your children?"

Ito sees Ali literally rolling around in mid-air, holding his hands to his mouth as he stifles his laughter. Even Bolo is grinning. It takes Ito a second more to figure out what is going on.

I glance at Ali, who isn't even bothering to hide his laughter now. "It's all your fault, you know, you and your Korean dramas."

"Don't blame me, it was your culture."

"Chinese. I'm Chinese, not Korean. I told you that before. And I am a CBC. Canadian-born Chinese, so not really but sort of," I reply.

Ito's eyes bulge and he starts shouting, so I flash my aura. He cuts off with a strangled squawk.

"I don't really know who you think you are, but I don't really care," I say. "Order someone else about this."

"You—"

He shuts up when I conjure my sword. Something about a four-foot hunk of steel, sheathed in Mana, dissuades him. I point away from me in a random direction and he walks off. I guess having a bit of a reputation for being an insane, rage-filled monster has advantages at times.

"Well, that was fun?" I say and look around once more.

Hundreds of members of the Erethran armed forces scurry around, some in robotic movers, others physically hauling away the beasts. Others are making roads, marking down locations for buildings, and tossing nanite formers. And in the distance, a familiar figure.

As Brerdain makes his way over, the Chief of Staff glances in the direction of where Ito has walked off to with a frown.

"Did you have to make my work more difficult?" he complains to me, but I notice he's not making any moves to speak with Ito either.

"The Empress bargained for five planets cleared and cleansed," I say. "She never said a word about me being polite or dealing with idiots."

"Some Paladins might consider that part of the unsaid requirements."

"More pity to them," I say.

"You do know your attitude carries over to the Paladins you trained. And they are training even more Honor Guards," Brerdain says, his voice chilly. "Your attitude is—"

"Perfect. I know."

Brerdain fumes for a second before he points upward. "In two hours, we will be ready to depart for the next planet. Make sure you're ready."

"Aye aye, sir!" I salute lazily, making the Chief frown. I guess his cultural download package didn't include Earth military salutes. Erethran salutes are different.

"We will be ready, Honored Strategist," Bolo says, cutting off any further discussion. "We are truly grateful for this opportunity."

I snort. The Empire is gaining as much, if not more, with this expedition in retaking lost planets in the Restricted Zone, but I can understand Bolo buttering him up. Most Heroic—or Master Class—individuals would find it difficult to find empty, uncontested planets on which to conduct such an attack. Politics and prior claims mean that most Heroics have to tread carefully and not just blip in and do what they want.

On top of that, this planet is the easiest of the lot. Most overrun locations have a mixture of monsters, including flying and magic-wielding ones. Elemental attacks, flying monsters, and gravitic implosions all make just hovering above the monsters and killing them without any major risk a non-starter. And let's not forget the fact that it kills your experience gain.

Without aid from the navy, without the benefits of boots on the ground to help quell rogue dungeons, retaking planets would be a fool's errand. Even blasting apart the swarms of monsters for pure experience becomes an issue when you don't have places to rest, to recuperate when a battle goes bad.

Never mind the long, long list of enemies waiting for your usual Heroic to waste their Mana, to lower their guard for a second. It's why such purges are rarer than you'd think. At least, on a Galactic scale.

"If we only have a few hours..." Bolo falls silent, looking around.

I snort and wave him away, letting him loose. Having gained his Levels the hard way, Bolo's got to grind a lot more than me to get anywhere. And while we might have taken out the main dungeon finally, there are still a ton of monsters constantly spawning.

Once Bolo rushes away, kicking up dirt and blood in his wake, I'm left alone. Alone, without monsters trying to kill me, in a charnel house of corpses and the collapsed end of the city dungeon.

***

While I wait, I look over my Character Screen. It's the first chance I've had to look at it since the battle ended. Even with all the death and destruction, I only got a couple of Levels.

More interestingly, that weird feeling about experience gain jumps out at me, displayed easily for me to spot on my Status Screen. If I wasn't so aware I'm in public view, my jaw would have dropped as I stare at the information.

Status Screen			
Name	John Lee	Class	Junior System Admin (Grand Paladin)
Race	Human (Male)	Level	1 (4)
Titles			
Monster's Bane, Redeemer of the Dead, Duelist, Explorer, Apprentice Questor, Galactic Silver Bounty Hunter, Corrupt Questor, (Living Repository), (Class Lock)			
Health	5450	Stamina	5450
Mana	5140	Mana Regeneration	459 (+5) / minute
Attributes			
Strength	385	Agility	458
Constitution	545	Perception	324
Intelligence	514	Willpower	559
Charisma	220	Luck	171
Class Skills			
Mana Imbue	5*	Blade Strike*	5
Thousand Steps	1	Altered Space	2
Two are One	1	The Body's Resolve	3
Greater Detection	1	A Thousand Blades*	4
Soul Shield*	8	Blink Step	2
Portal*	5	Army of One	4
Sanctum	2	Penetration	9e
Aura of Chivalry	1	Eyes of Insight	2

Beacon of the Angels	2	Eye of the Storm	1
Vanguard of the Apocalypse	2	Society's Web	1
Shackles of Eternity*	4	Immovable Object / Unstoppable Force*	1
Domain	1	Judgment of All	6
(Grand Cross)	(1)	System Edit	1
External Class Skills			
Instantaneous Inventory	1	Frenzy	1
Cleave	2	Tech Link	2
Elemental Strike	1 (Ice)	Shrunken Footsteps	1
Analyze	2	Harden	2
Quantum Lock	3	Elastic Skin	3
Disengage Safeties	2	Temporary Forced Link	1
Hyperspace Nitro Boost	1	On the Edge	1
Fates Thread	2	Peasant's Fury	1
Combat Spells			
Improved Minor Healing (IV)		Greater Regeneration (II)	
Greater Healing (II)		Mana Drip (II)	
Improved Mana Missile (IV)		Enhanced Lightning Strike (III)	
Firestorm		Polar Zone	
Freezing Blade		Improved Inferno Strike (II)	
Elemental Walls (Fire, Ice, Earth, etc.)		Ice Blast	
Icestorm		Improved Invisibility	
Improved Mana Cage		Improved Flight	
Haste		Enhanced Particle Ray	
Variable Gravitic Sphere		Zone of Denial	

I've gained enough Levels as a Grand Paladin that I've acquired a new Class Skill point. I can even add it to my Grand Paladin Class—or what acts like my Grand Paladin Class. But I don't actually have any experience for my Junior System Administrator Class. Like, at all. Which makes no sense.

Unless the System Administrator Class doesn't gain experience via the destruction of monsters or sapients. Which would be incredibly rare. Not unheard of—there are Classes like Pacifist or Fellow of the Universe that can't gain experience via murder—but they're truly rare. Like, I can recall maybe a dozen off the top of my head—and I've got the Questor's library in my head. Hell, even Artisan Classes get experience for kills.

Still, here I am, a ton of kills, an entire planet murdered, and I've received a portion of the experience and...

Nothing.

If that's the case, then the Administrator Class must be even more interesting than I thought. Considering I have the entire goddamn library of the Questors—a group so obsessed with the System, they went down some dark roads, and when they ran out of dark roads to go down, they cut down the trees, blasted the mountains, and paved whole new ones into the abyss—that's saying something.

It's saying something even more that over tens of thousands of years, there's no record of this position ever. Then again, the fact that the moment I gained the Class the Galactic Council went after Earth is more than sufficient evidence for me to scream cover up.

But...

My System Quest hasn't ticked up. Even as more and more information washes over me from the library, even as my new Administrator Class wields the System's gifted Intelligence to rip apart the library and provide the knowledge in bite-sized chunks, nothing. The silence, the lack of Quest updates is disturbing. Silence, as if I've hit a dead end.

But I don't know why.

I blow out a breath, shake my head, and glare at the Class Skill point I have to use. I have no access to the System Administrator Skill tree—if it even has one. So I'm forced to choose from the Grand Paladin Skill tree.

GRAND PALADIN SKILL TREE

Grand Cross	Extra Hands	Burden of the Worthy	Defense of the Fallen
⬇	⬇	➡ ⬅	⬇
Final Judgment	Combined Arms		Bonds of the People

As usual, I don't have to worry about the second tier for a long time. I'd have to hit Level 26 to gain access to it. While I gain Levels at a decent rate, especially for a Heroic Class, there's only so much grinding even I can do. Especially when said grinding involves taking out entire planets' worth of monsters.

All that means that each Class Skill point is ever more precious. And it's not as if I can afford to buy a Heroic Class Skill. Never mind the issue about off-loading activation since I've got the damn library in my head, it's also incredibly expensive. Like, not even our budget from the Erethran Empire is enough kind of expensive.

And this is the kind of budget—drawn down over decades of negligence, admittedly—that is taxed over multiple solar systems and billions upon billions of Erethran citizens. It's the kind of budget that let me spend on building up the newbie Paladins without much concern.

And a single Heroic Class Skill would wipe out the budget for the year.

I guess it makes sense. Each Class Skill is so powerful, continents get shredded with their use. If the System made it cheap, it'd be forced to constantly expend more Mana to trigger the effects of the Skill than it would have gained by forcing said Heroic Class to grind for the Credits. So the System has to make the Skill exorbitantly expensive, such that even wiping out a whole planet's worth of monsters is insufficient to buy a single Skill.

It's a logarithmic increase in Credits, such that a Heroic Class might grind for a decade or so before they could afford a single Skill on the first tier. Which means, in that period, he's pulled forth thousands of points of Mana and even more has been recirculated through the System, making it a net surplus.

And that assumes the Heroic even cares to grind. There are other ways to earn Credits of course. For example, just by existing on a planet, a Heroic is often sufficient deterrent against most kinds of shenanigans.

But none of that really matters, not to me. Right now, I've got to choose what kind of Skill to pick.

Grand Cross is powerful, and I know with a little push, I could expand the tens of kilometers the initial Skill range has set wider. Of course, it'd weaken the Skill further, but it's a great mass stomper. Even more powerful than Judgment of All in sheer damage, plus it works against environmental obstacles. More damage per Mana spent, and more focused damage.

But I don't need more damage. Not anymore. The ability to concentrate the attack on a single individual via Grand Cross is important for me, but if I'm punching my way through a fight with the Council, I'm already twenty kilometers from the nearest shelter in a Yukon winter in my pajamas.

Which is why, while I eye Defense of the Fallen, I decide against it too. It's definitely on my list of things to pick up eventually, because unlike my evolved Penetration Skill, there's no warmup required for its shielding properties. It's actually a permanent Skill, increasing my overall tankiness.

But... again, if I'm punching my way out of the problem, I'm on the wrong route. There are literal Legendary Classes in the Inner Council. I can't even hope to beat them.

The only good news is that because they are Legendaries, they won't take action directly. After all, the President of the United States doesn't come out to visit a rabble-rouser in a city just because they show up in the president's briefing reports. The president has better things to do—like dealing with other heads of state.

But that advantage only holds so long as I manage to stay far enough below the radar. Once I make too much noise, they'll likely take direct action and smack me around. And then it'll truly be over.

So back to Skills, since I ain't buying Defense of the Fallen, I definitely can't get the linked Skill. Burden of the Worthy is an interesting Skill that basically dumps damage onto my doppelgangers created by Extra Hands. It makes me much more unkillable.

And unlike most Skills, the doppelgangers in Extra Hands are real. Not ghosts like the ones that Hod makes, not semi-solid constructs or even shadow copies with a portion of my Skills. They're real.

Extra Hands (Level 1)

A Paladin can never be everywhere he needs to be. But with this Skill, the Grand Paladin can certainly cover more ground. Mana Regeneration reduced by 5 permanently.

Cost: 5000 Mana per duplicate.

Upkeep cost: 5000 Mana per day per duplicate. Must be paid by original Skill user.

Effect: Creates maximum two duplicates of the user. Duplicates have 90% of all (unboosted) Attributes, gain no effects from Titles, and may not equip Soulbound weapons but have access to all (non-purchased) Skills of user. Each duplicate has their own Mana pool but regenerates at 50% of normal regeneration levels. Mana levels take the place of health points for duplicates.

Original Skill user has a nonverbal connection to duplicates at all times. System will provide a download of duplicate's memories upon their destruction or cessation of upkeep costs. Fidelity of memory download dependent upon Skill level.

Note: This Skill cannot be used by duplicates.

My eyes narrow at the significant number of conditions in the Skill, but even then, having multiple versions of me is useful. I do recall the cautionary words passed on by Ali and Roxley about the System duplicate attempts though, so before I make my choice, I get to asking.

"How does the System create these duplicates? I thought you said it doesn't read memories?"

"It doesn't. The duplicates are Mana copies of you based off the System's best guesses," Ali says. "Keep them around long enough and they'll even form distinct personalities from you. It's why most individuals with such Skills dismiss the doppelgangers every few days."

"So when you say best guesses..."

"Everything you've shown the System, it'll show. In your case, they'll eat a lot of chocolate, obsess over the System, and piss off everyone they come into contact with."

"Funny."

"But true."

"Go watch your reality TV," I say to Ali and turn back to the floating notification window.

It sounds as though Extra Hands isn't the best Skill if I want long-term help. Memories and studies brush against my mind, offering further details about similar Skills.

The more data the System has, the better. The level of fidelity to the original increases for individuals who aren't as devious, while schemers and liars have difficulty with such Skills. The more you live with your heart in the open, the easier it is for the System to create people like you. Individuals who play multiple angles, who have significant mood swings or mental issues, or have spent significant periods in the Restricted Zone are all known to receive divergent doppelgangers.

It's one of the most often quoted examples of how the System isn't omnipotent. More than one Questor has even explored the possibility of using duplicates to further their System Quest by rereading the same information with duplicates themselves.

Sometimes it even works.

And we won't even discuss the truly disturbing research some have conducted on their very own duplicates to prove the difference in System-made duplicates and the original.

On the other hand, this is the only Skill that offers additional tactical and potentially strategic possibilities. I just need to make sure whatever— whoever—I create doesn't mess things up.

As I'm about to explore my newly acquired Skill, I'm interrupted by a cough. I frown, looking up, and realize I've been standing here for over an hour. Mikito's back, and with her is Brerdain.

"If you're ready, Grand Paladin…" Brerdain says, gesturing at one of the many attendants with him.

"Yeah, let's get to it. More planets to cleanse, more experience to gain."

And hopefully, gain the backing of the Empire. Or at least their neutrality as the Council comes after Earth and me.

Chapter 3

Interstellar travel with the System is weird. You can teleport anywhere with the right Skills or enough Credits. You can even take entire fleets if you have the money to do it. Credits are a power in themselves and can make even a small but prosperous organization lethal.

At the same time, even with the nearly instantaneous travel options available, most travel is conducted via hyperspace jumps and wormholes. The cost of instantaneous transportation is so expensive, it's only ever used as a strategic resource on a level above individual transportation or for small, high value goods.

And individuals with the Skill to transport entire fleets are in the Heroic level, so that's another level of rarity. Individuals are easier, but even then, the cost is significant. Which is why evolved Portal Skills are so important—and so easily blocked.

Want to use your teleportation Skills against monsters? You're good. The vast, vast majority aren't set up to block that. Want to use it against sapients? Not as easy.

All that is a long way of saying we're seated in our beige rest room, food splayed out across us on the steel board table, lighting adjusted for human norms as we traverse the interstellar vastness in a faster-than-light spaceship, bouncing from wormhole to wormhole.

Each of us have plates full of food. Even Ali is in his full-sized form, being just over eight feet tall. He, of course, has the most disgusting dish before him—a plateful of squirming bugs, piled high. Bolo's got three plates and works his way through his carnivore's delight, while Mikito's side of the table is much more contained. Not that it stops her from eating as much as the rest of us, just that she does it with a little more grace.

It says something about how long we've been in the Galaxy that none of us even blink as Ali pops the squirming bugs into his mouth and chews as though they're so much popcorn.

"Are you certain that Ambassador Ward is fine?" Harry raises the topic again. This isn't the first—or last—time he's asked, and I can understand his concern even if I'm frustrated by it.

"Yes. She's an Ambassador. They can't directly hurt her." I shake my head. "Even hiring mercenaries to destroy the embassy was pushing the letter of the law."

"The Redeemer speaks truth," Bolo says. "The Council and Irvina itself could not function if they destroyed the laws once more."

"Once more?" Harry says, leaning forward, sensing a story there.

"Ancient history. But twice before, the laws regarding the safety of planetary and governmental representatives and the peace of the capital were relaxed or removed. Both times, there were a significant number of casualties among the representatives. It devolved into all-out war among the greater and Inner Council." Bolo shakes his head. "We lost our inner council seat in the last altercation and the Erethrans took our seat then."

I grunt, surprised. I'd known there was some minor animosity in there, but considering how little Bolo cared about it, I thought it was a nonissue. This doesn't sound minor at all.

Spotting my surprise, Bolo waves. "In truth, I think the king was grateful for the loss. We care not for galactic politics. So long as we are left alone to care for our dragons and our planet, it is enough." Bolo pauses as if he considers something. "Also, without a Legendary to hold the seat, all such power is ephemeral."

"The Dragon Knights have no Legendaries?" Mikito asks.

"None that are public. The last known Legendary fell two and a half millennia ago during a dragon surge."

"Dragon surges sound way scarier than a normal monster wave," I say.

"They are. Dragons grow much faster during that period, going from adolescence to maturity in months instead of decades. Mature dragons become elders and elders become ancients."

I wince. The last time I met a dragon, it was but a mature dragon—and one that was pregnant and thus underpowered, along with being hampered by the lower Mana density of Earth still being in the transition period. Take away any of those things and I'd have been fucked.

On the other hand, it also means theres a baby dragon—or soon-to-be baby dragon—running around the Yukon somewhere. Curiosity has me poking into the System, and I find myself bookmarking the infosection on baby dragon pics. Nearly as good as cute kitten pics.

"So weird," I mutter. I push down the library, forcing it not to give me more data about dragon surges, Mana waves, and the System. A part of me— the part that has been boosted by the System—is happy to process that information, but I stay focused on the conversation. "Anyway, Katherine is safe. And some of her staff. They've managed to find a location to reside in which has guaranteed their safety."

"You say that, but I've been poking around, and something about the attack made me look at it over again," Harry says. "I found this guy outside. Watching."

A gesture, and a floating image forms of a big man clad in gold-edged, emerald plate armor and a flowing cloak, metal covering his body except for his actual face where small tusks jut from his jaw. Pink skin covers his face with its prominent cheekbones, but it's the glowing green eyes and wide smirk that catches one's attention.

"So who is he?" I ask.

"Kasva Dedprom, Champion of the Council, Level 38. Heroic Class. He didn't take part, but he was watching." Harry leans forward. "He doesn't show up outside of the arena battles"—Mikito perks up at the mention of her favorite sporting event—"in Irvina to protect his Championship Title or a few, special Council meetings. He is their ultimate attack dog. And he was watching the attack."

"Heroic Class Champion. Damn…" I frown. "And high-Leveled too. I wonder how he gets his experience…" I wait. But for once, the library has nothing to offer me. No direct information at least. I get a ton of knowledge about Champion Classes in general, but nothing specific. Which is fascinating in itself. "He's probably getting some latent experience gain just hanging around. But it's possible they keep him running around in a Council-only dungeon."

"There are rumors of a dungeon in the first district," Harry confirms.

"A Heroic." Bolo eyes the figure, tapping at the information Harry shared with us. His actions call up the sparse additional details about Kasva. Not much at all, considering his status and position. "A difficult fight."

"Well, if he's not acting directly, we'll have to worry about him later," I say.

"And in the meantime, we do what?" Harry says, pointing his fork at me. "I understand you don't feel strong enough to confront the Council directly, nor is violence the best resort. You are only a new Heroic. But if you intend to delay until you become a Legendary…"

"Not the plan." I shake my head. "The Levels are nice, but it's the Empire's involvement or support that's the reason we're doing all this. The Council is pressuring Earth, and even if I turn up, I doubt they'll just stop. Not since we became a bad example."

"About that…" Harry says.

I ignore him, not wanting to discuss why they dialed the pressure on Earth up to a twelve. Telling him would just make him even more of a target. "We need to rally support for Earth, to stop the vote to remove Earth and the rest of the Dungeon Worlds from participating on the Galactic Council. Which means helping out the Empire. And anyone else who is willing."

"I can understand the Empire choosing to help, what with you being their Grand Paladin and all, but the others—"

"The others will take more convincing," I say. "I know. Even if we give them the thousand hells, I doubt we alone have enough to convince any of the other Council members to help. Luckily, most Dungeon Worlds are in one empire or another. If we can convince the other empires, help them settle their Dungeon Worlds…"

"You think you can get their help?" Harry's eyes unfocus as his fingers work through the abbreviated information-only Shop he has access to before he nods. "The Movana and Erethran Empires each have two Dungeon Worlds. Including Earth, the Truinnar have two too now. The Dragon has one. The Twelve Clans of the Grimsar have another. There's another that sits in the center of the warring states that make up the Pooskeen empire. The last four are seated at the edges of a bunch of minor kingdoms, all of whom fight over the Dungeon Worlds among themselves and everyone else."

"Exactly. Any Dungeon World located in an empire's area of control could probably drive that empire's votes to us," I say. "Being able to control movement of visitors and settlers would be a significant economic, political, and Leveling boon."

"Which is why the Traditionalists will oppose you. As would the Fist, since they wouldn't want their members being stymied," Harry says. "In fact, they were one of the major sources of oppositions the last time, no?"

"Well, when they failed to get Earth for themselves. But if we could get one or two of those four—"

A snort rises from Bolo when I say that. "Don't get ahead of yourself. If you showed up, you'd just be escalating matters." I frown, and Bolo continues. "You don't know? Most Heroic Classes aren't allowed onto Dungeon Worlds without prior negotiation. Not that they care to turn up."

"What? Why?"

"Because Heroics are the atom bombs of the galaxy," Mikito says. "You can drop them on your own planets without an issue, but the moment you do it on another power's, you escalate matters."

"And Dungeon Worlds are contested zones," Ali says. "You can't have Heroics going in and tipping things one way or the other. Or else more Heroics turn up. And then a bunch of promising Advanced and Master Classes die as collateral damage from their fights, and the Dungeon World's infrastructure gets wrecked and costs every side billions of Credits in lost infrastructure, materials, and investment in their Advanced and Master Classers. Worst, no one wins anyway."

"For that matter, it's why Legendaries don't get involved unless it's to destroy a planet or two," Bolo says. "Tradition keeps the System running. It might not be perfect, it might have significant inequalities, but it has grown out from times when no such customs were around and planets were destroyed on the regular. And during those times, the Forbidden Zone grew unrestricted."

"The Beginning. The Time of Chaos. The First Insurrection. The Flight of Dragons. The Fae Revolution," Ali intones.

I hold up a hand as the library tugs at each name. "Enough."

"Library got your tongue?" Ali smirks.

But he does stop, while some pieces of information get downloaded. It's scattershot, since much of the information is just in reference to the events themselves and is in the earliest portion of the libraries where studies had just begun on the System. More observational than experimental.

"Just... no." I push aside the buzzing in my mind, finding it easier than ever now. A side benefit of my Class? Or maybe an improvement in my Intelligence? "Anyway, we just need to block the vote on the Dungeon Worlds, not pass a resolution. That's a lot easier, since the Mana requirement to enact such a change is pretty damn high."

There are a few nods, since we've all downloaded an information pack on how voting works. It's all done by Mana, with each planet having a set "amount" of Mana that they contribute to the running of the Galactic Council. More established planets, those closer to Forbidden Zones, often have more free processed Mana, so their votes are worth more. New planets have less. A Dungeon World has a ton, but it's a question of them reaching a threshold amount rather than a specific percentage or number.

"So the Fist will try to get on board, maybe by bribing them with exclusive access to some dungeons on Earth. Somehow. The Traditionalists might not like abstaining from the vote as a whole, but the Movana who do have two Dungeon Worlds will push for us. Katherine had some success aligning with the Edge by giving them access to Earth, and if we can somehow coordinate them, a single Dungeon World they can access would help." Another snort rises from Bolo as I blow past the ideas of how we're getting that done, but I keep pressing on. "That leaves the Technocrats, who don't give a damn really, and the Artisans as blocks."

"The Artisans will be opposed to it. Less competition on the Dungeon Worlds will see higher prices," Harry says. "And so will the Edge, no matter what you say. They were willing to go with Earth when it seemed everyone wasn't willing to push matters. But now that the Inner Council has acted…"

I slam my fist down, anger flaring. Harry flinches and I feel a flash of guilt, but I'm still too upset to stop. "I know, damn it. But what else do you expect us to do? We need to get allies on our side, and this is the best option I can think of. If you've got a better idea…"

"I'm no politician. But have you spoken to Rob?" Harry says, leaning forward. "Or Lana? Roxley? Even Katherine? Anyone?"

My silence is reply enough.

"Exactly," Harry says. "You're doing it again. Making plans without asking the rest of us. You aren't the only one who gives a damn about Earth! And this time, it's not just your head on the block." He stands, shaking his head. "Maybe working with the Erethrans makes sense. It probably won't hurt. But if you want to help Earth, you're really going to have to talk to them."

I watch him stalk out, the British gentleman tugging on his jacket as he leaves. I open my mouth then shut it like the doors leading out of the room as he exits. Bolo snorts again.

I round on the Dragon Lord. "You have something to say?"

"Nothing at all, Grand Paladin," Bolo says, drawling as he says my Class. "I'm just here for the experience."

I grunt. "Yeah, I thought so."

I stand, suddenly out of appetite and desire for company. By the time I hit the door, I realize no one has followed me. My lips curl up in disgust, but I say nothing, searching for one of the ship's training rooms.

I feel the need to destroy something.

***

The smoking ruins of the training room's short-circuited hard light projectors lie all around me, acrid and toxic smoke wafting from the remnants of the drones I've defeated. Some of the drones are nearly twenty feet tall, others no larger than the size of my hand. But they're all wrecked.

At six foot two and muscular for a human, those twenty-foot-tall, couple-of-ton drones should have been a problem when we clashed sword to pincer. But the System messes with physics and lets you mess with it too, which is why I can just as easily toss one of them one-handed as cut through them with my sword.

I look around, listening to the cackle of flames and the hiss and pop of broken drones attempting to rise, and I grimace. An insistent warning flashes in the corner of my eyes, a warning coming over the functioning speakers as they detail the loss of functionality in the training room.

Sadly, even on a capital ship, they just aren't set up to handle Heroic Class levels of destruction. Not for hours on end.

The door hisses open behind me, making me turn. In comes Mikito, who eyes the destruction before she tramps in the rest of the way. As she reaches me, a flicker of light by my side warns me of Ali's presence.

"Tantrum over?" Mikito says.

"Really? You think that's going to calm me down?" I say. But there's no heat in it, not anymore.

"I've given up trying to calm you down when you're angry," Mikito says. In direct contradiction though, she holds up a familiar triangular chocolate bar, one the size of my fist in cross-section.

I snort, but take the peace offering. I strip the cardboard and foil while answering her first question. "Calmer."

"Good. Then you're going to tell me why you aren't contacting the others?" Mikito says.

"You don't think I'm willing to do everything myself?" I say, lips twisting in sardonic humor.

"For all your overblown sense of responsibility, you've never been that egotistical. Not when you helped Lana set up that investment company. Or when you took others out training," Mikito says, voice dropping. "But you're trying to do this all yourself. You won't even speak to us about it. So there's a reason."

I grunt. I could contact Earth. But how do you explain, how do you say that the reason everything is broken is because of you? That you've let them down, that you brought the entire Galactic Council onto Earth?

Guilt. That's the reason why I've avoided contacting Earth. Guilt, and the hope that they have a solution. Because I can't find one, not really. Even if I turn up, if I let the Council have me, it won't stop the ball they've started rolling. It won't unring the bell.

"This is my fault," I finally say, closing my eyes as I feel the chocolate melt in my mouth. Not wanting to see her face.

"Because you're a Heroic now?" Mikito says. "You know, it was going to happen at some point. Maybe not this soon for some of the other Champions, but they're closing in on it. Another few years—"

"No. Not that." I shake my head and open my eyes, whispering, "Or not really."

"Baka. Stop speaking in riddles." Mikito's nose wrinkles, tiny creases appearing on the petite ridge and I wonder if the toxic smells are getting to her. It's not that bad, only a couple of health points a second.

I open my mouth then shut it. My head turns, looking around the broken training room, considering. The fleet, by virtue of the various navy and army intelligence personnel, is cloaked from most forms of espionage. Then again, considering who we're going against, I doubt it's sufficient.

"You can't speak of it, can you?" Mikito's legs part as she balances her weight evenly without thought. Readying herself. "What did you do?"

"I…"

"Boy-o really can't say." Ali floats down to her eye level, hands splayed. "This isn't the time. Or place."

"There will be one, yes?" I hesitate, and Mikito pokes me. "Yes?"

"Yes," I finally grate out. "But if you learn this—"

Mikito holds a hand up to stop me. "Blah blah, death, destruction, being hunted, more death. About right?"

"You're not taking this seriously."

"Death is not to be feared by a samurai. It will come for all of us, and as such, is no more important than tea." She looks at the triangle of chocolate in my hand. "Or chocolate."

"Death, tea, and chocolates. All of equal importance." I can't help but laugh a little before breaking off a piece to offer to the Samurai.

"I know you'll do your best for Earth." Mikito takes it and stares at me for a second then adds, softly, "But you need to call them. Coordinate."

I grunt. She's right. Even if, I fear, whatever we do is ultimately futile, we have to try. Even if I believe that the trying is the trap, that the Council expects me to jump to their rescue. That moving to Irvina is what they want. It's why I've held off, at least for now.

I watch her walk away as I contemplate our situation. She leaves me in the shattered training room, listening to the crackle and pop of malfunctioning machinery. Smaller maintenance drones sneak out of the walls and begin cleanup, now that they consider the training session over.

I sigh, turning to the Spirit who gives me a short but firm nod.

"Contact Earth, will you?" I say.

***

I speak with Rob first, the conversation being held in one of the ship's many meeting rooms. This one's reserved for the brass, but considering my titular rank within the armed forces, I have no issue accessing it. Among other things, there's an additional barrier against snooping. I expect it's not much better than a soggy sheet of A4 protecting my privacy from the Lady of Shadows, but if it'll cost them a little more, I'm all for it.

When Rob flickers into being, connected via the System bending the concept of quantum physics as I understand it, he appears in a hard-light projection of himself.

World President Rob Markey is in his late-thirties, if you pay attention to physical looks. But I know he's older, much, much older. If not for the genetic rejuvenation offered by the System and a bunch of points into Constitution, he'd be old and frail. Once ex-Secretary of Agriculture, then the only surviving member of the US Presidential Staff and now, President of Earth.

Rob Markey, 1ˢᵗ World Ruler of a Dungeon World, World President of Earth, Beloved, Loyalty Born of Blood, Sacrificed Existence, Efficient Manager, ... (more) (Planetary Leader Level 21) (M)
HP: 840/840

MP: 2430/2430

Conditions: Linked Health, Shielded, Location Sense (Earth), Freedom of Movement (Earth), Aura of Sovereignty, Mana Fount, Artisans Gift, Capitalist Dream, more…

"Rob," I greet the older man, gaze sweeping past his simple grey suit and the splash of color in his bright yellow tie.

"Mr. Lee," Rob says, hands crossed behind him. "You've gained a new tier. The first human to do so, it seems."

"I guess so."

"Katherine has briefed me on her troubles. And our losses, as well as the expected action taken against Earth." Rob's lips thin. "I expected to speak with you sooner."

I shrugged. "Things have been busy."

"Really?"

I explain what I set up, what we've done, and the agreement I've made with the Empire.

He doesn't comment until I'm done. "A fair start, but not what I'd hoped to speak with you about." When I don't fill the incriminating silence he leaves, he continues. "Why is it that Katherine says they want you in Irvina?"

"My good looks?"

"You're joking?" Rob's cold demeanor breaks in a flash of anger.

My shrug actually calms him, surprisingly.

"People are dying, if you did not know, Mr. Lee. Not just the diplomatic corp on Irvina, but people on Earth. They've redoubled their attacks. Many of our agents off world were attacked too. Merchant contracts have been broken. Guilds are pulling out of cities they are contracted to protect. Even mercenary companies are canceling their Contracts and giving up on their obligations. And you joke."

I offer him a weak smile, trying not to let him know how much his accusation hurts. "If I said I wasn't certain…"

"I'd ask for your best guess."

"And if I said I couldn't tell you?"

Rob's lips thin further. "This is not a joke, Mr. Lee."

"I know." I absently note the lack of Titles. A power play, to make it clear I'm still below him as a human? I'd say he isn't used to employing System Titles, but as a professional politician who has been doing it for nearly a decade, I doubt it's taken him that long to get used to the new reality. So, power play it is. "But some things, you're better off not knowing."

His eyes narrow before he gestures around him. I assume he means to showcase the world he sees around him, though it translates badly since he's gesturing at an empty board room here. "You put the whole planet in danger because of something you did, didn't you?"

"In a way."

"Again."

"Hey, boy-o's addition of the Galactic Citizens from the lower Combat Classers have helped you guys stay ahead of the increasing Mana saturation and dungeon formations. Hell, you've even begun to get Master Classers coming to offer service because John started the entire program," Ali says.

"The Master Class immigration program has nothing to do with Mr. Lee."

"Goblin shit. You only have applicants because boy-o made enough of a stink that the others are willing to give you a chance. He let Earth prove they aren't like the other governments. At least, not as bad and more desperate." Ali sniffs. "Though the way you're acting, I might be changing my mind on that."

"Mr. Lee has done us some good, but he also set the entire Galactic Council against us. Our inclusion in the Council as a Dungeon World was already precarious as it stood," Rob says. "Now, he has pushed even our allies to abandon us."

"Talking of allies, do we have any left?" I say.

Rob pauses for a long time, staring at me. Then, to my surprise, he shakes his head. "No. I don't think so."

"What?"

"I do not believe we will be telling you who we have allied."

I freeze for a second, then smile. "Oh. Security concerns, eh?"

"That, and your actions are less than optimal. I see no reason to subject ourselves to your actions again."

The smile grows strained. "I was trying to help."

"Yes, and your generosity is noted. But you do not always look out for what is best for Earth," Rob says flatly. "And that is what we need."

I clench my jaw, fighting the anger and the hurt. I force out a breath slowly before I raise my hand, ready to kill the hologram.

Rob's next words stop me. "There are things you can do though. If you are willing."

"Like?"

"*Boy-o, you're not going to just take that, are you?*" Ali says.

"*He's not wrong. I did bring the Council down on them because of my new Class. And I'm refusing to explain.*"

"*For their own good. And their seat was always precarious.*"

"Speak with the Duchess. She already has much to lose. A small push and we should be able to rely on her as a dependable ally through all this."

"Fine."

"One thing. You are not an official member of the Earth Planetary Government. Nor should you make any promises as such."

"Pooskeen twice born and regurgitated children. You want him to negotiate without any backing, putting himself on the line after that garbage?" Ali bristles. "No way in hell—"

"Anything else?" I say, cutting off Ali. I don't explicitly agree to the task, but I'm choosing not to disagree.

"Resolve whatever your issue is with the Council. Or we'll disown any connection with you," Rob says. "We can deal with the current problems. We have to. But this is their opening salvo. We will not be caught up in a third altercation."

"You ungrateful little golem waste, after all that John's done!"

"This isn't personal, Spirit. It is just necessary. Mr. Lee understands, doesn't he?" Rob fixes me with those pale blue eyes, meeting my own brown ones.

I let the silence draw out, weighing him, his resolve, and the situation. Finally, I answer. "I'll talk to the Duchess for you. And I'll deal with the Council. Because you're right, they are my problem. And Earth shouldn't be dragged into it."

Rob smiles, a flash of satisfaction crossing his face. He kills the feed a second later, leaving me standing alone in the room feeling a little abandoned and more than a little betrayed.

Then I shake my head and dismiss it. Whatever my feelings, the work ahead is still the same. Save the planet, figure out how to deal with the Council. And for that second part, I'm going to need help.

"Ready for the next call?" Ali says. "Or do you need to wipe your nose?"

"What?"

"To get rid of all that brown, after sticking your face so far up his ass."

"Enough, Ali. Just connect the calls."

"Yes, master!" Ali chirps.

***

"Redeemer," the voice comes softly, a chocolate and caramel caress on the ears. It sends shivers down my spine and brings a smile to my lips even when I don't want it to. And the speaker, the speaker's gorgeous. Unlike my own Charisma increases, his has made him handsome. Beautiful. Stylish.

Not hard and intimidating, not a force of nature or a broken, ragged edge of humanity. A weapon given flesh and form.

"Roxley," I say, bowing a little. "Thank you for seeing me."

"So formal." Roxley shakes his head. "When was the last time we met when it wasn't?"

I shrug, gesturing at him. At his new Status, his new Titles. "We're not who we were. Not able to do what we want, can we? Not without consequences."

Lord Graxin Roxley, Count of the White Pass, Hunter of Drakyl, Master of the Sword and the Black Flame, Corinthian of the Second Order and acclaimed Dancing Master of the 196th Ball, Slayer of Goblins, Movana,... (more) (Level 35 Truinnar Lord) (M)

Health: 3430/3430

MP: 2450/ 2450

Conditions: Pheremone Dispersal, Aura of Civility, the Grace of the Dance, Mana Channel, Right of the Lord, Liege's Favorite

"And consequences are what we are here to discuss, is it not?" Roxley says.

He wants to touch me, I can tell. But here, in this room, it would not be the same. The holographic projection we're using might give him a hard-light form, might display him in its entirety, but it won't convey touch or feel.

"Yes. I need to speak with the Duchess," I say.

"You know what that'll mean."

"Yes."

"I can't protect you," he says.

"I know. But if you can protect Earth now…"

"It's out of my hands. This, these are Levels I cannot climb."

"Cannot?" I offer him a half-smile. "Or will not?"

"Cannot. For now. My Levels have stagnated, compared to you." Roxley shakes his head, making his long hair—pale blue, almost white—flow behind him. "Some of us have responsibilities."

"Can you put me in touch with her?"

"I can. But John—"

"I know." I cut him off. "Thank you. For everything. You didn't have to help us, back then."

"This sounds very much like goodbye." The dark elf leans forward, locking my gaze with his. "I dislike goodbyes."

"And I, early mornings. And the apocalypse. But we don't get everything we want."

"Redeemer—"

"You know how to contact me. And thank you. Again."

I turn my hand to the side, killing the hologram. Roxley disappears in the blink of an eye and I find myself standing in silence once more.

Alone. Again.

***

Contemplation is broken by a shrill ring like an old rotary phone. I blink, surprise registering on my face, and spot Ali smirking. The Spirit does find ways to entertain himself. Idly, I accept the incoming projection, surprised that Roxley managed to work this fast.

"John." The voice is familiar, as is the buxom redhead before me. She looks older, more mature. Small bags under her jade eyes, from which she peers at me. "I just heard."

"About the attacks?" I say, surprised it took her so long. Surprised she wasn't targeted.

"No. About what Rob said to you." Lana's lips purse in disapproval. "He doesn't speak for all of us. You know that, right?"

"Sure."

"You don't sound very convinced." Lana's eyes narrow as she studies my face. Her voice drops, getting gentler. "You have friends here, you know."

"Hey, toots. What's it with Goblin-shit anyway?" Ali interjects, floating over to get her attention.

She smiles as she spots him, not taking offense at his words.

"Seemed a little more pointed than normal, the way he was talking to boy-o."

"Politics." Lana makes a face. "When you sold off your shares, to some people it signaled that you were done with Earth. On top of that, Rob's never been your biggest fan."

I frown, not recalling that. Not that I had a lot of interaction with the man. Sure, I put him on the seat, but he was kind of the last man standing.

"You didn't free him. Or really, be part of the reclamation of the USA. As much as we managed before we had to stop. And a number of his aides never got over the fact that they had to be rescued by Canadians," Lana says, eyes crinkling a little in humor. "Not that there's much of a Canada now, but—"

"But old ideologies die hard."

"Just about." Lana sighs. "On top of that, a lot of time has passed since you've left Earth. The fact that you didn't stick around afterward and then started sending people back, and well, a lot of people figure you're a bit of a loose cannon. And one that's just using Earth."

"Using how?" Ali throws up his hands. "If anything, you guys have been riding on our reputation."

"And Mikito's," she says. "She's got quite a few fans here due to her arena battles."

I grunt, recalling how even on Earth they've started in on that. Blood sports, a galactic pastime.

"That's part of the issue too. That you aren't really on Earth or tied to us in any real manner. Some people don't like the fact that their people aren't as well known as you. It makes them angry that they've wasted a ton of Credits and done, at best, half as well as you and Mikito," Lana says. "I mean, some of the Champions have done well, but as they're mostly on Earth, their Galactic reputation doesn't really increase. The few who have left…"

"Cause less trouble?" I say.

"Mostly." Lana's eyes twinkle. "But trouble adds to your fame. And so—"

"So I get blamed for being a troublemaker, making Earth look like one?" I snort. "And Rob doesn't like it. Though I'd have thought he'd buy into it, that entire scrappy underdog mythos and all…"

"Well, the populace does. But it's rather different when you have to run the planet."

I shake my head. "Fine. He doesn't like me and wants to hang me out to dry." I wave, dismissing the topic. "Whatever. I can deal with it. I do have to fix this."

"Yes, you do. I know you can't explain yourself. But was it worth it?"

The penetrating gaze she fixes on me makes me hesitate, forces me to consider my answer. Finally, I nod. She breaks into a smile that lights up the room and gets my heart beating a little faster. I tell that traitorous organ to calm down, and as usual, it ignores me.

"Let me know if you need anything," she says. "But I've got to go. Tell Mikito to call me when she can."

I nod, and Lana waves goodbye as she fades out. I stare at the spot, remembering times past. Remembering a head pillowed on my chest, lying down together in the middle of abandoned skyscrapers, staring at familiar stars. Of kisses and shared laughter, of comfort and peace.

There's no pain anymore, not from the memories at least.

But maybe a little regret. Of what could have been. Should have been perhaps, if I was someone else. Someone less broken. Someone less driven.

"That was nice of her."

"She was always nice," Ali says.

"Yeah…" I sigh. "Make sure we're patched in to Earth's news feed. But if we're going to fix this, we need to get a looking."

"For?"

"The asshole who started this."

***

It's a day of past flings, for while we work, we receive one last call. This one from a young lady who has every right to access the encrypted network. The one she speaks to me on is even more safeguarded, mostly because of who, what she is.

"M'ady Heir Apparent," I greet the visage of beauty that appears before me. I idly note the curves of her arms, the muscle in her chest and legs. She's put on some muscle mass, given a shapelier but more militaristic look to her body.

"Grand Paladin Lee," Catrin Dufoff, Empress Apparent of the Erethran Empire and ex-Companion, replies, her voice filled with amusement as she echoes my formality. "You are looking well. How goes the expedition?"

"Well. We've cleared one planet and are on track to finish the others," I say. "Your men are doing well too."

"I would hope so. There are quite a few resources expended on this endeavor," Catrin says. "Though I'm already seeing the results."

I nod, eyeing her new pair of Levels. As sponsor for this expedition, she's getting a small amount of experience from the kills and even more for the acquisition of the planet itself. Though I'd have to dig to check if it's because it's new territory or because it's the return of old territory. Or just the boost in reputation. Ruling Classes are weird in their experience gain methods.

"Thank you for arranging this. Again. And interceding with the Empress on my behalf," I say.

She waves it off, leaning forward in the purple and gold flowing robes she wears. I can't help but notice that they show a lot more skin than the Empress's, while at the same time being just as practical if she needs to get into combat. Since this is a hard-light hologram, there's no way to tell if the robes are enchanted from the Mana flows around the clothing, but I'd bet my sword on it.

"I'm sorry I couldn't do more. I'm looking into it but—"

I shake my head, cutting her off. As much as I want more help, I can understand their position. Even refusing to vote to kick Earth out of the Galactic Council is a big position to take. "I get it."

"No, I don't think you do." Catrin glances to the side, off-camera, and sighs. "And I can't explain it. But suffice it to say, I'll do what I can. But this is going to be up to you. Mostly."

"I know."

She offers me another smile before gesturing to the side. A second later, the hologram blinks out, leaving me standing alone with my research. I exhale harshly, pushing aside my rioting emotions, and get back to work.

Chapter 4

A month and a half. That's how long it took to clear out the other four planets. That included a bunch of time traversing the void, and a short period of actually destroying the monsters on the planets. I no longer hold back for testing, instead laying into the creatures and dungeons with abandon.

As we hit the planets, the speed with which we finish them off increases. Levels go up, the routine gets embedded in us, and the army and I learn how to grow ever more efficient. I don't wait around to make sure the kill and Skills are done, instead moving from zone to zone the moment my Skill activates.

In many cases, we do just enough damage to allow the Empire to move in and settle their people. To begin the process of reclamation against the monster hordes, letting the army and the hired mercenaries we leave behind to mop up.

Bolo and Mikito work together, blending their abilities to destroy lairs and dungeons at the Master Class Level. They have backup in a squad of Erethran Rangers at all times, though seeing me at work has lit a fire beneath them both. The Ranger squad changes out every dungeon, but Bolo and Mikito don't.

As for me, I rain down hellfire from above. Experience piles up as I kill and kill again, wielding my Skills with abandon. Mostly, Judgment of All gets the workout, though Grand Cross gets pulled into play when the world bosses arrive.

By the time I'm done, I'm up to Level 11 in my Grand Paladin Class and still at Level 1 for my Junior Administrator Class. I feel experience piling up there, experience from my use of the System Edit Skill itself, though not from kills. Whatever the threshold there is to the next Level, it's not easy to spot.

We bathe in blood and guts, in experience notifications, and at the end, we're done. The last location—a world that flies dangerously close to its sun, heated to the boiling point and cracked to showcase the lava within—is a hellhole of lava monsters, fire lizards, and flame elementals. It takes us over a week to kill them all, because they keep rising from the depths. Thankfully, we only need to secure a couple of mining centers rather than the entire planet. Even then, it's a pain in the ass.

When it's over, I find myself standing with my friends on a platform in space, staring at the glowing ball of fire. A shielding spell keeps air within the platform, lets us breathe and move. Bolo is beside me, and I can't help but look at the massive Dragon Lord. We both know what's coming now that the expedition is over.

"Coming?" I ask.

The Dragon Lord sobers, regarding me with a conflicted visage for a long second. I know what his answer is. Any reasonable person would turn me down considering who, what, I intend to face. But I still ask because I could use the help.

"I'm sorry. Twitting the Empire, cleansing these planets, it was all fun. Dangerous, near suicidal, but fun." Bolo looks away, making his hammer disappear as he shuffles awkwardly. "But I've realized I really don't have a death wish. And returning to Irvina to face the Council..."

"Is a bit much for you," I tease the man. When Bolo switches from embarrassed to angry, I smile and clap him on the shoulder. "It's fine. I understand. You've done, chosen to do, more than I could ask for. This isn't your fight."

"It isn't," Bolo agrees.

"So what are you going to do? I'm sure we could get them to open a Portal for you somewhere reasonably close to your destination."

"There is no need. I spoke with Dornalor before we started all this, and he's agreed to take me home. He should be arriving soon."

"Home?" I repeat dumbly. I still don't know what drove him away, why Bolo is considered persona non grata on his own planet. But it seems whatever else has happened, he's decided to face the matter directly at long last. I can't help but think that's a good thing. "Good luck then. If I can do anything…"

"My portion of all this will be more than sufficient," Bolo says.

I nod. Wiping the planets of high-Level monsters boosted his Levels significantly. More importantly, even a small portion of the loot has made him—us—quite rich. At least until he decides to buy another Skill.

"Then, best of luck." I offer Bolo my hand, which he takes and shakes by the forearm.

I smile at the seven-foot-tall Dragon Lord, memories flashing over the past year or so that we've known one another. I kind of lost track of time, what with multiple calendars running around in my head. That, and it's been quite a year. From obstacle to ally to friend, Bolo's shown me a path I could have taken. And sometimes, late at night, I wonder about it.

"And you, Grand Paladin. Safeguard your honor, protect your people, and remember…" Bolo pauses dramatically, before he lowers his voice, "When all else fail, burn it all down when you leave."

I snort, while the Dragon Lord leaves with a chuckle after bidding farewell to Mikito and Harry. I ponder his last words. For all the amusement in his voice, I remember the glint in his eyes, that hint of darkness that drove the Dragon Lord to hang out in a pirate station for years on end. There is a darkness in his past, one that even time with us has not driven away.

In the end, as the door closes and our Honor Guard escort arrives, we find ourselves alone with Ali alongside us. Knowing that what comes next will be a human affair once more. No one else would be dumb enough to choose to stand with us.

***

There are multiple types of Portal evolutions, ranging from the simple extension in range, to the ability to punch through teleport locks, to the more esoteric, like the ability to divert other people's teleportations. The simple kinds are the most common and are in plentiful supply among the Erethran Army. It's a popular specialization to take, since there's always work for teleporters, whether in the military or in the civilian world. In this case, the Erethran Honor Guard tasked with getting us where we need to go also has the requisite locations.

It still takes time though, as we jump across light years onto space stations, mining barges, military bases, and on one memorable occasion, the empty void itself. Each time, we wait in silence while the guard sits in meditation, waiting for his Mana to return before we take the next jump.

Getting back to Irvina where Katherine is under siege is a difficult process. The planet is deep in the Restricted Zone, ringed by solar systems that are close to being—and in a few cases already are—fully enveloped by Mana, becoming nothing more than Forbidden Zone candidates. If not for the significant number of resources thrown into the capital to keep it functioning, it would have gone under a long time ago.

Even then, every year there's a big discussion of moving the capital to a new planet. Or just moving the planet. Sadly, there's an inertia to Galactic politics that keeps major policy changes like this from becoming anything more than discussion.

On top of the distance from the Erethran Empire and the need to punch through the Mana static in a Restricted Zone is the solar system wide teleportation lock. There are carved out exceptions—like Portaling into the Erethran embassy by known and registered Erethran candidates—but my position with them is public knowledge. The Council and other interested parties aren't even trying to hide the watchers they have around the embassy, so any attempt of sneaking in that way is a guaranteed failure.

And while I could lean on my position a little, the amount of help the Empress is willing to offer is minimal. Part of the reason we helped out on the planets was because she wasn't willing to even stay neutral without both myself and the Empress Apparent leaning on her.

For that matter, things were a little touch-and-go in the first few days after we received Katherine's message, as the Empress received quite a few "suggestions" that I be handed over.

Of course, the fact the Empress didn't bend to the Council has as much to do with safeguarding the honor and prestige of the Empire as any liking for me. As a seated member of the inner council, the Erethran Empire has some pull. But it's a faded level of influence, with their lack of Paladins—until recently—and more of a matter of size and momentum than anything else.

Even so, they have some pull, which is why I've also not been abducted directly from Erethran space. Never mind the fact that the entire cover story is that Earth has gotten a little too big for its britches, with its Dungeon World status and their blockage of multiple parties trying to enter the planet to exploit its citizens. The greater concern is that even more Dungeon Worlds will do the same, essentially depriving entire groups from access to Leveling opportunities. It's that fear that is being exploited to harm Earth and draw me back.

"I get all that," Harry says after I finish explaining in party chat. "We can't go to Irvina directly because they'd know the moment we arrive. I can even see the need to deal with the highest-Level human threat."

I can't help but smile a little at that. Being a Heroic-level threat is no small deterrent for certain parties.

"But why exactly are we here?" Harry waves, encompassing the underwater city we've Portaled into.

Anlacwo is a water planet, where landmasses are few and far between and multi-kilometer-tall wave fronts swamp even the tallest peaks. Rather than deal with that, cities are built underwater, where the influence of tides high above are significantly decreased and layered bubbles of force shields and permeable crystal keep the air within.

The moment we arrived, the Erethran Honor Guard chose to part from us, leaving us to walk out of the hidden side alley he'd deposited us into. It says something about the city—and planet—that there are no safeguards against people randomly entering it like we did.

As Harry, Mikito, and I head down the street, a wide variety of Galactic humanoids mix and mingle, arguing over roadside foodstalls, merchant inventory screens, and men of the night. The smells are an assault to the senses, a mixture of musky fur, thrilling pheromones, and charred meat; all leaving a furry taste on one's tongue and a slight itch on the skin.

Those who move around are mostly dressed in Adventurer chic—armored jumpsuits with a variety of patches, straps, and pouches for weapons and other useful utility items. Enchanted items can be spotted strapped to arms, around necks or ears or tails, while high-tech communicators and low-tech melee weapons mix with gay abandon. It's a riot of colors—in some cases literally, as a furred, cat-hyena hybrid creature's nanowoven hair flashes through all the colors of the rainbow.

The buildings too showcase the wide variety of alien sensibilities and architecture, some bulging tens of stories high while others are living plants, hollowed out to teleport those entering to another location. The only thing they all have in common is the ability to widen their doorways to accommodate the sizes and shapes of the aliens tromping, gliding, and wiggling their way inward.

"There's someone we need to speak to before we try to enter Irvina," I say, answering Harry's question.

"Someone?" Harry says.

Mikito is idly eying the people around, head turning as she scans for trouble. Hitoshi is held in easy readiness over her shoulder as she surveys the crowd, seeking trouble. Her watchfulness is enough to put off the pickpockets and thieves that work through the crowds, using their Skills to dip into Inventory Spaces.

"Why don't you put your Skills to use?" I'm not just being an asshole. The reason why we're here originates from the library in my head. If Harry can figure it out though, so can our enemies.

Harry hisses in exasperation at me, but when I look around us, he falls silent. I'm not sure how much longer I can keep putting off telling them my secrets, but this is certainly not the place.

Focused for the moment, Harry's eyes flick from side to side, semi-autonomous flying camera drones recording the alien streets while he works. Idly, I wonder how much he's managing to record, since nearly everyone here has privacy screens running, blocking out simple recording of their features. Depending on the level of sophistication in their tech or Skills, some or all the information his drones might record will be false.

Even as Harry works his contacts, trying to ascertain what's special about this city, this planet, we keep walking. I follow the bouncing ball in my minimap, guiding the team through winding streets and across moving walkways. Mikito stays silent, only disappearing once to purchase some walking street food for us all. Trusting in me.

The moment our feet cross the threshold into the Barrens, the flood of Mana hits us hard. It's like stepping through an invisible bubble, and on the other side is pressure and pain as Mana floods into our bodies and crowds the System's connection to us. The two types of Mana—unmarked, raw Mana and System Mana—battle for control within our bodies, and the System itself flickers and distorts before the connection stabilizes.

Of course, that's when they hit us.

***

The Skill lock slams down first, blocking access to my Skills. Fractions of a second later, the attacks arrive. Fast-moving arrows, enhanced lasers expelled from mounted weaponry, a Psychic assault. They target me directly, with only a few attacks striking Mikito and Harry.

I survive the initial onslaught for a few reasons. Firstly, the same barrier that we passed through and messed with our System connections also degrades their attacks. The Mana differential on both sides means that the attacks that originate from the lower Mana side skew off slightly, are blunted or slowed down.

Secondly is the simple fact that I've been waiting for an attack. The enhanced Soul Shield I've been walking around with takes the attack before it pops, blocking about a fifth of the initial volley. The fractions of a second it gives me let me shift my body to ablate some of the attacks, let them skip off while I continue the dodge. At the same time, my secondary emergency shielding ring flicks on, blocking another fifth of the damage. Armored jumpsuit and my Class damage resistances help soak up some of the rest.

I'm still turned into a tumbling ball of fire and pain as the attacks keep slamming into me. Invisible chains explode from the ground, attaching to my body even as an additional dimensional lock blocks my Blink Step.

Rather than force my way through the block, I drop a pair of automated shield barriers around me. They pop into existence, giving me long seconds of protection. I push for Soul Shield, attempting to trigger the Skill and failing. Since I'm pinned, I borrow Ali's eyes, even as the Spirit slaps additional defenses in place, using my own Skill to pull forth earth from the ground to keep me alive.

I hold off on Sanctum for now, since triggering it would take me completely out of the fight. And, frankly, our ambushers are probably sticking around. It's not as if I have friends who can rush in to help.

Using Ali's eyes, I take in the surroundings. There are four attackers. A cyborg-like slug creature, the one who blasted me with the beam weaponry. A floating swarm of yellow-and-black-striped bee insects, whose buzz and drone conjure the spells that assail us. A purple-and-pink-furred Jarrack is the psychic, bands of metal rising into a crown of sparkling electricity that boosts its psychic attacks. Lastly, the trainer Ranger of indeterminate race in his gimp suit, who's drawing and firing his arrows at such a rate he might as well have an automatic in his hands. Each of those arrows are enchanted, displaying a wide variety of attack types. Some arrows hum with teeth-aching sonic attacks, others are wreathed in fire, ice, lightning, and other, more esoteric energies.

Luckily for me, the Ranger's focused on Mikito, giving me time to deal with the blood gushing from my nose, ears, and eyes as the Psychic smashes into my mind. Pain, confusion, a pickax to my mind. I breathe, trying to focus as I strain against the Skill block holding me down and trying to trigger Skill after Skill.

Skill block Skills are rare, and there are a variety of ways to beat them. But the easiest method is to just spend Mana until such time as the Skill block shatters. They are all generally Mana based, requiring the blocked individual to expend more Mana than the attacker. And unlike most Skills, Skill blocks all have a cooldown. Often, quite a significant one.

So I smash Skill after Skill into the block, burning away his Mana and the block, desperately trying to free myself.

In the meantime, Ali's split himself. One of his bodies starts with keeping me alive. He's not blocked, so he's casting Soul Shield with abandon—just in time to block the next series of attacks. Next up, he layers healing spells on me, propping up my plummeting health.

As for his other bodies, they take the fight to the group of attackers. Of course, he's not as strong as they are, even when he's lashing out with his Elemental Affinity. But he does have access to my Skills, which lets him throw attacks around wily nily, making him a great distraction.

Under assault, with the initial surprise ablated and stymied, the Master Class attackers attempt to pull back. Whether to retreat entirely or give themselves space, it's uncertain. Because that's when the next surprise happens.

A trio of attackers explode from the shadows and jump the Psychic, each of them wielding melee weapons. The first holds a familiar naginata, the other two katanas. They're all dressed in lamellar armor, painted red and black, with the overly large, distinctive helmets of Japanese samurai. The fight occurs at speed, initiated with a Charge skill by each of them, before they spin around in synchronicity and lay into their opponent.

The Psychic's mental assault on me stops as blood flies and his arm is nearly chopped off. Blood—yellow blood—splatters on the ground as the trio of attackers lay into him.

I breathe deeply, eyes wide as I check my own information. Fractions of my normal health level are left, but with a snap, I feel the Skill lock shatter as my passive Skills force themselves through. It's a mental plug giving way, and the Mana I've been pouring at my defense kicks in. It fills the space where my Skill should be and I get to work.

A Blade Strike from the weapon in my hand, combined with Peasant's Fury and Cleave, cuts through the air. A crescent of energy tinted with blue from Mana Imbue and crimson with Peasant's Fury cuts across space. It bisects the slug's body. The slug slides apart, blood gushing from the two halves as it dies. Its body twitches, but I feel a number of other debuffs disappear as it dies.

The moment the Skill lock shatters, the bee-attacker and archer run for it. The bees disperse, exploding into a fast-expanding globe of tiny insects while other portions of their body teleport away. The bodies dart into the ground, into the sky, and away in multiple directions, leaving the area in seconds.

At the same time, the Ranger fades out as he dodges Mikito's swing, blood flinging into the air and turning into phantom light as her cut passes through his faded body.

A flare of power, and the Psychic takes control of the trio's bodies briefly, making his attackers throw themselves out of the way. They tumble through the air, and the Psychic flickers. For a moment, I almost believe I see multiple copies of the Psychic dash off before he resolves properly into a single figure, blasting straight up toward the edge of the bubble dome. A mental notification tells me he's trying to hide his presence by overlaying mental projections, but it bounces right off me.

I clench my fist, pouring Mana into Grand Cross, and end him instead. The Skill activates, compressed into a small space, crushing him and forming a deep impression in the ground. As an afterthought, I throw up a Cleanse to clear out the numerous streaks of blood on my face and my body.

Mikito twists, glaring in the direction the archer was last at. She's on the balls of her feet. I can tell she wants to go after our attackers, but she stays, scanning for trouble instead. Playing bodyguard rather than attack dog.

"Let them go," I say. "We should keep moving."

"How did they know where we were?" Harry says, his normally dark skin the closest to pale he can be. He might be used to violence, but we have a history about being attacked randomly, the pair of us.

I'm not surprised I only notice him now, what with his Just a Bystander ability. It makes sure he's not directly targeted in battles, marking him a noncombatant in most cases. So long as he stays a noncombatant. And that includes things like throwing up buffs.

"Probably set up a tracker on the System for us," I say.

I drink more of my potions and renew my Soul Shield, making a face as I pull out the Hod. I step into the armor, watching it form around me and offer another layer of protection. I really should have been wearing it, as the ache of a burnt and blasted body tells me. If not for the System-created blocks in my mind for pain, I'd probably still be on the ground, crying.

"I'm surprised they tried and failed to kill you," Mikito says, frowning. "I would have thought they'd have run the numbers already."

"Probably didn't have the latest Skill information." The upgrade to my Soul Shield was done using the last of the discretionary budget I had access to. Now, I'm cut off from the Erethran budget entirely.

What I don't say is that the Psychic attack was blunted a lot more than it should have been thanks to my Administrator Class. It's not something a Grand Paladin would have, but that's probably what they were estimating on. Add the additional damage reduction from my hidden Class—again, not part of the Grand Paladin Class—and they probably were just using wrong assumptions.

The next attack won't though, since most of the damage data will likely be public. My next attackers are likely to assume I have some hidden Titles or Skills and pile on even more damage.

"Agreed, let's move," Ali says, floating alongside me. His other bodies are leading the way, moving along each side of the street that has since cleared out. Galactics are good at that—the first hint of a battle, they scramble.

"And us, honored one?" one of the Samurai trio asks. They're all on their feet, standing together with weapons out.

"You can come," I say. Anyone who risks their lives—especially at their low Levels—is not a real threat but an ally.

There's silence behind me and I risk a glance back, seeing that the three are not staring at me but Mikito. The Samurai makes a face as she repeats my words. They bow to her and fall into formation at the back of the group, keeping watch as we hurry away from the fight. None of us want to be around when the police arrive. I'm not inclined to bribe my way out of trouble with my precious Credits.

We keep walking, the main street we're on splitting again and again, becoming narrower with each split. I lead the wary group deeper into this portion of the city, the Mana growing denser each second. Soon enough, System notifications fritz out, the Mana density reaching that critical point.

I find a small park-cum-training ground and flare my Aura just long enough to get the few civilians to leave. A quick dispersal of formation flags and payment to the field sets up a privacy screen. Then, I turn and regard the three Samurai, all of whom stand at attention.

Ruvuds Tadauji, Way Down It Shines, From the Slums, Devoted Fan (Mikito Sato), Slayers of Goblins (Level 42 Samurai) (B)
HP: 1420/1420
MP: 630/630
Conditions: Mana Drip, Health over Honor

Vrasceids Tadauji, Thrice Blessed, Devoted Fan (Mikito Sato), Slayer of Goblins and Thrashers,... (Level 6 Middle Samurai) (A)
HP: 1970/1970
MP: 1220/1220
Conditions: Mana Drip, Health over Honor, Isoide

Agr'us Tadauji, Parent's Blessing, Devoted Fan (Mikito Sato), Slayers of Niktiku, Imma, Imps, Lis... (Level 47 Samurai) (B)
HP: 1870/1870
MP: 430/430
Conditions: Mana Drip

"Who the hell are you?" I say, holding the sword I materialize in my hand pointed at the ground.

If my anger and the pulse of my Aura bothers them, it doesn't show.

"We are Mikito-sama's clan, shogun," Vrasceids says, bowing to me.

Now that we're safe, they've all dismissed their helmets, which lets me stare at the gilled, green-scaled humanoid with his too-big eyes. I wouldn't call him ugly, just… alien. Years in the Galaxy have certainly altered my views on what ugly really is. What lies beneath a fair figure can be so much worse than the most open of sores and puss-ridden visages.

"He's not our shogun, he's our daimyo," Agr'us snarls. She's the shortest of them, a Grimsar katana-wielding fighter, broad like most dwarves but lacking the beard. Otherwise, I really wouldn't be able to tell if she was female at all.

"No, he's neither. Lord Sato is our lord," Ruvuds insists. Surprisingly, he's the closest to human, easily mistakable as one of us if not for the aqua blue skin and the cat-eyes. "He is her daimyo, but she is ours."

"Impossible. Samurai cannot be lords of other samurai!" Vrasceids says. "We are but her subordinates. He is our final lord."

"What?" I say, realizing they're bickering right in front of us. I turn to stare at Mikito, who is trying her best to act as if none of this is her business. Ali, on the other hand, having collapsed back into himself, has conjured a box of popcorn. "Care to explain?"

"They're my fan club."

"I think I missed that." I didn't. "Say again?"

"They're part of my fan club," Mikito says.

"Right. Fan club. Sure." I look at Harry, who seems perfectly unperturbed by all this. "Did you know about her fan club?"

"Of course. I did an entire segment on it," Harry says. "Nice to know all my hard work is being ignored."

"It wasn't… I… yeah. Sorry." I shrug. "You're right. I have been ignoring your broadcasts. But, fan club?"

"From my arena battles," Mikito says. "Some people have chosen to…"

"Follow in the way of the sword. For it is more than a simple weapon; it is an answer to life's very questions," Ruvuds said.

Mikito visibly twitches, then she draws a deep breath, calming herself. I watch as a mask drops over her face, as she stills her mind and emotions. The three are bickering again about quotes from some Five Ring book. I'm pretty sure they have it wrong, there being only One Ring.

Still, I get enough of the context. "Seriously, you made alien weebs?"

"I can kill you, you know," Mikito says.

I grin, but then drop the humor as I face the trio. "Hey!" Once that gets their attention, I continue. "How did you know how to find us?"

"The clan was alerted about the actions taken against Earth. Many are on their way to Earth already, but others have been on watch for Lord Sato. We keep track of her movements and we were luckily in the vicinity," Vrasceids says.

"I told you, that's not the right form of address. It is Sato-san!" Agr'us says.

I roll my eyes as they devolve into another argument and turn to Mikito. "Do you know anything about this?"

She shakes her head. I sigh, eyeing the trio. Finding out what they know is going to be painful.

***

Eventually, we get enough details to pacify my paranoia. Unlike myself, Mikito's never really had to divert a large amount of her Credits or Skills into hiding where she is or where she will be. Not to say she doesn't have any

Skill blockers, but in this case, it just wasn't enough. It helped that the fan base actually are registered as true allies for her, using some esoteric system that allows them to track her at a much reduced rate. It wouldn't be possible, at least at the rate that they were provided, for others to track Mikito and thus myself.

In either case, we pinned the idea that Mikito would require additional Skills for hiding for later. We still have an objective to complete and it's quite clear that now that we're out of the Erethran Empire, our enemies are taking action.

I am reassured that at the very least, Mikito's fan club members aren't a threat to us. Not in a direct manner. Since that's the case, and since they refuse to leave, I take them with us as we head for our destination. They follow along like three well-armed, lethal ducklings waddling after their even more deadly mother duck.

As we walk through the twisting turns of the city, they keep watch. We ascend a skyscraper, traipse through a winding skybridge, drop multiple stories to the ground to reach an otherwise inaccessible pathway, walk through shadowed alleyways, and duck through half-lit, barely open retail shops. More than once, we drop small surprises behind—some to hide our path, others to just cause havoc. Nothing lethal, but enough to disrupt pursuers if there are any. Always set to turn off after a certain period, knowing that we aren't the only individuals in town.

Not that the influx of Mana into this location wouldn't mess with people anyway.

"What is this place?" Harry asks as we walk through another worn-down corridor lit by luminescent moss. The War Reporter has his hand splayed out before him, recording everything with his Skill while walking.

His little camera drones have broken down, unable to handle the Mana saturation levels, forcing him to rely on his innate Skills.

"It's an artificial Forbidden Zone. The easiest way to deal with System spying, outside of Skills, is to create a Forbidden Zone around yourself. The overabundance of raw Mana means that the System is unable to function properly. Anything that happens in here is pretty close to not having happened at all, as far as the System is concerned," I explain to Harry.

"Pretty close?"

"Always exceptions. Special Skills, a lot of Credits, special individuals," Ali says, staring at me as he floats alongside.

I can only shrug, knowing what he's alluding to. I feel it too, the way my presence almost firms up the System around me. I wonder how far this effect stretches, how much variation it brings to the breakdown of the System's processes. But I'm also pretty sure that trying to track me this way would require significant resources, maybe even the kind that a Senior Administrator would have to bring to bear.

And no, I'm not entirely sure why I'm so certain of this. Some things, some knowledge pieces, seem to have been inserted into my memories as part of my Class.

"Are we using this place to throw a false trail?" Harry says. "Or a place to work out a way to enter Irvina better?"

"A little bit of both." I stop before a nondescript door, nothing marking it beyond the address stenciled across its face. I stare at it, then turn to the others and give them a half-shrug. "I'm going to have to do this myself."

Mikito stirs, looking a little upset.

I shake my head. "Trust me."

When I'm sure there are no more objections, I rap on the door, hoping that the one within will speak with me.

If not, we're really screwed.

Chapter 5

I walk into the room with a confident smile, one that belies the deep anxiety lodged in my gut. Behind me, I watch through Ali's eyes as my companions get bounced off the ward as they try to follow me in.

Told them so.

Briefly, I look over the new notification details even as my System Edit Skill provides further details on how the Skill keeping this place secret works on my friends' minds. It's not exactly mind control, just a nudge to make them forget what they read.

> **You have entered a Questor Library 174.6 (Corrupted)**
> *You have met the minimum requirements to make use of this library (System Quest completion rate >80% or Corrupt Questor Title).*
> - *You have full access to the library resources*
> - *You may speak with the Librarian*
> - *You receive a +10% bonus to learning speed*

The library itself is spartan, a series of small plinths spread across the empty room. There are no Questors within, though I know from experience, one need only place their hand on a plinth to gain access to the Questor's library. The room itself is shaded in a light green color, ambient lighting a soft, gentle, and disturbing color to my senses.

Of it all, it is my Mana Sense that is struggling. Between the greater-than-normal Mana levels and the adjusted Mana flows within, I feel as though a heavy fog cloaks that sense, making everything seem faint and muffled.

The dullness in my Mana Sense, the way even my System Edit is askew is why I don't sense the Librarian's presence until he is before me, just off-center from my line of sight. Long fingers clasped before a charcoal-grey-suited body, covering a white shirt and a thin black tie, whilst an overly large head, whose grey skin is pulled tight, stares at me. Large black eyes without an iris regard me, too-sharp teeth pulled into a permanent grin as the head cocks to the side.

"You haven't changed your taste at all," I say.

"Questor Lee. A surprise," Feh'ral says.

I stare at the man-thing head-on, shivering as I regard the Head Librarian. The sapient creature that stuck the library in my head, who is the cause of all my trouble. Staring at him, I drag his Status to the fore. I feel his Skill fight it, fight Ali and me. I see the Mana the System pours into the Skill, aiding him. Using him as a channel in this place, just as it uses my own presence. But the System is thin here, fritzy.

And I am an Administrator. I shove aside the System, find the Skill, and slip in a few words with the System Edit Skill. I alter the code that exists within the Mana itself that makes up the System and his Status blooms.

Librarian Feh'ral Vaqwe, Corrupt Questor, Librarians of Note v.18421, Deep Sense, Mana Pier, Slayer of Goblins, Leviathans, Gorgons, Hugag, Gumberoo, Adled, Nucklavee, … (Librarian of the Ten Thousand Paths Level 14) (L)

HP: 2380/2380

MP: 10168/10230

Conditions: Mana Pier, Domain of Words, Knowledge Fount, Skilled Personage, Aura of the Ten Thousand Paths, In the Deepest Abyss

"*Very nice, boy-o.*"

"*Thanks.*" I read his information quickly. Most of it isn't that surprising, especially the last Condition. It's a very powerful Skill that keeps him hidden, as much as his presence in this artificial Forbidden Zone.

"What did you?" Feh'ral says, sounding shocked. "Wait, this Skill…" His eyes go blank, lips moving as he processes the treasure trove of information at his—literal—fingertips. "Not that. Or that. Maybe but no…"

"Don't bother. It's not in the library," I say. "I should know. I've digested the majority of the information."

"Impossible. It has been months only," Feh'ral says dismissively.

"Yeah, well, let's just say my new Class gives me a bit of a boost to that."

That gets his attention. He peers at me, using his own Skill to read my Status information. I tell Ali to let him read it, curious to see what Feh'ral can pick up. I'm not sure he has a Legendary level Analysis Skill, but it'd be up there.

"A Grand Paladin? A prestige Class, but nothing special."

"Not that one."

Again, Feh'ral's eyes narrow. He floats closer to me, his feet never moving. Those dark eyes glitter with interest as long fingers move, the only movement in his own body. #creepasslibrarian.

"I see no other Class. But you are not lying."

"I'm not."

"Fascinating. And your System Quest Completion Rate… amazing." Feh'ral leans in, his face millimeters from mine. When he speaks, his breath brings with it the smell of cotton candy and caramel popcorn—a not unpleasant but disturbing smell. Especially when I involuntarily take a deeper whiff. "What is it that you have done?"

"A lot. A lot that we need speak about. But we're going to have to trade."

"Trade?"

"Information. And aid."

Feh'ral freezes, then his Aura crashes down on me. I might not be a Grand Paladin in truth, but the resistances of a Junior Administrator are even better in many ways. I stay standing on my feet even as the Aura of a Legendary Classed monster pushes against me. We stand, deadlocked, millimeters from one another, struggling in silence.

Eventually, the Aura fades. "Fascinating. Come. Let us speak." Feh'ral never shifts his gaze from me as he floats backward, away from the entrance to a hidden doorway that slides open at the back of the room. He never even looks away, knowing I will come.

And I do.

Because he's the devil I have to use against the Council. The man I've been searching for, all this time.

***

We take a seat across from one another at a simple table. It's wood of a form, green rather than brown, looking similar to jade but feeling warmer, more organic, like wood itself. I know it's a crafting material from one of the many living forests out there, popular with the rich due to its scarcity. It even has some moderate preservation qualities, emitting a field to help safeguard against damage.

We take seats on force chairs that form for us to rest against. It's the strangest thing, watching Feh'ral bend as if he's hinging at his hips to sit before his knees collapse and he is seated before me, still regarding me with those iris-less eyes.

"You desire a trade, answers for answers. Why should I not rip your memories apart instead?" Feh'ral says.

"Because you want the System Quest completed, and I think you know how to do it. But I also have a piece too, I believe."

"I have a theory. The theory seems to have received some approval from the System," he acknowledges. "But many have claimed what you have. Why is your claim different?"

I grin. My helmet from the Hod is down, so he can easily read my face, but I'm still resting in the comfortable embrace of powered armor.

"Confident. Answer for answer then. For I am intrigued."

"Good. But I'd rather have a different trade. My knowledge, the Skill, my Class, and that information." I raise a finger. "For answers to what the Council really wants you for. And help."

"Help?"

"With them."

Silence extends between us, and the atmosphere grows chilly. Only the rasp of my breathing, the gentle expansion of cloth and metal as I breathe breaks the pindrop silence.

"A small matter, to take on the Council." Feh'ral titters, voice high and squeaky. It's kind of disturbing, his laughter. "Did you think I would say that?"

"No. But I'm guessing if you want to finish the Quest, you'll need to do it anyway. And if I survive, what I learn might further aid you."

"High regards."

"You'll understand why, if you agree," I say.

"A blind request. Very well, I'll aid you as much as your information is worth."

"I'll hold you to it then."

It's not the straight-out agreement I wanted, but it's better than I had hoped for. Rather than delay further, I lean forward and talk. About what happened with the library in my mind, and furthermore, what happened in the throne room. The feeling I got when the Master Quest formed, and my desire to change it. Eventually, to how I changed it, borrowing from my Mana Sense, from the library's information and sheer will. The change in the Quest and the resulting Class alteration on my side, the enforced Heroic Class.

I talk for what seems hours, as Feh'ral probes my words and story, searching for gaps in my tale, searching for knowledge. He manipulates the Skill and Class information I display to him, even as I ignore the numerous warnings that appear when I show it to him. I'm a little concerned by the warnings, but I assume he's got a way of fixing the information flow back to the System. Or he's just intent on leaving later.

At some point, drinks appear, glasses formed from the table itself and refilled from inventory. The drink is some weird alien beverage, effervescent with carbonated bubbles but warm and soothing, a hint of a complex sugar like honey combined with a floral taste. I provide the cookies and chocolate.

He's dipping a chocolate chip cookie in his drink when I'm done, long fingers delicately holding the glass aloft as he regards me. I let the silence linger, chewing on my snack while he thinks.

"An Administrator Class. A hidden Class. The only truly hidden Class," Feh'ral says finally, leaning forward. "Fascinating. I would say impossible, but evidence proves contrary. Utterly fascinating." He leans back, his eyes going blank. I watch the drop of liquid gather on his cookie, raised halfway between cup and body, forgotten as he accesses data banks. "I wonder if Librarian Oaret was hinting... and K'sa of the Nine Gorges. He had just gained his...

"The library of Mus...

"... and the galaxy of Rexsa was destroyed...

"The Mana repercussions...

"Missing Mana flow, at the triumvirate experiment..."

He mutters and whispers to himself and I'm content to wait and listen, each overheard word bringing with it, its own wave of information from the library. I wait and sip on my drink.

After I finish my drink, I cough. When that fails to get his attention, I rap the table with my knuckles. That still doesn't get his attention. My next action is simple—I flare my Mana, churning it as if I'm starting a spell. That drags the Librarian's attention back to me. It's like a light switch flips on as his eyes lock onto me.

"Ah... my apologies. I was cross-referencing some previous work. This might explain a number of significant discrepancies in the records. Why, just the information about a true Hidden Class would explain the statistical anomaly detected at—"

"Your System Quest," I cut in, not willing to wait anymore.

"What?"

"What is it now?"

System Quest Completion Rate: 91.1%

"Fascinating! An increase. Finally." The Librarian leans forward. "It would seem that my hypothesis is correct."

"Hypothesis?"

"That to complete the Quest, further knowledge is unimportant. The final quest completion rate must be sought by action itself," he says.

"What kind of action?"

"You know as well as I do."

We sit in silence at that pronouncement before I bestir myself. As much as I'd like to pursue this conversation, to wonder why he is higher than me, why he's so far ahead... why I haven't gone up... there are lives on the line.

"Is what I have provided sufficient?"

"Sufficient." Feh'ral falls silent, lips pursing in thought. "Maybe. The Questors must test this. We must see if we can replicate this Class. Ascertain the information with replication... I wonder what the final proximate cause of your change would be? The library? The Levels? Willpower? The timing gap between choice and action? All of it? None?"

Feh'ral mutters to himself, eyes going blank. I slap my hand flat on the table, the loud thump making glasses jump. In the small, private room, the noise echoes.

"Later. We have a Council to handle."

"I will not—cannot—fight them," he says. "I am a non-Combat Classer. And the Council, many of them—"

"Are. I know. But you must have some idea of how to handle them. And we need the pressure on Earth to be lifted."

"Mmm... that I can help with. There are true Questors on the Council still. What you have provided... the actions... maybe if we..." Feh'ral's voice grows faint again, but this time, I let him fade out as he thinks.

"*Am I like this?*" I send to Ali. If so, this is incredibly frustrating.

"*Sort of. You're more focused when you need to be. But the library seems to muck with everyone who is connected to it,*" Ali replies.

I grunt and pull more chocolates from my storage space. Feh'ral's hands occasionally move. A portion of me, the part that allows me to Edit things, can feel him at work. I can't read what he sends, can't hear what he says, but I can tell he's accessing not just the library but a communication platform, one that puts him in touch with others.

Fascinating. Perhaps with a little push, I could even access the information he's reading, but I get the feeling that that isn't the point of my Skill. I'm not meant to use my Class for eavesdropping.

When he comes back to me, his voice is detached again. "I have informed others. Requested their help. Questors who are partial to our cause will lend aid. I have also called a meeting, a Great Gathering and Sharing. It is within my right, as a Head Librarian."

I blink.

"This will happen in three months. If the information gathered is sufficient..."

"Well?" I ask.

"Then it is likely another purge will begin."

I open my mouth to ask what he means, but the library beats me to it. Information floods into me, bringing tears to my eyes and rupturing blood vessels. Another section, another compartment I had not realized was hidden within my mind, within my portion of the System, breaks open. Information about the purge appears, and I break.

A galaxy, Rexsa, burns. Planets are torn asunder, moons cracked and pulverized. New asteroid fields are created, so dense with rocks and corpses that one could almost walk across the space.

Ships, so many ships that I cannot see the end of them, are marshalled, firing upon planets, solar systems. Hidden figures in shadows and bright, bold Champions march down streets, *tearing Questors from their hiding spots. Challenging those who stand and fight, offering no mercy.*

A child screams as its mother is killed before him with a single punch. The Heroic Class Gravitic Imploder pauses, then a voice squawks in his ears. It turns multi-faceted eyes onto the child and his fist blurs again. The scream cuts off.

Space ports spin, burning. Another implodes as gravity focuses deep within, and metal and mortal are crushed. A figure flies out, metal pulled from the wreckage reforming into machines that turn and blast at the Gravitic Imploder. He dies, but another takes his place.

Another galaxy, another solar system, another planet.

More death.

More destruction.

More endings met.

The purge plays out not in days or months or decades. It takes over a century, as Questors and those who support them are found and ended. As anyone who backed the current leadership, who might have learned something is killed.

The purge is declared necessary due to the Questors' actions. Their experiments, the sapients torn from home, sent out of the System, forced to lose Classes, to use Skills on a never-ending stage. Flames of prejudice are fanned, for the Questors do not hoard their information, the results of their tests. They steal Class information from groups that desire to keep it secret, they release Skill information for fractions of Credits, even cheaper than the System.

And the Galactic Council turns on them, burning them to the ground. Officially, a new Questor organization is formed, their quest, their search placed under the strict oversight of the Council itself. Those who escape the purges become the start of the Corrupt Questors.

In time, the oversight relaxes. Questors get on with their lives. They join together again as the desire for knowledge overrides politics.

Then the purges begin again. When the Questors go too far. More death, more destruction, more oversight. The same dance, played over and over again. Millennia apart, information about prior purges removed from the records.

Forgotten by all but the Questors themselves.

"Thousand hells," I say. My mind throbs even as System healing puts me back together.

Feh'ral flicks his fingers and the blood on the table disappears in wisps of smoke. "The purge?"

"Yeah. Why would you put that in there?" I say. There's no System information in it, just a long line of atrocities committed by the Council in its quest to destroy the Questors and any who might be considered their allies.

"To remember, to ensure others prepare."

"And you think the Council will enact another?" I whisper. A feeling of dread creeps up me. There weren't hundreds of lives lost or thousands. Entire planets were destroyed, an entire galaxy shattered. Billions would fall if another purge occurs.

"Yes. I am almost certain that part of the reason for the last was because of this information," Feh'ral says.

"But... why? I mean, sure, it's important, but isn't all information for sale?"

"Not if the Council makes the cost high enough to be infinite. And with the Lady of Shadows in play..."

I shudder, recalling that name. A Legendary whose ability revolves around secrets and hiding them. Yeah, I can see how a secret could be hidden, if such a person wanted it to be hidden.

But she's not that old. I know that for certain. She's a young Legendary—as these things go. Just a few centuries old. Nothing compared to the millennia of history the Galactic Council has. So perhaps the purge was the best they could do before.

Yet for all my dread, all my fear, I do not ask him to stop or to recall the information he sent to the Corrupt Questors. Not just because I think it'll help us, help reduce the pressure on Earth. But because I understand him, understand the "true" Questors. Those driven, like me, to find an answer. There is nothing we will not sacrifice for the answer.

Not ourselves.

Not others.

Nothing.

***

Hours later, I walk out.

We talked. We strategized. I was given a book. We came up with new plans and destroyed them with logic and creativity. He contacted other Questors, arranged for information to be purchased, support to be sent. I was provided even more data.

Outside, the group is still waiting. Harry's seated with his back to the wall, working on his show. Or gathering information. Never can tell with that one. Mikito, on the other hand, is meditating silently while her three fan club members are standing beside her in horse stance, sweating bullets.

I snort at the sight but choose to stay silent. Ali doesn't, flying over and already ribbing the trio.

"About time," Harry says. "Was he-who-shall-not-be-named in there?"

I look around rather pointedly. Harry sniffs, muttering something about paranoia. It's not, not when they really are intending to end you.

"Now what?" Mikito asks.

Her fan club get out of horse stance, moving to flank her. She rolls her eyes a little but says nothing.

"Now, we visit someone else." I take off, following the minimap marker that Feh'ral provided.

"Who?" Harry says.

"The person responsible for our current environment."

There are more than a few gasps, but I ignore all other questions as we keep walking. We've wasted enough time. And there's a lot more we need to get done.

Chapter 6

Stepping through the unremarkable doorway, I peer around the low-light interior. It's mostly colored in a light spectrum that's outside of the normal human range, making everything look pale blue and violet. Luckily, my power armor can deal with that, recoloring everything so that I can see without issue.

The first thing that meets me is a bare entrance hallway, one that stretches into the horizon. Following me, a step behind, are my friends. Or they should be. But two steps in, I turn around and see a closed door and no party members. In my party interface, they're still there with full health. Their Mana level drops as buffs appear under their sheets. I can't help but agree with the sentiment, throwing on a few myself.

A quick check shows that we aren't in comm range or even party chat. We've been separated as easily as a carnivore from vegetables.

"What's going on?" I say softly, listening to the echoes of my words bouncing down the hall.

"Games," Ali replies. He's the only one here with me, our link superseding whatever tricks were played.

I debate what to do, testing the extent of the trap. A punch to the wall has it crumple, but not give way. I should be able to cut my way through with my sword. It slides into the wall easily enough, but there doesn't seem to be an end to the wall itself. Might be a few feet thick, might be miles. There's also a rather obvious corridor.

Shrugging, I walk. I'm here to ask a favor, not destroy their home. I start walking and keep walking. Twenty minutes later, I'm still moving forward, my brows drawn together as Ali floats alongside me. From the map of the surroundings before we entered the room, the building itself should have been traversed within ten minutes, easily.

"This normal?"

"Spatial manipulation? For this guy?" Ali shrugs.

The entire location is locked down, so jumping forward isn't possible, even if the very same space is twisted by the Skill. All I can do is walk and hope there's an ending in sight.

I'm not certain how long I walk. The featureless light grey corridor, the low-light illumination, and the soft thud of my feet blending together. My feet don't ache, but the pressure of my feet, the shift in my weight never changes. Even the smell of the corridor—when I finally decide to put away the Hod—is the same as the scentless filtered air of before. Time blends together, and even the System clock in the corner of my vision offers no help, flicking between seconds back and forth.

When the ending arrives, it does so abruptly. One step I'm in the corridor, the next I'm in the midst of a towering amphitheatre that's open to the sky, a single table and a pair of lounging chairs in the center. Pink and yellow sand stain the ground below, reminiscent of alien beaches but without the mojitos. In one of the chairs is a figure in a white three-piece suit and a fedora.

The seated figure is humanish. Spray-bottle-tanned, unwrinkled in that over-application of Botox fashion you see in some celebrities, hair bleached unnaturally white. The eyes are the most disturbing—startingly green like a glacial lake but blank of emotions. Empty.

A push of will gets me nothing as I attempt to call information of his Status to being. I know Ali fails too.

No surprise.

I could push it, drag it forth as I did with the Librarian. But where I dared to do so with Feh'ral, I dare not with this man. For in this place, the one before me controls all.

"Honored—"

"No names. No Titles. Nothing like that. Now, how do you know of me?" the speaker says, his eyes fixed on my figure. There's no threat in the voice. It's perfectly calm and even a little bored. He doesn't need to threaten, for he holds all the cards here.

The more I stare at him, the more I realize that whatever he is, he's not really human. It's a form he drew from the ether, the Mana—a manipulation of my expectations, probably just how Ali popped up looking like he is.

Which is, in a way, a hint of what this man is. Who he is.

But I'm careful not to think that too loudly either. "I spoke with a man… alien… who is a part of a group that searches for answers. About a question…"

"Of course you are." There's a fatalistic tone to his voice. "You couldn't be a religious fanatic searching for another convert. Or a portal-to-portal salesman. No, you'd have to be one of *them.*"

"Yeah. Sorry… I had your location from, well…" I struggle to figure out what to say, how to say it, without using Feh'ral's name or the information on the library or anything else.

"I don't care. You people always find me, no matter how many times I shift things. I gave up a thousand years ago. Or was it ten?" The man's eyes go blank as he considers the question. "A hundred? No, it couldn't be a hundred. Maybe fifty… no. It was only recent, so it must have been six."

He prattles for a while on meaningless matters while I keep hold of my temper. There's no point trying to rush him, though there's a little bit of fear that I might have been here for… well… years now.

"Well then, tell me. What's your unique research project?" he finally says, focusing on me.

"Research project?"

"Study. Hypothesis that you want to prove. I'll warn you, if it's not unique, I'll be very upset at being disturbed."

I frown. "Really? Because it's not unique enough?"

"Well, of course. So what is it? Another theory on space and time and the System Shops? Or is it a Mana-focused project? Because I've got running all the ones dealing with Mana densities that you people can think of."

A hand waves, encompassing the surroundings. As if reacting to his movements, I feel Mana surge and twist, gaps opening in the ground and across the sky such that I might sense what was previously shrouded.

Locations where Mana is filled with System-marked Mana, held in stasis or moving in circles or hexagons or loops and swirls. Raw, untapped Mana at different levels, combining or interacting with System Mana. Spell forms, Skills, locked in place by enchantments. Hundreds and thousands of tests, all sealed off from one another.

The audience stands around us aren't just for show. They mark different studies, different tests. Each location in the arena we are within, each zone of the stands indicates a different type of study, a different experiment.

As I stare at it all, the library tugs at my attention, downloading information on each study as I stare at it. More than that, I feel myself reaching out, tapping into the information displayed by each study, filling in data points for the library as I gauge and take readings from the Mana sensors and elemental runes. Another portion of my mind spins, comparing the new data to previously held information.

Information updated only a bare two years ago.

"Interesting…" The word breaks me from my reverie, and I find the speaker staring at me, tapping a lip in thought. "You're not normal, are you?"

I grunt.

"Show me your System Quest."

"I…"

A raised eyebrow and I capitulate. I've not felt this powerless since I stared at a dragon sleeping. Even standing before Feh'ral or the Empress, I was never more aware of how outclassed I am.

System Quest Completion Rate: 89%

"Fascinating. How long?"

"Weeks now."

He nods. Then, without asking, he shows me his own.

System Quest Completion Rate: 89%

"What…?" I fall silent, because for the first time in weeks, something changes for me.

System Quest: +0.1%

"Something happened." His voice grows heated, his whole body leaning forward on his chair at an angle that isn't human. He's like a pointer dog having caught a scent, and unbeknownst to him, his inhumanity shows through in his eyes as they glow. "What is it?"

I wordlessly show him the update. And he laughs. Laughs and laughs, an insane edge to the cackling that makes my eyes widen and my palm itch for the comfort of my sword hilt. He laughs while I share a glance with Ali.

"*Are you sure this is our only option?*" I ask my friend.

"*You're the one with the plan.*"

"Yeah, because we need help against the Legendaries. But he doesn't seem very…"

"Stable? Sane? Human?" Ali shrugs. *"He's not. To any of those. But what's—*
"

"Sanity?" the suited man says, abruptly stopping his laughter. "Just another way of saying what others consider right and proper. You aren't even a century old, you earth-eating, plant-snacking child. Speak to me again when you're a few millennia old about the value of sanity."

"I'd say sure, but I doubt I'll last that long."

"No, not with your completion rate," he says, leaning forward. "I have sat here, running your Questors' tasks, for millennia. Doing what they asked, testing because…"

"Because?"

"Because I'm bored. And my number has risen because all you people can talk about is your Quest. And yet, for centuries now, it has not risen. And then you arrive…" I gulp, sensing the ire he radiates. Then, as suddenly, it's gone. "So tell me. What research project will you have me do?"

"None."

"I can… what?"

"None. I didn't come here for the Quest," I say.

When he frowns, I start speaking fast. Trying to explain about the situation on Earth. About Dungeon Worlds and Galactic Council ire, all before he decides he's done and ends me. I stumble a couple of times, trying not to use titles or specific terms, but it gets smoother, easier to do as I continue to talk.

When I'm done, there's a profound silence, a silence that pervades the amphitheatre. No wind, no chirp of birds or the hum of insects. It's unnaturally quiet, and I swear I can almost hear a heartbeat. Mine. Because neither of the other two are truly human. Or alive.

"Fascinating. I've gone from lab technician to errand boy."

A hand flicks and I fly backward, the force of the casual movement smashing me into walls. I shatter the stone slabs, imprinting my body upon the barricade and sliding down as dust and stone rain around me. I stagger to my feet, head ringing, blood dripping from a cut on my head, breathing hitched as I deal with bruised ribs. None of my defensive Skills are still active. In fact, they haven't been active for a very long time.

"What..."

"Lord of Space and Time, remember?"

"I told you not to use Titles, Spirit." He doesn't even move as Ali twists, scrunches down, and becomes a ball of compressed light. Then he's gone, destroyed. The only thing left is the mental scream Ali leaves behind.

"You bastard..." I snarl.

I cut upward, projecting a Blade Strike without thought. It's all instinct, thousands of hours in combat acting out. The attack never reaches him. Instead, I'm thrown forward, smashing into the ground as I feel my own back get torn apart as my attack reappears behind me.

"Foolish. But someone willing to defy the Council would have to be."

I snarl, pushing myself to my feet. Rage threatens to overtake good sense—again—but I pull it back. Force myself to breathe and focus. I can't beat him. I never could. I'm but a momentary distraction, a nuisance. And yet, for all his anger and irritation, I'm still alive. Which means...

"Fine." I dismiss my sword and hobble over, putting it back in whatever place it goes. Somewhere in my soul, within that portion of the System that is me. "You've let me live, which means you're interested. Maybe even willing to help. What do I need to do?"

The Lord smiles at me, lips widening and widening to an unnatural level. Then the grin disappears like a flame snuffed out by an errant breath. "Tell me the truth then."

"What truth?"

Another blow, coming from above. Unseen force squashing me into the ground. This time, it takes me a few minutes to clamber to my feet because the concussion he gives me makes me throw up the first time I try to stand.

"Fine. But this might be the end of you too," I say.

When his eyes narrow, I shrug. And tell him the rest. About why they chose to go after Earth now. About my true Class. And when he disbelieves me, I show him my Status, just as I did with Feh'ral.

He stares at it for a long time, and I let the silence linger while my body heals. Cracked bones reform, twisted spine straightens, and torn muscles reknit. I'm fully healed and even considering calling forth Ali when he speaks.

"A Class that should not be. A position that was rumored, but never confirmed." The Lord stares at me and shakes his head. "And you think this is the reason for all this?"

"Yes."

"What makes you think they wish not to recruit you?"

"Because if they wanted to be friendly about it, they'd have sent an invitation. Not threatened my planet," I say. "Not killed those I cared for."

He laughs then, shaking his head. "What makes you think this might not be a modest invitation?"

"I did talk about the death of my allies, no?"

"Yes. But these are individuals, groups, with powers greater than you can imagine. Many have lived for millennia, like me. To gain our final Class, to become what we are. Do you know what it requires normally?"

"A lot of XP."

"You murdered an entire planet and barely rose in Levels," the Lord says, his voice dropping. "A lot of experience, you say."

He laughs, and something changes. I turn my head from side to side as scenes of devastation, of death appear. None of the cities, none of the planets are familiar. None repeat. But they are all the same in intent and form.

A hand plunging into a chest, piercing the heart within. I can see it, feel the flesh, the bones, the beating organ around my too-big hand.

Screams as explosions roar and winds rise. Warmth on my face as the blood of a friend, an ally, splashes on me. Death rains down from above, and I find myself clutching at the incoming death, twisting space to send it back at our attackers.

A meteorite flying through space, and on it, I fight for my life against bipedal, armored, shell creatures that rise from its hollow center. A space dungeon let loose to fly through the cosmos, raining Level 200+ monsters on unsuspecting planets. I fly through space, sending shards of twisted space to crack the meteorite, speeding up my attacks and slowing attackers as they near. Fighting on as acidic blood splashes me, as it freezes and cracks and falls away. I beat upon the dungeon until the queen arises.

A planet, cupped in the palm of my metaphorical hands. I bring my hands together, and the planet buckles. Continents shatter, oceans churn, and a molten core is revealed. I keep closing my hands as I compress the planet, twisting space. When I'm done, I pocket the planet and dismiss the notification of experience gain.

Individual battles, wars waged, dungeons cleared. The battles are unending, all the space in the ampitheatre, on the ground, under it, and in the sky are filled with images, experiences. And as though it cannot be contained, the shattered mirrors of the past bleed.

Blood drips, and the amphitheatre fills. So much blood that it covers my feet, my knees, my head in bare seconds. I try to swim, paddle, but there's no surface. No place to go as it sucks me down, as the top rises to fill the entire location.

I struggle, twisting and bucking, lungs aching. My System doesn't work, my inventory doesn't open to provide me oxygen masks. Class Skills fire and are absorbed by the flood of sticky liquid. Even my reinforced Constitution is not enough in seconds, as time twists and buckles, when seconds become hours.

My mouth opens in a breathless scream and the blood floods in, filling my lungs, drowning me. All I can see is red. All I feel is the clammy wetness, the stickiness of the blood.

And I drown. Dying by inches. In all the blood he shed to reach the very apex of the System.

***

I come to on dry ground. I thrash to my feet, surprised to find myself alive. My mind is already blanking out the experience, the images, trying to save me from the screaming terror, my reborn phobia. My hands shake, my eyes are wide, and my breathing too fast. I struggle upright, my clothing clean, my lungs clear, my mind twisted.

"You melodramatic bastard…" I cough. "You could have just used your words."

"But would you have listened as well?"

I snort and shake my head, trying to clear it. Of the images, of all the sensations, of what I saw and felt. Because among it all, I also sensed what drove him. What made him, him. His own quest, as insane as mine—or perhaps even more so.

"So you think all this was just an invitation? Their way of saying 'come over for tea, we should have a chat'?"

He shrugs. "We do not interact, by choice. But there is little to be gained by setting oneself against the other."

"Yeah, okay. I'll take it under advisement. But I have a feeling it's more of a question of them not liking their secret being revealed."

"Also a possibility. A secret that has lasted millennia is one kept in blood itself. Your keeper of knowledge believes that for sure," the Lord says, his voice lowering. "That meddlesome fool. He was always such a problem…"

Again, I see glimpses. Of his interactions with Feh'ral, of long conversations and even fights. And in the corner of my mind, I note the tests that are Feh'rals, that are run for his sake.

"A dangerous secret, perhaps. And you gave it to me. Tell me, did you think to bring me to your side? What is that quaint human saying? The enemy of my enemy?"

"I warned you," I say in my defense.

"Knowing I would not be denied. Even intrigued." I shrug, and he laughs. "You overestimate how much I care."

There's truth in his words. I know it. I know his obsession and all that he has given up, all that he has sacrificed to reach as far as he has. And still, he has failed to truly master time. To step back into the past itself. And correct… something. What he intended, what drives him was missing. Unimparted by the Skill he used.

"A man must try, no?"

A chilly silence greets my words and I sigh. For all that he's playing unfriendly, the fact that he hasn't killed me yet—if barely—means I'm keeping him entertained. Which is good. Because the next step is the important one.

"Yeah, fine. So here's what I was really hoping from you…"

***

"Kuso!" Mikito swears as I appear right beside her. She doesn't even manage to stop her reflexive attack and buries her naginata halfway through my blocking arm.

"Thousand hells!" I swear as she yanks it out. I clutch my arm tightly, ignoring the way Hitoshi drinks up my blood, how tendrils of blood flow from my hand to the blade before the connection is broken. My eyes widen. I sense a new strength in the weapon, a little disturbed by its new abilities.

They widen even further when I realize that Mikito looks aged. More than that, her Levels…

Mikito Sato, Spear of Humanity, Blood Warden, Junior Arena Champion of Irvina, Arena Champion—Orion IV, Xumis,…; Time Slipped, True Bound Honor (Upper Samurai Level 40) (M)
HP: 4721/4721*
MP: 3567/3567*
Conditions: Isoide, Jin, Rei, Meiyo, Ishiki, Ryoyo, Feudal Bond, Blitzed, Future Projections
Galactic Reputation: 47
Galactic Fame: 47,864

"What the hell happened to you?" I say.

"Time." Mikito looks aside for a second, but there's a set to her stance, to her body that asks me to not ask further.

"A very short conversation. Then I was back here," Harry pipes up from where he's seated. "Mikito appeared a few minutes ago."

In the distance, the three fan club members are running through forms, never having been invited through the door with us.

"Where's Ali?" Mikito asks, changing the subject rather deliberately.

"Banished," I say. "But we should get going. There's a Shop orb a short distance away. We should make the visit. Might not get another chance."

"And then?" Harry asks from where he's seated.

"Then we make our way to Irvina."

"How?"

"I've made arrangements."

"Him?" Mikito says. "Did you make a deal, you baka?"

"I did. Had to," I say. "We need him. And what he can offer."

"At what price?" I shrug, and her lips purse. "We have yokai like that in our tales. Deals with them never turn out well."

"No." I fix her with a flat gaze. "But you made one too, no?"

Mikito shakes her head. "No. I didn't. It's why…" She trails off, shaking her head. "No promises were made. Just punishments doled out." I bristle and she shakes her head. "Forget it, John. It was expected."

I lean forward, looming over her only for her to glare at me, reminding me to keep my anger to myself. I'm not going to get an answer.

"Fine. Whatever." I tramp away, even as I poke at the link that connects me to Ali. Something pushes back and I realize that for whatever reason, he's not coming back just yet.

Well, maybe a little peace and quiet is good. For him and me. Because very soon, there won't be a lot of either.

My motley crew trail behind, and I hope that what I learned and what I have planned is enough. But before that, there's a secret or two that needs to be revealed.

***

It's a simple room, one that I access with the touch of my hand, a push of my will and a request sent. It's a place that cannot be found by the System—because of unregulated Mana, because of Skills, because he wills it—and because of that, it's perfect for what we need.

Once more, the main team enters. Once more, the trio of fan club members are left behind. They're not happy, but I don't give a damn.

"Where are we?" Mikito asks, staring around the blank white plane we stand upon. The horizon is empty too, a slightly different white that offsets the unnatural paleness we stand upon.

"Nowhere." I turn to the pair and hesitate.

"Why did you bring us here?" Harry asks.

"That…" I shake my head. "You need to make a decision. A choice. How much you want to know. About the System. About… the Council. And why they started all this."

Harry frowns, eyes narrowing. "And there's a price?"

"A consequence."

"Which is?"

"Your death."

"What?" Harry says, eyes widening.

"They'll kill you for knowing what I'll tell you." My lips thin as I gesture around. "All this, it started because I learned something I wasn't supposed to. And it's a secret they've killed before to protect."

"How do you know this?" Harry pauses, then shakes his head. "The library. It finally unraveled fully, didn't it?"

"Not exactly," I say. "But the library did play its part."

"And you know they've killed before," Harry states flatly.

"It's a secret tens of thousands of years in the keeping. You don't keep a secret like this without taking drastic measures," I say.

Harry slowly nods and falls silent. In turn, I look at Mikito. My most trusted companion.

"Do you need me to say it?" Mikito says.

I open my mouth to reply, then realize it's probably not necessary. She's reaffirmed her commitment in words and action again and again. Asking her again could be considered... well, an insult.

"Fine. Then we're just waiting—"

"For me?" Harry says, shaking his head. "No need. Tell me."

I say his name softly, wanting to dissuade him. Wanting to get him to choose otherwise.

"I understand. But I'm a reporter. Learning secrets at the risk of my life, that's what I do," Harry says with a tight grin. "And this sounds like a secret that I'm truly looking forward to hearing."

I draw a deep breath, calming myself. Forcing myself to accept that they've made their decision. Once I've gotten close to that acceptance, I tell them. It's a familiar refrain by now, even the show and tell. This time around, I feel the System shift, the Mana flare and twist as I push my true Status at my friends. As if it's watching,

When I'm done, the pair stare at me, before Harry snorts. "That's it?"

My jaw drops. "What do you mean, that's it?"

"It's a System. A program. That's literally what it's called. If there's a system, there's an administrator." Harry shakes his head. "It doesn't seem like much of a stretch to realize that."

Mikito nods.

"Hell, you were a programmer," Harry adds. "Seems like you'd have figured that out."

"But it's the *System*." I wave my hand around, trying to explain. "It's not an OS that you just boot in. It's… well…"

"It's what controls everything, yes. But I think, if anything, it's not so much the secret of your Class as wanting control of it—and its users—that caused this problem," Harry says.

I work my jaw as he speaks, as he explains the truth of my secret. But in the end, I have to wonder if he's right. Maybe it isn't the fact that I came upon the Class, but that I have it.

Not that it matters. Not really. Which I point out.

"Maybe it does," Mikito says, opening her hand. "If they just want to control you, then this might not be as bad."

I find myself nodding. "Maybe."

I recall what the Lord said, that maybe they just want to speak with me. And I wonder if the Lord and Harry are right. If so, what does that mean for my plans and Earth?

The silence continues for a few long breaths before Mikito breaks it. "That's it?"

"It?"

"Yeah, it. No other deep secrets we need to know while we attempt to save our friends and our home planet?" she prods.

I grunt. "No. That's it." I huff. "That's all there is."

My big reveal, and these two treat it as if it's just another damn secret, not a System-destroying revelation. I'm annoyed, petulant, but I shove it aside. We have more things to deal with than my hurt ego.

"What next?" Harry says, though I realize he seems to be deep in thought as he speaks.

"Now we really do go shopping. Then, finally, Irvina."

Chapter 7

Accessing Irvina always came with two major problems. First is entering the actual solar system itself. Being located in a Restricted Zone with the start of the Forbidden Zone within a few light years, most normal teleportation methods to Irvina are extremely expensive. The System has to expend a significant amount of Mana to teleport you, so it requires a significant Credit or Mana outlay.

It's why our first trip in, we did it via mundane technological means. Most ships can traverse the distance without issue, and even in the deepest areas of the Forbidden Zone, a properly shielded vehicle will run. Issues of Mana flooding can be handled with the right technology and channels.

Unfortunately, ease of access runs into the second major issue of entry into Irvina—the security concerns. Entering the solar system is regulated, with a variety of solar-system-wide dimensional locks and spatial sensors alerting them of incoming ships. For obvious reasons, security is a major concern.

The entire planet is under an extremely complex and robust dimensional lock, preventing direct access to the planet itself. Only a few exceptions are carved into the system, and all those involve the embassies themselves. In all other cases, you need to stop at one of the many space stations that orbit the planet as entry funnels and defensive grids.

All that said, and with the Council keeping an eye out for me, we need to sneak in. There are two ways to do that, of course: smugglers or a hidden teleportation. Smugglers into Irvina are either extremely high tiered—and thus extremely expensive and wary of the kind of cargo they grab—or are on a wink-and-nudge relationship with the bureaucracy. Unfortunately, without a ton of research, it's impossible to know which is which. Dornalor's contacts would normally be useful for this, but considering our position, I'm less than enthused about those options—especially since most of his suggestions are friends-of-friends-of-friends.

Even Harry can't help, coming up short as his contacts ran and hid at the thought of going against the Council. Harry holds a strange place in our group. He's a noncombatant and even has a series of Skills to keep him safe and ignored during a battle. Along with his membership with the Galactic Alliance of Reporters, he has a level of protection Mikito and I don't when things get hot—so long as he doesn't take part in the fight itself.

On the other hand, when we're out of combat, Harry is invaluable. He has connections, a wide base of knowledge, and often can learn of information that isn't public. The sheer volume of secrets the GAR are privy to is staggering, and many of those secrets are still kept for one reason or another. When it comes to arriving at a new location, there's no one better to have on our side.

For all those reasons and more, Harry is frowning when we enter the secluded, private travel room. The security check to get in was discreet but extensive, with everything from our DNA to our auras verified before we even made it down the white-walled corridor.

The room itself is reminiscent of a magic-ritual room combined with a steampunk mechanic's nightmare. Ritual circles on the floor in a configurable gear pattern allow fine-tuning of the ritual. Steam engines with exposed pipes chug away at the corner, supplying liquid Mana to the entire contraption, and wiring and exposed cables run toward a stone altar.

In the corner, the Gremlin who runs the entire damn thing is adjusting a variety of sockets with a wrench, Mana warping around him as he tugs on the stubborn machine via his Skills.

"You do know that they've got a Tier I, Heroic Class teleport blocker, right?" Harry says after eyeballing the location for a bit.

"No matter." The voice that speaks rises from our feet, making Harry jump in surprise. Out from the floor, a gooish substance rises until a trembling slime-like man stands, wisps of rainbow color floating within to form fragments of memory that replay on his skin. "You are not teleporting but traveling."

"What?" Harry exclaims, then draws a deep breath. "We're traveling?"

"Yes, this is a matter-energy discombulator," the slime says. "We'll transport you through space to your location."

"Discombulator?" the lead member of Mikito's fan club says. "That sounds dangerous."

"Not at all! We have a 98.4567% success rate at reforming our test subjects." The gremlin turns around, sliding his wrench into his tool belt as he walks over, offering a wide grin. "Call me Rachet Cord."

The slime makes a weird bubble popping sound. It then corrects the gremlin. "Customers."

"Right, right, customers!" Rachet says, almost bouncing. "So, who's first?"

"John..." Mikito speaks up, cutting off everyone else. I turn to see the Samurai wave me closer. "How safe is this? Really? And will it work? If it's the speed of light—"

"We have Class Skills speeding up the transportation of your bodies," Rachet says. "Myself and Burble."

"Burble?" Mikito says. "That's not—"

"My name. Yes. But Rachet cannot say my name."

"Why not?" Vrasceids frowns. The green-gilled Samurai turns to look at Rachet. "It's just—" he emits a shrill series of squeaks and bubbles, his gills fluttering as he makes the noise.

I ignore the group, speaking with Mikito and Harry, who has made his way over. "Estimated time for us to arrive should be around forty-three Galactic standard years." The looks of consternation on their faces make me smile slightly, but I decide not to push it further. "Don't worry. I have it handled. Through you know who."

Mikito sighs. "Baka. Fine." Without a further word, she walks over to the center of the ritual circle. "Shall we do this?"

"Really? That's it!?!" Harry shouts.

Mikito shrugs. "John's a bakayaro, but I trust him."

She stares as the gremlin runs around, twisting dials and adjusting steam levels while the slime taps at bubbling glass measuring devices and twirls dials on the stone altar. Under Mikito's feet, the gears spin and lock into place, settings adjusting. All through the movement, she keeps her balance with ease.

"This..." Harry purses his lips.

"You don't have to come this way. You're not wanted by the law," I say softly to the reporter. "If you port in normally, you should be fine."

"Har! With what funds?" Harry makes a face. "Did you see the prices?"

"I did." I'd poked at the Shop and winced, since the cost was in the tens of millions of Credits. A normal hyperspace flight was cheaper, significantly, but it'd take months for Harry to arrive. He'd have to swing out wide to avoid the Forbidden Zone since most ships don't want to deal with the creatures that exist within.

As if my question reminded Harry of something, he adds softly, "Hey, how are we paying for this?"

"All right, here we go! Engaging in three," Rachet says. "Oh right, this might pinch a little."

"We're not," I mutter to Harry. "We're voluntary test subjects."

Mikito glares at the gremlin as he provides the warning a little too late. The gremlin ignores her as he shouts the count for his fellow scientist. In unison, Burble and Rachet cry out the final number and a green tendril stabs down on a big yellow button.

Mikito's eyes widen as her body warps and twists, the edges of her body compressing. The entire process is over in a fraction of a second, the woman becoming no more than a single point of light that grows smaller and smaller, grows brighter in intensity. And then, the beam of light shoots upward through the ceiling through an aperture hole so small I missed it until now.

"How'd it do?" Rachet says.

"Full integrity. No issues," Burble says. "Told you we just needed to adjust the matter-kilo varix ratio by 0.14."

Harry's eyes widen further. "Where did you find these guys?"

"You don't want to know." Truth be told, I've never met them before. The Lord made the suggestion, and I'm just trusting that this will work.

"Next!" Rachet cries.

Ruvuds walks straight over to the platform. It grins and twists, adjusting as necessary while Harry stares at me, lips pursed.

"Time to choose, Harry. I could use you, but what's going on…" I shake my head. "I can't guarantee anything."

"Bloody hell," Harry says. "Blood, bloody hell." He watches as the gremlin and slime—the Galactic Tinkerers—get to adjusting and shudders. Eventually, when they're nearly done, he speaks. "If I get shot into a star, I'm going to come back and haunt you."

"Fair." My lips twist up. "But I'm pretty sure—"

"Three!"

"Whoa! Don't forget to adjust for his Levels next time!" Burble shouts out.

"—if things go bad, we'll all be haunting one another."

Harry rolls his eyes, but sensing a story, he walks over and questions the pair as the machine recharges.

***

The process of matter-energy transmutation isn't exactly painless, but it's not exactly painful. It happens in a flash from the inside, as nerves are twisted and torn before they are transformed. My body is compressed then thrown to the ceiling, exploding out of the planet, the solar system, then the galaxy.

The entire journey out of the solar system takes only minutes, as Class Skills warp the speed that the packets of light that are us are traveling at. We move faster than light, at least in relation to the rest of the universe. We go faster and faster, but it's still not fast enough. The galaxy is a large place after all.

I'm not exactly conscious, but I'm not exactly unaware of what is happening. A portion of me—that same portion that has been enhanced, upgraded, and supported by the System—is awake and paying attention. And it notes when the shift happens.

The reason, the only reason, this particular mode of transportation is viable is because of who we have in our corner. The Lord of Space and Time touches us, his Legendary Skill interacting with the world itself. And space folds, even as time itself slows down.

Twenty, fifty, a hundred thousand times as fast as the speed of light. We shift across time and space, and I catch brief glimpses of the world we cross. A rotund living ship whose hyperspace organ breathes the solar winds while forming a bubble of hyperspace is gently nudged aside as we pass it. The ship cries a greeting, a bleated note that wraps us around as we fly.

We slip by a planet, cutting so close to the edge of its atmosphere we're flashes of light, so bright that it lights the atmosphere on fire. Below us, monsters scream and cry, our passing lights making the sky burn briefly, saving a few Adventurers in mid-fight by forcing a distraction. Others, caught and distracted, are sent spiraling to their deaths.

A sun collapsed upon itself and, incredibly dense, tears apart the fabric of the planets caught in its orbit. It pulls gas and dust to itself, and we blur through its very heart, a cluster of fast-moving light dots. The Lord's Skill protects us, as we enter the sun and exit in a blink.

And most of all, most of all, there is the void. That deep darkness, that empty stretch of reality that is the gap between stars. We traverse it as moving dots of light, and in the infinite stretch of space, there is nothing for long hours, no souls, no matter, nothing.

Nothing but Mana.

And the System.

There's a truth in there, a fabric of reality. We spin through the void as semi-sapient dots and enter Irvina without issue. Nothing bothers us, nothing can bother us, not as we are.

We enter Irvina's solar system and slow down, slow again as we pass through one threshold after another. Slow and dim, becoming no more than ghosts, just another stream of light that hits the atmosphere and shifts direction, arcing to strike the bare earth.

Dots of concentrated light that plant themselves on solid earth, hovering above the ground like scattered solar seeds. We stop for a brief moment.

And blossom.

***

When the screams end, my friends are less than happy with me. It takes the trio of Samurai, with their Basic levels of pain resistance and experience, the longest to recover. But even for me, with the shielding and experience I've gained as a Heroic, the pain of dissolution and reconstitution which only happens as we reform is like being dipped in a sun, inside out. It took me long minutes to regain my senses, to recover.

It takes the others far longer.

"Yeesh. It's just a matter-shift," Ali says, shaking his head. "There's no reason to be so dramatic."

I resummoned the Spirit while I was waiting for the trio to recover. Mikito, rather than talk to me, had stalked off into the woods we'd been deposited within, searching for something to kill. Or a place to cry in private. Not sure which—nor am I intending to find out.

Irvina's a mostly developed planet, the galactic equivalent of Great Britain. A place once filled with wildlife and untamed forests turned into idyllic pastures and sprawling, dense cities. Except, of course, we're in the System, so dungeons dot the surroundings with distressing regularity.

You have entered the Opcet Forest Reserve (Level 75+ Zone)

This is a curated outdoor spawning area.

- *Access restricted*
- *Spawning levels increase by 125%*
- *Experience gains increase by 25%*
- *Loot drops decreased by 50%*

On top of your regular dungeons, there are also various options that allow one to manage Mana flow. Designated parks and reserves help focus

Mana production, and because this is the System, parks are more violent and murderhobo-like.

No surprise then that when Mikito wanders back in from the purple and neon forest, her ghost armor is speckled with blood and guts. She releases the Skill a moment later, the semi-translucent armor disappearing from her form and allowing the gunk to fall aside before she reforms the armor around her.

I've got my own Soul Shield up, and Harry's over in his corner, nursing a headache and delving into the neural net that surrounds the planet. He's pulling information and getting the lay of the land for us, whilst using his Skill to avoid being targeted.

I glance at the three Samurai, still surprised they're here. But it's clear that however they feel about me, I'm secondary to their entire objective of getting closer to Mikito. Or worshipping her. In any case, their presence should hopefully be a boon. As it is, those three are finally standing and stretching, still looking a little green—or very green, in Vrasceid's case—but functional.

"We ready?" I say.

"We are, but…" Harry frowns. "I thought the trip would take weeks. Or months. How are we here already? It's not even a full day."

I grin at Harry while the man puts things together. It's not too hard, since he has all the pieces, but he's still a little shocked. When he mouths the word Legendary, I nod.

"All right, so we're here. And if I'm correct, no one knows we're here." I point at the three. "You all will split off. Mikito will give you further marching orders, but we need you to speak with other members of Mikito's fan club—"

"Clan, Lord," Ruvuds corrects.

"—and have them ready to help us. Any additional help you can find would be useful. Mercenaries are probably our best bet here, at least those we can count on."

"Do you expect violence, Daimyo Lee?" Agr'us says, the tiny Grimsar grinning a little as she caresses the hilt of her katana.

"Expect?" I pause, considering. "Yes. But I'd like to avoid it."

"What kind of mercenaries do you require, Shogun?" Vrasceids says.

"What do you mean, kind?" I frown.

"Protection? Dungeon-delving teams? Occupation forces? Burn and churn?" Vrasceids says. "There are multiple kinds of mercenaries, Shogun. We mean no offense, by correcting you."

I blink and look at Mikito.

Luckily, she cuts in with ease. "Any kind that you can hire. We'll be fighting—if we fight—in Irvina. So whoever you hire has to be willing to do that. Or at least take the penalties in their rating and return our deposit."

"Deposit and standby fees, with last-minute activation terms," Vrasceids confirms. "May I suggest double penalties, on-site residence, one-month term, autorenewal? If that pleases you, Lord Sato."

"One month sounds about right." If anything, everything will end faster than that, so I confirm the timing with ease. "Can you hire without—"

"Letting them know the final objectives?" Vrasceids nods. "Of course, Shogun."

Agr'us's face scrunches up as Vrasceids continue to call me Shogun, though she doesn't object.

"Many units—especially those we'll be targeting—are used to unrevealed objectives and obscured targets." I frown, and Vrasceids grins. "They aren't the nicest groups, but they understand the risks."

"Fine, fine." I wave it away. I'm not going to worry about the potential issues right now, though I'm hoping that whatever we do end up using them for—and I'm imagining some violent strikes and rescue operations—they'll manage to keep civilian casualties down. But if we're fighting in the middle of the city, there's no guarantee for that. "Best get going. The longer we're together, the more exposed you guys are."

Once Mikito confirms my orders, the trio bows and heads off at a trot. She'll stay in contact with them, the entire "clan" having a secure communication to the Samurai, it seems. One that she has never told me about. I wonder if it's because she never knew or was trying her best to forget. I know I'd be embarrassed to have a fan club.

I wait for a few minutes, ensuring they're well and truly gone before I turn to my friends.

Harry beats me to the question before I can speak. "What's your plan for us? Are we contacting Katherine?"

"I want to, but initially, I figure we'll make our way to the outer edges of the capital. If we can lie low there, we'll see if it's possible to speak with her." My lips press together slightly before I continue. "However, contacting her will be tricky."

"She has Skills to block tracking. As do I," Harry says.

"Yeah, but…" I open my hand. "I have a feeling the Lady of Shadows and whoever else is tracking her anyway."

"Then…?"

I shrug, unsure. What the hell can I do?

"One thing at a time," Mikito says. "We need to enter the capital first."

"Fair." I cock my head.

Ali points, offering us the direction we need to walk. There's no other way to travel since I've been Dimension Locked since the moment we arrived. And even if I could punch through, we'd alert the very people we're trying to hide from.

So. Walk, or in the case of Mikito as she calls forth her horse, ride.

***

Along the way, we take precautions. Skills or enchantments are triggered, hiding our Statuses as well as what we look like, all little goodies we picked up at the Shop just before we left or from the Erethrans. Harry's got it easiest. A few of his Skills adjust how he looks and what kind of information people can get from him. Mikito, on the other hand, has a ring that makes her look different and a Skill that adjusts her Status information, while I have the opposite.

Once the initial Skills and enchantments are in place, I take the time to play with our Status information with the System Edit Skill. I feel my way through the data, having Mikito and Ali repeatedly call forth my Status information to get a feel of what is happening. Each time, I sense the pressure as the System bucks under my control, the flow of information and Mana wanting to escape my grasp.

It's only when I have a grasp of the flow, a twisting braid of multi-colored streams of information that are as intricate as a Gordian knot, that I dare to Edit it. It's a little like programming but less precise, more done by feel of flowing data points than any monitor and keyboard input. The System code is—as I'd once noted—not in any known language. Worse, the same words could mean different things depending on time, context, and individual.

It's only now, with my new Class, that I begin to understand the intricacies of the System and the reasoning behind the shifting symbolic language. The reason why some of the code, some of the commands feel so organic, why it alters consistently. And why and where such information is stable—just not in the way we'd expect.

The code, the information that those who delve into the System see, is not the true code. It's an encrypted form of data, one whose encryption constantly shifts and changes. The code underlying the layer of encryption, the way the System is built, on the other hand, is more like an actual program—but with some organic, almost living, leeway built into it.

By drawing forth the same commands, the same information, again and again and spying on the data flow using my Class and Skill, I begin to grasp the underlying true code. In doing so, it allows me to Edit it with greater precision and finesse.

When I'm done, we no longer have our names, Classes, Titles, or anything else showing up in our Status information. The data mingles with the Skills and enchantments that it'd take another Admin to see the difference.

Hours at a jog that would be faster than an all-out sprint back on pre-System Earth takes us through rough terrain. Monsters lunge for us, trying to block our way, and die just as fast. A cat-like creature with extra limbs jumps at me and I grab it by the neck, smashing it into a living tree thing. The tree breaks, as does the cat-monster, and I drop a firestorm spell behind me, letting it consume the pair and the forest.

The cat's a Level 70 creature, with Strengths in the hundred or so and a couple hundred in Agility. It is multiple times stronger than any normal human being. Even an Olympic weightlifter would be easily overpowered. But me? I can handle it like, well, a housecat.

As for the forest fire, it's of little concern. It's too damp here, too infused with Mana to let it get out of control. The forest will damp it out most likely—either that, or make it grow even bigger and form a fire elemental in our wake. Either works, since I'd get a small experience payment from the fire elemental if it did form.

We run, Mikito swinging her naginata in quick figure eights that catch leaping monsters and tear apart limbs as she leads the charge. Occasionally, she leans forward and takes a monster in the chest with the improvised lance, the extreme sharpness of the curved blade of her polearm and her use of Skills more than making up for its non-optimal form for lancing.

And Harry? Harry glides along on modified hoverboots, in the middle and completely ignored. Because that's his Skill, at least while he narrates a short documentary of the wildlife. His Class is weird.

In just under an hour, we make our way to the city of Siyoan, the closest hub city. From there, getting to the capital of Irvina will be simpler and mundane. Or as mundane as you can get when we're discussing scifi-fantasy travel.

There are a wide variety of options for travel, from the blimp with starship thrusters to hypertube capsules that are fired through the air like artillery shells and short-range teleportation portals. There are even a few biological travel methods like oliphants and trans-dimensional shades. The sheer variety is enough to make one's head explode if you think about it.

Head-explodingly variable being a good way of describing cities on the planet itself. Siyoan's a riot of architecture, drawn from every fevered dream of fantasy and science fiction writers and crumpled together. Crystal buildings stand beside towering trees which entwine with the silver-steel metal of living nano buildings and System-generated ultra-burnished architecture. Walkways of glass, adamantium, and wood sway between buildings while Mana lights flood the shadowed ground.

And the people. The sapient—and some sentient—members of the population are just as varied. Not only do you have the normal array of weird-ass fantasy individuals—elves, dwarves, gnomes, halflings, orcs, rock elementals, beastkin in all shapes and types—but you've also got their companions. This far out of the capital, there seems to be a larger variety of companion Classes, with the System-enabled residents riding, walking, flying, loping, and in a few cases burrowing through the city.

We're also just seeing the oxygen-focused side of the city. The non-oxygen (or carbon dioxide) side, domed and protected, is even wilder. We just don't deal with them as much, and their inherent lack of representation on the Council keeps them diminished in the System.

It's just another way the entire thing is unbalanced, how power accrues at the top and almost constrains it there. Much of it is because of the Galactic Council themselves, who have taken pains to keep such strength to themselves, to lengthen their lives and to concentrate experience, Credits, and Mana to those above.

Even if, at times, the System fights them. But it's not a hard push. The System is more concerned about overall effects, and for all that we're an important linchpin to the churn of Mana, to keeping System-Mana running, we're dwarfed by the monsters and vegetation the System creates. If not for our need to continually expand, to seed planets and form space stations in the void, we might not even be anything more than a footnote in the System's calculations.

Or at least, that's the feeling I get sometimes when I look at the System. Certainly, that pessimistic viewpoint is one of the leading theorems about sapient-System interactions. Others are less cynical, more optimistic. Pointing out that if we were that inconsequential, the Council would never be able to change the System at all.

We enter the city on foot, slipping among the throng without a problem. We get a few glances, but Harry's Skill—*Nothing to See Here*—keeps us from attracting too much attention. We've got enchantments altering our species too, so we don't look like three humans wandering around.

I guide the team with false confidence, Ali feeding me directions while we stroll. More than once, we move aside as adventuring teams return from the forest, bringing with them moving pallets piled high with corpses and other loot.

We're nearly at our destination when trouble comes a-calling in the shape of a three-foot, flapping, bulbous-nose creature and his partner, a conch shell crustacean with a head that pokes out and peers at us while slimy tentacles erupt from the end of its shell. They buzz down in front of us, and when I sidestep, they move to block our way.

"Halt, adventurer. Please display your pass," bulb nose says.

I look up, scanning his Status.

Jusbid Orea (Level 14 ~~Bureau of Land Management Enforcer~~) (A)
HP: 1430/1430
MP: 1172/1570
Conditions: Land Sense, Networked Connection

A flicker later, his Status changes.

Jusbid Orea (Level 14 Irvina Ranger) (A)
HP: 1430/1430
MP: 1172/1570
Conditions: Land Sense, Networked Connection

"What the hell, Ali?" I send to the Spirit over our connection.

"Figured this is a little more self-explanatory."

"Library, remember. I actually know what he is."

Having the entire damn library shoved in my head means I've got a much better idea about Classes and Skills than ever before. And, amusingly enough, the BLM official is an actual Class—one formed after centuries of bureaucratic service had solidified the hiring requirements. Now, the position itself is a Class.

There are entire studies based off which Classes have formed in Irvina due to the ossification of its bureaucracy. Furthermore, there are even notes of the Questors going out of their way to create niche jobs within the bureaucracy just to test how the System creates Classes.

Which is why there's a Class called *Galactic Stimulant, Sedative, and Psychotic Tester and Supplier* with attendant Skills and progressions. Their sole job, for centuries, was the dispensation of the Galactic equivalent of coffee. On a department level.

"Pass!" clicks the other creature.

I look at its name and its Class—similar to our friend—and decide to just call it Shelly. There's no way I'm trying to pronounce the click-hiss-burble mess that is its name.

"Careful! We can't get another bad evaluation," Jusbid buzzes to his partner.

"Pass!"

I'd laugh, but I'm not even sure what they mean. Luckily, Harry slides forward into the gap my silence creates.

"I'm sorry, we don't understand. What pass?" Harry says.

"Forest Reserve pass!"

"Ah…" Harry scratches his head, dialing up the charm all the way. He pushes out his official press pass. I didn't even need to adjust it, since the press pass automatically shifts to keep track of Harry's current name and face. Says something about the Galactic Press that it's coded to do that. "I'm sorry, it seems we did not acquire one. We were just filming a small documentary—"

"Then you need a media pass and an adventuring pass," Jusbid says. He floats over to Harry, eyeing him. "How did you make it past the forest wardens?"

"Uhh… we didn't see any?" I say.

"None? Impossible!" Shelly clicks, tentacles waving furiously.

"Not at all, since my friend speaks the truth," Harry says.

They've got Skills running, making sure they can tell if we're telling the truth. Or close enough, I'm sure.

"Impossible!" Shelly trembles, its whole conch shivering. "Invalid entrance! Slacking duty! Destruction of COLONY!"

"Easy there, partner, easy!" Jusbid floats down to Shelly, patting his hand on the shell. "Remember what Therapist Dofse said. Focus on yourself and the now."

We trade glances between one another as Shelly slowly stops trembling. When Jusbid turns to us, I raise an inquiring eyebrow, hoping it translates.

"Don't mind my partner, he's just getting over a small incident last month." Jusbid opens his hands and legs wide, displaying parts I didn't need to see. Not that it's arousing or anything, just… weird. The lack of pants is just wrong, but different species, different needs. "I hope it didn't inconvenience you too much."

"Not at all," Harry says smoothly. "But we really didn't know better. And we only taped a little before we came back."

"Well, that's not good. Illegal entry into the Forest Reserve is a crime," Jusbid says.

I find myself tensing mentally, wondering if we're going to have to kill them. Unfortunately, there's such a wide array of surveillance devices around us and people, many of whom are flowing around the small diversion we've created, that any combat will attract attention. I bite my tongue, wondering if all we've done is going to end because of a stupid pass...

"Well, I'm sure it's a problem. But is there something we can do...?" Harry says, his voice growing wheedling.

"Bribe! Wrong! Corruption!" Shelly twitches again.

Jusbid's eyes narrow too.

Ali floats over, waving his upper limbs. Even the Spirit has changed how he looks, going for a cubic representation of himself, with four limbs but no real face. "No, no, no. No bribe. None of us would dare bribe a Bureau of Land Management official." Ali shoots Harry a glare while he continues. "But isn't this just a fine? Or something lesser we can plead to?"

"Fine! Imprisonment! CLEANSING!"

Surprisingly, Ali's eyes lock onto Shelly. "Cleansing?"

"Community work," Jusbid says. "In this case, there's a parasitic mold that has invaded the lower sewer system that needs to be cleansed."

"CLEANSED!"

"I assume it's affecting your friend?" I nod to Shelly, whose back to trembling.

"It's... well, a delicate matter. But if you are willing to..." Jusbid eyes our Levels—mine and Mikito's in particular. I swapped out our Classes for Advanced ones, leaving us high leveled but not startling. "We could make use of you. It's a burgeoning lair, and we'll eventually get it sorted. But if we can save the department some money in hiring Adventurers..."

"This parasite, it's new? Unique?" Harry says, rubbing his chin. When he gets a nod from Jusbid, Harry grins. "Then we'll do it. Fine us, then assign us to this. So long as I get broadcast rights."

Jusbid hesitates, but at the clicks and chirps Shelly makes, he relents. A moment later, we've got a new map waypoint and a hundred thousand Credit fine each that we can work off.

Only when they've left us, heading for another group of scofflaws—aided by Class Skills and the omnipresent surveillance system of the city—do we dare to chat. In party chat, that is.

"That was nerve-racking. But why'd you agree to the Cleansing and not just pay the fine?" I send.

"Selling the story," Harry says. "Better to let them think I'm a press-hungry reporter with a couple of hires than... well..."

"Yeah. Better than that."

Still, I can't help but look back at the hidden forms of the enforcers and hope. Because if our cover is already blown, things are going to get a lot worse.

Chapter 8

"Get it off me!" Harry howls, twisting and scratching.

The living-mold thing crawls over Harry, its pink, furred, and mossy body shifting higher and higher toward his face, even as it grows from the ambient Mana in the sewer system.

"Oh, relax. We got this." I chant another spell, sending lightning—unenhanced but guided with my Elemental Affinity—roaring through the air, jumping to strike Harry and the moss before moving onward.

The pink "flesh" crisps, the moss burning away before it flops to the ground, shocked. Flame washes over it as Mikito, wielding a flamethrower backpack that we picked up just for this, finishes off the monster.

We've been down here for four hours, working deeper and deeper into the sewer system. The sewer system that also doubles as a creche for Shelly's race—and a few others. It seems the slime has taken over a few spots, destroying thousands of children.

It's kind of fascinating, the way the city has managed to use their sewer system to create a biodiverse environment for some species as well as a highly regulated and ideal environment for spawning. Well, regulated until things go wrong, as Mana is wont to make happen.

Harry's having the time of his life, narrating his research, giving me a glimpse of alien life that I have no desire to learn about. I might be more open-minded if the place didn't stink to high heaven and its environment wasn't caustic to our very existence. If not for System-aided regeneration, we'd be piles of bones right now. Unfortunately, I only realized after we were in that I couldn't take out my Hod like I would normally without giving the game away.

"Damn it, that's my fourth suit!" Harry says as he clambers to his feet, his outfit burnt through, exposing his skin to the flesh-eating atmosphere.

"Eh, told you to stop changing," I say.

"Not all of us bought enchanted underwear. Or are exhibitionists," Mikito says as she walks up to me, playing the flamethrower across the walls.

She's on her second suit, being one to buy better quality than Harry. There are gaps in her clothing though, which might be interesting if I'd ever thought of Mikito that way. But really, it'd be like thinking of your sister in a sexual manner—weird and wrong.

Of course, to keep our cover, we're also keeping our better pieces of equipment hidden. Along with the majority of our distinctive Skills. Otherwise, we'd be done already.

Really, playing as an Advanced Class is annoying.

"Hey, it was on offer! I'm surprised they had this set up, but I really can't complain." I grin and pull up the information about my clothing, even as slime drips and burns into my skin and the flesh underneath before it heals. It would be painful, if not for the significant amount of pain resistance my Class offers—well, that, and my resistance to acid damage.

Bainoff Enchanted Shocksilk Intimates (Tier I)

"Bainoff's so good, we're banned in 2,385 Countries!"

Chosen the world over by socialites and Adventurers, Bainoff's Enchanted Shocksilk Intimates guarantee both the most comfortable, self-repairing, and cleansed undergarments and come with lifetime access and connection to our fashion database.

Effects: +42 Defense, +240% Resistance to physical, acid, fire, and energy damage. Self-Cleanse, Self-Mend, Self-Tailor, Autofit Enchantments.

Attribute Bonus: +213 Charisma (when seen), Status Effect: Swagger and Well-Endowed

Amusingly, among the many benefits of having entire departments devoted to handling the Paladins was a sponsorship center that had managed to get Bainoff to provide all the Paladins with underclothes free-of-charge. And I'll admit, as I strut forward, there's something to be said about how comfortable it is. Almost makes one forget they're half-naked in a pile of goo. Of course, after all my attribute increases and the genetic wash, I've been known to take a few moments to admire myself in the mirror.

"Exhibitionist," Ali sniffs. "But don't worry, I got all this recorded, Mikito. For the future."

"Can't blackmail the shameless," I pipe up.

"Har! We'll see."

Mikito looks between Ali and me, then at Harry, who is struggling to get dressed, his open, burning wounds healing over, and shakes her head.

"Bakayaro." When that's not enough to relieve her feelings, she adds, "Men!"

***

Hours later, we're done. The last little bit, we'd had to pull out some bigger guns—literally—when we made it to the pulsing heart of the mutated moss lair. It burned and choked us, and even visibly mutated as we assaulted it, the mother moss attempting to shed its vulnerability to fire, then acid, then lightning. But it was outmatched and, in the end, succumbed to a gravitic mine.

There's almost no useful loot. Even the mutated mother spore drops nothing more interesting than some Credits—surprisingly—and a container of body parts that Ali tells me we can sell for a few thousand Credits as research material.

"No wonder no one was doing this," I grumble as we wait for the elevator doors to open. Thankfully, cleansing ourselves of the remainder of the spores was a simple matter of spells.

"Typical of living fungi. They're either gold mines of usable resources or a complete waste of time," Ali says.

"Cheap labor," Mikito grumbles. "And lousy experience too."

I nod. "I think we spent more on the actual gear than we earned."

"Well, if you hadn't thrown the gravitic mine at the end, we might have been up," Mikito points out as she walks into the elevator.

I chuckle, joining her. "Too true, M."

I laugh as she makes a face. Rather than go with remembering everyone's new made-up name, I've taken to using their initials, which I didn't change. Perfectly understandable, on all sides.

"At least you're dressed now."

"Hey, if you've got it, flaunt it." I say, taking a bodybuilding pose and flexing.

Harry and Mikito goggle at me, and I admit, I can't help but play the fool a little more while we walk out of the elevators. We keep joking while we make our way to the nearest network connection to fill out our report and buy our berths to Irvina.

Travel to Irvina is cheap(ish). We take a mid-grade option, one that lets us get to the city fast—a matter of hours instead of days, considering the size of the planet—but not startlingly so. Again, perfectly in tune with the kind of Advanced Classers we're trying to impersonate.

The blimp we board is grey-and-white for its body, with a dark green highlight along the metal struts that hold the airbags together. The struts and lighting strips run along the inflated body to the starship engines, where Mechanics and Airship Crew work on the craft.

We follow the System-map to our private cabin. After disabling the couple of listening devices in the cabin, as well as paying for additional privacy restrictions, we relax.

Not that anything we do could truly be hidden if anyone is looking at us specifically, but it's like finding information on the internet in the old ages. If you knew the website you were looking for, had its IP address or domain name, you could find it. But what if it was never linked? Never indexed? Then finding it requires you to know exactly the kind of questions to ask.

And we're just floating pages, one of trillions of individuals. Even if they knew to look for us initially, our journey through the artificial Forbidden Zone and our secret entrance makes us the equivalent of a website that changed its domain name and swapped out IP addresses without leaving an auto-forward.

Can we be found? Maybe. It'd take a lot of effort, but eventually, if they swept everything, they'd find us. For now though, so long as we don't pop up on any major security alerts, we should be invisible.

And that anonymity will be our weapon.

"Thousand hells, that was tiring," I say, flopping down on a nearby couch. It conforms to me, leaving me staring at my friends as they make their own ways to their seats.

"Acting like a fool?" Ali asks.

"Funny."

Mikito smiles slightly, before she grows serious, Hitoshi appearing in her hands. She strokes the shaft of her weapon. It's an unconscious motion, a comforting one for her. "What do we do now?"

"We get to Irvina. We find a place to rest. Then, carefully, we look for a way to contact Katherine," I say.

"How?" Mikito says.

I turn to look at Harry, curious if he has any suggestions. The Brit snorts when he spots me looking at him but then falls silent as he contemplates my question.

"Exactly," Mikito says, her voice growing heavy. "I'm not sure what we're doing, John. Or what even we can do. This isn't a bunch of hopped up corporations or an Empire. This is the Galactic Council..."

"Scared?" I say, a little surprised.

"Not for us." She waves between her and me.

"Hey!" Ali says, realizing he's not being included.

"But they're targeting Earth too. They're trying to take away its seat. They're attacking our friends. And we've got a plan you say, but it's not enough. Because it only solves the short-term problem. And it doesn't deal with..." Mikito waves at me, over my head.

I'm surprised to see Mikito say this out loud. She's often silent about her doubts, and it's rare to see her vulnerable. Then again, it's one thing to risk your life. It takes a different kind of courage—or a painful lack of empathy—to risk the lives of others.

"Truthfully, I'm not sure." I frown, leaning back. "Not in the long term. Not yet." I exhale, harshly, forcing myself to breathe. To circulate oxygen that I don't need because I have to. "Maybe I do need to talk to the Administrators. But if so, it's obvious the discussion has to be somewhere..." I trail off, unsure of what to say. Somewhere secure probably. That they control. Or I do. Problem is, they could have just contacted me if they wanted to talk.

Unless there's a reason they didn't. And if so, I don't know what it is. No matter what I do, no matter how much I test the Skill, the Class, or push at the library, there's nothing.

"But we need to sort this issue about Earth's seat first. After that…" I sigh. "After that, we'll have to get them to focus on us."

I pause.

"Me."

The pair nod. Knowing my secret, they realize what I'm trying to imply. That I'll have to chat with the Council eventually, somehow. Figure out a way to have a discussion without being caught or locked down. If it is a discussion they want, which I doubt. Their actions are impetuous, weird. If they just wanted to speak, a simple message would have sufficed. If they wanted me dead, they could have acted immediately and ended me. Used assassins.

This… this makes no sense.

Unless they're conflicted about their response. Or have other restraints I don't know of. Or maybe they're just trying to deal with more than one issue at a time. And this gives them a convenient excuse to finish off Earth.

Harry nods. "So firstly, contact Katherine silently. Work out who she needs. Then try to convince them to help. Or dissuade our detractors."

I pull out a piece of chocolate, this one gold-foil-wrapped, and chew. I dismiss the minor mental buff it gives, instead enjoying the warm gooeyness and the thickness as it lies on my tongue. When I clear my throat, the pair stare at me.

"I think we might want to look at it the other way. Instead of bribing or cajoling people, we play the other side of the coin. We try to dissuade those who are going after Earth from voting. Maybe have them abstain…" There are a few raised eyebrows, but I hold up my hand. "Listen. We got the Erethrans. And I'll speak with Duchess. But otherwise, what do we have?"

"Have?" Mikito says.

"Boy-o means leverage, right?" At my nod, Ali continues. "Political, social, economic leverage. Not Earth, just us."

Silence is all that greets his words. For all that we might be high-Leveled or dangerous on an individual basis, we're also, in many ways, unremarkable. Like most Adventurers, we pour most of our Credits into building ourselves up rather than building an economic engine.

We have little true political power. Sure, I helped the Erethrans and there's some leverage there, but it's leverage I've already tapped. Pushing further is probably a bad idea. The current Empress is less predisposed to like me than the Empress Apparent.

Socially, we have some strength individually. Harry has his fans and subscribers, his sources and contacts. Mikito has her fan club. But compared to the social strength of a single planet? Laughable.

"We have you." Mikito says, her eyes floating above my head. To where my Heroic status sits.

No Title, no accomplishment from the System for it, but a Heroic Class, even one that's broken like me, is still a power.

"Yeah... exactly."

A threat. Using me as a rogue element, just as we did before. Someone who can go out of his way to find, hunt, and kill those who would act against us. But if we can do that, so can our enemies. And taking that step might be one too far.

With that dour thought, we fall silent.

***

Of course, we don't sit there in silence, mulling over our lack of options. Harry does as he promised and researches Earth's opponents, working with

Ali to get a detailed analysis of the problem. Ali's also—carefully—accessing information about Earth and Katherine's status, looking for public data about her. We know where she and the surviving embassy personnel are living but figuring out a way to contact her is the tricky part. Thankfully, details about her aren't particularly hard to find.

"You sure this is accurate?" I raise an eyebrow, staring at the garish newspaper that fills my vision. It's displayed via my Neural Link, and one of a dozen different tabloids that Ali made me download. The one I'm regarding has a photo of Katherine on the arm of a rather robust gentleman who looks like a cross between a warthog and an anime character. In the Galactic equivalent of a suit, which involves lots of flowing tails and a hovering set of cloth-like wings.

"One hundred percent. Ms. Ward and the Grazish Heir are an item," Ali confirms.

"And they're going out."

"Yup."

"In public," I verify.

"And canoodling."

"Canoodling?"

"PDA. Getting handsy. Making the little spirit pay respects to the mother spirit."

"That..." I shake my head, refusing to be distracted. "Is it safe?"

"Why shouldn't it be?" Ali retorts.

"Because they killed Phil."

"He's not her," Ali says. "Officially killing the actual delegate is a major no-no. Unofficially, they might go after her, but you heard what Bolo said about anarchy. It might also stop you, boy-o, from coming to Irvina. Anyway, no one's taking potshots and potentially hitting the Grazish Heir."

"And why's that?" I say, only to catch Mikito muttering baka in my direction before returning to her research.

I glance over, but she's focused on her own notification, so I leave her be. She's got the job of working out potential vulnerabilities between our enemies—specifically, looking at those who voted against us before. If she can find a few we can convince to not vote against us, even if it means being neutral, that's as good as a vote for us. After all, while I might think of it as a specific vote, it's more a dedication of resources. So they're all already inclined to not paying the System Mana to make any particular vote workable since they'd then be less able to influence the next vote.

In fact, a few planets have been known to not vote at all, abstaining but holding the possibility of using their entire accumulated System-voting Mana at one time as a way to get what they want. Of course, it's a dangerous game to play since once it's all used up, their bullet is wasted. And there's always the danger of conquest... but some still dare.

"Because he's the Heir," Ali says slowly and clearly.

"You keep saying that..."

Ali throws up his hand. "Listen to me carefully. Grazish. Heir."

I open my mouth to scold Ali, but that's when the damn library in my head kicks off. I don't fade out, I don't lose sense of my surroundings. But I still get the download.

Heirs. A special Class within the System. Not always guaranteed to be given, not always available. And it is, in many cases, a crappy Class. It doesn't give you Skills for combat or even Artisan-type Skills. It is, however, extremely useful for survivability. The three pillars of the Heir Class revolve around survival Skills: increases in attributes, increases in resistances and immunities to poison and the like; networking Skills including Aura Skill's and Reputation bonus upgrades; and retribution Skills.

Like the penultimate Skill of the Basic Class under the retribution side for the Grazish Heir.

No Insult Unpaid (Level 1)

A Grazish does not condone insults. He does not allow those who have stained his honor or offered harm to him or his personnel to escape without retribution. Only proper recompense will see the ending of the feud with the Grazish. Mana Regeneration decreased by 5 permanently.

Effect: An Insult Marker is applied to each individual who insults or otherwise provokes the Grazish Heir. Each Insult Marker decreases cost of tracking spells, information purchases, and retributive Skills by 20%. Mark may only be dismissed by the Heir or those of higher Status than the Grazish Heir.

"And the Grazish are…?"

"Old money, as you humans might say," Ali says. "Powerful private corporation with its own Guild, security force, and Leveling teams. They keep things in-house for the most part, leveling the heirs—capital H or not—in safety, then they switch over Classes when they've hit the required Level." Ali shrugs. "At least, some of them. Some take a more active part in their own Leveling."

I see the threat this can create. Getting rid of a Marker like this must be difficult, and if they're old enough money, they're just as likely to kill those who insult them as listen to excuses. Scorched earth tactics are a favorite of the old families, especially against contractors. It helps keep things civilized.

I frown. "Why is she dating him?"

"Nice thighs?" Ali offers.

"Butt," Mikito corrects. Then tilts her head as she considers the picture. "Thighs are pretty good too."

"Seriously."

Ali drops the humor, flicking his fingers. A picture of Earth shows up, then it shifts. Small flags appear all across the globe as he continues. "Those cities have all special sponsored links from the Grazish corporation to the default Shop. As well as sponsored ads and sales prices for direct System-bought items."

"They can lower the cost via sponsorship?" I say, surprised.

Another flicker of Ali's fingers, and this time, small containers appear across the globe. Not as many by far, but some are in the middle of the ocean, surprisingly enough.

"Teleport and storage locations. If you get them close enough and provide the right kind of tech, you can lower teleport cost from the System."

"Smart," I praise.

Ali nods. "The Grazish corporation was the one that came up with the idea and exploited it, building out their teleport platforms near the start of the System. Since then, they've kept their first mover advantage."

"So you think he's helping her? Letting her meet who she needs in public while ostensibly 'dating' her?"

Ali nods.

I consider the possibilities. If they're in public, there'll be more eyes on them. At the same time, the Heir is rich enough that their social schedule will likely be extra secure. That's the thing about the capital—everyone's so used to clandestine meetings, most upscale locations have their own safe rooms. Never mind the more downscale ones I've used before.

And it might be safer to meet them in public than try to do so at their residence. That's definitely going to be watched.

"Find out their social schedule. We'll try to do a meetup that way," I say.

In the meantime, while the others work on the problem for Earth, I focus my attention on the Council. The inner Council of the Galactic Council, the nine (or so) permanent seats that make up the ruling council. They run everything on a day-to-day basis and they're the ones most likely to view me as a problem.

Nine individuals. Of the major political factions in the System, only the Galactic Edge and Artisans have seats as a faction. The Truinnar sit for the Galactic Edge—the expansionist group—while an old Nang Mai sits for the Artisans. The tree-like humanoid creature is one of the longest-serving members of the Council, and probably could hold his position by sheer virtue of strength and reputation alone if he sought it.

Neither the Traditionalists nor the Fist hold position on the council as a faction. You could say it's a weakness of their own philosophies. Or just an argument about how long they've been around as factions, requiring them not to have a grouped "bloc" to give them strength.

On top of that, we've got the Erethran and Movana representatives who are just that—representatives.

Of the remaining five, they sit on the council as independents, powers in themselves or for the planets they rule.

The Weaver is one. His body is bloated in the picture I've got, but his eyes—seven eyes on his face, another two that rise on tentacles from his forehead—draw attention. Fingers, long and nimble, twist and twitch, spasm in never-ending movement. Rumors are that he weaves fates in his fingers constantly, altering destinies of peasants and Legendaries with as much disregard.

The Lady of Shadows, she who few dare name, is another. Their intelligence asset, their Legendary spymaster. There are too many stories about her, many conflicting. Even her gender is in dispute, for information on one whose entire Class is focused upon cloaking and information dispersal cannot be trusted. Not even in the smallest detail.

The Dragon. Oldest of its kind, supposedly. It rarely shows up at meetings, rarely chooses to involve itself. It flies between stars, deep within the Forbidden Zone. As large as Jupiter itself, a monstrous creature whose Level is known to have breached at least five hundred. Maybe more.

Ares. Yes, that Ares—the one who runs the largest arms manufacturing company in the Galaxy, ruler of multiple manufacturing planets, the merchant of death. He's just as bad as the Dragon, always in the Forbidden Zone. Though he turns up for meetings more often. When he's not around, his daughter Nanaya sits in his place. Like him, she's a Legendary, though she's less direct warfare, a creature of deadly beauty and duels.

And finally, there's the Emperor. If you're unkind and feeling particularly secure, the Emperor of Nothing or Emperor of Ruins. For his empire is gone, his people scattered. He rules over nothing and no one, for the System has taken it all from him. And yet, he still lives. Wizened, ancient, he looks like an angel if your vision of an angel includes four wings, a pair of eyes on the end of his hands, and a blank, featureless face.

Nine individuals. Sometimes there are more, sometimes less. You get your seat by strength of arms, by influence, by acknowledgement. Any who desire a seat on the inner Council may do so. And if they chose wrongly, they die. Some last a few years, others a few centuries.

These are the people who would have started the problems with Earth. Except, something tells me it's not all of them. The secret of my Class, of being an Administrator, isn't something so easily bandied about. There have been hints, both in passing and in the library, that there is another circle, another group that rules. Made up of Legendaries and, I must assume,

Administrators. I need to figure out those names, but since I have only the main Council to go from, I start there.

I kick off the Erethran and Movana representatives from consideration. They don't matter. The Nang Mai might know about us Administrators, but he's well-known to not dabble too greatly in politics. A neutral party looking out for Artisans. Maybe an ally in that sense, but probably not.

That leaves pretty much the named individuals. The Lady of Shadows and Lies is the obvious first choice. Hiding a secret means she's part of it. The others are harder to tell. I'd guess Ares is out. He's a known meathead and this seems above his paygrade. On the other hand, he's a Legendary. It's hard to get that far by being a complete idiot. And he has a daughter who is smarter than he is.

The Dragon might be part of whatever inner circle there is that knows the secret. And the Emperor. Both are old enough that if they were searching for secrets—or through blind luck—they might have stumbled onto this knowledge.

The rest though… the Weaver is a Questor. Or at least, partial to us. Or was. Or maybe just out for the highest bidder. I don't know, it's hard to say with his history. He is what I would consider a moderate ally on the Council, if I have one. I doubt he's in the inner-inner circle though, or he wouldn't be a Questor anymore.

Then again, like my Society's Web Skill, his own Skills and Class might give him a head start on such secrets. When you're looking at the threads of society or fate, some secrets reveal themselves to you inadvertently.

But those are all guesses. The problem with a secret organization is that it's secret. And guessing might be a problem if I try to contact the wrong person.

As I dig into stories about each council member, trying to find a clue, a detail that might interact with what I know, what the library might contain, a loud beep startles us all. Hours have passed without us realizing it.

And we're finally here. In Irvina once again.

We stand and walk toward the exit, ready to enter our enemies' lair. And if we're flies heading in to see the spider, I just hope we're mutated flies. Or else this will end badly.

Chapter 9

Finding a place to lay low is easy enough. Hundreds of residences have been set up to handle the floating population of Adventurers, businessmen, and Artisans. So many Adventurers only come to Irvina for a short while to run a few specific dungeons before moving on.

Irvina itself has not changed much, being made of multiple ring districts. The first ring is where the Galactic Council holds its meetings, and the core of the city is within. Each ring from there grows in size and decreases in security.

This time around, we end up in the sixth ring. Far enough away that we're out of sight, and a little on the lower end for Advanced Adventurers but not uncommon. It's also only a short flight into the second or third ring if we want to meet with Katherine and the socialites.

Travel through the towering skyscrapers and myriad building designs of the city is as eclectic as the System. Some people fly on their own power. Others take the flying vehicles or creatures that ply the air, while transit options in terms of vacuum-filled bullet trains take the masses. For the most part, the plan is to take automated vehicles since Harry and I have had bad experiences with mass transportation.

The residence we rent is the Galactic equivalent of a four-bedroom condominium, the last bedroom adjusted to be a sparring ring. We pay a slight premium for such a residence, but again, nothing too surprising. Once we're in, we sweep the place for bugs, plant our own, and boost the security of the residence with a variety of pre-purchased items. Everything from talismans on walls to increase their durability and shielding spells to prevent spying as well as a few discreet nano-formed energy turrets.

Once we're settled, Harry makes his way out to meet with some of his contacts. For the reporter, many of his sources will only speak with him in person.

Which leaves Mikito and myself to get in contact with Katherine. And thankfully, Ali's found a decent option tonight. Even if it's not what I'd expect.

"A gallery opening?" I mutter, staring at the brochure and pair of tickets the Spirit has managed to score for us.

"Not just any gallery opening. It's Moyo Jin's gallery opening!" Ali snaps. When I shrug, he rolls his eyes. "Philistine. Moyo Jin hasn't had a showing in three decades."

I shrug again.

"There was an old work of his in my latest arena title defense. Meditating before it for a half hour gave me a bonus to my attributes and an additional passive defense Skill," Mikito says. "One with Air."

One with Air (Level 1) (B)

Legend has it that the first wind sylphs taught Evasoo, the martial warrior of air and void, this Skill directly before the advent of the System. When his planet was integrated, Evasoo gained his unique Class and this Skill, allowing him to float between the attacks of the monsters that dared to populate his planet. Reduces Mana Regeneration by 5 permanently.

Effect: Increases dodge skill by 20, increases environmental perception by 50, and allows one use of Peerless Dodge every ten minutes.

Peerless Dodge Effect: Increases dodge ability by 200 for one attack

I note the lack of a capital S on the skills, meaning that the increases are all effectively making someone better at dodging and perceiving the world rather than actively manipulating reality. It's a fine distinction, and there's an argument for Skills that affect skills. After all, for someone like Mikito, who relies on mundane skill to cross the threshold of raw power, the boost could make a big difference. Then again, raw power has a quality of its own.

A face-smashing quality.

"Do you lose Mana regeneration because of the bestowed Skill?" I ask. It's the first I've heard of an artifact from an Artisan providing not just regeneration or attribute buffs but a passive Skill buff.

"No," Mikito says. "But the buff is often short term. In this case, only twenty minutes."

More than long enough for an arena battle. Not so much if you were crafting. Though I guess if you were crafting, you might be able to put his artwork in front of you and get the boost anyway.

Huh.

"What level of work was it?" I ask.

"Heroic."

"Of course it is." I rub my chin, considering. I mean, I do have an Altered Storage space. If I could slip one of the works into it and stare at it before a fight, an extra Skill would be nice. Even if it is a Basic Skill. "All right, so we do the gallery opening. We find a place to talk to Katherine in the gallery and hopefully, find out who we can target. Sounds simple enough."

"You had to say that, didn't you?" Ali says, and I wince.

Oops.

***

Getting into the third ring requires a little work on my side, an adjustment on the pass restrictions that we received upon arriving in Irvina. The ones we originally received allow us to the fourth ring at most, and that with an additional payment. A minor push with the System Edit Skill changes them so that we can enter the third ring without issue and the second with a permit request.

The actual editing of our passes takes a bit. Partly because whoever designed the System for verification is paranoid. There are multiple safeguards in place, including a check against a central database, none of which I'd have known except for the fact that we had our previous permits. Using that as the basis for our amended permits, I was able to do the System-equivalent of hack the various databases.

Wielding the System Edit Skill is painful, as it floods my body with System Mana. Each time I try to read anything, try to Edit anything, I need to call that particular piece of code into my very body before I can begin the process.

It's painful and drains me of Mana at an astounding rate, but I get the job done. Once I'm finished, I verify that I'm not being logged before I move on. Thankfully, whoever decided to create Admin positions as Classes didn't also include a logging function. At least, not for our actual use of Skills.

It's an interesting factor, meaning that once you change something, unless you keep track of the changes yourself, it's never possible to go backward. Of course, I've got so many restrictions on what I can see or edit that this might only be for non-essential areas.

As I continue to play with my Skill, I learn the extent of my influence, and unsurprisingly, it's nowhere as large or wide as I'd like. I do wonder how much of that is because I'm a Junior Administrator and how much is because I've only got access to a single Skill thus far.

Questions, questions, questions.

"*Wake up, boy-o,*" Ali sends.

I look up in time for the private bubble car to slide to a halt beside the building. I resolutely don't look down since the floor is transparent and there are thousands of meters beneath my feet. The gallery we're visiting is expensive, which means it's located high up in Galactic society parlance.

In short order, we step out and join the small line of visitors. Wind catches and tugs at our clothing, threatening to blow us off the long balcony leading to the entrance proper with each gust. The constant hum and hiss of arriving flying cars floats down from the roof, where the rich and powerful arrive, and mixes with the whirr of constant video recordings. Muffled words, shouts, arrive in broken sentences, before another twist of the wind carries the words away.

Along with the noise and the cold of the altitude, there's the smell. It's floral with a hint of salt and thyme, piped into the open-air bay we stand in, along with a touch of heat to keep the place from being completely inhospitable.

Most of those who stand here don't seem bothered. I let my gaze flick across the numerous well-dressed individuals—and let me tell you, what is considered well-dressed in Galactic society is jaw-droppingly varied due to the mixture of cultures—and pick out the varied methods used to deal with the cold and winds.

Enchantments, glowing to provide strength and warmth. Deceptively light cloth or fur, taken from creatures in cold dungeons, that negate thermal penalties. Spells wrapped around auras. And in a very few cases, like the pair of us, just incredibly high Constitutions.

In fact, lack of clothing and protection seems to be as much a statement as the expensive materials some people wear. And while most of the clothing is civilian in form, in function, it could easily work as combat ware. Bonuses to Constitution, Strength, Agility are all in play, as well as the softer attributes. The most expensive pieces of equipment even boost Aura skills.

"Does no one understand subltety?" Mikito mutters.

Standing in line, we're buffeted by multiple Auras, pheromone- and scent-based attacks, and Charisma-based enchantments.

I grunt in reply, handing our pair of tickets to the crocodile-like humanoid attendant. Ali, even when pressed, refused to admit how he got those tickets on such short notice. I am somewhat concerned, but considering we've been here before, I take it on good faith they didn't come with too many strings attached.

"Flaunting your power is important," Ali says in a not-so-quiet whisper. "Especially since you can't do it inside."

"Why not?" I say, surprised as I take the tickets back. I step forward, only to halt as the crocodile speaks.

His voice grates and hisses, but it's also surprisingly well-enunciated. "Aura Skills would affect the artwork. Especially in large numbers."

"Ah!" I nod. "Thank you." And then, on a whim, I offer him a hand and send over a Credit tip when he takes it.

The crocodile-man grins and leans down, whispering, "If you speak to Trez on the third landing, let him know Idz says you're good people and to let you in."

I blink, but nod in thanks before moving away from the crocodile. Staying too long would make too big a scene. As it is, our clothing is close enough to being high quality, but I have a feeling close isn't exactly sufficient.

As we head in, I can't help but ask Ali for clarification.

"Private viewing. There's the kind of place you get in if you're invited. They'll have the better pieces in there. Or the stuff that has been pre-sold but the buyers still want to show off," Ali says.

I crane my neck upward as we wander into the gallery proper. The entire thing takes up three stories, with a central open-air area and wide winding ramps that snake around the periphery. Along the walls and sometimes smack dab in the middle of the ramps themselves are the art pieces.

"Now what?" Mikito says as we stare at the central piece, joining the audience.

The central piece reminds me of modern art, if modern art was sculpted in light and sound, in taste and Mana. It's impossible to see it fully without Mana sense, and even then, the more you stare, the more is revealed as the sculpture shifts and changes. Eventually though, there's a pattern to the movement. A story perhaps, or just guided fluctuations in Mana.

"We look around. And maybe buy something," I say to Mikito as we continue to stare at the artwork.

More than a few sapients stop and regard the work. Some take to the sky, floating above us. After a few minutes of regard, I get the buff that increases my Perception by tens of points and even gives me a passive Skill effect for the next hour that extends my physical senses and my concentration levels. Nothing more than a Basic Skill, but I could see a corporation purchasing something like this and leaving it in their lobby to give their employees a boost.

Idly, I look at the price of the piece and choke.

"You could buy a damn warship with that!" I splutter.

My outraged utterance gets more than a few disdainful looks and one fart noise from a ball-like creature. Mikito rolls her eyes while Ali is clutching his sides, rolling around in the air as I finally realize how expensive this work really is.

"You knew," I state flatly to Ali, dropping my voice as we head away.

"Oh yeah, boy-o." Ali sniffs. "This is artwork made by a Heroic Class artist! Of course it's expensive."

I can't help but shake my head as we make our way up one of the ramps. My minor outburst is thankfully soon forgotten. As we regard more of the pieces, I realize they're not all that expensive. Still stupidly so—the cheapest and smallest piece is still in the tens of millions of Credits—but not warship-level expensive.

Still out of my price range anyway.

As we walk along, Mikito and I do our best to blend in. Unsurprisingly, Mikito does better than I do. She's a little more socially savvy than me. She knows how to blend in, become part of the crowd.

I've rarely had the chance to do so. Not in these kinds of circles at least. It's a novel sensation, being relatively unknown. I actually don't mind it. It's a little reminder of my forgotten humanity, of a time when I was your basic geeky programmer. Infamy was never something I cared about, except as a tool.

There's also something weird about wandering through an art gallery when you're public enemy number one. Knowing that if you're caught, chances are it's the end of it all. Thankfully, nervousness from being an outlaw and nervousness at being in a social situation is all the same.

The artwork is varied. Mostly sculptures of one form or another, but in detail, it's different. The artist is working in multiple dimensions, not just within simple sight, but sound, smell, Mana, time, and sometimes even pure chaos.

Something made of stone twists and turns, rising up in the sky before swooping down, a never-ending spiral whose lines makes you fall with your eyes into a blank hole in its center that becomes something. An exhibit so hidden that you're not entirely sure what it is you're seeing. You smell it, leaning forward, then it's gone.

Another notification, another boost.

Mikito moves differently than I do. I stop, regarding each work for a bit, watching the various visitors dart about the gallery, paying attention to the works until I get a bonus, then I move on. Mikito, on the other hand, brushes past the vast majority of the work, only pausing once in a while to fall into deep thought before a piece. She's specific in her taste, whereas I'm dabbling.

And in the midst of all of this, attendants move with drinks, snacks, and notepads. Waiters feed us while salespeople try to talk up each particular work. After the first one I decline, they leave me alone. In fact, they hover around Mikito, almost as if they can sense that she's more of an opportunity than myself.

I have to admit, after staring at the prices, I've lost any interest. Frankly speaking, I'd rather pay for premade foods from Master Classers to give me a boost than run around with artwork. Consumables are still expensive, but overall cheaper. Not that I bother too often. Alchemists can generally generate the same effects with potions at a lower cost. Though if you really want to min-max, you could consume both since they're often separate stacking bonuses.

I know some of the more focused individuals do that, and while I'm not opposed to bonuses, the issue is cost, supply, and reliance. Grow too reliant on something that costs too much and when you don't have it, your entire performance level drops.

It's kind of like doping in the pre-System world. Sure, you can dope and you can do well—even better than your competitors. But what if you get caught? Or have to stop? The withdrawals and the lack of ability afterward is significant as you retrain.

In either case, we make our way up the art gallery until we arrive at the doors of the VIP section. Ali's been paying attention to the guests, but thus far, Katherine and her date have yet to make an appearance. We've been delaying our movements as long as possible, hoping she'll come out and see the rest of the exhibition. But it seems they've chosen to hang out with the VIPs, leaving us to wait.

It's frustrating, but luck is with us since we have a way in. A little more Credits, a smile, and a good word gets us in where we weren't meant to be. Though I assume, to some extent, there are exceptions already built in socially for cases like this. I can't help but wonder how much of our entrance is because of Luck or Charisma, how the System gently nudges things when it needs.

"Oh, this is much more like it!" Ali crows and darts over to the VIP buffet table.

I look it over and wince, since this is a Galactic event. The offerings are wide ranging, from meats of identifiable—read, with bodies and heads attached—and unidentifiable variety, as well as other forms of consumables. There are crystalline rods filled with raw Mana, electricity, and radioactive material. There are swirling globes of smoke that can be broken open and sniffed, and glass flutes of liquid nourishment.

While I'm pretty open about food I'm willing to eat, I do draw the line at sapient creatures. Which, in a few cases, are displayed on the buffet table. There are even a few living creatures, pain receptors neutered via Skills and technology, that are ready to be consumed.

Ali sweeps in, grabbing hold of one of the crystalline rods. He proceeds to open his mouth wide, swallowing the rod and the sparkling energy within in a sword-swallowing act that would win awards. For a moment, his tiny form shifts colors, growing more solid and opaque before he stabilizes.

"Whoa! Good stuff."

I snort and almost miss the waiter who replaces the energy flute. There's enough food on the hovering multi-tiered tables to feed every single visitor in the gallery three times over. But the gods forfend that it look as if they might run out.

"Gallery," Mikito says, elbowing me in the side.

I bring my attention back to the gathering and blink when I realize more than a few eyes are fixed upon us. More than one gaze is filled with disdain, and for the bodyguards, professional suspicion.

I wave, offering them a weak grin. "Hi?"

***

Thankfully, my smile and greeting seems to diffuse the situation. Not so much because it's what is expected but because they automatically label us as hicks and proceed to ignore us. Of course, that doesn't let us off entirely. A quartet of uniformed security personnel sweep in, their fixed stares daring us to try to run.

"*Oy! Find Katherine. Fast!*" I send to Ali while sweating mental bullets.

The Spirit does a little bob and freezes in place, flicking through sensor data.

There's no real danger in getting my ass kicked, but any altercation will lead to our identities being revealed. And that, more than anything else, is what I intend to avoid.

"Evening, gentlepeople," I say when they close. Of course, gentlepeople isn't the exact word I use in Galactic—the closer translation is something like "worthy and honored sapients," but gentlepeople is much nicer.

The four that close in on us are made up of three Hakarta—two men and a woman—and a single crystalline figure. It moves with a grace that belies its appearance, more liquid rock than sharp-edged body.

It's the living crystal that speaks. "Passes please."

I give them a smile and extract our tickets, handing over the two slips.

Crystal takes one look at them and hands them back to me, its voice still pleasant. "These are for the general viewing floor."

"There's more than one kind of floor?" I give them big eyes. "I didn't know. But the works here look so much nicer…"

"How did you acquire these tickets?" Crystal says, not at all affected by my poor attempt at charming them.

Mikito steps up next to me and places an arm around mine, almost leaning into me, and giving them a cool smile at the same time. "My husband's Spirit took care of it. We don't really bother with such trivial things."

"And what do you bother with?" Crystal says, its gaze sweeping over us and our clothing. Thankfully, with so many individuals, high culture for clothing isn't so much a specific type of style and more to do with cut and expense. Still, I'm getting the feeling that our attempt at fitting in is insufficient.

"And why would that matter?" Mikito says archly. "We're here to view Moyo Jin's work, not answer to impertinent questions."

"Found her! And contacting…"

Crystal glowers at her words. "Below, it might not matter. But this portion of the event is exclusive. Reserved for those who have the right Levels. Or connections."

I wonder then if perhaps we had been found out from the very beginning. Did I insult the man below, offer too little a bribe? Did I make a misstep then? Or was it now when Ali acted like a bore? Or myself when I said hi? Should I have just strutted in as if I owned this place?

Perhaps.

Spending years, nearly a decade, killing monsters, fighting Master Class and higher enemies has done little to aid my social acumen. I was never a socialite, but a simple programmer. And not even that successful a one. Parties like this, where I start out of my element just means I sink faster.

"Well, I've never been so insulted..." Mikito tilts her chin higher, staring down her nose at Crystal, who seems unperturbed by her actions.

But I also note Crystal and its people don't seem worried either. They're treating us like party crashers, not true threats.

"You may complain to my manager if you wish," Crystal says as he steps forward, a glittering, clawed hand sweeping to point at the door behind us.

"*Ali!*"

"*Katherine says go. And wait.*"

When Mikito opens her mouth to protest further, I tug on her arm gently and step back. She turns and glares at me while I lower my voice. Low enough to be a whisper, even if I know anyone here would hear it if they bothered. Damn Perception increases.

"Let's not cause a scene, dear. We couldn't afford the pieces in here anyway," I say.

"That's not the point!" Mikito says.

"The point will be them tossing us out physically, if we don't move."

Mikito sniffs again and detaches herself from my arm. She stalks out the door, and I turn to the group, offering them an open-handed and sheepish shrug. I can't read Crystal, but I catch a flicker of amusement among the Hakarta guards.

Outside, the pair of us move away from the doorway, down to a mostly empty landing where a twisted sculpture, when viewed, gives a bonus to Intelligence—specifically, mental arithmetic calculations. It also is made up of some annoyingly high-pitched auditory passages. It's one of the least popular showings because of that.

"So, that went well," I say, leaning in to speak with Mikito.

"It did not!" she replies, her voice still heated. "You always embarrass me like that."

"Oh, I do, do I?" I say. "As if I wanted to come to these things."

"Keep your voice down. They're still watching us!" Mikito says.

"And why should I care?"

Mikito growls and turns away, breaking off eye contact with me and looking instead ostensibly at the big center piece. I sniff, staring at her back, and turn to view a smaller piece, watching as Ali floats down to me. He's been ejected from the room too, though he took his time leaving.

"*Nicely done. People are looking away for the most part,*" Ali confirms.

"*You think we're good?*"

"*Mostly. Katherine's on her way. So just play the stricken lovers for a little more.*"

"*We still need a place to meet, in private,*" I point out.

"*Yeah, yeah. We'll figure it out.*"

I snort, then rub my ears. Hopefully the woman arrives soon. Because there's only so long I want to listen to this buzzing.

Chapter 10

Rather than meet us directly, Katherine sends a waiter who directs us to the top of the gallery. We cross by the stone-faced guard of the VIP room, who refuses to look at us, and end up in a smaller room, one whose doors slide open and shut behind us, leaving behind the waiter who escorted us.

Lights flicker on, and I find myself regarding a miniature city that dominates the room. I frown, walking forward and cocking my head, struck by the incongruity of the piece.

"What the hell is this?" I mutter.

There are even tiny figures, barely half an inch tall, who I could almost swear are alive, so lifelike are their motions. If not for the lack of any differentiation in the Mana flows through them, I would never have guessed them to be tiny golems.

"The next showing," Katherine's voice cuts in.

I turn, spotting her emerging from another doorway, and take a moment to assess the woman. She's looking good for her age, not seeming to have aged a day since I first met her nine years ago. Her hair might be a little paler and greyer, the eyes a little harder, but she's still the middle-aged secretary who'd introduced herself to me when I took over Vancouver.

"A miniature city, one that depicts life as it could be, or should be. There are a few more such cities, each revolving around another race, another political system. If you watch them long enough, you can see them play out day-to-day lives, revolutions and wars and social unrest. And then peace again. Or never-ending war," Katherine says.

"So, a real work of art, not a toy for Skills," Mikito says, walking over to Katherine.

Mikito hesitates for a second when she gets close, but Katherine doesn't, throwing her hands around Mikito and giving her a hug that the little Japanese woman returns.

Into her neck, Mikito mutters, "It's good to see you."

"And you. I've been watching your fights."

"You have?"

"Of course. You've got quite a following on Earth too, you know," Katherine says, making Mikito blush. She hangs her head, while Katherine lets her go and smiles. "You've done well."

Mikito steps back, shifting back to her impenetrable mien. To everyone but me, it'd be easy to miss the flush of happiness she is doing her best to hide.

"And you've made trouble," Katherine says, her voice growing colder as she faces me.

"I... didn't mean to this time?" I say, offering as explanation.

Katherine snorts, taking the couple of steps needed to close in on me and give me a hug. "Whatever, you idiot."

I hug her back, but I don't take my eyes off the fourth person in the room. Not that the hug is as long or as personal as the one she gave Mikito. Unlike Lana and Mikito, I barely spent any time with Katherine before I was thrown into the Forbidden Zone.

It's a good thing the hug's over quickly, since our silent watcher is hanging back and looking grumpy. Hiding in the shadows, as if he could hide. Considering he's neither human nor expected, the Grazish Heir is like a six-foot-tall man in a children's ballet class.

Like the picture I saw, he's dressed in a mixed-robe and ribbon outfit, with tails that float behind him, wings and ribbons twisting in a non-existent wind. The colors of his clothes and ribbons are myriad, shifting through the colors of the rainbow and yet coordinating with one another. Still, the warthog humanoid is distinctly inhuman as dark eyes stare at me, its pupils almost lost in the shadows of its overhanging eyebrows.

Reqm Harsem, Thirty-Eighth Heir of the Grazish Clan, Warden of the Eleventh Ward of Esuma, Lasard Mo-ki of the Rawce Clan, Corporate Raider, ... (Grazish Heir Level 19) (M)

HP: 2380/2380

MP: 2210/2210

Conditions: Linked Health, Second Chance: Rise, Shielded, Aura of Wealth

"You okay?" I say as I detach from her.

"Better, now that you're here. And you can relax, Reqm is on our side." Katherine beckons and Reqm walks forward, offering us a weird snapping salute with his left hand in greeting.

"You sure?" I say.

"You can rest assured, I would not betray my Gasjen," Reqm says.

"*Gasjen? A gas generator?*"

"*Funny. No. Uhh…*" Ali falls silent, accessing information while I watch as Katherine steps away from me and returns to Reqm's side. Closer now, they twine fingers together. "*Oh, wow. Yeah, that's…*"

"*Girlfriend?*" I supply.

"*Betrothed. First among his betrothed.*"

"Wait." I hold up a hand and stare at Ali before looking at Katherine. "You guys are an item?"

"Yes," Katherine answers.

"Of course," Reqm says.

"It's not just a cover?"

"Why would I do that?" Reqm looks honestly puzzled. "Do humans do that... oh wait. Yes. Of course. She is not my beard."

"That's not..." I splutter.

Katherine whisper something into Reqm's ear while he continues to regard me.

When he replies to her, his voice isn't as low. "He's not really that impressive. Are you sure it's him they want?"

"Oy. Pumbaa. Enough for now. This is a private talk," I say. "While this place might be private, I'm not sure I'd call it discreet. Or safe."

Katherine gives me a half-smile and holds up a single finger. A moment later, a notification appears before me.

Diplomatic Silence (Level 4)

Every form of government requires a way to keep secrets and negotiate in private. Using this Skill, the Diplomat ensures that what is said within the radius of the discussion is safeguarded. This Skill works in tandem with the government System-purchased buff National Secrets for additional effects. Mana regeneration reduced by 20 permanently.

Effect: Increases cost of information and other surveillance Skills by a factor of 4. Receives an additional 54% of National Secrets government buff.

"Fine," I grumble good-naturedly. "And I assume that's running all the time?"

"Of course," Katherine says. "Reqm has a similar Skill. His grandfather also has a constant counter-espionage Skill running on his family, as does Earth."

"Wait, counter-espionage Skill?" I say.

"It informs us if someone is purchasing information or attempting surveillance," Reqm says.

"Ah…" I nod. That makes sense. Still… "It's the Lady of Shadows…"

Katherine shakes her head. "There's a lot of misinformation about her. She's not infallible. She's just a Legendary."

"Just."

Ali snorts, but he nods at Katherine. "She's not wrong. Even a Legendary's power is limited."

"Do we even know what the limits might be?" Mikito asks.

"Her Skill details are hidden. But others?" Ali shakes his head. "If we took John's Class to the max, he'd have three choices from his Skill Tree. Each of which would be a penultimate for the Grand Master Paladin. Following the theme, they'd be able to boost any of the Paladins they command or even raise an individual to the Class or a tier, temporarily or permanently; he'd be able to use the Weight of Duty to shatter a planet; and the Skill the Might of Justice allows him to borrow any Skill, any System-recorded memory, any piece of currently owned equipment from those he served."

"Served?"

Ali nods and I pause. I recall that the Empress had a couple of Heroic-level pieces of equipment. Maybe even some Legendary ones.

"Actual borrow, as in teleportation or…?"

Ali shrugs. "Uncertain. I could verify at a Shop but…"

"It doesn't mater," Mikito butts in. "You're saying that a Legendary Skill can influence things on a planet or across an Empire, but with some degree of restrictions."

There are nods, and I frown, remembering what happened at Prax. The Lady of Shadows had taken steps to hide the movement of the fleet coming for us, making it so that we never knew it was arriving until it was too late. Hiding things at that level was powerful, but if you considered that she probably had to look at influencing multiple individuals at a time, instead of altering actual reality, it wasn't impossible. Or she might have just adjusted information flow for everything coming in and out of the space station.

"So we're looking at a limited number of individuals she can affect," I say.

Katherine nods. "And we know for certain that her Skills have been in use in a variety of other locations, including the current trade war between the Stadin and Maties Groups."

Req'm adds, "Ares has also requested her aid in dealing with a Mana outbreak along the Restricted Zone nearby the Fraskee Borders. There's a flood of Behemoth Crawlers and a living planet that has pushed outward, carrying with it a flood of Mana."

"*Fraskee?*"

"*Nautical creatures. Sort of like your mermaids, but not exactly,*" Ali supplies.

"Why would they care?" Mikito asks.

"Because one of the lies the Council tells is that the growth of the Forbidden and Restricted Zones are regular and controlled. Not contained, but controlled," Reqm says, his lips twisting in a snarl, his tiny tusks glowing with his displeasure. "They lie to us about the deaths that occur, the planets that are destroyed. And when they fail, they make sure no one knows."

"If no one knows, how do you?" Mikito says.

"Because the Galactic System is old, and no secret is truly secret," Reqm says.

I could beg to differ, but I keep my mouth shut. I don't know him, no matter how much Katherine trusts him.

"And such secrets are whispered among those of us in power," Reqm says. "It is only those without power who know not the lies they are told. Though many think they do."

I frown. "Yet you've got a whole planet experiencing things right now. What happens to them? Are they killed?"

"Or moved to another location. Their minds wiped, their memories altered, their histories changed," Reqm says. "If they fail. If they succeed in containing it, the incident is covered up, lies are woven such that no one knows better. Information is edited for many years, using individual Spies and Propagandists. The very nature of the attack is made a lie. Until the truth is no longer understandable."

"They do this so that more people stay. Wait. Holding still in their doomed planets because they think they're safe. Or at least, as safe as living in a Restricted Zone can be." I think over what I know of Restricted and Forbidden Zones and come to the final conclusion. "They need people to stay, don't they? Because without sapients, the borders would grow faster. Without individuals serving the Adventurers who move in to gain what resources they can, monsters won't be killed. Mana won't be churned."

"Yes."

Vicious but effective. It's not something I would do, not something I can even condone doing. But it's effective and it keeps things stable, which I am realizing, for most governments, is more important than what is good or right or moral. Practicality over morality.

Mikito drags the conversation back on topic, to the reason we're here, as she clears her throat. "We're safe from being spotted, at least we hope so. Unless she turns her attention on us, because we're a lot smaller than a planet—"

"Though you have your planet and my merchant empire backing you up."

Mikito continues, ignoring the interruption. "*But* we still shouldn't take too long. What can we do to help you, Katherine? You and Earth."

Katherine pauses, visibly recalling what she needs to say, then launches into what must be a rehearsed speech.

***

We leave the art gallery an hour later, with a lot less enthusiasm than we arrived. It's no real surprise, not with the information related to us. We're weighed down by the knowledge we've gained and what we must do. Being the organized woman she is, Katherine had much of the information ready to go in an information pack, so what we spoke about were the high-level aspects. The rest we'll read later.

As suspected, Katherine has been building alliances over the last four plus years she has been in Irvina. Even so, it has been difficult for the lady to build any true alliances due to concerns about longevity. While groups like the Erethrans or the Truinnar might want a Dungeon World under their control, making it happen is much more difficult than just wishing.

Like Earth when I returned years ago, many groups have formed their own enclaves, their areas of control. And unlike Earth, many such places in established Dungeon Worlds have significant resources poured into them. Even the lowest Level Dungeon World would still require a couple of Master Classes to conquer a lightly defended settlement. In higher Leveled, more established Dungeon Worlds, you'd require a full armed assault to have a hope of winning.

On top of that, you've got internal politics—who gets control of the Dungeon World? Which faction is in charge? What kinds of benefits would each faction gain? After all, if they won't get any benefits from those in charge, would it not be better to make a deal with those on the Dungeon Worlds already and get something from them for opposing the Dungeon World sole-government?

As I said, it's complicated. Even when Katherine made headway, managing to get a few allies on our side—various governments, races, merchant groups and guilds—the direct opposition by the Council has driven many of them away. Suddenly, the benefits no longer outweigh the cost.

When we suggested my plan of physically dissuading voting groups, Katherine was quite adamant that it's a horrible idea. Reqm threw his weight behind her, pointing out that any action we take on the vote will reflect badly on Earth.

The only good news Katherine had to offer is that to make a major change in the Galactic Constitution requires a significant Mana flow. It's the equivalent of 80% of the Mana generated by the System-planets in a month, making it a big ask.

Because of the cost involved, Katherine's actually found a number of people who are willing to vote against or abstain entirely. In some cases, only for a single vote. But a single vote of abstinence from each party is what we need now. Which is where the list and information she gave us comes into play.

As for future votes, we'll have to get past this one before worrying about it.

In truth, the Galactic Council have tried to take away Earth's seat before—by contesting its legitimacy in courts, its standing in the Council as a Dungeon World, and even the legitimacy of the actual vote. In the end, all of that failed, leaving the Galactic Council with this final maneuver—striking off all rights of Dungeon Worlds to hold a seat on the Council and marking them as contested territories for now and forever more.

The stakes have never been higher, and the problem is more insurmountable than ever, it seems. Thankfully, we've got a few options. And once we return to our residence and emplace our defenses, we go over those options, combining the knowledge Katherine has provided us with our own research.

"This is a very long list," Harry says. The reporter managed to make his way back halfway through the next day, adding his own findings to what we were given.

We've been mostly reading, taking in details of political games that we have no idea about. Even as fast as we consume information, we can only take in an overview, since there are so many players involved.

Still, the information we garner is enough for us to do our job and, when things go south, hopefully not mess it up too much by improvising.

"Katherine's highlighted one hundred sixteen different groups that might be open to convincing," I say in confirmation. "We've got less than a month to convince as many of them as we can. Maybe as little as two weeks, if Katherine can't stall the vote further."

"One hundred eight," Ali corrects, flicking over the new list. "I just finished the info dump Harry brought back. If he's right, those eight are no-gos."

I grunt and accept the correction. One hundred sixteen or one hundred eight, it's too many for me to tackle anyway.

"Either way, too many. We have to split this up if we have any hope of doing any good," Mikito says.

"Just like before, triage."

I poke the information, sorting it out by number of seats. At the same time, the spreadsheet keeps the details of what kind of needs they have pre-sorted. At least, what they've told Katherine what they need. Reading over the list, I can't help but shake my head.

- *Title: Master Duelist (Beat a Heroic Class in a formal duel)*
- *Title: Galactic Gourmet (Consume 2,500 different kinds of monster meat within a year)*
- *Class: Breaker of Chains (Advanced Prestige. Must break a Master Class Binding Skill)*
- *Class: Paen of Pain (Advanced Prestige. Receive over 1,000,000 points of damage)*
- *Class: Inheritor of Secrets (Master Class. Be given a dozen Tier I secrets)*
- *...*

"What happened to sex, power, and money?" I mutter. "Isn't that what most people want?"

"You want the sex ones?" Ali says, raising an eyebrow. His fingers flick and my jaw drops as he sorts the information.

"Not doing that. Or that. Maybe that…" My gaze moves down the list, making Mikito pause and look at me.

"There are some of those you'd do?" she says, sounding surprised.

"It's just sex." I pause. "Well, that one was just sex. If I have to, I'll put a bag over their head." As the group stares at me, I face their incredulous gazes and open my hands wide. "It's my fault, people. Taking one—okay, six—for the team isn't that bad.

"Though I might need a bath or two." I scratch my chin and add, "Also, have you noticed how, if you've not had sex for a bit, it's fine. You can deal with it. But once you get used to being… ummm… regular, then the next few months or so is rather difficult?"

Mikito blushes slightly, muttering curses under her breath at me. I grin at her, though I must admit, I'm blathering on a little to cover up my own embarrassment. Sometimes, the only way through it is to head in deep.

Harry snorts, the Brit—who, come to think of it, I know indulges with his fans and other races regularly—ignoring my segue. "Perhaps we should consider selling your body last. Many of the more carnal desires are more tentative, as Katherine has noted. People in the positions of power like that often have access to such…"

"Conveniences?" I offer.

"Dalliances?" Ali says.

"Fetishes?" Mikito supplies.

"Opportunities," Harry says with finality. "It's more a case of finding the right timing for them."

"So what you're saying is that they might not be willing to offer their vote for boy-o's sweet, sweet body," Ali says.

"Exactly. Whereas providing access to Titles and Classes…" Harry shrugs. "Those can be more difficult. Especially these…"

- *Class: Jesuit Priest*
- *Class: Hair Metal Drummer*
- *Class: Babalawo*
- *Class: Micro-Expression Interrogator*
- *Title: Neither Rain nor Shine*

- *Title: Virtual Killer*
- *Title: Triad Leader*
- ...

"Restricted Classes and Titles," I say, sighing. "I guess that's a form of power, isn't it?"

"Especially when it's unexpected," Ali says. "The System might not like to balance each Class against another, but with the variety out there, there's always a balance to be found against another. Or an exploit."

I nod. While most types of Skills come down to the System-equivalent of punching someone in the head until they fall, when it comes to non-Combat Classes, there's a lot more variety. And sometimes, certain Classes and Skills just slip under the radar of other Skills.

Being the new kids on the block, we've got a bunch of new Classes waiting for exploits. Add in interesting Titles that might provide either prestige or stackable bonuses, and I can see these Titles being desired. Still, there's no way to know for sure without actually gaining a Class or Title and testing it to see if they can be exploited. I'm sure the vast majority of them won't be anything particularly new or interesting, but as any good fighter knows—it only takes one lucky shot to end a fight.

Except that's not really true with the System. Health Points give us an unnatural level of resilience, such that even a cheap shot or one that lands perfectly cleanly won't necessarily take out someone with high health. The tyranny of Levels can keep those below chained to the bottom.

Or it would, if not for the fact that Mana and health regeneration is finite. That's where the System's ability to provide information is a leveler. Knowing how much you need to hammer someone means that, if necessary, you can work out what you need to do to end them. And in a few cases, the best revenge hasn't even been direct attacks but the wide release of an individual's build. For those at the highest Levels, most have gotten where they are by stepping on a few necks along the way.

A borrowed knife slits a throat just as cleanly.

"I'm assuming Credits aren't high on the list because we don't have enough?" I say.

One of the interesting aspects of Katherine's list is the focus on the individual rather than the government. She's got that covered. What she wants us to exploit are the people who do the actual voting—the man on the ground, if you will.

"Actually, it's mostly because the people on the list are paid an extremely high salary to ensure they aren't bribable." Harry says. "At least with Credits, that is."

I chuckle a bit. It's the Singapore method of public service. If you pay your government servants the same as any CEO, not only do you get good government servants, but the need for bribery decreases. Not that the high salaries get rid of bribery entirely—as we're going to exploit—but it does reduce it.

"Well, at least there aren't any white elephants," I say.

"Elephants?" Harry asks.

"Just something I read about. How some gifts are white elephants that stroke the ego more than anything else," I say.

"Oh, like these?" Ali says.

A moment later, I'm reading a rather long list of materials, none of which I've heard about and most of which I have trouble even pronouncing.

"Gah!" I throw up my hands. "What would you need the marrow of a twelve-headed hydra for?"

"Alchemical compound. Useful for a variety of regenerative effects," Ali replies.

"So, a health potion?"

"Affliction removal. Or regeneration from old age in particular."

"Right."

When he mentions the one thing the System will not remove, even if it slows it, I eye the materials with renewed interest. Once I poke at the details, what seems like a bewildering array of gifts become a series of weird, specific Master or Heroic crafted items and a bunch of materials for longevity potions.

"Great. So how are we doing this?" I prod the sheet. As fascinating as all this might be, it doesn't solve the problem of how we're dividing the work.

"I can do the gifts," Harry says. "Between my contacts and whatever Dornalor might dig up, I might be able to locate some of these things."

Unspoken is the added caveat of locate and acquire. One of the issues with much of the material is that even when their location is known, they aren't being sold. Dornalor might not be here, but his contacts could be useful—not to forget any criminal contacts Harry might have made on Prax.

"Classes and Titles for us," Mikito says, pointing between her and me. "We can teach or train them. Some might be more difficult. And there are the obvious ones John has to do."

"Like the Heroic requirement kind." I nod. Annoying, but those who require specific kinds of Skills can be dealt with. So long as they're willing to subject themselves to the abuse, which requires trust. Which is often the sticking point.

"You also have one other thing to do…" warns Mikito.

I sigh. Truth. For all this, we still need to figure out what to do about the inner Council. And…

"The Duchess."

I make a face again as the pair of humans voice their agreement. If there's one person who can aid us in all this, it'd be her. The question is, of course, what she wants.

Time to find out what's taking her so long to contact me.

Chapter 11

Of course, like most of my existence these last few months, it isn't as easy as asking Roxley what the hell is going on. He didn't even deign to meet with me, instead sending back a note that the Duchess will see me when she's ready to do so.

That issue resolved, the team splits up to begin the process of getting votes. Luckily, the vast majority of the time, we have easy methods of contacting our targets, supplied to us by Katherine.

One of the things about working in such a big, political city is that those in the know all set up multiple methods of communication. Not just the official channels and the unofficial official channels, but unofficial secret channels and secret secret channels of communication. All of it is broken out into multiple levels, given out to various acquaintances and allies and even enemies as needed, depending on what you think is required.

After all, you might not want the government to know what you're saying. Or you might not want to officially be speaking to certain people, even if unofficially, your government agrees with your action. And so on, so forth.

What we were given are the semi-public secret channels, with the requisite notations on how to let them know their information isn't burned, just passed along properly. Which is a whole different level of secrecy.

"*And why does Katherine have all this?*" I mutter, staring at the Galactic equivalent of a burner phone. "*Isn't there a spy head or something?*"

"*Contingency planning of course. Also, pretty sure Earth's spy head is dead,*" Ali sends back.

"*How'd you know that?*" I reply.

I let my gaze roam over the park we're waiting in, mentally grumbling about the idiocy of having a secret meeting in public. But since this is the initial contact, they didn't want to be in a hidden place, so here we are.

This park isn't that big, just over a few hundred meters, but with multiple dips and rises so that direct lines of sight are cut off. This is aided by the local fauna, many of which grow to twice or thrice the height of the sapients ambling along. Other than the occasional giant, of course—a pair of which ducked behind a convenient wall of shrubbery and masonry to canoodle.

"*Do they really think they're hidden?*" I send to Ali, watching the trembling foliage.

"*Sometimes, it's more the illusion of privacy than the reality, boy-o.*"

"*Fine. But the spy master?*"

I keep scanning while we wait, searching for our contact. I hope he isn't too late. I've booked another meeting in another public location—a bullet train transit station—in an hour. And then another after that. And the burner phone is for the next set of calls I need to make, while I'm scrambling from one location to the next.

Even peering around, I see nothing. There are flying creatures, insects, winged angels, half-beast or monster equivalents, even a few elemental-bodied fellows. And on the ground, you get the usual plethora of humanoids walking, rolling, and jumping along. But not my next meet.

"*Mikito actually told me about it. According to her, he was targeted during the attack,*" Ali explains. When I send back a wordless grunt, he shrugs. "*We've been digging a little into the actual attack. She knew who he was before because she'd been in contact with Katherine and Lana. And we reviewed the attack, just in case.*"

"*Just in case what?*"

"*They use the same teams.*"

Before I can ask for details, a voice speaks up behind me. I don't start, even if I want to. Because whoever it is has taken the seat on the opposite side of the park bench, facing away from me on the circular bench-cum-table-cum-elevated rise, without me knowing.

"You're not human."

"No. But I can get you the individual."

"Really? Because we've yet to get one to agree to leave Earth," the creature says.

I glance over, spotting the creature as it inhales. It's a short, stubby alien whose grey skin and flat features are dominated by the trio of large nostrils situated around its body. Small flaps open and close, allowing the creature to block off potential smells and attacks, while even more fleshy flaps and strings of flesh deeper within strain out other gaseous particles.

"I can. My word on it," I say. "But you know what we want in return."

"Expensive."

"But for your Clan, this would be quite the win, would it not? After all, bringing a new scent-based Class to the Kinanti…"

"We'll need a serf contract for seven years. System-registered."

"No," I flat-out refuse. "Work contract for five years. System-registered, based off you fulfilling your bargain. In turn, we'll provide a System-registered proof of Class."

"Ten years."

"Agreed."

"Transport costs?" the Kinanti asks, its voice low and husky.

I note it snuffling more, as if trying to ascertain my identity via smell. Good luck with that. I have a spell and an enchantment both killing my scent for just this reason.

"We can handle it," I say. "But you'll pay going rates for their work. And take care of their accommodations and safety. Along with their family."

"Of course. Standard contract for Artisans. But this is an Advanced, yes?"

"Yes. By the time the vote is completed, you'll get your Advanced Class Perfumer."

The creature lets out a trill, a snort, then stands. "Don't contact me again until the documents are ready."

I don't look at him as he stalks off, but I do borrow Ali's field of vision to note his bouncing step. It's only when he's gone, when I've finished reading the threads from Society's Web and the changes in his demeanor, that I speak.

"What do you think?"

"He'll do it. Now, come on. Next!"

I groan but stand, heading out. We'll have to contact Lana to get this done, but thankfully, we know a Basic Classer who will jump at the chance. All we have to do is boost him through his Levels, which means VIP access to our dungeons and a Leveling team.

A small price to pay for an abstentation.

Now, if only the rest of our deals are this easy.

***

Underground. This is the galactic equivalent of a sewer line, but it's a lot cleaner and less smelly since everything is actually contained within sealed effluent lines. The maintenance room we stand in is in a confluence of such maintenance shafts, giving us more room to work within. Even if it is big, the presence of a half dozen bodyguards crowds out the room. Especially when a pair of them are sapient trolls.

"Explain again this Skill of yours," the older Movana standing before me mutters.

He's not the target, of course. It's the young Movana girl behind him, all of twenty-three. She's already two-thirds of the way through her Basic Class thanks to her banked experience and being dragged through dungeons. But that won't get her a good Class, especially since she lacks any good Titles.

Thus, this meeting.

"I can layer the Skill multiple times, depending on wording and intent," I say. I know this to be true, in a way that even knowledge and use of the Skill wouldn't have offered without significantly more experimenting, thanks to my new Class. "But it'll do damage."

"How much?"

I grunt, running the math in my head and inform him.

He winces and shakes his head. "Very high."

"Yes. But that also means it'll increase her chance of getting the Prestige Class, right? The harder it is to break, the more damage she takes, the better the Class."

"Expensive to get them the right enchantments," her overseer says, crossing his arms. "And you still haven't mentioned the name of the Skill. We need to ascertain it doesn't overlap with others."

"It won't."

"How do you know?"

I point over the girl's head while she ducks her head and pouts. There's a sullenness to her actions, to the way she stands that makes my heart ache. I understand her standing, her importance to the family is guiding the actions here. Favors for favors. She has no choice in this, in the oaths and the bindings and, yes, the pain required to break those bindings.

But as much as I want to help her, I know I can't. Because I can't fix every problem I come across, and because she has the tools to fix it herself. All she has to do is walk away. From a life of comfort and security.

This isn't my fight. And my help would probably be less than desired.

"Conditions. I can see them. Nothing special," I say. "And no conflicts. You barely have a half dozen running on her right now, and only one other Master Class."

"I broke the rest," she snaps, crossing her arms. "And I can break yours. I've done worst. It's just damage." Her voice drips with derision.

I make note to perhaps find something particularly inventive as my binding. "Now, about our payment…"

The overseer smiles, turning to me as I brightly begin the negotiations.

***

"*Trap?*"

"*Trap,*" Ali confirms.

I almost sigh and give away the game as we follow the man into the courtyard. The building is reinforced, the sky a false projection—even if it does go up at least five stories. The entire courtyard in a building thing is very Irvina, what with the need for space and yet the illusion of control. When one has money, alterations to the internal portions of a building are simple enough. And our current guest has money. The courtyard is another example of them showing it off.

It also creates a good killing ground, but we don't talk about such things.

"I'm surprised you contacted us. Our interactions with Ambassador Ward and Earth have been less than pleasant before," the speaker says, furry hands crossed behind his back. The Zarrie—gnoll-like creatures—smiles widely. "In fact, there are a number of blood promises bound around some of your people's heroes."

"Representatives," I say. "And not my people. The humans."

"Of course, of course," the Zarrie says, bobbing his head. "I'm grateful you were willing to meet us here. Few would be so trusting."

"It's hard to be, when betrayal seems to be a common coin in the realm," I say. "But I've always felt it better to give trust when you can."

"Oh, for certain. It's a very honorable viewpoint," the speaker says. He turns around now, having put us in the middle of the courtyard.

In my minimap, Ali floods the information screen with dots. Lots of dots, many of them Advanced Classers. I don't see many Master Classers, though I'm not surprised. Not only are Master Classers rarer, they're also expensive to hire and not something you expect to throw together in a few hours.

"I've always felt that. And when someone does betray you, you just have to make sure they don't do it again." I wonder if the warning will help, but I doubt it.

"There is no true betrayal though, when you are enemies already," the speaker replies, smiling wide. "Don't you think so, Redeemer?"

I keep smiling even as he uses my Title. "I have no idea what you're speaking of."

"That enchantment you're using is very good. We can't pierce it, not at all. But there is no one else we can think of who would dare contact us. Not so blatantly, not so soon. And with such an obvious companion." He nods to where Ali hangs over my shoulder.

Ali's shifted his form again, looking like a floating tree trunk, and is supposed to be invisible since he's only partially dimensionally shifted in.

I raise an eyebrow, still trying to play it cool. But I sense the Mana fluctuations above me as the ambushers buff themselves and charge up their attacks. "Again, no idea what you're talking about."

Ali flies upward and to the side, tiny hands shifting as he gets ready to layer Skills and his ability to protect me. A quick flash of information over our communication channel indicates that he's being tracked by a couple of our ambushers, putting to rest the question of the viability of his invisibility. They definitely can track him.

"Now, I came here with an offer. You wanted some Titles that weren't available otherwise, all human-centric. I know how to get them for you." I open my hands sideways, smiling. "But it'll cost you."

"Yes. A vote…" The Zarrie shakes his head. "We are not interested. What was taken, we will have back. And the blood debt will be repaid."

His final words are the signal and his friends open fire. I throw myself forward—not at him, but sideways past him, then change directions again, putting myself behind the speaker's back. The movement isn't fast enough to dodge all the shots of course, but Soul Shield provides enough protection when combined with Ali's twisting of their attacks.

Even as I move, I trigger Judgment of All. One good thing about working for the Erethrans is they've been blocking purchases of their Class Skills since forever. And while the Zarrie's main government probably has details, this is but a branch of a branch. Their budget has nothing on what the Erethrans have paid to keep Skills like Judgment for All hidden.

And while they might be able to buy my Status Sheet, if they even bothered, it wouldn't necessarily tell them what the Skill does. Not until I use it. Like now.

Light flares as Ali and I spin around in opposite circles. We use my Skill, both of us, pouring damage onto our attackers. With Penetration's ability in play, they don't stand a chance.

I watch damage pile on, the support Classers falling first. One of them has a retributive Aura Skill, reflecting a portion of their attacks onto me. Another attacker drops a cloying plasma attack that refuses to stop burning. A series of beacon darts dig into my body and draw fire from other attacks while overlapping fields of debuffs slow me down and drain Mana.

There's more, a lot more.

The very air around me burns. The poor Speaker's ability to avoid the attacks—similar to Harry's—is subverted by the sheer volume of fire. He dies as collateral damage, rather than my Skill, which he manages to avoid triggering.

My dodging works at shedding some of the damage, but my attackers shift to area effect attacks that combine with the defenses implanted in the building. Then things get a lot more difficult to avoid. I leave my sword uncalled, instead smashing apart the emplaced weaponry with spells and well-placed body slams, my Soul Shield replenished continuously by Ali.

A short and hectic minute later, as Judgment of All finishes its job, the Spirit is buzzing through open windows, looting bodies and dumping them in my Altered Space. I do the same with the Speaker's body, both of us more than cognizant that we have to be gone within minutes.

"*Up here. Teleport circle. It's locked to the users here but…*"

"*Got it.*" I bounce upward, using my hoverboots to slide through the balcony and into the room. A hand on the console and I'm accessing the System-controlled lock-outs.

System Edit flashes, and I feel another tiny tick of experience slide into the Administrator Class as I adjust the settings. I slip in a small program that'll delete my access, the logs, and itself after a set amount of time after I finish editing access levels, then we get on the platform.

The encompassing Dimension Lock disappears as I stand on the teleport circle and grin. Then we're gone, leaving behind nothing but a burnt and shattered building.

Moments later, the gravity bomb I left in the center of the building implodes, taking the building and what evidence there might be with it.

***

I push against the bottom of the pool, shooting out of the water and breaking into fresh air. My breathing is slightly ragged, more than it should be considering how little I truly need oxygen these days, but following the selkie through the water has been quite the workout. I swim until we reach the small island in the middle of the giant water playground—large enough to be a lake—they consider a swimming pool and rest against the warm sand.

The selkie shivers and twists, bones popping and cracking as it transforms before it climbs onto the sandy beach. It turns around, the smooth, slightly dimpled nature of its lower body a weird sight even as the transformation completes, hiding its fur… somewhere.

"Satisfied?" I say.

The selkie tilts its head from side to side, the whiskers of its seal body one of the features not having disappeared. They twitch in the breeze as it spies on its own people, before it turns back to me. "Yes."

"Good. So do we have a deal?" I say.

"No."

I frown, but the selkie doesn't elaborate, forcing me to ask why.

"Details," it says.

"Well, yes. I guess." I bite my lip, remembering what I've been warned about. "Details are required. But we can work that out in someplace drier, no?"

"Sample."

"You want a sample? A demonstration?" I consider. "That can be arranged."

"Good." Then the selkie walks away, leaving me slack-jawed.

"What the hell?"

"They don't like talking much to dry-landers," Ali supplies. *"By the way, make sure that sample is sufficiently sized."*

"Sufficient for what?"

"Both of you to consume."

"Both of us!?!" I frown and sense Ali's amusement. *"Why?"*

"Don't you guys have a food culture too? It's the same thing. You can't trust people you don't eat beside. It's why Rob hasn't managed to make a deal."

"But Katherine's here. As was her trade representative."

"Politics. They only work with those with sufficient influence. And that's Rob. Or, well, you."

I frown, triggering my Flight spell as I head back to dry land now that I'm certain the Selkie won't speak further.

"Don't send that disapproval. You wouldn't even count if you hadn't gotten your Heroic Class. It's why I had you alter that for him."

I shake my head, shedding water as I fly and getting a few shouted imprecations from those below my flight path. I ignore them as I land at the entrance, already conjuring a Cleansing spell.

There's more work to do and even more people to meet. Thus far, we've been tackling the easy jobs. It's just going to get harder as we go down the list.

I expect I'll trigger Extra Hands after today. I'd have done it today, but I wanted an idea of the kind of thing we were going to be dealing with, the kind of people and problems. I won't send them—myself—into this blind.

But as I'm finding out, the more people we contact, the more we meet, the higher the chance there is that we'll be located. The fight with the Zarrie was bad enough, but at least they're assholes who have a long, long list of enemies. Eventually though, we'll be found out.

Which is another reason to consider how to contact the damn Galactic Council before things go to hell in a handcart.

Chapter 12

"Are you sure this is a good idea?" Ali says.

He hovers over my outstretched hand, making me pause as I reach for the Shop orb. We're not in Irvina anymore, having made the trip in the early hours of the morning to a sleepy holiday town to use their Shop orb. The population is high enough they've got multiple such orbs in play, each linked to the main settlement orb but rarely used. Especially at this time of the night.

"No. But we don't seem to be getting anywhere, do we?" I say.

Ali gives me a half-hearted shrug, the pair of us alone in the sealed-off room that offers the orb and its users privacy.

We've been running around for the last week and a half, doing the best we can to get votes against or abstentations. At first, it was easy. Or it seemed that way at least.

But soon enough, the low-hanging fruit of votes are gone, leaving us to deal with people who want things that are harder to source, harder to convince we can fulfill when no one else can.

I've been beaten black and blue three times, and still the System has yet to register the Heroic "duel win." The kid who does it to me packs one heck of a wallop, since they've geared his entire build to single-hit knockouts, and still, the System doesn't consider it a win. We've tried multiple ways now— from direct fights to a registered dueling ring—and nothing. I keep holding back too much, such that the poor fellow can't convince the System he's winning properly.

We've run into other problems, like the Babalawo Class, which requires us to not only find living practitioners of Santeira on Earth, but also to convince them to transfer a number of their prayers, loa, and their blessings to an individual they've never met. Lana and Rob are finding that impossible.

As far as the practitioners are concerned, what we're asking them to do is the worst kind of cultural appropriation. I don't blame them, but it doesn't help our case.

The Virtual Killer title should be simple to acquire, but there's a piece missing no matter how many games of Doom, COD, and tower defense battles the Title Hunter plays. I've promised to dig into it further, and Rob's looking into the backgrounds of everyone on Earth with the Title, but no luck thus far. I might have to dig into it myself, with my Skill. But we're beginning to wonder if it's a pre-System-only Title.

There are a bunch of Titles like that, things that are only available for people who weren't in the System when they started it.

There's also the negotiation for an exclusive on coffee production from Brazil that the Fifteen Spire Guild is demanding. Specifically, a certain enhanced bean and the individuals producing it. We have to play go-between, even arranging for a strike team from Erethra to drop in to destroy a bunch of dungeons to even make the producers consider the offer. If we get the coffee for the Guild, they'll use their influence to get us a couple of votes.

And there's more. So much more. Assassination requests that we either have to undertake ourselves or contract out. Of course, there are no guarantees in those cases, just nicely worded assurances that don't read as anything more than platitudes since both sides don't want to say what they want outright, leaving themselves a certain level of deniability.

I'll admit, in a few cases where the attacks are close enough to make it worthwhile and the individuals morally bankrupt enough that it doesn't impact my twisted morality, I've agreed to it. And then promptly arranged for one of my Extra Hands to deal with it.

Amazing what a doppelganger with no care about his life is able to do. That's the problem when you're playing security—if the other person really doesn't care about surviving, their options open up vastly.

Of course, I'm also very careful about how often I send my Extra Hands on assassinations. Too many sudden deaths would be another sign we're around. So the targets are people who are obvious, who make sense. And I do my best to ensure, when I can, that the deaths aren't traceable to me.

It doesn't always work, but that's fine.

Artifact retrievals and dungeon clearings, both of which would take more time than we can afford. We make promises, guarantees of retrievals and clearing backed by the System, but there's reluctance. From Earth, to commit to travel—or Portal cost—and from those who might benefit. If Mikito and I could leave Irvina entirely, it'd be easy. But we neither have the ability to run off and return without alerting others nor the time to clear or do retrievals.

We're stymied by the time frame, by the needs of our targets. And even if we do manage to make the current vote go our way, it doesn't solve the other issue. It doesn't deal with the Council.

At some point, I need to talk to them, to ascertain what they want. After numerous attempts at cudgeling my brain for a way, I've come up with this idea. It's borne from my constant testing of the System, the gentle prod of my System Edit Skill.

"All right, but if the Mana floods…" Ali says warningly.

"You told me so." I punctuate my sentence by placing my hand on the Shop orb.

As it prompts me to see if I want to teleport to my usual Shop, I delve right into the information flow with my System Edit Skill, bypassing the main interface to access the admin section.

The Shop itself is both one of the most complicated pieces of programming in the System and incredibly simple. At its base, the Shop is just a listing of information, each piece of information drawing from a database. But considering the sheer volume of information required, there are numerous subroutines and programs set up to reduce the load whenever an individual accesses the Shop.

Among some of the most prominent are the personalization routines that are hooked directly into an individual's Status. In this way, certain options are automatically suppressed while others are brought forward. While it looks—and in some ways, acts—like a method of helping users optimize their development, it also benefits the System.

As the most basic example, there's no need for humans to buy "oxygen breathing" Skills, genetic alterations, or enchantments. It's pretty much guaranteed humanity can breathe oxygen. Same with regrowth options for limbs—unless you've recently lost one. At which point, the System would likely move those options up on the display.

There are numerous little formulas and subroutines running, each of them balancing out one another and the use of the System just so that the Shop itself can be more efficiently managed. Add the fact that some truly complex programs are linked to the Shop—teleportation, Credit-Mana cost-benefit analysis, and the time distortion windows, among others—and you get a System that should be monitored pretty closely.

And when there's a System that's monitored closely, there's development notes and bug reports.

As I swim through the data fields of Mana—because that's what the System codes in, Mana—I grasp at tiny bits of information, staring at runic configurations that alter in meaning as I stare at them before discarding the programs for more. I feel myself burning up as I struggle to cope with the flood of information, the processing of raw Mana until I locate what I need.

Then I go deeper.

Because I don't want the specific directory for this Shop location, but the generic administrative notes and bug reports for the entire Shop subroutine. Once I get there, I take the time to verify that administrative notes are logged by individual but not location and grin.

Gotcha.

As I get ready to do what I need to next, I feel my body jar, bones creaking and my neck whiplashing around. My hand, clutching the Shop orb, breaks free and I stagger to the side. Purely by instinct, my sword appears in my hand and swings. It bites into skin and flesh, and a portion of my attacker flops away.

"Aaaaargh! You goddamn Gremlin-feces-loving son-of-the-abyss!" Ali shouts, dodging backward even as he reforms his leg.

"What the hell!"

"Teaches me to save your ass!" Ali snarls, his wound sealed, the stub of his leg reforming. As a creature of thought and energy more than actual mass, damage to Ali is more conceptual than biological.

"What do you… mean."

I take into account my body and health. I feel wretched—much more than getting body-slammed by the rapidly shrinking Spirit would entail. As the pain finally makes itself known, I find myself sagging to my knees as every single nerve, muscle, and cell within my body screams.

Mana Sense is tingling, overloaded by the sheer amount of System Mana my body contains now. I'm overclocked on Mana itself and my body is doing its best to purge itself of the excess amount. For a moment, I try to trigger a spell, a simple Light spell to help bleed off the excess Mana.

I only do it for a second before curling up on the floor, choking off screams as betrayed nerves inform me that attempting to cast or utilize Skills at this moment is the worst idea I could have.

Long minutes, maybe hours, pass as my body washes the System Mana from my body. When I finally stagger back to my feet, I find Ali hovering beside me, biting his lip in anxiousness.

"Well, that was new," Ali says sardonically, the trace of concern disappearing under his usual nonchalant expression.

I can only offer him a half-smile before I push my way to the exit. As much as I want to finish what I started, we need to leave before someone finds us hogging the Shop sphere.

It's only pure luck and some planning that has allowed us to get this far.

***

Waves lap at my feet as I sit beside the water, small carnivorous fish and cephalopods attempting to rip through my reinforced skin. They fail, their Levels too low to breach my innate defenses. I ignore them, for they're too low-Leveled to bother killing either.

Not when I have bigger—metaphorical—fish to fry. In my mind's eye, deep within, I exist in a painless void that lets me tap into the only Skill I have available right now—System Edit. And using that Skill, I review my body, the data stream of my Status Screen and log files to find out what happened.

Beside me, spinning in slow circles, Ali watches the world pass by. He's in a diamond-shaped Spirit form, invisible to most eyes and keeping track of potential dangers while I work.

Long minutes pass before I finally surface, more knowledgeable than ever of my own Skills and the System. If no wiser.

"*So?*"

I look around and wonder if it's smart to discuss it here. But there's no one watching, and once again, our best defense is anonymity. Pushing aside the never-ending paranoia that living in the System engenders, I answer my friend. "*In summary—I was overloaded with Mana.*"

"No shit, Gremlin-breath. What I want to know is why now?"

"*That's more interesting. I've always been flooded with System Mana when I access the information. The first time I got burnt was when I got the Class, but we just thought it was a case of the Class change. It's not. It's a… feature, not a bug of the Class.*"

"Why?"

"*The System itself is coded in Mana. System Mana, to be specific. So when I access it, I'm actually drawing in System Mana. The more I do, the more I drain. However, as a Heroic Class, I also churn through the Mana much faster, so it's never been a major thing. But the Shop has a lot more that I can deal with, and…*"

"You got burnt."

"*Exactly.*" I fall silent for a bit, rubbing my chin. "*I wonder if people do stumble onto this Class earlier. But the moment they try to access the System in any way, they burn out. I mean, I'm tougher than your usual Heroic Class in many ways. Certainly more than any Artisan Heroic. The sheer amount of Mana being sent when accessing even a small program would likely kill a Basic Classer.*"

"*So you think that's why you don't hear of the Class, because they die too fast?*" Ali sends back.

"*That, and the Council probably covers it up. But if a Heroic Class can barely handle poking at the basic information structures—*"

"*The Shop isn't that basic.*"

I ignore the mental interruption. "*—of the System, even accessing low level information would probably kill a Basic Class. Heck, it'd probably damage an Advanced pretty fast, and a Master Class might only be able to handle it in very controlled doses.*"

"*But why would the Council set it up in such a way? It seems like a bad idea for your Junior Administrators to form from such a small pool.*"

I chew on my lip a little while I think over Ali's question before I offer the only answer that makes sense to me. "*Maybe they didn't choose to do so.*" I turn over the idea in my mind further. "*What if the current Council is just, I don't know, interlopers? Or the third or fourth iteration of the programmers? And they're stuck with whatever the idiots who first created it did. The gods know, I've had to clean up messy programming before.*"

"*You know, not everyone is as sloppy at finishing their work as you, boy-o.*"

"*Maybe they didn't have a choice. The Shop, Classes, Spells, and Skills. They're both super simple and super complicated at the same time. Anything and everything's written in Mana. So anytime you want to edit, code anything, it's a huge burden. It's all part of the System after all.*"

"*Right, but why even bother with Classes, Skills, Levels? We know the System's churning unaspected Mana into itself, through living things, but why make it so complicated? Why not just… I don't know, force you meatbags into becoming giant slug things that grow, die, and consume Mana?*"

"*Take away free will and options?*" I rub my chin. That would make sense in a sense. Though… "*We consume more Mana the more we Level. And our choices to build Levels are predicated—generally—upon who we are. But there's no reason it might not make more sense to make us just Leveling machines, or the equivalent."*

The library brings to mind images of planets warped by the System into giant, living blobs of flesh or greenery, growing without end and merging to become a living mass that just consumes Mana, and I shudder. Even the Forbidden Planets aren't as insane as that, though monsters might run rampant and behemoths walk the land.

Yet Classes, Skills, and Leveling seem like an inefficient manner of using Mana. Unless...

"Does Mana need to be used? Not just to grow but used for... things. The System, us." I wave at the lake, the greenery, and the marine life that continues to try to eat me. *"Maybe it needs sapient life to give Mana form, otherwise it..."*

I shrug. I'm not sure what it does. Grow unceasingly? Destroy life?

Knowledge, once more from the library. This time, ancillary reports from Technocrats who stay on the edge of System space, testing and learning the limits of this world.

Old recordings of worlds caught up in the Mana expansion. Worlds without the guidance of the System, or with only the barest. Mutations, change. Warped cultures, dimensional rifts. Creatures with powers that defy reasoning, ruling over worlds until they abruptly lose their powers or die to its overuse.

Skills and Classes, without form, run rampant. Monsters the size of a fingernail that destroy entire continents and titans that grow so big they are unable to move anymore.

Mana, without the constraints of the System, gives life. Gives magic, but without constraints or logic. Like a kindergarten classroom given a pile of paint and let loose. Free to make or do anything they want. With all the resulting sense and chaos.

"John?" Ali asks softly, bringing me back.

"I get it," I say softly, wondering if I should speak the words. *"I get why the System needs form. Because Mana needs structure. Without it, it's chaos. Untamed possibility. The System rebuilds Mana into a structure, forces it to form and flow in constraints. It's why Spells are so much more flexible, because they tap into Mana direct. But they're also more prone to destruction, to blowing up. And are weaker..."*

"Because we have to control all aspects of it at the same time, including the actual Mana flow." Ali nods.

That's not new spell theory. It's spellcasting 101 really—at least for spell researchers like Aiden. People like me, who buy their spells from the Store, kind of skip the theory and just use the spells like plug-and-play rituals, no different than Skills.

But just because I use magic that way doesn't mean I don't understand that it can be used much more flexibly. I just never had the time or desire to learn. And, as mentioned, for the equivalent Mana cost, your spells are weaker and slower.

I'm not even surprised when the System Quest updates. This time it's a full 1%. That puts me at 90% now. Just under the trigger point for when they went after Feh'ral.

And a part of me—a reckless, insane part that cares not for the current troubles we are in, that demands I find out—wonders what it would take to trigger that last 0.1%

***

The very next day, after running around and trying to sort out Titles and Classes and committing grand larceny in one case, we found another small

Shop to complete the plan. This time around, I knew exactly where I needed to go.

While waiting and transiting between our meetings, I spent the hours in-between creating the System Mana equivalent of pre-packaged viruses and code. It was a strange thing to build such code in twists of System Mana that's connected to me and my personal Status Sheet. Each program I formed and stored was loaded into a separate location on my sheet, hidden from normal viewing and access and yet, there in my new Skill Edit sense.

Just as interestingly, the act of creation and storage of such programs gave me experience in my Class. Not a lot, not nearly as much as actually processing and interacting with the System outside of myself did—not like the flood of experience I gained from touching the Shop for example—but it did give experience.

And in so doing, made me wonder if I was wrong. If that was the way you'd Level the Class. By creating programs and viruses in one own's Status Sheet, not exploring anything beyond that.

Except of course, the flood of System Mana was still significant. Perhaps not enough to bother me as a Heroic, but for a Basic? Certainly too much. But perhaps a Master Class.

I'm not certain, like so many other things, so I can only prepare myself. Prepare such that when I access the Shop, I breach the defenses, clear the logs, and slide in to deposit my note, it happens in one continuous surge of energy and concentration.

And then, I exit, long before the Mana accumulation is sufficient to injure me. It helps that this particular program-cum-note is simple. Left in the administrative section of the Shop's interface, where a cursory check would find it.

A simple program with an eye-catching title—"*Hey Assholes!*"—where a single program repeatedly forms a single sentence and appends it into the end of the note. A single sentence repeated over and over. Taking up more and more resources, the way a virus would. A single, direct sentence.

Let's talk.

Chapter 13

They find me as we travel through the air. Rather than deal with the delays and waits while using public transportation, I've rented an aircar. Being able to head straight for the location I want is so much more convenient, even if you have to provide your route beforehand.

In this case, we're headed out of the city again. It's late at night, which doesn't mean as much as you'd think with people with high Constitutions, an overcrowded metropolis, and nocturnal inhabitants. But it is quieter, and since I'm looking for another Shop access to check on my messages, I'm moving through less savory parts.

What that translates to in terms of the environment are shorter buildings—only twenty stories tall or so—with a lot less air traffic. And what air traffic there is, it's in vehicles like mine. Solo flying permits are just too expensive for those here.

My first clue is Ali, who is watching a reality TV show about hot men and women vying for attention on a deserted island. I'm not sure which one it is, and really, I don't care. I do care when he stops spinning in place and stills, head tilting.

"We have multiple Class Skill lock-ons." Even as Ali speaks, he's drawing upon my Skills and tossing a Soul Shield on me.

I trigger a secondary shield option on one of the rings I wear, a cheap ablative Shield meant for an Advanced Classer.

Not a moment too soon, as the aircar shatters around me. A glowing comet slams into the body of the car, the glow from the dropping orbital cutting through the thick, durasteel armoring of the aircar moments before the impact arrives. Durasteel melts and tears apart, whereupon the heat and illumination of the comet fills the inside of the car. Overheated air expands, tearing the car apart as kinetic energy imparts through the still falling attack.

I am smashed aside by the approaching shockwave, then burnt from the contact heat. Leather seats smolder and crisp, my shields fall, and even a hasty addition to my Soul Shield barely lasts as I'm thrown aside.

On instinct, I conjure my sword and throw out a Blade Strike, realizing only too late what I've done. My attack tears at the comet as it begins its return journey, turning about in space at an unnatural angle. For a moment, the glow around the comet parts and I get to see within. As flames disperse, I see the wide-eyed visage of a golden-haired, masked female with ram horns before the flames close again and the cut I've made is sealed by heat and flame.

As I tumble through the air, the second attack arrives soon after the first. This time around, it's a giant green hand that swats me out of the sky, the green energy clinging to me as I spin through the air in another trajectory. In a corner of my eyes, a notification flashes as I attempt to locate my attackers.

Lantern of Decay Resisted

"Got him. Keep being a good punching bag, will you? I'll find the others soon," Ali sends to me, highlighting my second attacker.

I tumble through the air, dealing with the now multifarious green hands that bat me away from the edges of buildings and keep me in the center of the open space I've been forced into. I get to casting, ignoring the burning, cloying green energy of decay that wraps around my shields, around me.

First comes Fates Thread, anchoring the comet to me. Then I toss Toothy Knives, a couple embedded with Cleave. The melee attack slams into the poor bastard, distracting her from me reeling her in. Which means she's striking the green flames too, burning up with the energy of decay.

Instinct has me block the next attack, the crossbow bolt deflecting off my sword. It doesn't help though, as the bolt implodes. Instead of falling, I'm drawn into the miniature gravity well. My hand, holding the sword, reaches it first and I feel bones twist and warp as skin and tendons are crushed and shrunk. My sword actually lasts longer than my flesh and bone, but not much.

Another crossbow bolt, targeted at my foot, is dodged but implodes as well. I'm suddenly drawn in two different directions as gravitic wells tear me apart. My chest and groin strain, and I fight back with the full Strength of the System.

"*And got him too!*" Ali crows.

Another light blinks on my minimap as my body goes through intense pain. Health regenerates at the same time as tendons and muscles tear.

The green hands, no longer needing to keep me busy, wrap my body in their flaming fingers while Cometgirl hovers close by, peppering me with flame-imbued Mana attacks that tear off her flame body to crash against me.

Blood pours as constrained flesh and bone rip open and holes appear in my body as the concentrated flames punch through strained flesh. My shields are gone and I'm wide open to attack, which means my health is dropping. Pain tugs at my consciousness as the decay energy finally latches on, breaching my resistances. Surprisingly, it doesn't damage me directly, but instead retards my regeneration.

Normally, I'd Blink Step away, but with multiple Dimension Locks in place, options like Blink Step are much less viable. I've not had time to switch to my Hod either, so I'm hampered in terms of other options. Never mind how distinctive the Master Class work is.

"That way!" Ali gestures to the side, and I see them. They've split into three compass points, each at nearly a 90-degree angle to the other. Which means...

"One more?"

"Probably waiting."

Unable to get away and hoping against hope that my presence is still hidden, I stop playing punching bag and get to work. A mental yank pulls on Fates Thread. It drags the comet closer, and she blazes higher in an attempt to burn me away.

I'm not done though. The paired gravitic imploders hold me still, forcing me to be passive in this fight. I turn within, to the Strength within my body and Status Sheet, and flex. This time, with my System Edit Skill, I can see how that changes, how the shift works and the aid that the System provides.

Rather than let it just happen via will and a slight sense of the past, I guide the shift in my Strength attribute via the System Edit Skill. Instead of a forty or fifty percent shift, I crank it all the way up to eighty.

I scream as my hand, closest to the actual gravity well, comes apart. I leave bone and skin behind as I physically yank my arm away. Then, using the freed stump, I punch Cometgirl in her face even as I fall, my body pulled toward the other gravity well. Skin sears closed, blood boils away even as blood vessels curl up from the flame. Bones crunch, her nose shatters, and she flies backward.

Then, shifting Fates Thread, I yank on her again, spinning the thread around my arm so that she twists like an oversized yo-yo. Into my gravity well near my feet.

She screams, twisting and trying to fly away. But there's nowhere to fly, and the actual well is so powerful that I had to leave my own hand behind to escape it. I'm still trapped, my foot caught, my body curling in toward the second gravity well, held aloft only by the flames and the other well's effects, but I figure…

"Thanks!" I shout when they do what I expect.

It takes a certain kind of person to leave your friends to die in your own attacks. And everything I've seen—the way the attacks coordinate, the way even now the decayed hands try to block my sight, try to stop my movement, the way more bolts fly toward me, intent on tearing me apart—shows that they're a good team. A long-standing one.

"Not this time!" Ali flies in the direction of the bolts. He twists his hands sideways, and I feel him pulling and twisting at the air via electromagnetic force. The air flow turns erratic and the bolts are thrown off course, some veering to strike nearby buildings.

Unwary and slow flying vehicles get caught in Ali's manipulation of reality, some of them crashing into the buildings and falling. Security systems kick in, many buildings closing down, others forming sanctuary shields to protect themselves. Bolts are buffeted, some missing only by inches as they're diverted by the flowing air. But a little is all that's needed when you're shooting from kilometers away. And this time, he isn't using gravity bolts.

It's a smart play, leaving only a single player close on hand to keep me trapped. And if Cometgirl had been able to keep her distance, been able to keep flying back and forth to attack me, it would have worked.

Now that I'm freed, I can see her properly. I stare at her Status Screen, drinking in the details, grabbing at what's important. Grateful that Ali has dropped the Titles.

Cometgirl (Level 13 Enervating Orbital) (M)

HP: 1421/3413*

MP: 843/1818*

Conditions: Lantern of Decay*, Mana Fount, Orbital Flames, Atmospheric Conditions, Anchored Trust, Birth of the Stars

As the gravity wells disappear, as we fall together, I can't help but smirk. I've fought speedsters before, and Fates Thread is perfect for dealing with speedy asses like her. It keeps her close and that's more than enough, for I've realized that they don't have a friend-and-foe option for their own attacks. That's the thing about fighting in teams, of being friends like these guys.

It can make you weak, if your enemy knows how to exploit it.

Sia La (Level 4 Lantern of Third Square) (M)

HP: 1230/1230

MP: 2753/4210

Conditions: Sworn to NML, Lord of Decay, Times to Twist, Flame Heart, Mana Manipulation, Reforms

Crossbowperson (Level 11 Weight of One) (M)

HP: 1743/2380

MP: 1347/2530

Conditions: Elemental Affinity: Gravity, Delayed Choice, Focused Point, One Point to Return, Till the Last.

We drop, the gravity well gone, and normal gravity reasserts itself. I pull Cometgirl close with Fates Thread, plunging my undamaged hand into her chest. I squeeze, crushing skin and organ—including a rather weird pulpy thing that twists and throbs like a heart. It might even be her heart, but alien. It might be her stomach for all I know.

"Master Class team?" I'm surprised, I admit. I've fought Master Classers before, been ambushed by them, once a long time ago. And knowing that, I don't understand why they sent such low-powered Master Classes if they truly know who I am.

"Unless the Heroic's hidden." Ali sounds busy, his hands weaving together as he dodges the grasping flames, his presence now spotted. He's channeling a light-based spell, using focused energy attacks to hammer at the spot where the Lantern is hanging out.

Holding onto Cometgirl, her flames eating at my skin even as I twist Soul Shield to protect me, I pull her around to take more of the attacks from the grasping green flames. She twitches and screams as she burns, the decay decreasing her regeneration, her total health and Mana. I feel it too, tearing at me, but my own Skills, my own Classes protect me at a greater level than Cometgirl's. I wait, picking my time.

"You picked these other guys out easily enough," I send back, snarling. I'm still holding back, worried about the last member of their team. *"Can't you find him?"*

"If it's a Heroic, no. I've got the Levels to deal with Master Classers now but not Heroics." Ali is technically a Master Class, as far as the System is concerned. *"If there's a fourth, they're hiding too well."*

My health hits half, Mana still high. I throw a Healing Spell, casting it so that it stays channeled even as I wrap the stump of my hand in the Frozen Blade spell and punch Cometgirl.

I'm pushing the team, pushing to see how far they're willing to let me beat on their friends. Our fall has halted, Cometgirl's powers keeping us aloft. For the most part. Each time I punch her, each time I coat her with my spell and slow her down further, we fall.

Meters from the ground, our speed arrested, I sense the threat before Ali speaks. The pair of long-range attackers have focused their attacks, forcing him to pay extra attention to help alleviate some of the incoming damage. Some, since Bolt Boy has shifted tactics and is using more energized light bolts that are less affected by Ali's trick with air.

"Let my bondmate go!" She slams into me with a spike shoulder, tearing my arm out of Cometgirl's chest. Along the way, I take the organ too.

I skip across the ground and off the nearby building shields, bouncing around with so much energy that I feel as if I'm playing Pong with my body. I dig in my feet, tearing up the ground, shifting my Strength to stabilize the ground and bleed off energy. As she clutches her coughing, heavily injured bondmate, I snarl at the tiny, two-foot-tall furry rabbitlike creature.

Cunwoz (Obliterating Vector Level 34) (M)

HP: 4478/4480

MP: 3210/3210

Condition: Hasted, Blurred Lines, Two Step, Between the Raindrops, Physics— what physics?

"Enough!" I snarl as I recall Ali closer. I throw up another Soul Shield, feeling my body fight the energy of decay pushing at me. "If you keep pushing, I'm going to stop playing nice."

Cunwoz's eyes narrow, then she tilts her head up. Long ears, which I realize have multiple eyes on them, twist about, staring around. Taking in the damage we've done—the flames that eat into residential shields, the blood that has rained upon the ground, the twisted wreckage of flying vehicles that smoke. The air is filled with the stink of death and decay, the flames somehow throwing off that smell even further, causing those too poor or too unlucky to choke on the poison.

And then Cunwoz stares at Ali and me. She takes in my health, the flames that still lick at my body and my missing hand where red blood drips to the ground. I watch it do the math, debating if it can win. A part of me worries that I might not. But only a small part.

I give it a grin, and the little rabbit tilts its head. "Enough."

Silence greets the rabbit as it picks up its friend. Tiny hands expand, gripping the woman, and it takes a careful step back. I watch as blood—slower now—pumps out of Cometgirl's body, spilling to the ground. But the green flames around her wounded body have died, peeling off to surround me. The rabbit takes another step back, still watching.

And I speak. "Wait." Tension ratchets up, the flames stilling before bursting into further, angry motion. I can almost sense the targeting carats of the archer, but I keep talking. "We're going to talk first. Before you leave. All of us."

"And if we refuse?"

"Then she dies." I nod toward the one in her arms. The tiny rabbit vibrates, but I keep talking. "Then you do. And I've got a lock on the other two. Maybe they can run, but they certainly can't hide."

"You think you can finish us."

"I think you think I can." I nod at the twitching Cometgirl. "And I'm certain you know she won't live."

Silence.

Cunwoz's ears twitch, shifting. The body in its arms glows as healing spells layer over the heavily injured body, trying to fix the damage done by the flames. A pair of flaming hands detach from the swarm, landing on Cometgirl, changing color to yellow and flowing up and down the body.

"They're chatting. Lousy op-sec. I could break in if you want."

I'm curious, but I decline Ali's offer. I split part of my attention, shifting my own Constitution around, adjusting the way I handle damage. The damage from the decay attack stops accumulating and starts dispersing as the System aids me. Of course, I help it along with a tiny Edit, but mostly, I watch.

Eventually, Cunwoz looks up, long lashes on overly large eyes meeting mine. "We talk. But not here."

I can't help but grin, waving her to lead the way. She moves and I follow, running to catch up. Luckily, the rabbit's burdened by her friend, so she's a little slower than normal.

Now, time to find out who the hell set them on me.

***

I watch with interest as we run for our lives. The team is smart, and once Cometgirl recovers, she drops behind us a series of tech and magical tools to make things difficult for our trackers. They range from the mundane, like gaseous cannisters of mixed smells, to high-tech nanite cleaners and magical Mana burst devices to destroy our Mana signatures. On top of that, a trio of localized chaos mines are added to the mix, leaking the raw energies of the chaos dimension into normal reality. It's the most thorough cleansing I've ever seen, and I've participated in more than my fair share.

"What about the security cameras?" I say as we run.

We've ducked underground by this point, running through the maintenance tunnels that link the vast majority of the city, allowing easy access for droids and automated robots to ensure the city ticks over as normal.

"Diverted and turned off," Cunwoz says, bouncing beside me. She's eyeing me warily, but considering I've never let her or Cometgirl out of my sight, she's playing it nice for now. The way she looks at me makes me think she's getting the idea that my threat to end them all was no idle pronouncement.

And it wasn't. The Skills I've gained as a Heroic have given me the ability to end them. Heck, if I got them right, Judgment of All would end things by itself, especially if I went all out with my other Skills.

That's the difference between a Heroic and a low-level Master Class. Those final Skills as a Master Class adds another level of insanity. But violence isn't going to win the war, even if I might win the battle here.

"Good. How long now?" I ask.

Ali, floating beside me and invisible once more, has been tracking the other two Master Classers, straining to stay focused on them and no one else.

In the meantime, I keep an eye out for trouble with my Greater Detection, low level as it is. Then again, I'm not expecting the local security forces to arrive under cover but large and loud, cocksure in their certainty of righteousness.

"Soon."

She's true enough to her word. We pass through a series of glowing, enchanted walls that strip us of any contaminants and also help block any scrying. When we get to the secure room, it's hidden behind a non-descript maintenance office. Within, the break room has a small table suitable for eating or doing notes, a wall full of decontamination suits, and a map of the surrounding tunnels.

The place has a mild antiseptic smell that combines with the taint of rusted metal and stuffy clothing and makes me wrinkle my nose. More interestingly, a light hum in the air makes the hair on my skin stand up. My overworked Mana Sense tells me it's a badly tuned active enchantment, one that covers up the other, subtler enchantments beneath its ostensible air purification. A mental pull at my Status Conditions shows a wide series of anti-scrying, anti-viewing spells in play.

Along with the furniture, I catch sight of my other attackers. Sia La and the Crossbowperson aren't exactly what I expected. Sia La is a four-foot-tall, six-legged salamander-like creature that uses its flames to move around. And the Crossbowperson is a weird snail-monster hybrid whose back actually houses the crossbow. I realize that part of the musty, stuffed clothing smell is originating from the Crossbowperson itself.

"Well, we're here," I say, taking control of the meeting.

"Cunwoz, he's yours." I tilt my head as Cometgirl walks right over to the fridge as she speaks, yanks it open, and scoops out armfuls of food. Even as she walks, the individual containers turn on and heat up their foodstuff.

Cunwoz glares at me, then hops up on the table so that she's closer to my eye-level. "What do you want? Assurance we've given up the job?"

"The name of your employer."

"No," Cunwoz, Crossbow, and Sia La say at the same time.

"You know, I can find out pretty easily," I say.

"Our cutouts, certainly." Cunwoz's ears twitch. "But not our real employer."

"True. But you do know who that is," I say softly.

"I didn't say that!" Cunwoz says while Crossbow curses in realization.

I smirk. "You guys aren't used to intrigue, are you?"

"We aren't used to talking to our targets!" Cometgirl snaps at me as she continues to stuff her face. She's got half of the containers open, dipping the Galactic equivalent of a spork into the dishes and spooning-cum-spearing the food out. "They're normally dead."

"Well, obviously that didn't happen."

"Because our information on you was wrong," Sia La says, his flames burning brighter with agitation. "You're no Master Class. No matter what your Status says."

I grin, opening my hands. "Sure, but I want to know who it was who set the kill order on me. I mean, you can understand my curiosity, right?"

"Understand, but it's not our problem," Cunwoz says. "If that's it…"

"*Don't push it, boy-o. Merc honor and all that,*" Ali sends.

I hesitate, wanting to push the matter. Learning who sent them after me is important. I need to know if my cover is blown. Then again, the fact that they were going after a Master Class is clue enough, perhaps.

I wonder if our fight was too much. Maybe… but I did hold off on using any Heroic Class Skills.

I shake my head, dismissing those thoughts as the group grows impatient and Cometgirl finishes another container. "One other thing. You've seen some of what I can do. So I'm going to want to make sure you don't discuss that."

My words raise the tension in the room, with Sia La's flames concentrating and brightening while the Crossbowperson shifts so that the bolt it carries in its frame is pointed directly at me. Even Cometgirl stops eating for a second before going back to shoveling food.

"*What is it with her?*"

"*Regeneration Skill. She's rebuilding overhealth reserves. It's the reason she didn't die when you tore out her heart and she kept losing health and blood.*"

"And how do you intend to do that?" Cunwoz says.

"A Skill. It'll force you to not disclose anything about our fight or allow you to attack me or my allies again."

"Your allies?"

"You know who I'm speaking about."

"Earth," Cometgirl interrupts, food falling out of her mouth. Still now, the flames from her Class Skill are gone. "If we disagree?"

I meet her gaze flatly. She returns my stare for a bit before she turns away and goes back to eating. I turn to each of the others slowly, facing them down. Sia La growls, his flames flashing and intensifying but eventually, dimming. The Crossbowperson I fail at staring down, what with it lacking eyes that are easy to spot, but I get a squishy, squirmy bob. And last but not least is Cunwoz.

"Get it over with."

So I do. Of course, after my first cast of the Shackles of Eternity on Cunwoz, she can't help but speak up.

"You're really him, aren't you? The one they warned us about."

"They had a warning?" I say, raising an eyebrow.

"A half dozen individuals, moving around to help Earth. One of them could be the Redeemer of the Dead, the Grand Paladin himself. A Heroic Class opponent."

Cunwoz hesitates, and in the gap, Sia La interjects with his high-pitched voice. "You're on a non-contact, inform-once-sighted list. Someone wants you found. And they're paying a lot."

"That's nice," I say, watching my Mana climb. I left enough to trigger Judgment of All if necessary. In this crowded area, I have the advantage over this ranged attack team. I'd prefer not to kill them, but you never know. "You wouldn't be trying to contact them, would you?"

Cunwoz makes a little trilling sound that is so high-pitched, my ears hurt. "No. But you've got some major enemies. There's not just a flat bounty on you Earthers. There's a Galactic bounty on you specifically. Hush-hush, but it's there."

"*Why not public?*" I send to Ali, curious about that discrepancy.

"*No idea. Maybe they don't trust your average citizen not to try for something more?*"

"You wouldn't happen to know who's after me, would you?" At their silence, I sigh.

"But we got the contact information for the bounty. We could give it to you," Sia La speaks up, buzzing closer to me. "For a price."

"How about I not kill you? That work as a price?"

"You won't be able to kill me before I get word out. And I'm pretty sure you don't want that to happen. Because all you've been doing is to stay hidden, isn't it?" Sia La says.

I consider taking him up on the offer. Ending him. He doesn't know all that I can do, including Grand Cross. But... "What do you want?"

"Credits. You cost us a job. Figure you should pay for it."

My lips twist into a snarl. "Fine. Escrow account. We'll get you paid."

"Get?"

"Don't push it." I let a little of the rage that I keep contained, that is part of me, leak. I don't bother with an Aura. I just do it with body language and my eyes. The simple, clear knowledge that if he pushes me, I'll end him, his friends, and then watch the rest of the city burn down.

"Fine... escrow," Sia La says.

I offer him a tight smile. "Good. So, to summarize. You won't tell me who hired you, you want me to pay you for the contact information on the bounty on my head and the failed hit, and we just need to finish chaining you all. That about right?"

The susurration of resigned acceptance makes me half-smile. It's not the best option there is, but what is, is.

Chapter 14

Meeting up with the team and informing them of my recent altercation happened hours later. I verified I was safe before I made my way over, but it was clear, anonymity was no longer a guarantee. Relating the fight took only a few minutes, but the conversation itself required more time.

"I don't get it," Mikito says, shaking her head. "You could have finished them off. Why meet? And bind them all?"

"Information," I say.

"But they didn't tell you anything."

"Actually, they did," Harry corrects Mikito, rubbing his chin. "And I have to say, John, you've gotten quite sly."

I sketch a bow. "Thank you."

"What am I missing?" Mikito says.

"Subtlety, obviously," Ali teases. When Mikito hefts Hitoshi in warning, Ali ducks away with a laugh. "We know whoever hired them suspects John is here but isn't certain. If they knew, they'd never have used a bunch of Master Classers as a first strike. So it's not the Council."

"Exactly," I say. "They probably think we're hired guns, people that maybe I contacted."

"And not ourselves." Mikito shakes her head, short hair twisting in the motion. She runs a hand through her hair, eyeing the red in it, the thicker, almost dread-like nature the spells and enchantments made of it. "But why would the Council not be watching for us? Why are they not the ones acting?"

"Ah, that'd be Feh'ral and the Corrupted Librarians' fault." I open my hand sideways. "One of the reasons I met with him was to get his help, and theirs. They're used to hiding—and making a mess when they need to.

Having them slide lies about our location into the System is actually easy enough, with the right Skills."

"And that's enough to deal with the Lady?" Harry says. "Or are you counting on her lack of attention?"

"A little of both," I say. "Feh'ral might also be making himself a little bit of a target."

"Why?"

"Because it doesn't cost him much," I say. "And because I might have a chance of learning something he could use for the Quest."

Both of my friends roll their eyes. The fact that it's the truth, that the possibility of solving the Quest is what drives us Questors, well, that's just what we are. Fanatics perhaps, but reliable fanatics.

It's also how we got the rest of the Corrupted Questors on our side, risking their lives. A promise of knowledge, of an answer is enough to drive them to action. At least, in a limited fashion.

We're still waiting for the final verdict, for the testing to be done on the knowledge I've passed on to them. Until that happens, they're willing to extend some help, but not all that they can offer.

"Fine. So they have guesses on why we've not come to Earth's help directly. Which is why you delayed us going in, because running straight in would leave us trapped." Mikito ticks off on her fingers as she speaks. "You've got the Questors creating distractions as us. You've got Feh'ral being a distraction. And you snuck us in with the Lord's help.

"But that still leaves us being attacked by people who don't want Earth to keep its seat. And they're still looking for us—or what they think are us. The more fights we get into, the more likelihood our cover will be blown."

I nod. "Aye. Good news is that we've only got to survive a few more days."

There are quite a few relieved nods at that, and I grin slightly.

I pause, my head snapping to the side. Something happens in the far distance, in the fifth ring, outside of the scope of my immediate awareness. I feel a connection snap, a portion of me disappear, and I blink. "Oh."

Mikito tenses, seeing my face, then her eyes glaze over a little as she scans for trouble around us. But there's no immediate danger, as Ali informs them.

"We just lost one of John's doppelgangers."

I'm silent as data streams in. I pull at the memories, System-formed and provided to me in a block. It's kind of like the library, the way the data is parsed. Strange, since it's not really my memories.

"What happened?" Harry says, his voice filled with concern.

"Not sure yet. I'm still trying to understand what happened. I just know he's dead now." I cock my head, giving Ali a look.

The Spirit rolls his eyes, but his fingers twitch as he looks into public broadcasts.

"And your other one?" Harry says.

"Doing his job," I say. When Harry raises an eyebrow, I shrug. "He's disposable, and we need to keep moving. He's on-planet right now anyway."

"That's… not very nice," Mikito points out.

"Mana construct."

"You know, that sounds a lot like slavery," Harry says. "And sacrificing what we don't like."

"Except he's not real. No soul. Just a program. A very, very complex program, but a program." I shake my head. "Trust me, I know."

"How?" Mikito asks.

"My Skill," I say.

It had been rather fascinating, using the Skill while triggering Extra Hands. I'd been able to view the process the System used to create my Mana doppelganger, watched how his body was formed. Even his physical body was, for all intents and purposes, non-existent, a replica constructed of Mana itself. That Mana could duplicate the entire process of life so easily was fascinating, especially since it almost seemed as if it hungered to do so. The body was biologically sound, as far as I knew—though how far that went, I wasn't certain.

The memories I get, they're edited. Portions. Not real. More like bullet points or flashes of insight.

"We're getting off track here. We can discuss John's lack of ethics with regard to his doppelgangers later," Harry says. "I'm more curious about what we're going to do about the information we've acquired."

"That's why we're here to discuss it, no?" I open my hands. "It seems they've got multiple attack units out. Some high-Level Advanced Class teams, some Master Class teams too I'd bet. And whatever it was that took out my doppelganger."

"Not whatever. Who," Ali speaks up.

We turn to the Spirit, who is looking troubled. He shifts his hands and security footage blooms. The video comes from multiple angles, providing full details.

It's a good thing too, since the fight itself is over in seconds. My doppelganger is moving down the street, Soul Shield active, Greater Detection in play. It doesn't matter though, because his assailant doesn't try to hide. Instead, he walks right out into the middle of the street, throwing his cloak back and striking a wide-legged pose. Gold edging on his armor glints and sparkles in the streetlamps, showing off his pink skin and small tusks.

Memory stirs, a flash of emotion from the doppelganger's memory. Arrogance. Towering arrogance.

"Halt! In the name of the Galactic Council, you are ordered to stop your activities and come back with me," Kasva, the Champion of the Council, says.

Irvina residents are scrambling, leaving as fast as they can as a sixth sense tells them to get the hell out. I don't blame them. I wouldn't want to be around when a pair of Heroics fight either.

"Yeah, no. Why don't you just fuck off?" my doppelganger snaps.

"Well, I tried." Kasva shrugs.

And then he moves. One second, Kasva's hundreds of meters away from my Hand. The next, he's right next to him and swinging. Kasva calls forth a double-bladed sword, one with blades jutting out from both sides and each blade as thick as a good-sized tree. It's what I'd call an anime weapon—too large and weighty to be practical for anyone who didn't have the boosted stats of a Combat Classer in the Advanced stages.

My doppelganger brings out his own weapon, a simple sword that's unenchanted but of good make. Standard wear for your average Erethran soldier when they don't have a Soulbound weapon. It doesn't even last a second as Kasva's blade cuts right through the weapon, the Soul Shield, then halfway down my Hand's body. A savage yank rips out the blade, detaching my Hand's arm in the process.

A part of me wonders about all the lost limbs I keep getting. Involuntarily, I look at my regrown hand and flex it, a phantom pain briefly making an appearance before the System and my higher stats push them aside.

Of course, my Hand is like me. Pain isn't something that stops us—not after all this time, not with the sheer number of defenses the System has built into our minds against it. The remaining hand pushes forward, a Chaos mine aiming to attach itself to Kasva's body.

It fails, because Kasva isn't there. He's moving fast, faster than almost any other fighter I've dealt with that isn't a pure Speedster. He's also smart, having already started shifting the moment his attack was finished.

Another cut, another dodge that misses. The mine goes off, raw Chaos energy spilling into the environment and tearing at the pair of bodies. It forms into ropes of intestines that sizzle upon contact with ground and flesh. It doesn't kill, it damages, but it doesn't end there. Another sword is conjured by my doppelganger, cutting at Kasva, but again, it's dodged.

And another cut, this one bisecting my Hand's head. It flops to the ground, rolling away. The body stays for a second before it disperses, bloody bits breaking up as Mana is taken back by the System.

"Disappointing. But at least we learned something new." Then Kasva looks up, right at where one of the security cameras is recording. He's smiling but there's a blankness to his eyes, a cold finality that reminds me of large predators, the kind that lie waiting rather than stalking you. "You're going to have to do better if you want to beat me. You'll need to stop holding back, Redeemer."

Then the recording cuts off, leaving us in silence.

"Welp, I don't need to change my pants. Not at all," Harry says into the silence. "Now, if you'll just excuse me for a second…"

***

Harry returns to us discussing what we saw of Kasva and his abilities. Perhaps most prominent of all was one simple fact.

"He wasn't using any major Skills." Mikito frowns. "You sure that's all you have on his Skill use?" That question is to Ali, who nods. "Then I'm leaning toward a passive build."

"Like Bolo?" I say.

"Yes. With maybe a couple of Heroic Class Skills held as trumps."

"Can we find out what they might be?" I ask.

"Already tried, boy-o. Not possible. The Council clamped down on that real hard."

I'm not particularly surprised. What we've seen of his Skills speak to a lot of passives. Not just in terms of damage dealt or speed, but also in high attributes. Higher than normal for certain—or else he's learned to adjust the flow and guidance of his attributes to just speed. Which might be possible, but I consider it unlikely. After all, we still have to leave some level of control to the System to stabilize the physical world around us. Or else we'd burst into flame, shatter the ground, or heck, slip and fall on our faces.

"There's something strange about the way he moves," Mikito says softly, shifting the fight again. She replays the part where I—my Hand—tried to clamp the Chaos Mine onto Kasva's body and lets it repeat.

"He's smart enough to know to not be there when I'm going to attack." I shrug. "Means he's trained."

"No." Mikito shakes his head. "Look at his momentum, the way he shifts. If he really thought you'd attack that line, he wouldn't have put all his weight down. He actually has to force himself into a new line to dodge..." Mikito looks at me, a half-smile forming. "You've actually gotten pretty good at that."

"That?"

"Anticipating movements and momentum," Mikito says. "See how he shifts there? It's like he suddenly realizes what you're going to do and shifts to adjust. Rather than planning for the shift beforehand."

"You can plan for that?" I say.

"I can," Mikito replies confidently. "I do." She lets the rest of the short fight play out. "He doesn't. I think he's got a future forecasting Skill."

I frown. "You sure? That doesn't look like his kind of build..."

"Bought. Or maybe it's part of the Council Champion. Might make thematic sense," Ali points out.

"I thought those Skills aren't very useful?" Harry cuts into the conversation. "At least, that's what most fighters tell me."

"They aren't," I say. "Normally."

"It's the problem of attributes. You need both a high Perception ability to 'see' properly and a high Intelligence attribute to understand what you're seeing without going insane," Ali says. "In normal circumstances, people like the Oracles and the like either get cryptic prophecies that are provided to them as a whole, or they see the prophecies as visions and end up trying to explain them as either bad poetry or too straightforward words. Since they can't 'see' fully, often those kinds of prophecies are hard to understand. Or trust. On top of that, of course, it's all a matter of guesstimation off current known events. It's not 'true' future seeing."

"I know that," Harry says. "But if you're seeing only a few seconds ahead, isn't that easier?"

"Is it easier to see the cells on a leaf or the tree itself?" Mikito says. "Stare too close, and potential actions explode in number."

"Too far into the future though and you can't even see the tree anymore," I add.

"So seeing into the future isn't possible because there are too many options to judge normally? And requires too many attributes?" Harry says to confirm.

"Exactly. But he's moving like a bullet and dodging ahead of time. And that Strength…" I shake my head, pointing at the attacks. "It's not a momentum-based Skill that adds to damage either. It's raw Strength."

"So how is he doing this?" Harry says.

I share a look with Mikito and Ali before the three of us give Harry a shrug. Without more to go on, we can only guess. And we'd already offered that—a series of Passive Skill builds. Whatever the answer is, it's certain that he's a very dangerous opponent.

"Do we continue then?" Mikito says, making another window appear.

I look at the numbers Mikito shows, frowning. Even our best estimates show that we've convinced only two-thirds of the people we need to get a null vote.

"Do we have a choice?" Harry says unhappily.

"Can we even make it?" I say softly, tapping the screen and tossing out another screen. This one has a list of those we still have to contact. "We've got what, sixty-four still on the list? And of those, the majority were in our 'well, maybe it'd work' list or we suspect they're stringing us along?"

There are nods from the group, and I flick my hand, pulling up another list. The pair peer at it, having never seen this list before. It doesn't take them long to realize what it is.

"This is a kill list." Harry sounds disapproving.

"Yes," I say. "Everyone whose asked us to end someone else for their votes which I haven't accepted or who we think might be worthwhile ending anyway."

"And you want to agree to it?" Harry shakes his head. "You're good, John, but some of these guys have Master Class bodyguards. And without the ability to teleport from location to location…"

"Or verify security procedures, backup plans, doppelgangers, Skills, or set-up times," Mikito says. "Never mind automatic reprisal plans. This is a bad idea."

"I know." I shake my head. "There's no way for us to finish all of this. Not even with my Extra Hands."

"Then?"

I nod to Harry, smiling widely. "We just need to screw up the votes, right? And there's never any guarantee that they'd vote for us. So let's overturn the apple cart."

"You want me to publicize this list?"

"And the recordings of the requests we have," I say, confirming his guess.

"I…" Harry shakes his head. "This isn't a good idea. Many of these might be our friends, or at least are moderately inclined to help us."

"Inclined but not going to. We're already fucked, so we might as well finish this," I say, lowering my voice as I try to wheedle him into doing what I want.

"I…" Harry straightens himself and shakes his head. "No. I won't do this. Not without speaking with Katherine."

"That's—"

"Not a good idea?" Harry crosses his arms. "Because she's going to say no?" He harumphs. "Exactly. And you're not going to do it either, not without getting Earth's agreement."

I raise an eyebrow at his tone, the way he's so certain I'll agree. He glares at me and I return his gaze, the pair of us facing one another down. Seeing who will break first.

Into the silent contest of wills, Mikito arrives with a smack on the back of my head.

"Owww!" I say, looking at her. I touch my head where the bloody wound is already healing. "That hurt."

"Of course it did, you baka tank!" Mikito says. "You think I could get your attention with a love tap?" She wrinkles her nose. "I'm not Roxley."

"Or Lana," Ali says.

"Lana would step between him and Harry and lean forward," Mikito says.

"True. She had great... ass-ets," Ali finishes with a waggle of his eyebrows.

I roll my eyes. "We were in the middle of something here."

"A measuring contest. Yes, we know." She points at Ali. "He's the biggest, because he isn't human. Get over it." She glares at me. "You're asking Earth's permission before you burn all their bridges." When I open my mouth to protest, Mikito steps closer and drops her voice. "It's not your life you're gambling with here. And you don't have to do it all by yourself."

I shake my head. As if I didn't know it isn't just my life. Does she think I take these kinds of risks, accept this kind of insanity when it comes to just my life? This is a new level of chaos. If we had any other choice...

But I can't think of one.

"Fine," I say, throwing up my hands. "We'll ask them. We'll see what other ideas, what else Katherine has chosen to do."

"And if she says no?" Harry says.

"Then..." I'm uncertain of what else to say.

In the end, I shrug. We have only a few days left, and I'm out of ideas. Perhaps I'll think of something at the last minute, but what it is, I have no idea. We need to make sure that vote doesn't pass.

***

Meeting up with Katherine is no easy matter. We have to be careful about how we contact her. And even more careful of when and where we set up the meet. In the end, it's two days later, two long days where we lay low and send out my Extra Hands to do what they can and we—quietly—remeet with some of our failed targets.

The only good news we receive is that the vote has been delayed again. There's a big flare-up of trouble as a dungeon outbreak occurs between the border of the Truinnar and Movana empires. It's quickly revealed that the Movana set off the outbreak, which then devolves into a giant squabble between the parties.

Emergency resolutions after emergency resolutions are thrown around, with no end in sight. The entire thing might resolve tomorrow or a month later, according to Harry.

Now that we're finally able to meet up with Katherine, that's, of course, when I get the message. It's a simple text message, but it's one I can't turn down.

14:45pm at the System Helix Shrine.
— Duchess Kangana

"Thousand hells," I swear. "I got to do this."

"Perfect timing..." Mikito mutters, making a face. She stares at the notification for a long time before she nods to me. "Go."

"You guys..."

"Will be fine. Just go."

I nod and accept her word. I switch directions, heading for a bullet train that'll get me to the second ring and in the direction of the Shrine rather than into the fifth ring like the team. Hopefully their meeting goes well, but I'll have to get briefed later. I've been waiting to speak with the Duchess forever.

The ride to the second ring is quiet, if a little tense. The security procedures in the third ring are much tighter than anywhere else, but the Shrine is one of the few places anyone can travel to—if they can afford the cost. There are even special conveyances that go directly to the Shrine and nowhere else.

Of course, calling the multi-hectare, fifty-story tall structure a Shrine is kind of like calling the Hagia Sophia a little roadside chapel. The entire Shrine is made of crystallized Mana, solidified Mana in which data, knowledge, is embedded. Each person who pays a visit to the Shrine of the System leaves a small Mana crystal at each visit, a gift of their best knowledge, their best craft. Something that may be gifted outward to another, as the priests and bishops of the System deem fit.

Over the centuries, the Shrine has grown from a small, single-room building into this towering edifice. Often, the Shrine is the last chance for an individual to make a difference as they beg for a new Class, a new Skill, knowledge on how to gain a Title that will change their life.

And all too often, they fail. But we don't talk about that part.

Thousands of supplicants walk into the building, streaming through the numerous doors to journey within. I step to the side, watching as sapients walk, hop, glide, and lope forward. Some walk with confidence. Others shrink and slide within, scared of their own shadows. But the glowing blue building swallows them all without hesitation, accepting their worship without judgment.

"First time?" The voice catches me by surprise. Not by the speaker's presence but that they chose to speak to me at all.

"Yes." I turn to the speaker, blinking a little at the masked, android-like face. I stare, realizing a bit late that he breathes like a living organism. Whoever, whatever it was, it's now more machine than organic.

"I see you're one of the blessed." It inclines its head toward Ali in his glowing, crystal form.

"You can see him?" I raise an eyebrow. An unusual ability, but not uncommon.

"The System has gifted me such sight." A spark, a flood of Mana that does nothing as the creature speaks. "But I'm rude. I am Ote, the Six Hundred Eighteenth version of its line."

I want to ask but suppress my curiosity. I have other things to do. "Nice to meet you, Ote."

If Ote seems perturbed by my lack of introduction, it doesn't show it. "It is a small thing, to ask the System for its guidance. Just walk the halls. When you feel it is right, offer your gift. And if you think it appropriate, you may ask it for guidance. If the System wills it, it will answer."

"How long a walk?" I'm wondering how I'm going to find the Duchess in the building, because she sure as hell hasn't told me.

Ali's busy looking for her, but with the sheer amount of Mana the Shrine represents, both of our abilities to scan the surroundings have fallen to meters.

"That is a matter of contention." Ote opens his arms. "Some walk the halls for decades, making their plea. Others say that the System is all-knowing, all-giving when it wants. And as such, a single brief sojourn is all that is needed."

"And the bigger the Gift, the better chance you'll get an answer?" I say wryly, even as I tell Ali to keep looking.

"Not at all. The System does not care for what you gift. It is, after all, already known to it. It is the act itself, rather than the contents, that matter." Ote drops his buzzy voice and leans in. "Or so the priests say. Me, I try to give the best I can."

I snort but watch as Ote wanders off. Practical and religious. "Interesting guy."

"*More than you know.*" Ali updates my minimap with a map of the entire building. Along with it, there's a pathway that's marked out and an x with a timer on it. "*A little gift.*"

"*Sneaky.*" I eye the time and distance, then the crowd. I sigh and walk. Not much time if I want to make it there as scheduled.

We walk through the crystal hallways in silence, the air within chilly, lower than human comfortable. Occasionally it's warmed by a passing sapient creature, one burning with the flames of its own body like the salamander-man or a living lava ball. Each passing sapient Systemer adds to the mixed aroma of the building, creating a unique stench that has me breathing through my mouth while I attempt to forget about the stink. It's the least pleasant parts of a skunk's tail, an uncared for barnyard, and a compost pile mixed together and amplified.

Most penitents move in silence, which makes the few who chant, sing, or orate all the more stark in appearance. Passages of Systemer-creed are spoken, sung, or otherwise announced, while others beg for salvation and help from the crystal walls. Occasionally, stifled sobs break the silence, only to be ignored by the uncaring public.

As I turn the umpteenth passageway, Ali breaks our internal silence. *"I'm a little surprised how few of you humans have taken up the Systemer creed."*

"Why?" I send back.

"Just seems like you humans liked your religion."

"We're rather a stubborn bunch." I briefly wonder what it's like for those who still hold onto the old religions. But it's not something I've ever bothered to look into.

Having edged his way into the conversation, Ali drops his next statement. *"Surprised you didn't take it up either."*

"Was never religious."

"Why?"

My answering silence is met by a rather impatient hmmm across the mental network. When Ali continues to send the same hmmm, I give in. If nothing else, it'll cover the rather boring walk.

"I don't trust people. Not really. And all those religions, they're touched by humanity. Religious text copied over and over again by self-serving, short-sighted, careless, and dumb humans. I've seen code a year old messed up beyond all recognition. How am I supposed to trust books hundreds of years old?"

"So you don't believe in god? A higher power?" Ali asks.

"Didn't say that. Just that I'm not sure that anyone has ever gotten it right. It doesn't matter anyway."

"Why not?"

"If there's a god worthy of following, then he's worth following if I believe in him or not. And to paraphrase a wise man, if he isn't, then to hell with him."

The look Ali gives me makes it hard to keep my face straight. While I'm not lying, I've never really thought much about gods before the System. And afterward, for a long time, I was too busy trying to stay alive to worry about what came after. Even now, with all the evidence of the System being something artificial, I haven't been convinced either way. The problem with religion is it requires a leap of faith. To ignore the logic of science and good sense, the contradictions that arise, and just believe. I've never been able to do that.

As for the Systemers themselves, in many ways, they're the complete opposite of Questors like me. They take the System to be a god, to be something all-powerful. And I admit, by factual evidence and effect on everyday life, the System has meddled much more than any remote god. But Questors like me believe there's a reason, a truth to what the System really is. And Systemers just believe.

At least for the main religion. There are obviously offshoots, heresies, and individuals who combine the insanity and the obstinance of both parties, focused on both worshiping and understanding the System itself. Many of those have become Corrupt Questors, known for their unbending pursuit of the truth without care or morality.

I have way too many memories of those people in my library.

We walk together, traveling the hallways of Mana, passing supplicants as we follow the map. Subconsciously, I adjust the speed of our passage as we move to ensure that I arrive on time.

The longer I walk, the more I realize that this is an ingenious method of meeting. We're all walking through the shrine, and only through chance or planning would one meet another within.

We get to the passageway just a little early, and somehow, I'm not surprised to see a familiar figure. Hondo Ehrish, Weaponmaster for Clan Kangana, makes his appearance, walking ahead of who I expect is the Duchess. He looks well, like himself. Big, strong, slightly scarred. Grumpy.

So many years have passed since our first meeting. And he is no longer an Advanced Class, but a Master Class now. A low-Level Master Class, since his duties keep him away from the dungeons and the planets where he could Level. It's strange, to me, to think that I have passed Hondo in personal strength, when years ago, he was such a fearsome opponent.

But it's part of the problem of serving another. When you subsume your own needs for others, you also reduce the speed of your Leveling. Certainly safer, certainly more likely to survive, and as a Master Class, he probably has a very comfortable life ahead of him. Not one filled with pain and suffering, danger and tragedy around each corner like we have lived for so many years now.

And the reward for all my emotional toll, for all the risk-taking, is in the widening of his eyes, the twist in his lips as he begins to sneer then stops himself. When he realizes the vast difference between myself and him now. Because even if I have adjusted my Levels and hidden my Heroic Class, he knows the truth. As does his mistress.

She sweeps into the room, proceeded only seconds ahead by her Aura. The Aura of the Frozen Winter Queen pings off my resistances, reminding me of who she is. Like her servant, the Duchess Kangana is not a Heroic, just a late Master Class. Though she might gain experience from doing her duties, from ruling, such experience gain is much slower and less plentiful, if steadier than throwing oneself into the middle of a Forbidden Planet.

As interesting as her Class is, so are her looks. The Duchess is gorgeous. And I'm talking gorgeous in relation to other Master Class level Charisma-influenced individuals. She's tall, nearly six and a half feet tall, with the dark skin of the Truinnar and the striking, bright eyes that come with her kind. Her hair is long and lustrous, swaying just above the swell of her behind in a tightly wound, compact braid. Legs for days, and a shapely figure like a model underneath a sharp, angular face.

As for her dress, it's a flowing, multi-layered cloth piece that reminds me of a saree—the more risqué kinds that reveal as much as they hide. She draws more than one hungry gaze, but I know it's from the Aura she uses as much as her beauty.

Snorting, I turn from her with a visible yank, moving away from the woman. How the hell we're supposed to meet without people noticing, I have no idea.

After half a dozen steps, my pace slightly slower than hers, a slight touch on my arm startles me. I turn my head even as I drop a Toothy Knife into my palm.

Beside me is a young lady, another Truinnar. Plain-looking, just about as tall as me, dressed in Adventurer chic. She bobs her head, and I feel a slight shift in the Mana around us. A Skill kicks on, but it's so subtle you wouldn't realize it was there if you didn't pay attention. A new condition appears in my Status display.

Condition: Secret Liaisons

Sometimes, midnight assignations have to be done during the day. Secret Liaisons allows a lady to speak and interact with her lover in public without drawing attention. A combination of magical, psychic, emotional, and System influence makes others ignore the interactions within the field of the Skill.

"A pleasure meeting you, Redeemer." The greeting is whispered, a simple low, throaty growl that makes me shiver and pings my Mental Resistances.

My eyes narrow as I read the Skill notification, the Resistance notification, then her Status. Which, surprisingly, is filled with question marks. Even for her name.

"Duchess," I say in conclusion.

"Good. Graxan did say you were smarter than your actions would lead many to believe," the Duchess-in-disguise says. She steps forward, making sure we keep walking, pulling away from the fake-Duchess but still within proximity.

"*Smart. Doppelganger and Skills to take away attraction. Add in the Shrine's natural abilities to hide scrying and a routine for coming in, and I'm surprised more people don't use the Shrine for their meetings,*" Ali says.

I can only send a mental shrug to him while I speak with the Duchess. "I'm sure you've had time to consider my request."

"So direct…" The Duchess smiles and nods. "I have. I have spoken with your Earthen representative too. He has offered much, but all of it dependent upon successfully seeing off this challenge to the World's sovereignty."

I grunt a little in surprise that she talked to Rob. When she sees my surprise, the Duchess sniffs.

"Did you think I would deal with a middleman in such matters? I am loath to waste my time."

"Then why are you talking to me at all?"

"Maybe not as smart."

I growl in response to her taunt.

"You have something they do not have, of course."

"My Class."

"Insignificant." The Duchess shakes her head. "I can acquire one of your stature if necessary. Credits do have their own strength. As do favors."

My eyes narrow as she falls silent. I walk with her, crossing one hallway after the other, eyeing the various supplicants. I see one golem-like creature made of sand pushing its fist into the wall, the Mana crystal dissolving to take his arm. When he pulls back, the wall hardens, leaving his hand within, where it slowly transforms into crystal too.

Eventually, the Duchess speaks, naming what she wants. "Answers. You have answers to why the Council acts with such impertinence. They have upset centuries of political norms, attacking diplomatic locations, making their wishes known."

"It's a dangerous secret," I say.

"All secrets worth having are dangerous."

And once more, we walk in silence as I mull over my options. "Fine. I'll let you know what they want to keep hidden, what this is all about." The start of the lady's smile is squashed as I continue. "After the vote."

"You'd have me waste political resources for a promise?"

"Or for me to provide a secret on one?" I counter.

She turns her head, and I meet her gaze too. Violet eyes bore into mine, an unyielding will pressing against me. But I find it easy to dismiss the pressure she exerts. I've faced down an Empress before. A mere Duchess is nothing—even if she controls as large a volume of space as the Empress does.

"You could use your Skill," she offers.

"As you said, Credits have their own power. Be a simple matter for you to break it, with the right kind of hire. Or using the System." I shake my head. "This secret stays with me until you vote. But whatever the result, I promise you this. I'll tell you the truth."

The Duchess turns away, staring at the walls as we walk. Behind us, a loud thump, then a body comes flying past me. Hondo strides after the body, but the walls of the Shrine act first, picking up the plastic-creature that dared to approach the fake-Duchess and absorbing it.

As I reel with surprise at the actions, Ali slides into my mind. *"Relax. It's just depositing him in another corridor. No killing."*

I nod dumbly, relaxing. Only to tense as the Duchess speaks. "Very well. I shall take your word. I expect you will make arrangements that such information passes on, no matter what happens to you?"

"As best as I can."

The Duchess nods and, without bidding me farewell, takes an off-shoot passage. Leaving me to stroll on alone. Hondo and the fake-Duchess make their way over to her passageway. And just like that, our meeting is over.

"She never did say how much help she'd bring," Ali muses.

"Nope. Also, another important question," I send.

"What?"

I stare down the featureless blue crystal walls, the passageway that splits and splits again as it leads me through the multi-hectare, multi-story building. Packed with sapients, praying, chanting, singing, and exuding pheromones.

"How the hell do we get out?"

Chapter 15

If this was a Hollywood story, when I finally deposited my little nugget of information, my crystallized warp of Mana and information into the Shrine, it would have bestowed upon me some great Skill, some nugget of information that would have solved all my problems. Sadly, even when I left the Shrine with my most closely guarded secret, it offered me nothing.

Not even a feeling of pleasant exchange.

Forced to join the exiting throng of disillusioned supplicants, I move in the crowd of hopping, floating, walking sapients. Two transits and one long walk to verify I'm not being followed later, I'm relaxed enough to check on the status of the team. Since they aren't home yet, I divert myself to a nearby Shop sphere, accessing a private room and using Extra Hands to form another copy.

While my doppelganger picks up various equipment to resculpt his face and make himself not so human-looking, I take the time to review my own Status Screen and consider my next steps. My Credit pool is sadly bereft, though only by the standards of a Heroic. I still have more than enough to pay for daily events and even pick up a couple of lower-end Class Skills, but… what's the point?

Status Screen			
Name	John Lee	Class	Junior System Admin (Grand Paladin)
Race	Human (Male)	Level	3 (12)
Titles			
Monster's Bane, Redeemer of the Dead, Duelist, Explorer, Apprentice Questor, Galactic Silver Bounty Hunter, Corrupt Questor, (Living Repository), (Class Lock)			

Health	6000	Stamina	6000
Mana	5740	Mana Regeneration	474 (+5) / minute

Attributes			
Strength	422	Agility	495
Constitution	600	Perception	403
Intelligence	593	Willpower	574
Charisma	225	Luck	256

Class Skills			
Mana Imbue	5*	Blade Strike*	5
Thousand Steps	1	Altered Space	2
Two are One	1	The Body's Resolve	3
Greater Detection	1	A Thousand Blades*	4
Soul Shield*	8	Blink Step	2
Portal*	5	Army of One	4
Sanctum	2	Penetration	9ᵉ
Aura of Chivalry	1	Eyes of Insight	2
Beacon of the Angels	2	Eye of the Storm	1
Vanguard of the Apocalypse	2	Society's Web	1
Shackles of Eternity*	4	Immovable Object / Unstoppable Force*	1
Domain	1	Judgment of All	6
(Grand Cross)	(2)	(Extra Hands)	(3)
System Edit	2		

External Class Skills			
Instantaneous Inventory	1	Frenzy	1
Cleave	2	Tech Link	2
Elemental Strike	1 (Ice)	Shrunken Footsteps	1
Analyze	2	Harden	2
Quantum Lock	3	Elastic Skin	3
Disengage Safeties	2	Temporary Forced Link	1
Hyperspace Nitro Boost	1	On the Edge	1
Fates Thread	2	Peasant's Fury	1
Combat Spells			
Improved Minor Healing (IV)		Greater Regeneration (II)	
Greater Healing (II)		Mana Drip (II)	
Improved Mana Missile (IV)		Enhanced Lightning Strike (III)	
Firestorm		Polar Zone	
Freezing Blade		Improved Inferno Strike (II)	
Elemental Walls (Fire, Ice, Earth, etc.)		Ice Blast	
Icestorm		Improved Invisibility	
Improved Mana Cage		Improved Flight	
Haste		Enhanced Particle Ray	
Variable Gravitic Sphere		Zone of Denial	

I'd made a few changes on my Status Screen, spending a ton of the free attribute points I'd saved to test how it affected my ability to handle the Mana code. Unfortunately, even adding points to each of my attributes slowly, one after the other, and running the tests, it seemed that attributes had only a marginal affect on my ability to handle System Mana. Constitution, Intelligence, and weirdly, Luck all gave me a little more time. Perception let me handle and understand the flow faster, but it didn't increase the amount of time I had before I started taking serious damage.

No, the biggest determinant of how long I could stay within the System and edit things? My Level. And interestingly enough, this is one case where my Junior System Administrator Level counts as much as my "fake" Levels.

Sadly, even when I Leveled up my Administrator Class, I didn't double dip and gain additional attributes. I found it strange that I received attribute points when I leveled my other Class, but didn't want to look a gift horse in the mouth. But when it didn't double dip and give me those attribute points for the Administrator Class for which the actual attributes should have been linked to, then I was real curious.

Of course, it's not as if I can actually ask the System why it's doing what it is. Nor do I have anyone else to experiment or compare with. The only thing I can think of is that the System has to give me those attribute points immediately—otherwise, my fake Class would be a poor fake.

On top of that, I've got the adjustments to my Class Skills, including the unhappy experience of learning how to upgrade my Skill Edit ability. Specifically, when I was meant to get a new Class Skill point at Level 3, the free point I hadn't used beforehand had been taken and used immediately to level it.

Now, I have a second point in Skill Edit and no free Class Skill point to use in case I need it for something else. The good news is that the upgraded System Edit Skill allows me to adjust code easier. I even get the feeling that with a few upgrades, I could edit certain types of code I've been locked out of thus far. But...

It doesn't help with my ability to kick ass. And the fact that Kasva is running around makes me feel the lack of ass-kicking Skills even more than normal. It's kind of amusing how I keep fluctuating between feeling like a goddamn demigod and feeling useless and underpowered.

Sure, having a total of three doppelgangers that I can use might be useful—if it didn't drain nearly my entire Mana pool to conjure a single Extra Hand. And even though Grand Cross's second Level is powerful, adding even more damage to what is already a ridiculous Skill, I still feel underpowered.

Grand Cross (Level 2)

The burden of existence weighs heavily on the Paladin. This Skill allows the Paladin to allow another to share in the burden. Under the light of and benediction of the Grand Paladin, under the weight of true understanding, wayward children may be brought back to the fold.

Effect: Damage done equals to (Willpower * 22) per square meter over radius of (1 / 10th of Perception^2) meters. Damage may be increased by reducing radius of the Grand Cross. Does additional (Willpower) points of damage per second for 11 seconds.

Cost: 2000 MP

Now, that doesn't seem like a lot of damage for a single point attack. After all, my Advanced Class Skill already does over fifteen thousand points of damage. If you don't include resistances, armor, and the like, even I'd fall to one of my own Advanced Class attacks. And I'm a "tank."

So when you look at it that way, doing roughly fourteen thousand points of damage is nothing. And sure, there's a damage-over-time effect, but most Paladins would have the Judgement of All for a much better damage-over-time effect.

That is, until you get to the part where I'm able to increase damage by concentrating the attack. And since it is very rare I need to use it at the full size of seventeen kilometers radius, the ability to concentrate damage stacks. And it stacks at an incredible rate when you consider how fast my attributes are increasing.

Of course, the issue with a Skill like this—much like Sanctum—is the need to control size and placement. It's not like Beacon of the Angels, where I point and activate, letting it do its things. Beacon might take longer to charge up, but the attack doesn't require much in the way of concentration once I use it.

Whereas with Grand Cross or Sanctum, I have to pre-fill in the details before activating or else it defaults to its base setting. In Grand Cross, that's smacking down everyone at maximum size. With Sanctum, it's forming itself around me at maximum size, enveloping everything.

Both are powerful but have to be used carefully. I've also noticed, upon inspecting Sanctum with my Skill, that the "all" portion of the Skill description is a little misleading. In its entirety in System Script, it's actually a formula calculation—much like I'm seeing for my newer Skills—that indicates the amount of damage it can absorb per second before it falls apart.

In fact, upon inspecting most "absolute" statements from the System, there's often more detail. Sometimes it's just a matter of translation. Sometimes I can see the workings of a System Admin in there, adjusting descriptions to something that's a little more user-friendly.

Reviewing my Status Screen is really my way of procrastinating. I can't buy much in terms of new Skills, and with my penniless nature, I don't have the funds to buy anything really cool. Never mind the fact that I'm filled to the brim between the System Edit and Class Skills. In fact, my Grand Paladin

Class Skills are all side-loaded, meaning they're even slower to activate than I'd like.

No, I'm just wasting time reviewing my Status Screen because there's something else I have to do. Drawing a deep breath of the stale, recycled air of the Shop anteroom, I place my hands on the Sphere and slip into the System layer. Repeated tests have shown it's relatively safe for me to access the admin level of the Shop, thus far. I could almost swear the System is built so that finding other Administrators is hard, the way it naturally obscures logging functions. And makes it even easier to obscure your own further.

Still, I don't have a lot of time to go over such details, not with the need to layer my protections and ensure I'm hidden before I slip within and look for a message. And this time, I'm surprised to note there is one.

It's pretty simple, though I do have to disable a nasty little locator virus before I open the file.

Meet at 198.55.xmu.$@90.55

There's a date afterward, but the moment I see the address, it feels as if it's branded into me. I reel backward out of the System, cutting the feed and the Mana draw, shutting down any tracing as I stagger back.

My doppelganger stares at me and sniffs. Which is just weird when his face is mine—if I was in full V-lizard face makeup. You wouldn't realize it was me if you didn't know what to look for, but because it's my face, I do.

"Idiot. You should be more careful. And wipe your nose," the Hand says. The voice is mine, but grouchier, lower.

I blink, touching my nose and feeling blood running down it. I wipe it away, grateful that I'm not bleeding further as System regeneration fixes the damage.

"What was it?" the Hand asks.

"An address."

"System address? You should be careful. That Skill is dangerous," the Hand says.

"No shit." I'd love to have the doppelgangers use it, but funnily enough, they don't have it. While they might replicate my attributes at a lower percentage, they don't have the System Edit Skill. Which is, in itself, fascinating. "Now, please stop talking to me. It's **really** weird listening to me talk."

Doppelganger John rolls his eyes but does shut up. One good thing about the System making it based off me, it seems to accept that I really don't want to talk to myself. And makes the doppelgangers respect my wishes— the same way I would my own.

No, that sentence doesn't make much sense. But it's not a very sensible world.

"Well, if that's it. I'm off." The doppelganger waves goodbye off-handedly before walking out of the room, silver doors sliding open.

I nod absently, watching him leave and feeling a weird sense of déjà vu. I hurry after him a moment later, not wanting to stay at the Shop any longer than necessary, especially after what happened.

It's when we're well away, moving in a random but trained pattern to pick out potential shadows, that Ali asks the obvious question.

"What the hell happened?"

"The Council—or the Administrator side of the Council, or the Inner Council, or whoever it is—gave me an address."

"And it made you bleed?"

"Yes. I'm pretty sure it's not just any address."

"Then what is it, boy-o? I'm not here to play twenty questions, you know."

I work my jaw, getting some saliva back into my mouth. Even thinking it dried my mouth, and I'm not particularly happy with the idea of thinking it out loud. And yes, it's weird to want to be able to say the words, even when you're thinking it. And I could suppress such actions, but why bother? It's small things like that that help me stay human.

I hope.

"If I'm not wrong, it's a System programming station."

There's a long, long silence after that as Ali works through the implications. It's particularly concerning, since even though we've had a hint of them before, we've never seen hide nor hair of them. Not even when we've gone poking among the planets we helped reconquer.

"Well, that's not worrying at all."

***

Meeting with the rest of the group at our residence comes soon after. The group finds me eating, having ordered a large meal to assuage my hunger and my restlessness. The overly large dining room is filled with takeout boxes, each of them individually heated to keep the meats, pastas, vegetables, roasts, and other forms of sustenance warm. There's even a gooey sludge that looks like slime and tastes like liquid sunshine.

I'm wrangling a drumstick whose bone is made of crystals and metals, the meat tearing off in strips with each bite, when they walk in. I take one look at Harry's more expressive face and kick out a chair.

"Didn't go well, eh?" I say.

"It could have gone better," Harry admits, catching the chair's back. He spins it around and sits, flopping down to stare at the food.

Mikito snorts as she takes her own seat, pulling the Galactic equivalent of fried rice over to her side of the table, along with a shallow and large bowl. She ladles in the carbs while she explains.

"Katherine ran the numbers. Has been running the numbers. Even with the Duchess's help, she doesn't think we have enough to stop the vote." Mikito side-eyes Harry before she adds, "She thinks at least half of those we have done work for aren't going to come through with their side."

"Even with the System contracts?" I snarl.

"Even with," Mikito says.

"Goblin shit," Ali says. He's in his full-size mode and visible since he's helping himself to food that he doesn't need to eat. But he likes the taste and who am I to say no? "Is there no more honor among politicians?"

"You're not serious, are you?" Harry sighs. "Fun fact. It seems that for high-Level Politicians, Diplomats, and the like, they have Skills that mitigate the effect of broken System contracts and oaths."

"What!?!" I say.

"Yeah, surprised us too." Harry shook his head. "Katherine forgot to tell us because she's gotten used to it. Wouldn't matter anyway. It isn't as if we know who's going to break their word until, well…"

"They do."

"Exactly." Mikito spears a shrimp, chewing the deep-fried, battered goodness.

We fall silent for a bit, each of us following her example and eating a little more.

"So, you've heard about what the Duchess did?" I ask.

"Yes. Which is why her wanting to meet you was surprising," Harry says. "She's extracted quite her pound of flesh from Earth."

I grunt, not surprised. It's not as if they all don't have us over the barrel. But… "She wanted to know why they're after us. Me."

"Told you," Mikito says to Harry.

He shrugs. "I was just offering other options. But I did say that was most likely."

"So?" Mikito says to me.

"So what?"

"Did you tell her?"

"Not immediately," I say. "I promised I would if she came through on her end."

"Big promise," Harry says. "You think it's a smart thing to let her in on it?"

I shrug. There's the obvious conclusion that if the Council really doesn't like what's going on, they'll end her, my friends, and anyone they even think I provided the information to. But… "She's a big girl."

Harry shrugs, seeming sufficiently settled. I guess he's used to seeing adults throw themselves into seemingly dumb situations. Taking risks that others would decline because that's just the way it goes. At a certain point, you have to accept that risk is part and parcel of the job description and stop worrying about it.

"You didn't tell us what they thought of John's brilliant plan," Ali says, sipping on a drink-cum-meal via a bendy straw that injects a portion of the meal's taste as it passes through.

"Katherine wasn't thrilled," Mikito says. "But she'll take it to Rob."

"And he'll release the information?" When they look up, I clarify, "If he decides to do it."

Mikito shrugs.

I frown. "He shouldn't. He should be using… well, a patsy."

"Us, you mean," Harry says.

"Well, you." I grin at the reporter and he rolls his eyes. But I'm surprised to note there's a level of uncertainty in there too. "Problem?"

"This isn't breaking just any story. This isn't even news reporting, not really. It's weaponized information," Harry says. The man has a very large slab of meat, still raw and bloody, sitting on his plate, being delicately sliced with knife and fork. Next to it, carefully set aside, is a small, colorful handful of greens—well, yellows and purples. "I'm not comfortable with the idea of using the news like that."

Huh. I would have thought it was the target being painted on his back. Then again, Harry's always been a little more moral than smart. "Fair enough. Doesn't sound like he's going to use us anyway."

"He probably has others," Ali says.

When we look at him, the Spirit shrugs, having traded for another soupy dish which he uses a tureen spoon on. Small, floating chunks of meat that still squirm and reach can be seen in the soup as he pops the entire, so-cold-it's-smoking ladle into his mouth.

We aren't the only players in the Galactic scene these days. And as a World Ruler, Rob has his own contacts. Maybe he uses a group that does things like this, or maybe he uses another human team. Or maybe, just maybe, I'm overthinking things.

But for now, there's not a lot we can do but wait. Which, I'm finding, is an extremely uncomfortable place to be in.

We sit, we eat, and we do that in silence. When the meal is nearly done, when we've cleared the majority of the plates and another of my doppelgangers has died, Ali speaks up.

"You going to tell them?"

I glare at the Spirit, angry he's pushed me to speak when I would prefer to be silent. At least for a little while more. But the threads of the doppelgangers in my mind, the missing one weighs upon me. Telling me that what we're outnumbered, outplayed, and no matter how much we hide, what we've done, all our efforts are worthless. They know we're here.

"The Council. Or the Administrators at least. They've left me a message," I said. "An address."

My words cause a stir, one that has Harry and Mikito shifting uncomfortably and offering me suspicious looks. I can only offer a half-shrug in apology for the length of time I've taken to speak.

"You going?" Mikito says.

I nod.

"When?"

"You're not coming," I say.

"I'm not letting you go alone, you bakayaro!"

I shake my head again. "It's not your call. Where I'm going... you can't enter."

She frowns before shifting tactics. "Then I'll go as far as I can."

"Mikito..."

She crosses her arms, daring me to push it further. I meet her stubborn gaze, and I find myself at another crossroads. One of trust. Because I could sneak out, but loyalty, trust, belief... it's a double-edged weapon. What is given must be returned, or one day, the well will run dry.

"Fine." I turn to Harry, who snorts.

"I'd love to, but I think I'll get this news later." Harry chuckles ruefully at my incredulous look. "The juicy bit is in the room, and if I can't get in, I don't think it matters if I get the news five minutes or five hours later. And you're probably also going to want me on the outside as insurance, no?"

I half-shrug. In truth, I'd considered it, but I wasn't going to presume. Asking him to release what I know, to cover my bases, to let the galaxy know, it's more than presumptuous.

"I thought so," Harry says. "How many days do I have to set up the news release?"

"Eleven hours, four minutes, and thirteen seconds."

"Well, isn't that accurate," Harry drawls, but I see the worry in his eyes.

And I get it. Because the countdown in my vision, the one that has refused to disappear ever since I received the address and invitation, continues to tick ever so slowly.

Down.

Down.

Down.

Chapter 16

An empty alleyway, shrouded in the shadows of the buildings that loom above it and bereft of light even from the main streets. In the middle of the night, the dark passageway offers no illumination but for the single, hovering light spell I sent ahead of us. Unlike a pre-System human alleyway, there's no detritus on the ground, no broken asphalt or concrete or scrawled graffiti from neglect. In this place, there's not enough traffic for sapients to lay their mark upon the alley before the System cleanses it.

We're in the third ring, close enough to the center that there are actual dead spaces like this. In the outer rings, empty alleyways like this would be impossible, as every scrap of land is used, even by the homeless.

"This it?" Mikito sounds doubtful, even though she's seen the overhead imagery from the drone we deployed ahead of us and its conjured map.

"Yeah."

I tilt my head, watching the Mana flows, the way it interacts with the environment. Something weird is going on, but I can't figure it out. In the end, I dismiss the matter. Not because I don't want to know, but because if I tried to work out every strangeness in Mana flows I encountered, I'd never take more than a dozen steps.

Mana moves as it will, and sometimes, System Mana and unaspected Mana conflict, almost as if they're fighting one another. Other times, they flow past one another without an issue, mingling. And sometimes, one or the other just subsumes the other entirely. There are even a few studies—2,413—that have delved into the matter with the leading theory...

"Boy-o..." Ali coughs.

I blink, shake my head, and pull my mind back to the present. I'm less prone to side-thoughts now that the damn library is being processed by my new Class, but it still happens, especially when I'm a little nervous.

"Sorry." I shake my head. "Now, remember, just watch. Stay hidden, if you can. If things go to hell—"

Mikito snorts.

I chuckle ruefully but step into the alleyway, then stop. I turn to her and touch the side of my bracelet, pushing the Skill over us to hide our conversation as I continue. "About the three stooges..."

"Musketeers," Mikito says.

"That make you D'Artagnan?" I raise an eyebrow. Mikito shrugs, and I push past the irrelevant question. "Any word?"

"Yes. They're good. They are on it," Mikito murmurs. She looks around and shakes her head. "I'm still a little uncomfortable with using them."

"It's safer than being with us," I point out.

Mikito nods, smoothing out her face and shoving me in the shoulder to get me moving. I sketch a bow, dropping the topic, and walk away. I watch the little dot on my minimap grow closer, the dot located almost two-thirds of the way down the empty alley.

Each step I take seems to take forever. There's a slow building discomfort that scratches at the back of my throat, clenches my guts. I cough, clear my throat, clench and unclench my fist as I walk. Ali beside me keeps flipping between his TV channels, going from reality TV show to reality TV show, before finding a musical.

"Something..." I frown. I poke at my resistances mentally, testing the borders of the System-generated defenses. I find nothing, but my footsteps have begun to drag, each movement slower than the other. "Something's wrong."

Ali frowns, then he slowly stops spinning. He opens his mouth then shuts it, notification windows appearing then disappearing, flicking on and off. He struggles, then suddenly, just up and disappears.

Banished.

My sword appears in my hand and I turn around slowly, searching for the threat. For what banished him. Long minutes pass, where I have to fend off a worried ping from Mikito and the growing dread. But nothing happens.

And I find myself growing angry. Angry at whatever it is that's affecting me, that's slipping past the defenses the System has put in place. That has buffered my will and driven me on.

That has made me, me.

I'm angry, and because I'm me, instead of turning away, instead of running, I turn back. I walk farther in, shoving my anger at the damn feeling, at the cloying tendrils of fear that wrap around my heart and guts that try to push me away. Anger unleashed, the dread and fear, the need to depart, shrivels before me.

Step after step, I make my way inward, the empty alleyway a void of dark thoughts and darker threats. I push forward with each step before the tension snaps like a rubber band at my latest step.

I stagger as the weight, the pressure disappears. Only to find myself nearly where the location given to me should be. The place where I am to meet the Council. Or whoever it is I'm to meet.

"A thousand and one demons," I snarl, realization arriving belatedly.

Of course this feeling bypassed the System. The gods damned Administrators are in play here. The weirdness in Mana, the Skills not working. It's their way of hiding themselves. Which means…

I eye the empty space before me, the innocuous piece of land that marks the meeting spot. There's nothing there, nothing I can see, nothing I can sense even when I push my Mana Sense forward. It's empty.

Utterly empty.

"Well, let's just hope I'm not a frog looking up the well." Two quick steps, and I'm there.

Then.

Light.

***

When my sight resolves again, I've taken three steps to the side, crouched low with my sword held before me and trying to activate Soul Shield. Surprisingly, it doesn't activate, which has me worried. Almost as much as my blindness.

But System healing is powerful, and the teleportation—and it was a teleportation—wasn't meant to blind me, just shift me. To this place. A simple room filled with hanging notification windows with System script scrolling across, multiple bar and line graphs, and what my many years as an IT worker can tell immediately is a ticketing board with colored priority task lists.

My stomach falls, my breathing hitches, and I push—and fail to activate—Blade Strike. Just for a second, before I get hold of myself. Flashbacks are bad, and it's surprising that my short period working at an IT help desk can be more scarring than getting eaten by a giant monster.

"So. You really are on Irvina," a voice cuts through my subsiding panic, dragging my attention to it.

I turn my head from side to side, taking in the room and the simple steel-grey mezzanine floor without a railing, the glowing blue notification windows that dominate the walls before turning to the only figure within.

He stands before me, a humanoid corvid creature with black feathers, a long beak, and large, pupil-filled eyes that focus upon every motion of mine. Wings jut from his back, a contrast to the taloned fingers that he keeps crossed before me. As for clothing, he's dressed in belts, and a loin cloth and nothing more.

My eyes narrow further when I see his Status.

Sefan ared Lebek'jjas (Senior Administrator Level 14)
HP: ???/ ???
MP: ???/ ???
Conditions: ???

"Who are you?" I push once more at my identification Skill and find it doesn't activate further. Another push and System Edit kicks in, showing me that my entire series of Skill uses are being blocked. An Administrative block.

What the hell?

"If you read your location notification, you'll understand," Sefan says.

I realize I swore out loud, but while keeping an eye on him, I call forth the System location notification as he suggested.

You have entered Administrative Center 194-8-15 (Security Access Level 3)

Warning! No violence may be initiated in Administrative Centers. All Skills (outside of Administrative Skills) and System-assisted Spells are blocked. This includes all enchanted items and System-registered technological aids.

Effects: +2 Skill Ranks in System Edit Skills, +200% increase in Mana Sense skill, access to Level 3+ System Administrator Quests, access to Administrator Network (temporary)

Congratulations Junior Administrator!

You have accessed an Administrative Center for the first time! You have gained access to the System Administrator Quest notice board and the Administrator Network (temporary localized basis)

Level Up! +1 Junior Administrator Level

I stare at the notifications before coming back to myself. I realize that Sefan's still making no move to bother me. In fact, his eyes are no longer even focused on me, darting from side to side as he reads notification windows, talons twitching in small motions as he controls the data.

Thus far, if this was a trap, they've missed multiple opportunities to close the jaws of it. And really, I can only hope it's not a trap. If it is, I walked in here knowing it could be. Without answers, I'm not leaving. And this is my first chance for true answers.

I dive into the notifications, pulling up the System Administrator Quest board. And then I have to quell my rising panic when I realize it's the very same task list I spotted on arrival.

"Cut me apart and boil me in the thousand hells. You have got to be fucking joking with me." When the corvid stares at me, I growl. "The damn System Administrator Quest board is an IT help desk!"

"Well, yes. We are System Administrators." Sefan's voice is slightly musical, a little clicky—as if the top of his tongue keeps hitting the roof of his mouth at the most inopportune time. That his tongue is sharp and angular and perhaps not used to Galactic might be the reason for that. "We fix the System, when necessary."

I twitch. The first ticket I try to touch—one that's glowing green—sends a painful jolt back at me. I stagger, feeling my nerves burn as the ticket rejects my choice.

"Why would you choose one you are barred from?" Sefan says.

"It's green. Green is go!"

"No. Green is barred. You are black." Sefan shakes his head. "Everyone civilized knows that."

I hear the unsaid "barbarian," but I leave it alone. Even if, I know, there's no such information in any of the Galactic civilization packs I've purchased.

I'm a little hesitant to touch the ticketing board again, but I have to know. So, mentally reaching out, I touch a black ticket. And get a notification.

There's Something Wrong in Tumiaaq (Status Level 3)

Experience and Mana exchange is imbalanced in Tumiaaq. Conflict caused by inclusion of dungeon 132.8, revision 511581251267844.881.52, and the presence of the Skills Experience Tap for the Lazy and 5,565 Minutes Used Properly.

Do you wish to take this quest? (Y/N)

I hit the No, skipping out of the mental notification, and check a few more. They're all the same, all coding issues where Mana, experience, Levels, Skills, or attributes are messed up. Sometimes for the better, sometimes for the worse. A dungeon spawning too fast. A building not fixing itself, instead spewing out System Mana as it attempts to handle a persistent enchanted item. A warp engine with a design error that churns through unaffiliated Mana while also draining System Mana at the same time.

Error after error after error. I watch as some of the notifications disappear and others pop up, replacing them. The ones that don't change, the ones that sit there, are the ones coded green. They just sit, unmoving.

Untouched?

I purse my lips, but noise from the corvid makes me glance at the unspeaking Administrator. I shift my sight away from him and check the Administrator Network. Only to find myself less than impressed.

"I'm blocked from everything but the local node," I say.

Silence greets my words. I start to speak but notice his clawed fingers flicking in routine. I shut my mouth, watching silently as I test the edges of this Administrative block with my System Edit Skill. It doesn't take me long to feel how hard, how rigid it is.

If it can be bypassed, it won't be by me.

"You are blocked because you are but a Junior Administrator," Sefan says finally, his fingers stilling. At the same time, I see a green ticket disappear. "An unauthorized Junior Administrator."

"And here we get to it. So will it be door T or B?"

"What?" Sefan says.

"Threats or bribery?"

Sefan lets out a little screeching noise. The grip on my sword tightens and the tip bobs up and down under my grip. I try for Ali, hoping I can get an ally, and find the very same block in place. Not that it matters to the corvid who ignores my caution as it continues to screech. It takes me a bit to realize he's laughing.

"You are blunt as a warhammer to the beak." Sefan cackles. "Do you humans not know subtlety? Grace?"

"I'm North American. Our version of subtlety is checking if you're fine after we kick your ass," I say.

"And you think you can 'kick my ass'?" Sefan cocks his head. Down, down, down until he reaches his shoulder, his head tilted until it goes past the edge of his shoulders. My neck hurts just looking at him.

"I'll give it the good old college try." And hope that the question marks are due to our location and not the fact that he's a Legendary. Because otherwise, this will be an incredibly fast fight. And not in a good way.

"College. How quaint," Sefan says. "But you have gained knowledge you should not. Endangered an order you should not. You and those Corrupt Questors continue to be a pain in our order."

"Then why not just kill us all?"

"Because we occasionally get something useful." This voice is high-pitched, female. It's accent is unnatural and stilted, a Latin American one of some sort. I never did visit before the apocalypse.

I jump, looking up at where the voice comes from and get a spideresque nightmare. It's a reminder of Xev, my old mechanic. The creature is similar to her in the vaguest sense that a house spider compares to an invisible tarantula. Because this one, above, is invisible except for the barest outlines. It's not even a Skill, just its natural ability to play chameleon.

Wex (Senior Administrator Level 17)

HP: ???/ ???

MP: ???/ ???

Conditions: ???

"Who the hell are you?" I back away, only to stop when I realize that Wex is moving too, making sure to hover right above me. I growl, but if my displeasure makes any difference to the spider, there's absolutely no indication.

"You may call me Wex. Senior Administrator." The bulbous head, with its multi-faceted eyes, turns slowly. Then, disturbingly enough, it conjures a bundle wrapped in spider-silk and sinks its jaw into it. A little of the liquiefied remains drips out from where its fangs pierce the bundle, missing me by a foot or so.

I keep my face neutral at the display, just letting my lip curl up a little. Intimidation. Petty intimidation.

I turn over its words, seeking understanding. If there's an argument about how useful I can be, that explains why I'm not dead. I wonder how often Administrators are made, what the usual methods are of creating such individuals. It's a Hidden Class, but is it one you could get from just knowing that you can alter the System? Certainly a level of mastery over Mana Sense is required. But is there more? I would guess so, or else there'd be a lot more and it would be a less well-kept secret.

If there is more, if it's hard to make Administrators, maybe I have more leverage than I think I do.

"Something useful, you say." Yeah, fine. I'm as blunt as a virgin asking for his first kiss.

"But I fear there's nothing useful in this one," Sefan says. "He's a bog-standard Administrator. One with problematic connections and an even more problematic attitude."

I bite my lip on my instant retort, keeping an eye on Wex above. I'm getting the idea that these two are the representatives of opposing viewpoints. And Sefan is never going to warm up to me. So…

The spider makes the bundle disappear back into its inventory before it answers. That the bundle is half the size, I try not to note. "We've yet to see what he can do. Or why the System chose him."

"The System?" I say, only to see Wex nod a little.

So. That's interesting. A notification window blooms before me, the ticketing system appearing before my eyes.

"Enough talk. Let us see then. Or be done with this," Sefan says.

I could ask what they want to see, but I'm not that dumb. And since what they want from me is what my own curiosity is killing me to explore, I take to it with gusto.

First, I plant my feet apart, making sure I'm well balanced. Then I shift the window to the main focus area before I pop out tickets. I toss them to the side of me, leaving them hanging in mid-air without accepting, without closing them.

I do that for a half dozen before I stop, then I probe the connection between the ticketing window and me. I look for more information, more details that can be brought forth. To little surprise, there's more information that could be added to each ticket.

The stream of information, the flow of Mana it denotes, was hidden by default. I delve into the view, looking for details, looking for what I need. Previous administrator comments—added. Number of times tickets have been accessed—added. Security access requirements—added. Time in queue—added.

I customize my interface, pulling more information and discarding others. I automatically filter away anything I don't have access to. Then I filter out anything that requires significant access to multiple databases. I filter by previous comments by administrators, putting those at the bottom of the list. And then filter for new tickets that haven't been accessed.

All of it to find work that I'm more likely to do well. I can't guarantee that it'll work, but it's better than accessing tickets where previous Administrators with more experience have started and left unfinished.

Maybe it's not what they're looking for. Maybe they want someone brilliant and gifted, who'll tackle the hardest jobs and somehow, miraculously, do what others can't. But those kinds of individuals only exist in movies and TV shows. And sometimes, rarely, in really life. For the rest of us mere mortals, who have to wade through mud when it pours, who have to learn to dance by taking classes or put on pants one leg at a time, we've got to start easy.

And work our way up.

The tickets I've opened help with that. I pull data from them, digging into details before I accept anything. I get more information, more columns to show me what I need. The System can show more than I could begin to guess. Number of databases accessed. Number of Classes involved. Number of individuals involved. Sphere of effect. Amount of Mana involved or stored within the Class, or Skills, or enchantments, or whatever else is being affected.

I sort and adjust, filtering again and again. All the while, the pair of Senior Administrators watch me, saying nothing and letting me do what I want. The tickets before me change, adjusting constantly as they update with new information.

And at some point, I'm done. There's no more delaying. Nothing else to stop me from picking something. I draw a deep breath and I find my hands trembling.

Suppressed fear or excitement? I'm not sure. But it doesn't matter, because it's—

Time.

***

Damage Calculation for Class Skill Open Ocean is Incorrect
Calculations when interacting with the Skills River Flows and the Greater Depths as well as during formula calculation of resistances to fire and elemental ice damage; damage calculations are providing x83-variance in Mana.

The first ticket seems simple. It's an edge case, happened twice in all the time it's been in play. It's a relatively urgent ticket though, because an individual is running this particular underwater ice dungeon. Once he leaves, it probably won't matter ever again.

But it still needs fixing.

System Mana is bleeding from the bad calculations as the System compensates for the bad data with raw power. System Mana fixes issues, paves over the problems so that those affected don't see what's happening, don't realize there's a problem—for the most part. But it costs. Costs more than it's worth for the System to keep the Skill and individuals alive.

So we fix it.

Administrators, that is. The information flows through me, into me, an answer to a question I didn't know I was asking. I fix the calculations, working by instinct, using Intelligence attributes in ways I never knew it could be used, Wisdom and intuition when raw processing power is insufficient. I twist the Mana strings, encode the new formula, the exceptions, and send back the results.

There's a hum, almost a feeling of gratitude when the answer is accepted. I feel experience trickle into my body, going straight to my System Administrator role. The ticket closes.

And I grab another.

Regeneration of monsters in Class XIVI dungeons, at the Hamton and Brasmith dungeons compromised.

A simple matter of adjusting Mana flows around Mana lines that the System laid down due to damage from a recent Master Class fight. Stupid

Geomancers, with their alteration of the Mana and physical environment. I adjust the flow, increasing it for the normal monsters, reducing it for the Alpha, and put the bleed-off into the nearby river. That'll make the water slightly more Mana-rich, maybe mutate a few more things in the future. Make an alchemist or two happy.

Another prompt, another agreement. Another rush of experience.

Next ticket.

Attempted access to time displacement technology (5.7s) by the Varia White Institute on Yuhupe Satellite IV.

I dig into the information. It's interesting—the notification isn't because the System doesn't want them to try to go back in time. It doesn't care. There's almost a smug sense of guarantee that it won't work.

No, it's not that the System doesn't want them to try. It's because the attempt itself is the problem, because the drain on System Mana and the subsequent destruction of the materials makes the experiment cost vastly more than what Skill, technological processing, and regeneration the individuals involved—even peripherally—have put into the System.

It's inefficient.

I get the database, the full cost and variables. And I have to balance it all out. It's part accounting, part manufacturing process management, and part Administrative Skill adjustment as I dig into all of the data. I make adjustments on the backend, not on the System itself. But there are so many variables that we never see—especially when creating—that it's not easy to balance it all.

It's not an easy ticket, because I can't just make the artifacts they create more expensive. Otherwise, they'd get around it by creating something similar. And I can't penalize their entire Skill because then it'd penalize everyone else. Nor can I do it on an individual level or else our adjustments would be noted.

My work slows down then as the library, the Questors' library, assaults me. It floods me with information about times when an Administrator, or perhaps even the System, did a bad job. It gives me information, guesses, formulas that the Questors have used to understand what is going on.

Information.

I admit, I crib from the notes. I make alterations, twist the strings of Mana that are the program codes that tell the world how to work. I get to fixing, smoothing out the data, applying an older solution with some minor adjustments.

Next ticket.

Ares Gravitic Grenade v183.9 interaction with Mana-infused Dragon Silver—Overdrawn

Formula. Math. Calculation. Adjustment.
Next ticket.

Rhapsody of the Siren current degradation too slow

Just over two dozen individuals, all of them having found this once abandoned Class. Now they're back and creating a... cult? Groupie group? I'm not even sure. It's a problem, especially with the way they're exploiting the Rhapsody. I dig into it, and once again the library comes to my aid. Research studies, Skill lists, details about mental and musical Skills.

All of it at my fingertips.

I adjust the degradation, add details of how and why and when, make it easy to explain away why it wasn't noticed before. I give users a built-in resistance. And maybe I overweigh it a little bit so that they get a mental resistance for everything too.

The System rejects and fixes that overplayed hand. Sends back a feeling of… wrongness. The experience I get is less. The final ticket is adjusted by the System before the ticket itself disappears.

And I'm on to the next ticket.

Star 489151x199967y889987z-1 has begun to dim. Mana uptake is at 87% of expectations.

I falter a little when this one comes up. The System deals with suns? Not surprisingly, the library has something to say about that too.

I hesitate at adjusting this, wondering at a System where fixing a star is considered a trivial, low-level Administrative task. But the Senior Administrators are waiting, watching. I feel the weight of their regard even as I unconsciously note that they're at work too. Coding.

I dive right in, forcing aside doubts.

For what is an enormous project, the code itself is simple. A simple comparison is all that's required before I see the problem. The Mana equivalent of copy and paste fixes the issue, then I send it over.

Assessment, agreement, and experience.

Next ticket.

There's always another ticket.

***

"Enough."

Sefan's voice pulls me from the fugue I've fallen into, grabbing tickets, fixing the problem, and moving on. An unknown period of time has passed, my abnormal Constitution, buoyed by the intense focus my attributes have provided, allowing me to work without interruption.

Multiple tickets are open before me, each of them in the process of being completed. I've gone from one ticket to three, search processes and databases open for each of them. At some point, the Administrative equivalent of their data repository was made available and I've got multiple windows into that open, allowing me to review and assess code. Adding remarks of my own, like the one I finish leaving as Stefan's sentence recalls me to the present.

The next time you leave a code recommendation, make sure you check it over first. Otherwise you'll cause a cascading failure in the third tier of the System database archives. References attached.
Code revision attached.

I finish the updates with a grunt and drop back into reality. I put bookmarks on the tickets, leaving links for reference when I get to them again. But a part of me burns with rage at being interrupted. Do they know how long it takes to get back into the right frame of mind for coding?

Actually, as I eye the pair of Senior Administrators, I realize they probably do. They deal with the System code much like I do. And while the System code is as much poetry and biology as hard programmed lines, the mindset required is the same.

"Seen enough?" I say. When in doubt, go on the offensive.

"You have some skill," Sefan admits, looking to the side.

I follow his gaze and realize I can see the window he's looking at. On it are a list of tickets I've tackled and a timer beneath it.

258 Class 3 tickets. 4 Class 2 tickets (misclassified).
97.8% code fidelity. Loss of 1.8764k SMU.
Security rating upgraded to Class 2 (Provisional, within Administrative centers only. Pending approval).
14 hours, 38 minutes Administrator Time

"Fourteen hours!" I yelp a little. "Wait. What's Administrator time?"

"Time within this zone is compressed. Only an hour and a half will have passed when you exit," Wex says. "A decent number for a first-time delve."

"Decent?" I raise an eyebrow.

"Decent. I cleared two hundred seventy-five," Wex says.

"Three hundred fifteen," Sefan says smugly.

Beyond the radiating pride from Sefan, I don't see any indication they're lying. Which makes me a little annoyed. Even if I know I'm not a gifted coder, it's never nice to have it rubbed in your face. Especially since I was in the flow when they interrupted me.

It's possible that was for the best though. Even if the flow, the damage, from interacting with this much System Mana is reduced in the Administrative Center, my body burns, aches from being damaged and regenerated continuously.

"However, the System seems pleased with your work," Wex says. "Few Junior Administrators do as much. Or as cleanly."

"As cleanly for sure." Sefan stares at me, as if by just looking, he could dig out my secrets. Maybe outside of the Administrative Center he could, using Skills and psychic abilities, but in here, there's just my smiling mien.

"Then did I pass?" I smile grimly. "Will you end your actions against Earth?"

"Earth?" Sefan looks puzzled before recollection sparks. He caws again, in shortened amusement. "That matter is already resolved. The vote will be done and another problem dealt with."

"I don't see a ticket for it, so it ain't an Administrator problem," I say, flicking my hand and refreshing the ticket. "Doesn't seem to be a problem to me."

"Not everything is dealt with via the Administrative Center," Wex says. "Managing the Galactic System requires more than the ability to resolve tickets. Though that is not a matter that *Junior Administrators* should trouble themselves with."

"Then again, I'm not your normal inductee, am I?" I say, turning from one to the other. "And that's the point of why I'm here."

"Yes." Sefan's wings rustle, opening and closing as he stares at me. In the end, he shakes his head to Wex. "He has talent. Whatever he did to get him the Class, it makes him a good technician. But he is too much of a risk. Even now, he taunts us. He will not bow. He will not bend. My vote stands."

"The Weaver will be unhappy," Wex states calmly, clicking its mandibles together. But it lowers itself on a thread, getting closer to me.

"Hey now, no need to be hasty. You could try asking before making pronouncements," I say, edging away.

To my utter lack of surprise, the damn spider-creature has invisible threads strung above, letting it shift sideways too. It just reattaches as necessary. I eye the surroundings, taking in the mezzanine floor, the walls.

There's no exit that I can see. I cast around discreetly for a way out as the corvid stalks toward me. Sefan's feet click with each step, even as the spider above me moves, watching my every motion.

"We are not hasty." Sefan's wings open and a breeze arises.

"We are deliberate." Wex twitches, and the notification windows collapse, shrouding me in darkness.

"We are inevitable." Energy talons extend from Sefan's fingers.

"We are what makes the System work." Wex rears back, bunching legs as he readies himself.

Together, they finish their creepy villain dialogue. "And you are a bug."

Chapter 17

I throw myself out of the way well before they finish their words. Sefan is already darting forward, the wings on his back beating as he flies low toward me. Wex above on its invisible threads, barely discernible with its camouflaged skin, spurts out new thread, hoping to catch me.

Skin tears, blood staining the white floor of the Administrative Center. The energy talons Sefan uses don't burn, leaving my torso wound to dribble red blood, nanowoven battlemesh coming apart as easily as Christmas wrapping paper. As Sefan twists in mid-air, I smell the musky stink of his feathers, hints of heavy spices and clean wind.

A raised sword catches the thread as it splashes around me, allowing me to tear myself away from Wex's attack. The sudden jerk and change in momentum forces me into a roll, small strands of the spider thread catching at my clothing and tearing free. My sword I dismiss, leaving its thread to flop around uselessly before I recall the clean weapon to hand.

Soulbound seems to mean something more than just plain Skills. That's good, because I'm at a disadvantage here.

I hunt for an exit, pushing at the System, searching. After a second, a notification flares into my vision, ever so briefly. A door flickers then disappears, forced away by the Senior Administrators.

Distracted, I don't see Sefan bearing down on me until it's too late. A sword catches one talon, my free hand grasping his shoulder as he bowls me backward. I fly back under the mezzanine I've been angling toward, feeling his talons sink into my body. At least we're briefly hidden from Wex above.

Taloned claws clench in my stomach, tearing at intestines, slippery innards sliced apart and turned into Silly Putty as the Senior Administrator easily overpowers me. I struggle, but he's stronger, much, much stronger.

Even adjusting the Strength attribute, throwing everything into pure strength does nothing to his grip.

If they had Skills, if I had Skills, this fight would go differently. But we have nothing but our attributes, our skills, and whatever innate abilities we might have given our bodies.

Sefan's mouth opens in a long screech that makes my ears hurt, my arm tremble. I shift the direction of his other attack, letting his arm slip over my shoulder even as I crash into the wall behind me. My teeth slam shut, blood fills my mouth, and my bones creak in dismay. The wall itself does not give way, Mana construct that it is, but his talon is briefly captured.

I drop down, feeling more of my body tear, rip. But the overly sharp nature of his claws plays against Sefan now, the skin in my torso opened wide. I rip free, screaming in agony. His now-free hand swings down. A sword in the way cuts into his arm a little, stopping the attack as I'm flattened on the floor.

Out of the corner of my eyes, beneath the mezzanine roof, I see Wex creeping over. Its body can barely be seen but for flickers of motion. It's taking its time, placing its feet carefully as multi-faceted eyes watch as I struggle.

And struggle I am, for Sefan keeps lashing out. I have a single sword that allows me to block his attacks somewhat. But each blow throws me around, crumpling my defense and leaving me bleeding.

Seconds pass, enough time for Wex, with its increased attributes, to near. A kick—a new addition to Sefan's arsenal—throws me back into the unyielding wall when I attempt to escape. I crack my head again and see stars. My health is halfway down, my torso a gaping wound that attempts to reconstruct itself, but a part of me, the part that is connected to the System, buzzes.

It's angry, upset over the breaking of its rules. I almost swear I sense a touch of frustration in the connection, but I can't focus on it. Just my impending doom, as Sefan raises his hand to strike me down.

Time slows as I taste iron, as stars resound and his screech of victory pierces my eardrums. I watch talons, glowing yellow and red with shafts of energy, rise and fall, both oh-so-fast and glacially slow at the same time. I feel my hand, bereft of my sword, rise up to block it. I know it's wasted effort.

Time slows, and for a few infinite seconds, I have time to think.

Energy.

Force.

Affinity.

Lightning bursts from my raised hand, channeled through it. Electrons are excited, released from their bonds, resistances lowered. The world changes and brightens as my attack strikes Sefan and arcs through his body, grounding in the floor, in the mezzanine roof, in Wex.

I tap into my Elemental Affinity, the connection strong and powerful and not at all gifted by the System. There is no block on it, for it's not something offered to me by the System but via my connection to Ali at first, then by time and training.

Sefan staggers back, surprised. As is Wex. The attack doesn't kill. It barely even damages. But it gives me an opening, and with that and with the aid of the System, I push against the block they've set up. The door appears, open, against the wall I lean on. Behind me.

I fall through it, still unleashing uncontrolled energy. When Sefan and Wex move to follow, I take away their grip, the friction between them and the floor. It bothers them for a second as they fail to find purchase on the floor, the ceiling. They slip, fall, and reassert their own control of reality through the System.

Then I'm through, the door slamming shut as I let their block reassert itself.

I tumble to the ground in the same alleyway, bleeding, bruised, broken. Blood pools around my torso, ropes of torn intestine falling out, shredded clothing by my side. I have multiple broken bones, a shattered collarbone.

I'm hurt and in pain. But I'm alive.

I stagger to my feet, feeling my Skills reassert themselves. As Mikito rushes to aid me, I grin predatorily at the empty spot.

"Inevitable, my ass."

***

My moment of arrogant challenge dissipates as fast as the blood escaping from wounds. I pull myself together, using healing potions to aid the System that struggles to heal me. I drop a bunch of mines, shield barriers, and other friendly greetings in front of the door as I stagger toward Mikito. She's stopped, a deep frown on her face as she deals with the Administrative injunction to enter the alleyway.

"Sloppy code…" I mutter, watching as Mikito grows more and more frustrated. She struggles forward, pushing against the enchantment even through the lack of notifications. "Don't. I'm coming."

She jerks a nod, relief evident on her face. Rather than worry about the state I'm in, she conjures a beam rifle and points it behind me in support while I stumble to her. Injuries that should cripple me seem to be healing faster than normal. I could poke at it but getting away is more important.

Yet, nothing happens. Not when I get to Mikito. Not when we retreat, while I plaster myself with healing spells and wrap a cloak around my torn clothing. Not even when we get on a nearby private aircar to be chauffeured away.

Long, tense minutes pass as we evade pursuit. We change cars and transportation methods, even going so far as to pay for a short-range teleport out of the city.

Once we're away from civilization—or the closest Irvina equivalent—we conduct short-range hops. I push past the Dimension Locks on the planet, overriding it with my System Edit Skill.

We run and keep running until we're in the middle of an ocean, floating in the middle of the air. Alone, with the ability to see potential problems coming from every angle. Paranoia wanes, and I find my hands trembling uncontrollably while the sour taste of acid floats in the back of my mouth.

"What happened?" Mikito says, eyeing me with caution.

"Trap." When she grunts, I continue. "A pair of Administrators were within." I shudder, remembering their visages, the power they wielded. "They had to be high Heroics. Maybe Legendaries."

"How are you alive?" Mikito asks.

I don't answer the insulting question, not immediately. I call forth Ali, who pops into being, arms crossed. He spins around, taking in the world, then relaxes. Only to tense again when he sees my face. I'm clean now, all the blood gone, but the shredded remnants of my clothing are still on me.

"What the hell happened?" Ali says.

"Trap," Mikito replies.

"Duh! But why's boy-o looking like he's been told he's got a kid? And what are all these notifi—" Ali shuts up as his eyes glaze over, data streaming before him. He reads and ignores us, catching up in a more direct manner.

"They didn't have access to Skills. None of us did." I touch my side where I can still feel the sensations of my body being torn apart. "And they weren't taking it seriously. Didn't think I could do anything."

Mikito purses her lips. "Learn anything useful?"

"A lot. But most importantly…" I draw a deep breath and let it out. "They've made up their minds. I don't think they're going to hold off hunting for us. Not anymore."

Mikito's eyes widen and I nod. She shivers, but I smile. A hand is raised and a book recalled. I weigh it in my hands, feeling the power within as I let the book fall open. A Skill, harnessed within, waits to be unleashed. And I let it.

The book rushes into my mind, seeking information, knowledge. I offer it what I can, everything I just learned about Skills, Administrators and Administrative Centers. How the System works, how its encoded.

With a snap, the book closes. I hold it for a second more, Mikito side-eyeing me and the leather-bound, parchment-based weapon of mass destruction and knowledge. Then I open my hand, letting the book free. Light swallows the book as it shrinks, twisting in on itself before it disappears.

Returned.

"John?" Mikito asks quietly, and I smile grimly.

"Time to pull out all the guns." I draw a deep breath. "Tell Katherine, Rob. They're not going to stop pushing Earth, no matter what we do. Best to be ready."

She nods jerkily, and the wind picks up over the open ocean, splashing us with water. As dark storm clouds roll in, we get to work.

If chaos, if death and destruction are all they're searching for, then we'll give it to them. In spades.

274

***

The Questors get moving. Corrupt Questors or orthodox, this information gets disseminated. Not the actual information about my Class—not yet. But that there might be more to the System, to the Quest? Definitely. The new information, hints and real data are thrown into void space to chum the waters.

Long dormant conversations about the kind of world we live in, the nature of the System and our reality rise once more. News articles appear, reporters and investigative journalists having long-held questions answered. Reports about the movements of the Council, the things they've done in the past—and are doing now—are published all across the galaxy.

Secrets are revealed. From the residence of Legendaries who value their privacy to share holdings in private companies, forcing runs on shares and the sudden questioning of certain contracts. Other companies and guilds, who have long alluded to powerful backers, are revealed as frauds, their share prices dropping. Guilds are destroyed, headquarters gutted.

Civil order becomes discivil. Races whose worlds were stolen, their lands taken, question the validity of the actions taken against them, their place in society. The line between what the System—an uncaring, unfeeling, remote program—and the Galactic Council—supposedly a body to serve all sapients—is questioned once more.

Libraries of hidden knowledge, of Classes and Titles that the Questors have accumulated suddenly appear in public forums. Secret Skills, used to control and hamper competitors, other individuals, other groups, become known.

Assassins and bounty hunters, searching for their targets, for weaknesses to exploit, find that once closely held information is now freely available. Vengeance seekers looking for those to blame, looking for a path forward find their ways illuminated.

The Questors make their move, and the galaxy is thrown into chaos. Because while the Questors might not be able to wield a sword, the weapon they hold—the trove of knowledge they have access to—is as dangerous, if not more, to the society they live within. They but lacked the will to use it. Now, they act. A truth dangled before them, a hint whispering through the halls.

That there are not one but two individuals who have reached ninety percent in the Quest. That the Quest is possible to complete, perhaps. That information, that final step, if asked for carefully, if desired, might be available. For those who dare.

Questors act, and the Head Librarians meet. And what they might make of my little book, I know not. Because I've got my own problems.

***

They find us a day later. Mikito, Ali, and me. The attack tears the sky apart, boiling water, cooking the jelly-like monster we've been attempting to reel in and creating gale force winds that toss us aside. Servos whine in the Hod, my power armor struggling to keep me aloft. Engines shriek and scream as I stabilize myself, as the sky lights up again.

Blink Step takes me out of the way while Mikito tanks another blast, her conjured horse riding out of the beam of light with her on it. Ghostly armor forms as she rides through the stabbing beams of light, joining me as we run. Ali reforms beside me, attaching himself to the Hod as he floats on his back, staring at the sky. As we keep running, he bends light itself, making the next strike miss us by miles.

"Where is he?" I snarl, searching my minimap for our attacker and finding nothing.

"Out of sight. This is a Heroic artillery Skill," Ali says. "Untargeted—sort of—but wide ranging. Keep running, we'll get out of range soon enough."

I cast Soul Shield on myself and Mikito before I reach out to my doppelgangers, hoping they're doing okay. I could call another now, but I get the feeling I'm going to need all my Mana. Anyway, their job hasn't changed. Keep trying to get us more seats, and failing that, try not to get killed and waste my Mana.

The air heats up around us, waterspouts attempting to form from the overheated air and failing as even more beams crash down. Occasionally, I see the edges of the holes that the attacks create, deep abysses of boiled water and injured aquatic creatures before the ocean rushes back in.

"Underwater?" I send to Mikito over party chat.

Rather than answer me, she dives. Maybe it'll help, maybe it won't, but we don't have a lot of options, so we go down. Deep into the water, feeling the liquid press upon us, slowing us as we kick forward.

Until I reach outward with my affinity and take away the friction. We speed up, faster than ever before, angling deeper and away. The beams continue to attack us, but they're less coordinated, the water and Ali bending them, the lack of direct sight disallowing direct adjustments. It's easy to tell when Artillery boy switches methods to watch us, since more of the attacks land.

Damaging or not, the Hod and my Soul Shield hold up, aided by the dispersed level of the attacks. We run, and we keep running, health and Mana see-sawing as the artillery attacks keep landing.

As we escape the edge of the Skill, the next attack comes. The Sea Serpent rises from the depth, swallowing Mikito on her horse entirely, rows of teeth chomping down and masticating the woman and her ride. Dark green-blue scales swirl, its swimming form smacking me in the side and sending me away as I catch sight of its Status.

Ancient Sea Serpent (Level 283)

HP: 28155/28387*

MP: 1253/1253*

Conditions: Controlled, Heroic Passive Pet Buffs (Partial)—increased Mana regeneration, Health regeneration, damage resistance and damage penetration. Water Mana Damage.

"Mikito!" I throw a couple of Blade Strikes, holding off on my other Skills, uncertain of where exactly the Samurai is. I know she's alive—her health still stands. But my Skills would damage her too if I miss, and the kilometer-long body obscures her location. "I hate water!"

It was the right option to go down, to fight where we believed they'd have fewer options, fewer civilians to harm. But less is not nothing…

The Sea Serpent turns toward me, mouth opening. I expect it to swim toward me, and it does. But deep within its mouth, a glow forms, an attack beginning.

A hand shifts and I toss out grenades. Absolute-zero cold grenades and mines trigger as they float away, forming shards of ice between us. The mini-glacier is created within seconds, even as I boost back and aside.

The Serpent's attacks tear away my protection, tossing me around as it shatters the Hod's security shield and strains my own. I snarl, relayering Soul Shield, but I'm surprised as the blast continues to veer away. The Serpent struggles, twisting and curling in paroxysms of pain.

Then from its belly, a third of the way down, a shining light. A curved, illuminated blade pokes out, blood flowing into the edge of the weapon as it tears a way out for its wielder. Samurai and horse exit before turning around and driving downward. Hitoshi's blade end plunges into the body, unzipping the Serpent.

Before I can exult, the artillery beams from before reappear. I'm tossed aside as the waters boil.

"Time to go!" I shout as I regain control.

Mikito pulls away, the Serpent left to fall to the ground, dying or dead.

And we're running.

Running and wondering when the big boys will arrive.

***

One day. They take an entire day to harass and attack us. It's not just the Heroic artillery attacker and the Beast King in play but a trio of Master Class mages who lob attacks at us, well outside of our range. Using ritual spells, Skills, and beast pests to keep Mikito and I running, they never get close enough that I can hurt them. We cross the ocean, flying, fighting, and dodging, transiting between air and water from moment to moment.

We get a short break when I contact the Questors, who manage to pull the Heroic artillery attacker away by dropping a bomb on his location. It won't do much to the actual Heroic himself, but it does destroy his connection to the satellites above Mikito and me. A series of sabotages sent the remainder satellites spinning away at the same time, repositioned or destroyed.

And while he went chasing off after the Corrupt Questors and System Watchers who are busy playing hide and seek, their respective Skills and enchantments making them perfect to play saboteurs, the rest of the Irvina military takes over the job.

We get swarmed a couple of times by Galactic military personnel, the equivalent of planetary security. They don't last long, not when I can throw Judgment of All at the group. I was tempted to use my System Edit to kill the Heroic artillery and Beast King, but I held off, concern about potential feedback affects, about who they have waiting in the wings, holding back my ire.

Twice, the Council's army try swarming us. Twice, I rack up kills without our enemies doing much to us.

After that, it's summoned monsters, drones, and long-range attacks over the horizon. We're harassed and attacked constantly, the damage accumulating to the point that I give up on the Hod, storing it away so that it can regenerate while I tank the damage.

Mikito suffers the worst from it, and I add Two for One at opportune moments to share her pain. Luckily, her Ghost Armor and higher mobility keeps her from taking the brunt of the attacks. But it doesn't stop all of it, and she lacks the sheer number of resistances I have. She gets thrown around a lot, and toward the latter half of the day, we split up more since their main target is me. It gives her a break, even if it makes her grumpy.

But unlike the movies, she's not stubbornly opinionated, willing to risk her life for no good reason but pride. She's practical enough to understand that she can't do any protecting if she's dead.

One day, and by the time they finally decide to act, we've landed on one of the semi-abandoned islands that dot the ocean. The entire place was initially swarming with monsters, but the constant bombardment while we ran around has thinned the herd, even as more continue to emerge from the overflowing dungeon.

"Why the hell would they let a dungeon break happen?" I snarl, feeling the pulse, the open wound of Mana that is the dungeon and its overflowing monsters like a needle in my System senses.

"Level management, if I had to guess. Let it break, let the monsters kill and Level up outside, then when the place is packed, let a Heroic or some senior Master Classers go to town and farm the XP." Ali looks harried, exhausted like Mikito and me. He's reverted to his normal form rather than the floating crystal he was, but he's hazy, broken at the edges. It's one of the ways I know he's struggling. As a creature of energy and concept, what he looks like is more a matter of choice and will than physical truth.

As Mikito rides up to me, blood dripping off the edge of her naginata and the edges of her translucent armor, I look around. It's silent for the first time in a while, though in the corner of my vision, I see a pair of dots moving toward us unhurriedly.

The vivid colors of the planet's vegetation are marred, crisped by flames and overwrought energy, stained with dark purple and red blood. Corpses of monsters that attempted to attack us or were caught in the crossfire litter the ground, lustrous scaled skin and peacock feathers crisped. Once upon a time, I'd have picked up the high-Level waste, used every inch of their hides to earn a few Credits.

Now, I just wonder if they'd work as cover.

"Decided to stop running?" Kasva says. The Champion is bedecked in his gold-edged plate armor that sparkles in the sunlight, pink skin and small tusks perfectly burnished. He looks as if he just walked off a magazine shoot, his hair billowing in the wind.

"Decided to come out to play at last?" I reply, conjuring my swords. They form around me, hanging in mid-air, and I smile grimly. Level 38 to my own Level 14—quite a big difference. Especially since Kasva's got a bunch of additional Class Skills.

Beside him, a short whiplike creature slithers forward on his tail. He hisses and shifts, staring at Mikito. A crystal diadem floats above his earless head, yellow scales glinting in reflected light. Ali provides his Status, making me wince a little.

Buidoi Samaaoi, Winner of the 219th Koopash Tournament, Banned of the Casinos, Marked Gambler, Marked from Birth, Mind Flayer, Outcast, Slayer of Goblins, Movana, Truinnar, Hakarta, Erethran, Grimsar, … (Psychic Master Level 42) (M)

HP: 2140/2140

MP: 4230/4230

Conditions: Psychic Storm, the Waves of the Soul, Mana Fount, Empathic Senses, Mind to Body

"I was held back," Kasva says. He looks as unhappy as I am as he walks forward and plants his feet before me. His cloak catches the wind, fluttering behind him. I spot a half dozen small drones, barely larger than a fly, floating before him. Recording him. "By those who feel you are worthy of being taken seriously."

"Bomb me to bits first then." I shake my head. "But then you take the time to let my Health and Mana regenerate."

"Killing you was never the expectation. Though it would have been convenient," Kasva says. "Your companion perhaps. But even that was not within the range of forecast outcomes. Wearing you down, mentally, was."

"Some people might point out that lowering my intelligence might be the opposite of good," I say, idly twirling my sword. "I'm more an instinctual fighter."

"Some might. Few who have truly studied you, Redeemer." Kasva's eyes narrow as he regards me. "You might fight instinctually, but you win your fights with your mind." He pauses, then adds, "And with unexpected help at times."

I grin.

"Those Questors. What did you tell them?" Kasva says.

Before I can answer, pressure pushes at my mind like a building headache. It's annoying, and there's an understanding that if I push, I could make it disappear. I almost do, before I pause and consider the pain, the pressure. I test it with my System sense, feel the edges of the attack with my System Edit Skill.

And watch as a flood of notifications arrive.

Mental Intrusion Detected
Skill: Secrets of the Mind and Soul in use.
Modified Skill Detected
System Edit (Level 2) Used to Edit Skill.
Would you like to see edits?

A mental assent is all I need before details on the Edited Skill arrive in a tangle of Mana.

Mental Resistances Lowered

Mental Manipulation Detection Opportunities Lowered

System Resistances Altered

Intelligence Attribute—Compromised

Each of those are summaries, high level headlines for what is a much more complex bundle of information. I absorb it all within fractions of a second as the Mana threads flow within me. Armed with new knowledge, I push back, slamming shut the mental intrusion.

Mental Influence Resisted

"Nice try," I say while Buidoi cocks his head.

I wonder how much Kasva knows, how much he suspects. He is the Champion, but in the conversation, there were hints. Hints that the Council and the Administrators are not the same. That there might be another council, another group behind them.

"Will you answer the question?" Kasva says. "You could save a lot of lives. Already we are forced to undertake drastic actions. The terrorist attack on the military base containing Guard DeeArz was highly inflammatory."

"Who?"

"The individual striking at you from above." Kasva gestures above and I nod. Artillery boy. "Many were killed in aiding you. Men, women, slugs. Ordinary guards who were just doing their jobs. Killed by the bomb that did nothing to injure Guard DeeArz himself."

I make a little face at that. I'm not thrilled to hear of the deaths.

As if sensing my hesitation, Kasva continues. "If you provide us details, information about your friends, we can end the deaths early. Lower the body count, the numbers that must die."

"No offer of mercy for myself?" I tilt my head toward Mikito, who is silent, watching the pair on her horse. "Or my companions."

"Too late for you or your companions. But not for the civilians, for the innocent Questors you have dragged down with you." Kasva gestures again, his movements expansive. I note the little cameras moving. "No need to drag others down."

I find myself staring at Kasva and Buidoi for a long moment. It's a tempting offer, one geared to tug at my heartstrings, at the remnants of my conscience. My eyes narrow in thought, and perhaps I'd have continued talking.

As always, I'm saved by my friends. By those who have aided me.

"Six assault teams are surrounding you, cutting off all escape. He's just buying time!" The voice is familiar, but one I'd forgotten mostly. It's Vrasceids, the Middle Samurai's voice crackling over my helmet's communicator. He says something else, but it comes across garbled as the Council shuts down his hack. But the map download he sends expands my minimap.

It shows the truth of the attackers coming for us. And suddenly, that moment of peace ends as the silence becomes edged with dread and the upcoming threat.

"Ah… too bad." Kasva smirks and gestures for the drones to move aside. The next motion he makes is to explode forward, legs fountaining dirt behind him as he charges us.

***

He's fast. Faster than I realized, watching the recordings. I get the feeling he was holding back for this reason. He bats aside two of my floating swords, the one I wield, and my blocking arm, and hits me in the chest with his fist. No weapon, just a fist.

Cold, penetrating cold, tears away my breath and locks my muscles from the attack. It digs deep into my chest even as I fly backward, the attack bypassing my Soul Shield, Hod's armor, and my resistances. He doesn't stop, launching a second, third, and fourth strike.

I manage to block two of the others, take a glancing blow on the fourth. The cold radiates from the top of my shoulder from the fourth strike, slowing me down further. I trigger Penetration's Evolved form, hitting back as hard as I can to make the Skill shield work. Somehow, his attacks punch right through my Soul Shield without destroying it entirely, though I can sense its integrity has dropped.

"*What the hell is going on?*" I get the thought off even as I do my best to deploy the rest of my Skills.

Aura of Chivalry turns on, its effects slowing my opponent by fractions of a millisecond. But it costs me nothing, so I let it run. Vanguard of the Apocalypse gives me speed and strength, boosting me, as does the Haste spell I've already laced myself with. Vanguard drains my Stamina, which will take a beating under the stress of fighting. For more speed, I use Unstoppable Force as well, boosting my damage output and attributes even further.

Domain engages after that. It takes a while to fully trigger as the System extends who and what I am over the space I'm in. The Champion slows down noticeably when Domain does kick in, and my Penetration Shield glows and firms up, shards of ice and frost noticeable along its shell. The damage per second effect hammers him and the few monsters we pass, flames erupting from trees and plants while reinforcing my Penetration Shield.

The sky spins and blurs around me as we battle. I keep blocking, conjuring and dispersing my swords as I block his attacks, forcing him to dodge or take the cuts. Pink and purple vegetation burns, trees shatter, and we keep adding Skills.

Disengage Safeties triggers next, overriding the Hod's output regulators. It gives me greater strength, speed, reaction times. When I swing and attack, cutting at the Champion, he's forced back now, with all the accumulated boosts I have. I'm stronger, faster than him—briefly.

Then he triggers his own Skills. Passive effects that build upon his strength, that grow stronger the longer we fight, Skills that have limited durations. My advantage disappears. We're equal to one another for now, even as Kasva takes damage from my Domain.

Our fight takes us farther away from Mikito and the psychic. We move at such speed that hills are destroyed, trees and vegetation flattened. Everywhere we pass, monsters are hurt, injured, and killed. I attempt to guide the fight to the edges of the island, to where his people attempt to surround us, to deal damage to them as well. Kasva blocks my attempts, punching me down, throwing me aside and guiding the fight with contemptuous ease.

We're equal in attributes, but not in skill. Or Skills. He has decades of combat experience over me, training by the finest masters in the Galaxy, and an unimaginably large Credit pool to draw from. His strength builds with each moment, his attributes increasing the longer we fight. The gap between the two of us constantly increases.

Funnily enough, neither of us are bothering to Zone or Dimension Lock another. Even the planetary lock is of little use, bypassed on a short-range basis by myself and removed for the Champion. But neither of us is bothering to run.

I need to finish this fast before all the on-going Skill use drains my Mana and Stamina pools. With so many Skills turned on and with the use of my damage-eliciting Skills, my Mana Pool is draining at an alarming rate. I'm losing nearly three hundred Mana per minute just for my current Skill use, never mind Stamina drain or damage to myself.

Worse, he's wielding an affinity. One he has a Greater Affinity for. It's cold, or frost, or something along those lines. It's making me slower, freezing muscles and tendons, locking up my limbs and organs and forcing me to injure myself with each movement. Unstoppable Force bleeds the edge off his attacks a little, but not enough. Each time he hits, he's slipping past my Evolved Penetration Shielding and hurting me. Not much, but enough that his affinity takes hold as it slips past even the physical containment of the Hod.

Perhaps I could fight it back, use my own affinity on it. But I don't have time to experiment, not in the middle of the fight. Even as I block another attack, he's shoving his arm right through my blades, shedding blood and skin in an attempt to grab me.

I pull back, dropping my sword and snatching it as it reappears in my other hand, shifting angles so that he's forced to impale himself on it. Kasva does, the blade bending around his reinforced armor a little even as blood drips.

A surge of power shoots a Blade Strike out from the tip of the blade, firing from the point of the weapon into his open wound. It burns Kasva, crisping his flesh and muscle before tearing a new orifice in his body.

Then Kasva hits me, his hand wrapping around the edge of the Hod's armor. Grey metal groans and tears as he twists, throwing me through the air before I impact the edge of a hill. The angle is sufficient that I tear a deep furrow before skipping off into the sky, legs aching and numb. As I crest above the hill, Kasva is chasing me on foot, already at the top, ready to punch me again.

Abyssal Chains trigger, forming from around the hill and reaching upward. He flinches a little, thinking the black chains are meant for him. But they're too low-powered to slow him. Instead, I wrap myself in the chains, change the arc of my flight, and dodge him even as I conjure and layer the air between us with weapons.

Kasva turns, searching for me, scaled armor sparking as it batters aside my swords. Blade Strikes tear into his back as I angle myself over his body, and as I land and spin around, Beacon of the Angels strikes down on his charging form.

Another moment to focus as I trigger another Skill. I have him held, for a brief moment, as he hunkers down around the blast of Beacon of the Angels. It's enough time for more swords to form, for me to use Army of One.

I swing my hand down, the enhanced Intelligence and my control of the System making the once-elongated process of casting faster than ever. I admit, I'm surprised to find that true, but only in a very small corner of my mind.

Army of One hammers into the Champion. He blocks it on his arm, expending one of his enchanted items to form a spherical green shield of energy to tank the attack. It's insufficient, given the amount of damage I can do, especially with Penetration.

Bright cracks form, then the energy dome shatters. White light pierces his shield, catching him on the arms, mutilating skin and muscle. Bones the color of brick are revealed as my attack breaches his defenses.

Kasva lands in a heap farther away from me, body smoking, the air shrieking as overheated air forms around us. As he stands, I can literally see flesh and muscle forming around his flesh. Healbot nanites, Skills, and enchantments all work in tandem to keep him on his feet. But he's dazed, recovering.

Another time, I might have said something. Taunted him. Here, now, I just call upon my next Skill—Grand Cross. I spin the Skill, the formula together without thought, taking the brief moment to finish it.

A bright light, a column of energy. Small, no larger than the man I target. It crashes down, gravity and electromagnetic force and Mana. So much System Mana, focused on one small area.

It glows, growing brighter with each second. The flapping cloak, the emerald chest plate burn and melt beneath my attack. Kasva collapses onto his knees, forced down by the attack. The ground compresses in a circle around him, showing orange clay beneath. Light grows even brighter, cauterizing and crushing at the same moment.

So bright I can no longer see him.

Wind rushes outward, kicking at the Hod, threatening to knock me off my feet. The few remaining trees are knocked over as the kinetic energy of the attack disperses. The ground itself heaves and tosses, disturbing my balance.

And then, no more light. No more sound. The Skill ends.

When it's gone, it leaves a crater centered around the Champion, eight feet deep, orange clay edging the crater. The wind moans, but there are no screams, no howls of anger.

And Kasva, still standing, still alive, grins at me as he floats out of the crater, burnt and damaged but alive.

"That all?"

***

I drop the majority of my Mana-intensive Skills, letting my Mana regeneration pick back up. Using all my Mana-intensive Skills means I'm close to tapped out, having spent over half my pool on my last three attacks.

I need the Mana now, need to refill the tank. Potions are slammed into my body, hypodermic needles flooding my body with Stamina and Mana potions. The cold tries to slow down the regeneration, slow my healing. I fight it back, but my body is trembling involuntarily as muscles clench and release.

Kasva doesn't care as I ready myself. He stalks forward, his grin cracking wide. Metal, twisted and melted, regenerates around him, puddles of broken liquid flowing upward and connecting to the breastplate as it reforms. His cloak restitches itself before my eyes, flesh reforming and bones shifting back into the right position.

Above his head, his Status flashes, Mana and health climbing at an alarming rate. It's not regeneration, because this is at least ten times the rate should be increasing from what I recall from the last little bit of our fight. Worse, he still has a quarter of his life yet.

I toss out a few Blade Strikes, but instinctual recognition of the glow around him is proven true. The attacks deflect off an invisible shield that flashes to life briefly. My eyes narrow as I read the System data that flows to me, the library filling me in on the rest.

Second Chance (Level 1) (H)

Champions do not fall that easily. There's always another chance, another opportunity to keep going. How could a hero, a champion of the people, fall that easily, when the world believes in him? Second Chance makes that concept a universal truth.

Effect 1: Second Chance automatically activates when user has less than <1% of Health.

Effect 2: Skill User regains Health, Mana, and Stamina to maximum upon use of the Skill over the period of one (1) minute. All equipped equipment is restored to full durability. A portable second chance shield that grants invulnerability to damage is in effect during that restoration period. All Skills are reset.

Uses: 1

Recharge rate: Variable ($_championrepxhealthxManaregenxqualificationxlevelx…)

Annoying. Unlike the other second life Skill I've run into, this one regenerates the individual's lifeforce. And something in the way the System information is coming to me says that the Champion has dumped multiple points in this, giving him more than one use.

I shake my head, pushing aside the idle thought of what an Evolved Skill like this would be like. As it stands, I'm pretty sure whatever he's using to pierce my Shields is an evolved Skill, a damage multiplier effect or an evolved piercing attack or something. It combines to be a real cheat as he drives his Affinity into me.

Kasva strolls up, his body, his clothing, his weapons almost fully regenerated. He grins, cracking his knuckles, his neck. He even bounces a little on his feet as we wait for the shield to drop.

"Round two."

The words are barely out of his mouth when he shoots forward, right at me. I drop low, pushing down hard on my Elemental Affinity, letting him hit me as I crouch. The bubble of my Penetration Skill bulges, flexes even as

I adjust the angle of his strike and his momentum, the friction between himself and the world. I stabilize the ground beneath me, lock myself down with Immovable Object and heave.

He flies, arcing through the air, and even my head rings from the collision. I turn to track his flight, only to see him disappear from my sight.

Kasva reappears briefly to hit me as I twist around. I'm flying through the air, my Immovable Object Skill's threshold exceeded. The belated feel of impact on my back arrives with a burst of pain and cold. I tumble through mid-air, spotting Kasva grinning at me. Before he disappears again.

Impact.

Cold.

Pain.

I try to block, try to defend myself with my swords. But he's faster now, faster than ever. Another Skill, a passive that builds the longer he's in a fight. He's also using his equivalent of Blink Step, except his doesn't confer momentum. So he's teleporting, striking, and following up whenever I manage to reposition myself.

Even Blink Stepping myself—shoving past the weakened planetary Dimensional Lock around the island—is insufficient. I just damage myself porting through the sky before he is on me, smashing me around.

Fate's Thread breaks the moment I latch it onto him, shorn apart by another Skill.

Impact.

Cold.

Pain.

The only advantage I have is that he's taking less care around my weapons now, accumulating injuries. He's healing around them, but each portion of damage adds to my Penetration Skill Shield. It holds, for now, as the Champion hammers at me.

But I'm realizing he doesn't care about my shield. It's his affinity that is doing the real damage here. My body is slowing, and no matter what I do to churn my Mana, to push against it, I feel myself freezing over. Slowing down.

Which lets him hit me more.

Which freezes me further.

Which lets him hit me more.

A vicious circle of pain as I am blasted around the island. Even Immovable Object doesn't help, its parameters unable to stop the physical dislocation of myself or the ground I stand upon.

Trees tear, hills and cliff faces are destroyed. Sky and ground intermix in my view, nausea threatening to overtake my guts. He pummels me through the edge of a waterfall so hard that I collapse the cave behind it, crashing through the edges of an incipient dungeon, collapsing the mountain on the lair as I'm blasted out.

Blood dribbles from my chin and fills my mouth. Ribs grate, and I no longer tremble as my body stops fighting back against the encroaching cold affinity.

"*Ali!*" I scream for my friend, looking for help. But he's nowhere to be found, hasn't been anywhere since the start. I wonder what happened, a little, before I'm struck again.

My head throbs, blood leaking from my nose, my eyes. Vomit spills from my mouth. I struggle through the pain, searching for a way out. I reach for my Elemental Affinity, trying to excite my cells, to push against what he's using. Instead, I end up injuring myself as I tear apart my very own cells.

Blood fountains from my arm as I block another attack and bones tear free of my muscle and skin. I fall down on my side, still partly protected by my shield. He's still striking me with short, repeated jabs, hooks, and cut kicks.

Another blow and I bounce over to where one of the groups ringing us stands. My eyes widen when I notice they've got manacles, enchanted to capture and suppress my Mana regeneration. I push against the cold, triggering the start of Judgment for All. It starts slowly, even the Mana within me seeming to move slowly.

"No," Kasva says and slams his hand down on the remnants of my shield.

The core of cold pierces me, and something flickers into my vision.

Mana Spike—Skill Disruption Attempted
Skill Interrupted Successful—Judgment of All

The Mana I gathered disperses and Kasva grins. "Take his shield down. I'll make sure he doesn't use anything."

Another quick strike, and his affinity continues to burrow deeper into me.

I struggle.

I fail.

The cold takes me, darkness pulling at my consciousness.

And then, warmth.

Heat.

Flames everywhere. The cold affinity breaks, replaced by the heat, the warmth, the raging inferno of flame.

I scream, for it burns me. And the darkness that was approaching takes me.

Even as the world burns.

Chapter 18

I wake up, which is a surprise. I'm healed, which is less of a surprise, considering it's the System. But as I struggle to wakefulness, as my arms shift to take me up, I find myself free of restraints. Another surprise.

Eyes crack open and I stare at the smooth white ceiling of a vessel of some form. I hear the engine running quietly in the distance, the slight shudder that is suppressed to all but the most delicate of Perceptions.

The fur blanket covering me trembles, shivering with each motion, the heated warmth of the fur bringing back flashes of my dream of rolling around in the depths of a canyon, fighting, struggling against a swarm of furred creatures that bite, chew, and claw.

I push away the nightmare, the relived memory, and breathe deeply. I swing my feet off the bed, leaving the soft, almost sensuous comfort of the mattress. The blanket rolls itself back up, fur parting a little, and I frown at the enchanted stitching it shows off. Expensive. Decadent. And wasteful.

"What the hell is going on?" I wonder.

I admit, I'm hoping someone will answer me, but the room is empty. In features, the room is much the same as the blanket and bed. Over-the-top luxury but understated in form. Nanite-based furnishings that form with a thought, restrictive arrays all around to ensure privacy and increase Mana density within. Soft lighting that is perfectly suited for human normal levels of sight. There's even the faintest hint of vanilla, lavendar, and chocolate in the air, meant to calm.

"Awake finally?" Ali says, drifting out of the wall.

"What the hell happened to you?" I say, feeling a flash of irrational anger. Where was he? Where was Mikito when I was being beaten? Humiliated.

"Getting my ass handed to me," Ali replies. "The Psychic had a Spirit of his own. Trapped me almost as soon as the fight started. I couldn't get out."

I frown, not recalling the enemy Spirit. Then again, that doesn't mean much. Unlike me, who can make do with buying Skills and the like, Ali is constrained to some extent by the System. His strength is directly proportional to my true Level—so about one entire grade down. He's the equivalent of a Master Class Level 14 Linked Spirit, which means if the other Spirit was Linked, Ali would be at a major disadvantage.

Still...

"I guess you're not as good as you think," I say. Ali glowers while I wave at him. "Mikito?"

"She's fine. A little banged up and nursing the mother of all headaches, but she's good. Being linked to you means she's got more defenses than most against Psychics, but it wasn't an easy fight."

"What was?" I mutter rhetorically. I then ask the most important question. "Now, where the hell are we?"

I barely notice the wall open, falling apart as the nanites act upon the unspoken command of the one who enters. She's tall, beautiful, regal, and scary at the same time. Golden hair tumbling down behind her back, pointy ears that suit the angular, heart-shaped face, and piercing blue eyes that strike a chord deep in my soul.

"Perhaps I can answer that." The speaker's voice is low, throaty, sensual. The kind of voice some women get naturally and others via a pack-a-day habit.

My loins stir involuntarily as a flood of notifications roll by my eyes. Most are beaten down, but the charms she wields leave their mark upon my mind, my body, and my emotions. I find myself turning, disregarding my lack of proper clothing as I face her.

That I conjure—successfully—my sword into hand only elicits a small, mysterious smile from her. "Who are you?"

She arches an eyebrow and tilts her head upward. I flush, realizing what she means, and look up to stare at her Status.

And find my jaw dropping.

The Lady of Shadows and Lies, ???? (??? Level ???) (L)

HP: ???/???

MP: ???/???

Conditions: ~Emotional, Mental and Physical Skill Manipulators~ (Put some pants on, boy-o!), ???

"Thousand hells."

***

After she crooks a finger at me, I find myself following the swaying, green-dressed, form-fitting figure down the corridor. Out of portholes, I catch the occasional glimpse of surf and deep water, blinking creatures with way too many teeth and not enough points in Charisma. I watch it and her, all the while conjuring myself some clothing.

Because.

We don't walk long before I enter an oval dining room. I manage to make it three steps before my eyes land on the figure dominating the room. And I find myself sinking to my knees, my legs giving way beneath me. If the Lady of Shadows is regal and queenly, a dream of a goddess of beauty given life, the one who sits, lounging with his feet on the table, is her opposite.

But more so.

The pressure he exudes, the dominance of the room crushes me, like being forced to give a speech before millions of disdainful mortals. Like the first time I tried to ask Angela out on a date in tenth grade, as her friends cut me down with their eyes. Except this time, the eyes can truly cut, the contempt crushing my will and bones. My heart hitches, pausing between beats.

No notifications, no indications the effects are driven by the System. Even my new System-enhanced senses are quiet. This is not a Skill or an Aura. This is the man's sheer presence, the legacy of what he, who he is.

He's a stake driven into reality, a reminder of who I am, what I am. How little I truly matter.

My head bows, my eyes close, and I find myself biting my lower lip. Anger roiling and thrashing deep within me smolders, catching fire. Reminders of past failures compress around my sense of self, and it doesn't extinguish my ego but gives it fuel.

"This trick again," I growl the words out. Or try to. It comes out slurred, mangled. But it doesn't matter. I don't say it for them.

Just for me.

I push, shoving back against the pressure, against the metaphorical chains that attempt to bind me. Fingers clench into a fist that pounds the floor once, then again. Pain flares down broken knuckles, but it's pain I can use.

I use it to stand, to meet the man's eyes. Meet and realize they're reptilian in nature. Golden, with slitted pupils and a fire burning deep within. Meet and note he's smiling.

It's smiling.

So I smile back, though mine is more a snarl. I shove back as hard as I can and my heart speeds up, having restarted at some point. It beats fast, but it beats. My breathing evens out, even if it's deep. The pressure, that was at first too heavy to bear, becomes manageable. Like most tragedies, time and will make it bearable. If painful.

"The Dragon," I state, naming him.

My eyes travel to the side, blink as I spot another anomaly. Floating above a chair is a single twisted eye clad in a robe. The eye looks, feels familiar, bloated with fat and power. The library aids me, offering details.

"The Weaver." I incline my head toward the eye.

It blinks but offers no other indication.

"You might as well let her up too," the Lady cuts in. I follow the small gesture, the way she turns her body, and finally notice Mikito.

She's kneeling, one hand gripping Hitoshi, the other on her knee. She is grimacing in pain and determination as she struggles to stay upright. Something in her eyes, something in the way she holds herself makes me wonder if she is trying her hardest.

Or waiting for the opportunity to thrust that polearm through the oh-so-tantalizingly-close dragon.

The pressure releases like a pop and Mikito draws a deep, unhindered breath, as do I. I offer her a half-smile before regarding the trio, making one more quick sweep for others. None that I can see. Which means almost nothing among this company.

"So. You saved us," I say. "Why?"

"Not even a thank you?" the Dragon asks. Like the Lady, his Status is empty of any useful information.

"If you did it from the kindness of your hearts, without agenda or expectation of return, sure. Thank you." I let the silence drag out a little. "But that's not why you did it."

The Lady slides into a chair, leaning back in it ever so slightly. The chair reforms to make itself more comfortable and, conversely, also emphasize her figure. Not that she needs any help.

The Weaver blinks. Once.

"No, it's not," the Lady says. A slight movement and a drink appears, forming above the table and allowing her to snag it. The pale, amber drink within the dainty fluted glass with a handle reminds me of whisky or tea.

I stay silent while she sips her tea and the Dragon stares at me as I stand there, waiting. Mikito shifts slightly, putting herself directly behind the most obvious threat. The silence drags on until such time as the Lady conjures a wooden, tiered display of snacks reminiscent of a snooty high tea restaurant.

"Am I supposed to call you the Lady, the Weaver, and the Dragon?" I change tactics, striding over to the table and taking a seat. I ignore the Dragon's predatory gaze by dint of sheer willpower, letting the anger still smoldering within me be my shield.

"It will do as well as any moniker you might use," the Dragon rumbles.

"Shiny." I gesture and pull out snacks of my own, conjuring them from my own inventory. It's nowhere as smooth, the plates and containers making noise as they drop onto the metal table. I snatch up a chocolate cake, pulling it to me as I spear the entire thing with a fork.

Yes, the entire cake. It's been a long day.

Ali floats over my shoulder, making little motions with his hand to float one of the Lady's snacks over to him. Mikito stays standing, watching in silence.

Chocolate cake, carafe of coffee, and a chaser of Mana-imbued water. I eat, ignoring the trio while I wait for them to answer my question. I'm amused to see the Dragon taste-test everything I dropped, while the Lady keeps to her own food. The Weaver just watches, rarely blinking. I'm half-done with the cake before she speaks.

"Few would dare to act like you." The Lady gestures at me, and I flash her a tight-lipped grin. Mikito makes a wiping motion on her face and I find a napkin to clean up the mess around my lips. "Do you not fear what we might do?"

"To what? Me? Mikito?" I say. "Seems to me if you wanted to torture us, you'd have done it already. If you wanted me dead, you'd have waited a couple of seconds. Which means whatever you seek, it's not something that force will aid you in achieving. And if I had to guess, you have the same question we've all been trying to answer all this time."

"I care naught for your System Quest," the Dragon rumbles. Golden eyes sparkle with flame, and the fork in my hand trembles a little as he showcases his displeasure. "It is enough to exist. Seeking the why is a fool's errand."

I feel a minor flash of irritation—more because of his casual dismissal than because he doesn't care. I've known for a long time I'm on a fool's errand, that I'm tilting at windmills of my own making. But stopping has never been something I'm good at. "Foolish or not, you saved me. So you want something."

"What any good dragon wants." He grins wide, showing me all his teeth. I'm reminded that he's a predator as I note the pointed, sharp edge of the majority of them. "I desire power. And you Administrators, with your secrets and hidden agendas, are in the way of that."

My mind spins, putting together numbers. Nine Inner Council members. Here are three members of the Inner Council in their own secret club.

The two Administrators I met aren't part of the Inner Council numbers, which confirms there's another, hidden power set. But there's no way the Administrators would leave the Inner Council untouched. Which means they'd need at least four, if not more, members to outvote these three.

Six potential suspects.

"Emperor, Nang Mai, the Truinnar representative—their King..." It makes sense he'd be an Administrator. It'd give them power and it'd be an easy way to shape things. "Ares? Or his daughter."

The Dragon inclines his head a little, marking my guess.

"Four against your three. The Erethrans are out—they're barely holding on and I'd have been caught. The Movana? Maybe, but dangerous to use a faction," I say.

Memory from the library comes back, filling me in on details about the seat, the number of seat changes for the faction. Surprisingly stable, with the Movana mostly holding the seat. But occasionally it changes. I run the numbers, gauge the politics, and decide they're likely not controlled.

Not directly.

"Go on," the Lady of Shadows says softly. Her eyes lower as she regards me as if I'm an intriguing bug. Or a dancing bear.

I keep talking out loud. "Four against three. But there are more, hidden Administrators who can join the Council if they wish. They probably tilt it in their direction, when they want, through bribes. But that doesn't work, not all the time." I sweep my gaze over the three. "And I bet you don't always work together either. Too obvious. And probably too many conflicting agendas." I remember Prax, fixing my gaze on the Lady, and frown. "In fact... you vote for them too at times, don't you?"

She inclines her head.

I turn to the Dragon, somewhat certain of my conclusions. "You want me to distract, kill some of them, don't you? Maybe help adjust the seats, make some of them lose power. Give you an opportunity to gain further control."

"That is sufficiently correct for our purposes," the Dragon says. "Your survival and the aggravation of your existence keeps them distracted. If you are able to end them or create opportunities for such an attack..." His grin reappears, feral and predatory. "My investment will have paid out."

"But why act yourself, honored lord dragon?" Mikito says, her voice soft and demure.

He turns his head toward Mikito, head twisting all the way around like an owl's. He looks puzzled for a second. As if he'd forgotten she was even here.

Before he can speak, the Lady cuts in. "Because the *Lord Dragon* does not countenance the use of others. He feels it is demeaning to his honor to deal regularly with those beneath him. As for myself"—the Lady places a hand on her chest—"I am required to hide you and him."

That last makes sense. She's who we were the most worried about all the time. And her presence here explains why the Council hadn't found us too quickly, if she was working at cross-purposes the entire time. It does amuse me a little that the Dragon doesn't have minions, but looking at the lounging, confident man, I can see it.

"Honor is important." Mikito bobs her head in agreement.

I smile slightly as she butters up the Dragon while standing right behind him, ready to cut him apart with her polearm. Of course, I'm not sure it matters since he's already turned from her at this point. But it's useful to have at least one of us trying to be polite.

"So he wants Power. And you, the Quest?" I say to the Lady.

"Yes."

"Why?"

"I'm the *Lady of Shadows and Lies. Keeper of Secrets. Mistress of the Obscure,*" The Lady drawls, her voice filled with sarcasm as she names her various unofficial titles. Then she becomes serious. "But there is one secret I do not have. Do you know how irritating that is?"

I open my mouth and, deciding against a direct answer, stuff it with chocolate. While the chewy, chocolatey gooeyness melts in my mouth and the ship we're on cuts through the water silently, I consider my next questions.

To buy time, I swallow and look at the Weaver. "And you?"

Silence greets my question, which isn't surprising. It is a floating eyeball after all.

"*What do you think? Do we trust them?*" I send to Ali, who shifts, staring between the group.

"*Do we have a choice? Also, throne room.*"

I pick up the water, washing down my latest mouthful at Ali's warning about our silent conversations being not so hidden. I slide my tongue along my teeth, picking up crumbs as I turn from the trio. They don't seem particularly in a hurry to push this conversation along. But a part of me, the part that's still agitated by the damn Dragon and his power plays, with having my ass handed to me by Kasva, can't help but push things.

"Then let's stop playing footsie. What exactly do you want?" I say as I lay down my fork and fix them with a flat stare.

***

"You had to say that, didn't you?" Mikito says, hands on her hip as we watch the Lady's vessel submerge itself and motor away. We're standing on the shore of the beach off a peninsula a good thousand-plus kilometers from where we started.

A breeze kicks up as I contemplate her question and the last two hours. I draw a deep breath, smelling the salt in the breeze. I note the barest tinge of sulphur and rotten meat in it and wrinkle my nose at the smells, even as I answer my friend. "I doubt anything I said was going to change what they did."

"Probably not." Mikito shakes her head. "You do seem to attract hyper-focused individuals."

"You know, I wonder if the fact that we have actual Levels and Skills kind of removes the need to posture as much. At least, when you hit the Levels those guys have," I muse. "It's not as if they don't have a very clear understanding of how powerful they are."

"You mean planet-swallowing levels of strength?" Ali says. "And instead of giving him a planet to eat, you offered him chocolate?"

"Hey, he liked it. And I only gave him the name of the chocolatier."

"Which he's now bought."

"What!?!"

Ali gestures and a notification flashes up in front of me.

News Alert—Savoy & Sons, Her Majesty's Chocolatiers, have now been purchased and renamed Savoy & Sons, His Dragon's Chocolatiers.

"Thousand hells. He works fast."

"Best remember that." Ali taps his wrist. "And you should get moving too. That cloak she put on you won't last forever."

I nod, turning inland and beginning the hike. We head as fast as we can for the peak of the small mountain range ahead of us. Knowing where we're headed, Mikito takes point, safeguarding me while I consider our most recent encounter.

For all my glib conversation with the Legendaries, in the last two fights I was involved in, I had my ass handed to me. The very last fight, I was as good as dead if not for the Dragon's intervention. Sadly, while he had intervened, he'd left Kasva alive, citing security concerns with killing him.

Personally, I think he just likes to see me squirm.

While I might have help in beating the Administrators, if I meet them again, I do need to work out how to deal with Kasva. That Affinity of his was nasty, and figuring out what it was and how to beat it will top my list of things to do.

Fortunately, I'll have more than sufficient time to work that out. Katherine and Rob have, from what the Lady tells me, taken my suggestion and run with it. There's quite a bit of a ruckus growing right now, but even so, there's no guarantee anything we do will be enough for the vote. Estimates—and these are the Lady's estimates—put us too close to call. There are too many variables since a particularly annoyed planet could throw all of its backing into making the vote work.

But the advantage of the chaos we've caused is that many are now hesitant, concerned about being backstabbed. Or using their resources to lash out. It's delayed the vote again, giving us time.

For now, me staying hidden is for the best. The idea of a Galactic Bounty Hunter—Silver Class running around and lashing out against our enemies is useful. So long as I'm alive, I can spawn my doppelgangers to kill and wreak havoc.

With the Lady's help, I expect my doppelgangers will do even more damage than normal, potentially tipping the scales. And though Harry has been captured, imprisoned under the orders of the Council, his interrogation is currently on hold. A power play going on between the Administrators who wish to learn how much I've told him and the Lady, who insists on being in the questioning, as is her right as the Secret Keeper of the Council.

That her insistence on regulations is but a threadbare fig for her naked curiosity, it is a curiosity and interest that is well-known. And as such, unremarkable. In this way, my friend is safe.

For now.

In the meantime, while my doppelgangers are busy playing hardball and Katherine and Rob are trying to convince everyone else to keep to their promises, we're here. Holding up our end of the deal with the Legendaries.

Doing the one thing they cannot.

We've traded knowledge, information on the Administrators that we've met for information too. The Dragon was more than happy to gain confirmation of members of the shadow council. Together, the Lady and Weaver will use that information to track down more of the Administrators, figure out who is and isn't part of the shadow council. Confirm—or not—their pawns on the Inner Council. It's a good trade.

All things they can do that I can't. But out here, this place, this exploration of information, this is ours to do.

Our feet grind into the ground as we turn around the switchback, pushing past the hanging foliage on the deer—har, probably something a lot less innocuous than a deer—trail we follow and find ourselves before our goal. Amusingly enough, for all the alien architecture I've seen, for all the soaring skyscrapers, living trees, crystalline temples, this structure is all too familiar. A dome with a single, deep slit sits upon a cylindrical base. An observatory, meant for viewing the stars.

An innocuous-looking structure.

Which hides the Administrative Center we're about to break into.

Chapter 19

We stand on the small, flat outcropping, shattered granite sand beneath our feet as we stare at the observatory. To all external senses, it's abandoned, empty of sapient personnel. A light wind blows, catching at our clothing, bringing with it the taste of the sea.

We stare at our objective until Mikito shrugs and walks forward. She does so hesitantly, back tense, bracing for an attack that never comes. A few more steps and she turns around, frowning at me.

"What?" I say.

"No attack. None of…" She waves as if trying to explain the mental, emotional pressure the last Administrative Center had forced upon us.

I stride over, head cocked as if I'm listening for the attack. As she said, nothing. I turn around, sensing something unusual. Over my right shoulder, where I'm used to a floating presence, I find nothing.

"I'll just be back here, if you don't mind. Getting banished sucked," Ali is quick to say when I spot him, still a distance back and floating farther away with each passing second.

"Traitor!" I shake my hand at him before turning back to the looming observatory. Mikito has not waited for me, continuing to close on the silent structure. I hurry to catch up with her and turn my head as I pass her. "You know, I'm the Administrator here."

"Junior." Mikito speeds up, pushing ahead of me. "Also, bodyguard."

"Better resistances." I speed up again.

"Faster." She overtakes me once more.

"Soul Shield."

"Ghost armor."

In this manner, we race toward the observatory. We're sprinting in a silly attempt to outpace one another. But for all our joking, neither of us is really going all out, and we're keeping an eye out for problems.

Of which there are exactly none.

Standing before the closed door, a hand on the entrance plate, I glance at Mikito one last time. Upon her nod, I send the surge of Mana it waits for, opening the damn thing.

To find the inside empty too.

"Well, that's a little disappointing," Ali says, making the pair of us jump as he appears behind us.

***

We walk the empty halls, chatting quietly, heads turning from side to side as we manually search for problems. There are no sapients within, though there are numerous dumb machines and semi-sentient droids taking care of the place, jotting down notes, cleaning the mirrors, and repairing issues. There's even a single security droid that attempts to chase us out. The insides are busy, if empty of living creatures.

"Makes sense with their tech to automate everything," I say. "No point in being here when you can just get the readings sent over."

"And the overall Level is low enough that the security droid and the exterior walls keep things secure," Mikito says.

"Needing space and clear skies to run the observatory makes sense," Ali adds. "Along with the Mana-sensing equipment."

"But that doesn't explain why we can't find the Center." Once more, I look around the building as we keep climbing.

We make it to the top of the building, to where they house the telescope and other Mana-sensing equipment, only to find nothing. No sense, no indication of an Administrative Center.

"You sure there's one here?" Mikito finally voices the question we've all been asking.

"The Lady believes so," I say. It's not as if I have a better clue. The only time I found one was when they told me the exact coordinates.

"There's no… mind messing," Mikito says.

"I know."

I stomp around the perimeter, poking idly at the equipment and walls and triggering nothing. I end up back where Mikito is standing, watching me while Ali floats around, his notification windows beside him. Searching in his own way.

"But this is our best lead," I say.

"Then maybe you are looking at this the wrong way," she says.

Her words force a reluctant nod of acknowledgement from me. I draw a breath then another, slowly cycling out irritation and impatience before I tap into my Skill. Skill Edit blooms and I reach out with it, using the additional System Edit sense it gives me for… something.

The results come so fast, I could kick myself for not doing this earlier. The Administrative Center's entrance is like a blazing beacon in my mind, one that screams for attention. Half-cognizant of what I'm doing, I walk down the stairs, away from the main rooms, into a familiar office.

The door slides open, revealing a boring-ass manager's office. But it's not the desk that I see, nor the single, strangely shaped chair with its extra-long seat and sloped back. My attention is fixed on the empty exterior wall that should lead to the outdoors. I'm nearly there, nearly touching it when a hand drops on my shoulder.

"You're taking me with you this time, yes," Mikito says. The sentence might be phrased like a question, but it's clear she really isn't asking one.

"I don't think I can," I say. My head turns, facing Ali. "I don't think even he can come."

"Don't think or do you know?" Mikito says.

I consider the information pressing on my mind. Glyphs, runes, whatever you want to call them, each with further information encoded in each rune, their meanings manifold. Details about exceptions, regulations, methods of creating exceptions, security considerations, minimum thresholds, data and more data.

I try processing it consciously, fail, and give up, letting my subconscious mind take care of the information flowing within. It's the only way to deal with the System, only way to understand... everything.

"Know. Sorry." I tilt my head upward, considering. "But I think, yes. I should be able to augment and alter the security protocols. Keep you hidden, just like the Lady did."

"You sure?" Mikito says, frowning. "You know, I could go with her..."

"And be beholden to that witch further?" I shake my head. "We already owe her for Harry. And your club."

Mikito makes a face. "We don't know if she's lying."

"No, we don't. But do you think they'd leave even that stone unturned?"

Mikito shakes her head.

"Right. So we trust that she's protecting them as best she can. By making them less of a threat than they might be."

"I...." Mikito bites her lips, shaking her head. "Do you think they know what they're truly getting into?"

I hesitate, thinking of her question. Thinking of all those we've burnt, will burn. All those who've been sacrificed on the altar of my Quest. Who will be sacrificed. I see Lana's face, Roxley's dark skin, the pictures of Kyle's and Sarah's kids. I remember an old friend, a tired First Nation lady and a vibrant one, now dead.

Harry.

Richard.

Bolo.

Even Catrin, perhaps.

So many lives at risk or lost already. And for what?

For what?

"Boy-o?" Ali calls.

I shake my head, seeing Mikito's face, brows scrunched, lips tight with worry. I offer her a half-smile, then tell her the truth.

"I don't know. Probably not. But did any of us?" I say. "I don't know if there's anything that could ever make us truly prepared. But we've made choices, and those choices have brought us here. And there might be more prices to pay, more lives lost. But if we stop moving forward now, everything we've done will have been for nothing."

Mikito nods, then meets my eyes. She says the next words slowly. "Then you best get moving, baka."

With those compassionate words ringing in my ears, I touch the wall.

***

The inside of the Administrative Center is similar to the last one I was in. Same white décor, same large windows of notifications giving details about

the local System code and tickets. Same mezzanine. Good news though—
what's not the same is the lack of homicidal Senior Administrators.

Once I confirm my life isn't at risk, I turn my attention to the buzzing
notifications. I flip through them quickly, ignoring the welcome messages,
searching for new information. A surprise is the small experience
notifications I get when I find a pair of the tickets I was working on having
been completed. I get partial experience and credit for that.

I almost pull up the tickets to see what they've done to my code. To
see what kind of obtuse solution they entered for what would likely be a
simple solution. Then I smack myself mentally. For not trusting others and
for the fact that I'm not here to code.

At least, not immediately.

Instead, I dig through the notifications for more information. I'm still
puzzled about why the Senior Administrators didn't exit after me. Nor do I
think that just trying to kill me is all they could do if they were blocked from
exiting.

Unsurprisingly, I find my answer in my notifications.

*Senior Administrators ared Lebek'jjas and Wex have been penalized for violating
Administrative Center protocols.*

No information about what kind of penalties, but I'm assuming it
involved being unable to follow me. Potentially being put in a time-out. I can
only hope it's a long time-out. Still, that's one mystery solved. Not that it was
a big mystery, but I'll take the wins where I can find them. I haven't been
getting a lot of them recently.

Senior Administrator ared Lebek'jjas has input a demerit for Junior Administrator Lee and instituted a decrease in his security clearance.

Those Gremlin-shit eaters. Wait. Am I hanging out with Ali too much? I'm beginning to curse like him.

Security Clearance for Junior Administrator Lee is now at Level 5.

Root Administrator has reviewed security clearance decrease for Junior Administrator Lee.

Root Administrator has rescinded security clearance decrease.

Security Clearance for Junior Administrator Lee has been adjusted by Root Administrator to Level 1*.

The last three notifications scroll past without comment as I find myself too stunned to move. I stare at the last notification that slowly disappears, my jaw hanging open, my mouth and throat drier than the underside of a vacuum cleaner in the Sahara Desert.

Administrative Center maps have become available for Junior Administrator Lee. Please access Administrative Center consoles for further details.

Root Administrator.

There's a Root Administrator.

I find myself on the floor, shivering. Emotions, long pushed aside or subsumed under that most useful of cloaks—rage—erupt and resolve. My hands are shaking, and I find my eyes wet with unshed tears.

Because if there's a Root Administrator, and one that rules against the Senior Administrator, then that means there's someone out there who might be able to help us. Someone who, with their knowledge, might be able to answer my questions. Someone who can stand against the Council in its entirety. Stand against even my so-called allies.

It means there's hope.

Of salvation.

And an answer to the Quest.

As though the System reads my mind, my System Quest has another update waiting for me, one that appeared when I read the other notifications. A simple update, a small rollover of numbers.

System Quest Completion Rate: 90.1%

"Gods above and below…" I breathe the words, staggering to my feet as I prod at the notification. But there's no further data to be had, just a simple notification. No more useful than a plain piece of paper.

Just a series of numbers.

Which change everything.

"I knew it." My grin grows savage as I look around the Administrative Center, my smile widening. Gloating at my success. At the hope I can now grasp, which I thought lost. Lost, even though I dared not say so to Mikito. Or anyone else.

And then my face falls, for the library reminds me that my success, the knowledge I've extracted, is not unique. Other Questors have reached these heights. Others must have gotten this close. And to keep their secret, to protect their powers, the knowledge I've gleaned, the Administrators have enacted purges. Billions have perished to cover up this secret.

"How far will you go?" I repeat Mikito's question out loud.

And for once, I have no answer. For my resolution is shaken.

***

I walk upstairs in the echoing silence of the Administrative Center, ignoring the unanswered question I leave behind, headed for the mezzanine. There's nowhere else I've not seen, and rather importantly, I'm looking for information on the map. Tapping the details in the notification had not provided me further details, so I'm leaning toward the mezzanine having the answers.

The mezzanine, when I finally make it upstairs, is empty of everything but a gleaming silver console. I walk over to the console and frown, for it's empty of buttons or markings.

I prod it with a finger, only to watch notifications bloom before me. But my eyes are glazed over, for I'm busy focusing on the Mana stream, the System information being displayed to me via my Skill.

Information about the facility, about the people who have used it, about the settings for the facility surrounding the Administrative Center. A slight touch of power extends the zone of exclusion. Another ensures that Ali and Mikito are allowed to work within that zone. I set a timer on this, before letting it revert to its previous settings.

My friends' safety assured, I pull up further information. I find details on the zones in close proximity, information on monster Levels and aggression settings. Details about spawn rates, habitats, Mana flow to each of the species, unmarked Mana and System Mana inflow and outflow.

My lips twist in amusement as I make a few adjustments. The lure I deploy ensures Mikito will have something to do while I'm busy, the System-enforced shielding around the building giving her a safe place to rest when necessary.

Another focus of will, and I drop a note for her to read over Party Chat. It requires more effort to do so as I'm forced to bypass some of the safeguards in the Center, but being at the console, I'm finding I have more options. And one of them is a way to "spoof" my location to some extent. The manipulation wouldn't hide itself from other Administrators, but it does make things like explaining what I'm doing to mundanes easier.

More importantly, as I stare at the console, I'm brought to focus on another aspect of my time in the previous center. I'd done a ton of work, gained a bunch of Levels, yet when I came out, it seemed only a few hours had passed. Like the Shop, the Administrative Centers each have time dilation effects, but the level varies and is, in general, significantly more powerful than most Shop time dilation effects.

Of course, I immediately try to adjust it. More time to train, more time to think, would be an advantage to me. But I hit a hard wall in the code as the System refuses to budge that number. Not for a simple Level 3 Administrative Center.

If I want a higher time dilation, I need to find an Administrative Center with a higher Security Rating. Which brings me to the last notification waiting for me.

I touch it, and information blazes into me. I crumple to the floor as nerves burn from Mana flooding into me along with the information. It's as if the System is literally carving the information into my body with liquid fire.

Fingers clench and tremble, and I let out little whimpers as I spasm on the floor. I'm really beginning to hate being a System Administrator. Even if I've learnt to ignore the pain, the damage, it's not *fun*. As pain finally recedes, I touch the imprinted information tentatively. And realize why the damn process hurt so badly.

The System Galaxy blooms in my mind in its entirety. Not just the planets, but the space in between too. There are even Administrative Centers in the deep reaches of space, places where swarms of space wraiths and leviathans float, asteroid-laden phantom stalkers and electric stingrays float on solar winds.

The empty vastness of space is not so empty, not with creatures such as those. And other, smaller, almost impossible-to-notice things. Clouds of creatures, as fine as dust, who exist upon Mana itself. These clouds float in the vastness of space, churning through unaffiliated Mana and creating System Mana.

I knew all this. Even fought some of these creatures in my time in the Galaxy. Now, with the galaxy map forming in my mind, I see the galaxy as the System sees it, and with it, the spaces that we, as Administrators, must care for.

In this map, I have the location of every Administrative Center I may journey to. And there are so many, so many for those with security clearances of three or lower. A single thought will show me any single spot, any single world, with full directions and a map of where to go.

"Couldn't have just given me a damn paper map, could you?" I grumble, struggling to my feet.

I stare down my body, at the wet patch on the floor, and cast a Cleanse. Watching as blood and other unmentionables disappear. And I grin grimly.

For among all the information burned into me, there's a single dot that glows. That burns, calling to me. A dot, an anomalous security clearance and a notification.

Administrative Center 14-1-1 (Security Access Level 1*)

A single place, the only one that I can access that is higher ranked than three. The asterisk in my Security Clearance. Located in the deepest regions of the Forbidden Zone, in the center of the System galaxy. Where planets should be overrun, destroyed by the pressure of unaffiliated Mana.

A lure. A goal. An objective.

On a planet full of dragons.

***

Once I've regained my bearings, I explore the security console further. There are more functionalities in the console, but for the most part, its aspects hold little interest to me. It does give me a deeper understanding of the System, of how it controls the flow of Mana. And it reinforces my belief, my understanding that the entire System is nothing more than a sieve.

Unaspected Mana goes in, aspected Mana comes out. Living creatures, matter, it all acts as a sieve. But creatures, living creatures, are better sieves than most, while sapients are the best. And the higher the Level, the better.

Titles, Levels, Classes, all of it are just a method for the System to push sapients to advance, grow, and become stronger to handle more Mana. There's an aspect of sapient creatures—call it the soul, call it Mana saturation—that changes when people Level. When people push themselves. And in so doing, expand what they can hold.

It's this aspect that the System wants to expand upon. And so Titles, Levels, Skills, spells. All of it, available to give everyone as much opportunity as possible. Experience is just a way for the System to judge growth and force it. The entire system is the most laisez faire capitalist system in the galaxy.

More than that, it's also corrupted. For I can see the fingerprints of the Administrators all over it. Adjustments made by Senior and Junior Administrators to benefit one Class, one Skill, one person over another. Minor adjustments that pass the System's verification. Galactic Council edicts that twist the—relatively minor—levers the System offers them to their benefit.

It's not a good System. The more I dig into it, the more I notice the slipshodness, the haste with which it seems to have been implemented. There are errors, but the errors are covered by expenditures of Mana such that no one notices them in the moment. Until an Administrator or the System itself puts in a more permanent patch. Sometimes causing even more trouble further down the line.

It's not a fair System. But I don't think it cares to be fair. Or just. There's no overarching edict, no rules or conditions.

Yet for all the information I glean, for all my new understanding, even when muttered out loud, I gain no change in my System Quest. That Quest, that question lies unanswered.

What is the System?

I know what it is in terms of Mana, in terms of function. I can see the code. But I don't know the why. And the deeper secrets of what it is, what the System truly means. Or so the System judges.

Perhaps just as important, what is Mana? And why does the System go through so much effort to integrate it, control it? Why can it do what it does, change the very fabric of reality?

"And why does it keep increasing?" I say softly.

Because it's very, very clear, looking at the information provided to me here, that the Mana keeps increasing. Every second, every moment, the numbers climb. And it's been going on for thousands, hundreds of thousands of years. Eventually, at some point, like the heat death of the universe, Mana itself will fill the world and kill us all.

If there is an answer, it's not one that I can find here. Once more, my gaze drifts to the simple map notification.

Administrative Center 14-1-1 (Security Access Level 1*)

If there's an answer, it's there. An end to the road. Just a hop, skip, and jump away. Past the yellow brick road, at the end of the rainbow. Over the eastern sea where the immortals live.

All I have to do is get there…

"And be willing to sacrifice everyone else along the way."

Because that's what it would mean. I can see it now, the Administrators beginning their purge. Sending armies to destroy Earth. Bounty Hunters and assassins after the Questors. The Galactic Council's army, their guards searching down everyone connected to my quest.

"But I'd have my answer."

For why they have to die. For why a world had to be twisted. For all the death and destruction. Why, after all this time, I'm still standing. Still here, where so many others who should be alive are dead. Individuals more deserving, more virtuous.

An answer.

An ending.

I close my eyes, searching for my anger, my conviction. And finding it missing, banked. Anger has no answer for me here, rage no solution. Desperate action can only take you so far before it sputters to an end, leaving you standing empty and hollow. Gutted of dreams and hopes, lost in the blaze of energy and action, washed away in streams of weeping blood and unshed tears.

In the desert of my soul, I search for something to hold on to, some compass to give me an answer. Resolution or benediction.

Time passes, and in that hollow space, I find it. The simple truth of my own existence.

My eyes snap open. And I laugh softly at the simple answer I have found. Because there was never really a choice. Not and be who I am, what I have forged myself into after all these years.

"What is, is. And it's time to make that clear too."

I look up at the softly glowing, blank ceiling. I crane my head, searching for a sign of the Root Administrator that might be watching.

I find nothing, but still, I speak. "Fair warning given then. I'm coming for you and for my answers.

"And if I have to, I'll let your Council burn to get it."

Chapter 20

Of course, it's not that simple. Time dilation means I have time to kill. To learn and Level. Prepare and plan. I make full use of it. Because there's more to be done to ensure I'll be able to do what I need, to reach where I have to go.

First things first, I use the communication hack I have to coordinate with Mikito and those I need to work with. Katherine's initial list, of those who oppose us and those who might be swayed, becomes my guide as I make calls.

There aren't many, just a few here and there. People who have what I need, who might be open to gaining a lead over their opponents by betting right, by having some information provided to them earlier.

I ask them to do certain things, to open up gaps in security cordons, to provide aid. When we get down to the brass tacks, I tap into my Skills. Forced Link with System Edit and Shackles of Eternity to cross the gap between them and me, riding along the communication and control lines of the Administrative Center. It's a pain and I do it only a few times, but it's sufficient to lock down the help. They might be able to break my Skills, but there's so little time that it doesn't matter. I don't bet on any single person anyway.

All of that is ancillary, things that are done while I work on the truly important aspect of my plan—leveling my Junior Administrator Class. I spend hours Leveling via the ticketing board. I pick my tickets with more care now, finding ones that might have something to teach me. That are more than just simple patches. The ones that give the most experience.

I find tickets to help create programs to fix minor tickets, to build processes to sort and fix regular issues. I spend interminable hours building the programs, debugging its code, and spitting blood when I overdraw System Mana. Eventually, I release the program as a completed solution.

Even more hours are spent debugging the program as it runs into more unforeseen issues and interactions. I untangle the snarl of error codes and new tickets when my program runs into other automated solutions, recode priority signals, trim down my program in its scope, and save the hacked code for future use. I delete other programs and incorporate their functions into mine.

Hours, interminable hours, when I eat on the move, pacing, lounging in the air, then snapping to attention as a solution comes to me. Reworking strings of Mana, watching my hands tremble, bleed, and crisp as my vision doubles or triples while Mana ravages my body and code refuses to function as I wish.

Never-ending hours working base tickets to understand what I did wrong, what I needed to learn. Gaining experience, fixing problems, and finishing ticket after ticket.

Levels fly past me, as do days, and when I release the program, I receive another surge of experience. A surge of gratitude as it goes to work with minimal errors. Immediately, the program begins the process of cleaning up snarled processes, conflicting Skills, and more.

My Level as a Junior Administrator climbs again, overtaking my Level as a Grand Paladin. It jumps as I'm gifted experience for the final program, but not for the tickets it solves. Annoying, but understandable.

As I Level, additional Skill points arrive, only to be allocated just as quickly. There's a bare moment of anger at the loss, at the lack of options given. Then I shove it aside, for I know now which is the greater Skill.

When my body cannot take anymore, when even my will and drive is insufficient to push me further into the jaws of System Mana as it shreds my body and soul repeatedly, I sit and meditate. I find my center, and I contemplate the fight. I investigate the dregs of Kasva's Affinity, query my feelings and the System for what it logged. I pull at my own Affinity and pit it against my memory of the battle, searching for a solution.

Then I experiment on my own body.

I bleed. I tear. I burn. I scream and roll across the floor in pain. But I inch toward a solution, an understanding of a counter. In the near-timeless space of the Administrative Center, in the safety of Leveling, coding, and experimentation, I find what could be a solution.

And when I'm healed, when the Mana overflow is cleansed and my mind restored, I get back to coding. I throw myself back into the flood of Mana and swim, doing the best I can to make my way to the source, to an answer.

Endless days before the timer I set finally goes off. Weeks, maybe months within the unchanging world of the Administrative Center before Mikito contacts me, letting me know its time. The chaos we created in the outer world has died down and the vote is finally going to go through. No longer can I hide. No longer can we wait.

I clean myself up using Cleanse, setting the System to wash away the grime and the clues of my residence within the Center. I have the System help me with that, cleansing log and data sets. Then I change, dressing in my armor, my weapons.

As I leave, I glance at my Status Screen, grinning maniacally at what I see there. Because there have been a few changes, some of which I'm sure the System and the other Administrators would be less than impressed with.

Status Screen			
Name	John Lee	Class	Junior System Admin (Grand Paladin)
Race	Human (Male)	Level	16 (12)
Titles			
Monster's Bane, Redeemer of the Dead, Duelist, Explorer, Apprentice Questor, Galactic Silver Bounty Hunter, Corrupt Questor, (Living Repository), (Class Lock)			
Health	6300	Stamina	6300
Mana	6350	Mana Regeneration	479 (+5) / minute
Attributes			
Strength	448	Agility	521
Constitution	630	Perception	435
Intelligence	635	Willpower	574
Charisma	225	Luck	296
Class Skills			
Mana Imbue	5*	Blade Strike*	5
Thousand Steps	1	Altered Space	2
Two are One	1	The Body's Resolve	3
Greater Detection	1	A Thousand Blades*	4
Soul Shield*	8	Blink Step	2
Portal*	5	Army of One	4
Sanctum	2	Penetration	9c
Aura of Chivalry	1	Eyes of Insight	2
Beacon of the Angels	2	Eye of the Storm	1

Vanguard of the Apocalypse	2	Society's Web	1
Shackles of Eternity*	4	Immovable Object / Unstoppable Force*	1
Domain	1	Judgment of All	6
(Grand Cross)	(2)	(Extra Hands)	(3)
System Edit	4		

External Class Skills

Instantaneous Inventory	1	Frenzy	1
Cleave	2	Tech Link	2
Elemental Strike	1 (Ice)	Shrunken Footsteps	1
Analyze	2	Harden	2
Quantum Lock	3	Elastic Skin	3
Disengage Safeties	2	Temporary Forced Link	1
Hyperspace Nitro Boost	1	On the Edge	1
Fates Thread	2		

Combat Spells

Improved Minor Healing (IV)	Greater Regeneration (II)
Greater Healing (II)	Mana Drip (II)
Improved Mana Missile (IV)	Enhanced Lightning Strike (III)
Firestorm	Polar Zone
Freezing Blade	Improved Inferno Strike (II)
Elemental Walls (Fire, Ice, Earth, etc.)	Ice Blast
Icestorm	Improved Invisibility
Improved Mana Cage	Improved Flight
Haste	Enhanced Particle Ray
Variable Gravitic Sphere	Zone of Denial

But that's their problem.

***

To my surprise, I don't find Mikito waiting for me outside. Only Ali stands there, arms crossed, foot tapping on the floor, rotund belly pushing against his orange jumpsuit. I idly note that it seems to have shifted slightly, looking more like a onesie than a jumpsuit. Seeing my attention, Ali growls and wills it back to its normal configuration.

"Miss me?" I say, walking forward. That he stands at his full height, dwarfing me, makes me kind of amused.

"Who'd miss a Goblin-loving, toad-warming Mana-crystal waste like you?" Ali says. He waits for me to pass by before he floats, shrinking as he does so such that he finds his place at my shoulder once more.

"Perhaps a socially inept Spirit?" I say. "Did you get what I asked for done?"

"I contacted them. Still waiting to hear back from the Dragon Lord, but the other arrangements, well…" A flash of uncertainty crosses his bearded face. "You sure?"

"I am." Whatever doubts I have, I've let them die. It's the best solution I can find, even if it's one that no one will be happy with. Not even me.

We make our way out of the building and see the sky filled with puffy pink-shaded clouds for the first time in ages. I spot Mikito, standing at ease out there.

"The arrangements?" I ask.

"Completed," Mikito says. "If you want this to work though, you're going to need to start producing your Hands. We lost all of them days ago."

I nod, calling forth my Skill. Mana pulses through me, rippling outward to touch the space beside me. What pops out is a replica of myself. A few short words, and he's off to keep an eye on our next guests while I turn to Mikito.

"Thank you. Did you have fun out here?" I say, gesturing around.

In the distance, I see the mounds of flies, the shifting corpses of monsters that Mikito has killed. Small—and not so small—scavengers tear at the corpses, eating their fill. Thankfully, the System wipes the smell well before it reaches us.

"It was productive," she says.

I grin, eyeing her Status.

Mikito Sato, Spear of Humanity, Blood Warden, Junior Arena Champion of Irvina, Arena Champion—Orion IV, Xumis,...; *Time Slipped, True Bound Honor (Upper Samurai Level 42) (M)*
HP: 4818/4818*
MP: 3657/3657*
Conditions: Isoide, Jin, Rei, Meiyo, Ishiki, Ryoyo, Feudal Bond, Blitzed, Future Projections
Galactic Reputation: 84
Galactic Fame: 38,983

"So it seems." A pair of Levels might not seem much, but at the amount of XP she needs to Level, it's considerable.

"Oh, the second Level was when you walked out." Mikito's eyes glint with amusement. "I think there's a bug between the Bond and your dual Classes."

That would make sense. I could even check and fix it. But in this case, I'm just going to leave well enough alone. We need every advantage we can get, and her leeching experience from both of my Classes whenever I get experience works. I just have to hope no one fixes the issue.

I could take the ticket and mark it as being worked upon. But considering I'm persona non grata to the rest of the Administrators, that might make the issue even more obvious and highlight it for others. Decisions, decisions, decisions.

"John?" Mikito draws my attention back. "Are you sure about this?"

I meet her concerned gaze and consider what I told her. What she now knows and what I haven't mentioned. In the end, I can't help but nod.

"Yes. I have to do this," I say softy. "And we'll need all their help. Just... make sure they're ready to run."

My words are punctuated by the whine of an engine and the gusts of blowing wind as a plane, with giant rotating motors encased within oval shields, arrives. Four swirling propellers on each corner, on top of a sleek vehicle and jet engines at the back land the plane straight down, landing struts deploying just before they touch the ground. A door rolls open and a familiar trio waves to us from within the vehicle. Other unfamiliar faces peer from behind, all of them looking to spot their idol.

"Then it's best we get going," Mikito says, walking over and waving back to her fan club, closely followed by myself. My doppelganger is already in the vehicle, scanning for trouble, mask down to hide his features. "We've got a friend to rescue. And a vote to gatecrash."

***

They keep Harry in a secret prison, one off the books. They want to interrogate him, pull out information about where I am. And, probably, set it up as a lure for when I come to rescue him like the fool I am. Considering he's a Galactic Reporter, his capture is currently a closely held secret, one they don't want getting out. He has protections in his role that they're ignoring, for now.

Which is an advantage for us. Because the problem with secret bases is that you can only put so many people within and still keep it innocuous. Of course, teleportation pads and quick scramble units alleviate some of those issues, but it means on-site, the number of personnel—enemy combatants— are low.

Relatively speaking.

Then again, there's also the additional problem of Levels. A single Legendary could make our lives truly miserable, which is where having an inside man—or in this case, Dragon—helps.

We're two-thirds of the way to the prison, joining the air traffic that dominates the skies above Irvina, when we get the call.

"The meeting is called," the Lady says. It's a video call, though it is of little use since her background is shrouded in shadow, leaving only her breathtaking beauty to be seen. For a lady known for being the most secretive, she really does like to preen. "Our mutual friend will handle the Council. Now, about the information..."

"I set up a message drop. Don't worry, it won't ever not release. It comes through my specific skill set." I'm not exactly certain I want to speak about my special Class in public. There's not a lot of privacy in this ship. "It'll arrive after the vote. So long as you do your part."

"Very well. Everything you've asked for, so long as you complete your objectives, will be in play." The Lady shares a small smile with me. It's a cute smile, almost endearing, as if she's a little child with a secret that she cannot wait to share. "You know, such confrontations, they're rarely my thing."

I open my hands sideways. "It's always nice to change things up, isn't it?"

As she smiles in approval, I flick my hands and dismiss the communications channel. I turn to Mikito, eyeing the swarm of fan club members around her. It's a surprising number, but the three have been hard at work, pooling the locals—in terms of a solar system—into Irvina. Just over two and a half dozen individuals, most of them in the late Basic to mid-Advanced Class stages. No Master Classes though, not yet.

There are more fans, from what Mikito and Ali tell me. But being a new fan club, it's still building. Most of those who follow her, at the level of adoration given like these guys, are at the lowest Levels. Give her another decade or two and if she continues winning, the numbers and Levels might be quite different.

That being said, I turn to the group and grin. "All right, you guys. When we get there, leave the big boys to us."

A small gesture from Ali and a slew of notification windows appear for everyone. Among other things, the Lady has dropped off information about who exactly is on guard, as well as their backup plans and reinforcements. Using that information, we adjust our plans to remove some of those distractions, which is why we need my doppelgangers.

"Your job is dealing with the regular administrative and security personnel and intercepting any additional security that arrives. There are also at least two other prisoners. One of them, we want to free. If you can, get it out."

I think of the information about the first prisoner. Political rather than criminal, the picture Ali displays is of a bright bug-like creature who's another sapient from a nearby galaxy. He was reported disappeared by the powers-in-charge of his planet just over half a year ago. As a contender for planetary governorship, his disappearance meant that his opponent achieved reelection with minimal fuss.

Hopefully his release and escape will engender a level of gratitude that will help the fan club, as well as add to the chaos. Of course, I'm not betting on it, but it's a nice side benefit.

"And the second?" a voice calls from the back of the crowd.

"Kill him."

There is a susurration of whispered words at my blunt statement. But it's cut off when Agr'us gets to the personnel file of the second prisoner.

Her exclamation silences the craft. "That's the Flayer of F'fauheok."

"Impossible. I heard he was in the Rusanox sector." Another voice, among the crowd.

"No, he's dead," Ruvuds says, his tone doubtful.

"You're wrong. The Leontine Gris caught him, tore his arm off. But he escaped using the Skill Blast Off. After that, he had it regenerated—"

I listen to the hubbub, the conversations as they argue about one of the galaxy's most notorious mass killers. The Flayer was a homicidal maniac crossed with the Joker and a Friday night horror flick, all squished into one insane package. The fact that he gained strength not only from the atrocities he committed, but from the fame he gained, drove him to higher stages of violence.

It was kind of worrying, the way the Council had him locked away. I'm sure there are a load of reasons why. Whole conspiracy theories, ready to be born out of that single fact. If it was any other time, I might even try spinning some of them myself. I'm sure Harry will, when we free him. But for now, the more important aspect is…

"Oy! I said kill him, not become his fan club."

You would think I'd shot their dog, the way I spoke. They glare at me, though some are chagrined. It's amusing, the way they interact with me. Mikito, they adore and listen to without thought. Me, I'm either considered her Lord or her abuser, depending on who you ask.

At the glares, I'm tempted to continue insulting them, just to get a rise. To pick a fight I know I can. It's the part of me that isn't particularly nice, which I try not to indulge. Too much.

Before things can devolve further, Mikito elbows me in the side and I force an apologetic grin around the wince.

"Best make another Hand, boy-o," Ali reminds me as we dip out of the clouds nearby a new building.

My first Hand has already moved to stand by, readying himself to leave.

The first part of a plan is getting prepped right now. And as always, with any of my plans, it involves a healthy dose of violence.

***

Step one is dropping off the pair of doppelgangers. They know what I plan to do, mostly because I told the System—and Mikito—the breakout plan already. The doppelgangers know they're headed off to die—which, by the way, elicited a few nasty looks from them to me. I'm beginning to wonder about the moral implications of all this, even though I know they're not really real. Still, a part of me doesn't feel great about this.

But needs must, and right now, the gates of hell have been thrown open and the hungry ghosts are coming. Better to get moving and to stay out of the water rather than concern myself if this is perfect.

As my last Hand walks away, blending into the crowd around the rooftop parking spot, the plane takes off again and we jet over to the prison. We can't land too close, but there's a useful training center in a nearby skyscraper—one geared toward newbies. They had been more than happy to receive a last-minute group booking to learn the art of survival scavenging.

"Welcome to Mioga Dosa Training Center." The snake monster greeter slithers up to us, iridescent purple and green scales glistening as it hisses its greeting. Its lips widen as it arcs up, thin arms held open and wide. "If you'll come this way, we have the virtual training room—"

"Thanks... Chad." I blink as I read the Trainer's name. I feel a weird sense of vertigo at the name before pushing it aside. "But we've got other plans. Just let us park the ship here for the moment and we'll be out of your hair."

Chad blinks—vertical eyelids snapping shut and open—as it takes in the team streaming out. Clad in full combat gear, weapons out, they head to their assigned locations, streaming to elevators, stairs, and in a few cases, shooting locations.

"I'm sorry. Your booking doesn't include a terrorist incident," Chad says, drawing himself up. "If you don't vacate our premises, I will be forced to contact the authorities."

"As if you haven't tried," Ali says, floating up and wagging his fingers at Chad. "Good thing I blocked you. And your friends." He shakes his head. "We've deployed a communication router. Also, if you haven't realized it, take a good, close look at boy-o over here."

Chad stares at me then looks up, spotting my revealed Status. He rears back, mouth dropping open as he hisses, fangs dropping in surprise. His hands drop next as he readies himself to attack or defend.

Mikito appears next to Chad, moving so fast she's almost teleporting. She hits him with a series of short, quick jabs and elbow strikes that chain together, taking his health down and putting him in a stunned Status. Another series of blows and a Skill use and he drops, unable to do anything.

"I thought we were trying this without violence," I complain even as fan club members drag Chad's body aside.

"We did. You failed." Mikito points at the floor and the floors below. "Now come on, we're on a schedule."

Shaking my head, I follow Mikito as she leads the alpha strike team. It's kind of different, having her take charge, but this is her fan club and her plan. I just gave her the overall objectives and passed on information. The details of the execution are hers.

By the time we hit the skybridge that connects to our target—a series of condos set in the middle of the skyscraper opposite us—the first part of the plan has kicked off. We get to watch it all, since Ali has a news feed playing next to him, set to display for the team.

— a familiar figure, striding across the ballroom floor. A hand rises and clenches, and people going for him fall. Bodyguards scream and curl up, private security shields flare and crash as Judgment for All takes effect. The diplomat, one of the ones known to be against Earth and a prime instigator due to his ties with the Zarry Cartel, starts bleeding. Even as the alarms go off, emergency personnel punch through the cheap dimension lock that the dimension stabilizer the Hand carries emits. Weapons are drawn and fired, but the Hand isn't staying still, moving through the group with his swords, cutting and dicing.

Another screen, another video of destruction.

This time, it's the Beacon of the Angels striking the living tree that houses this target. Shields gleam and glimmer as they fight off the attack, even as the Hand continues to cast Beacons and strike with his sword. Automated defenses open fire upon the Hand, but the evolved Penetration Skill shield holds up easily, giving the Hand more than enough time to dish out damage.

More guards, more emergency personnel scramble. And fall right into his trap, as the Hand triggers Judgment for All, killing them and adding to his shield. He stops for a bit, just using his sword and striking the shield with it as he regenerates his own Mana, tossing out the occasional nanoswarm grenade to reduce the shield regeneration rate.

The Hands draw emergency security personnel with their brazen attacks. Sadly, they only manage to draw away one of the six teams that ring our target. The rest of the reinforcements come from other locations. Still, it's better than our expectations of none, though nowhere as good as what we hoped.

The interception teams slide into place around the buildings as we arrive at the skybridge joining the two buildings.

One of the fan club members, dressed like a cyberpunk-ninja with wires and glowing dots along her head and arms, finishes the hack of the security systems just in time, killing the forward alerts. That doesn't do much for the physical sentries who spot us and attempt to raise their friends.

The scouts who are part of the vanguard are already across the bridge, having either walked across innocuously or invisibly. They launch their backstabs as the guards scramble, even while those of us in the main group keep strolling forward. The scouts and guards enter into a short, bloody brawl. Made even shorter when the rest of the vanguard arrives and adds their burst attacks.

As for me? I'm stuck in the middle of the group, watching as the fan club sweeps ahead like a well-practiced special forces team. Even Ali's busier than I am, doing his best to block off System notifications and communication channels, aiding the comm team. Mikito, the three musketeers, and a number of other fan club members are all around me, blocking my way.

My fingers twitch. I'm eager to step in and do something. I feel the System notifications, the buzzing of System Mana flowing all around me. I could reach out, Edit the information and Skills, kill notifications and reduce Mana regeneration rates. I could help.

But I hold back, because this is not the time.

"Relax, we have this," Mikito murmurs. "And try to look a little more confident."

"I am relaxed," I bite out.

"Really?" Mikito looks downward, where I'm white-knuckling my sword. I make it disappear, feeling guilty, while explosions and screams echo toward us. "They really do have this."

"A bunch of Basic and Advance Classers?" I raise an eyebrow. "You know the guards are mostly Advanced Classers, right?"

"Yes. But we have numbers, surprise, and skill on our side," Vrasceids says, joining the conversation from where he walks beside me. "The only way to gain our Samurai Class was to reset ourselves. We are all, significantly, more experienced than our Levels would indicate."

Each step takes us deeper into the rising skyrise, its defenses broken. Smoking bodies, struggling figures are all around us, appearing and disappearing as we walk past them. The alpha team, my group, peels off at intervals, joining fights as necessary.

"Levels aren't the only gauge of strength," Mikito says sniffily. "As you should know."

"*Skill*, not Skill, eh?" It's true enough that she has kept up with me through all this by displaying more skill than Levels. Still, Levels are an absolute unit of strength that is hard to overcome. Almost impossible at the highest tiers.

"Also…" Mikito grins, shifting her stance slightly. Hitoshi appears in her hand even as her Haste Skill triggers and wraps itself over her body, shrouding her in a cloak of Mana. Then, Blitzed. She leaves behind a garbled message as she blinks away, leaving me alone. "Theyhaveme."

I watch her leave before I turn to the remnants of the alpha team who have been left behind to guard our retreat. It's only Vrasceids and the cyber-samurai now, the other pair of musketeers in charge of their own strike teams.

"You not going?" I ask.

"We have other orders," Vrasceids says, his pale-green-and-black gills flaring open and closed as he tastes the air.

My eyes narrow even as the continuing screams, the shouts, and the addition of a high-pitched whine as Hitoshi comes out to play echo through the building. Explosions, the telltale shattering of tiles as people lose control of their Strength, the smashing of walls and the pop-hiss of failed shields all tell a story of combat around us.

"Hells doors. You're babysitting me, aren't you?"

We pass through the entrance foyer, blasted and torn, and turn toward the fighting in a marked corridor. Upstairs, more fighting occurs, the battles more contained as the beta strike teams slide in from above to deal with the office and off-duty personnel who reside there.

Vrasceids's face is smooth, calm at my irritation. "I would not describe our duties like that."

"Maybe not, but that's what it is." I close my eyes and touch upon Society's Web. I follow the threads that reach out from me, watching the way certain threads hidden from normal sight appear under my System Edit Skill. Threads that I know lead to certain high-ranking members of the Galactic Council.

But one thread isn't shadowed. It shifts and strikes at another, a more personal thread. My Hand disappears, and I watch as the green-and-red thread that leads toward Kasva shifts, intent on dealing with the next Hand.

"We better get moving," I say, opening my eyes again. "We just lost one of my Hands."

Vrasceids's eyes flick up, noting something, then he nods. "Yes, Shogun. Lord Mikito has been informed."

I snort, but we both shut up and hurry forward. To join the fight or free the prisoners. Whichever comes first.

***

"Harry. You've looked better," I say, grinning at the reporter.

I cast a Cleanse to punctuate the point, wiping the dirt, blood, and snot from his body. The dark-skinned British reporter is gaunt, seeming to have lost thirty pounds in the two weeks we've been gone. He's clad in prison garb—yellow clothing with stripes of green and grey—meant to restrict his Mana regeneration and leave him in a low Mana state.

Harry Prince, the Unfiltered Eye, Galactic Investigative Reporter—Barium Level, the Unvarnished Truth, Heroic

Survivor, Friend of the Erethran Empire,... (Galactic Correspondent Level 19) (M)

HP: 174/780

MP: 21/2740

Conditions: Reporter's Luck, Nose for Trouble, Just a Bystander, Information Locus, Network News—Barium Grade, Mana Withdrawal (Severe)

"Let's get you changed, shall we?" I touch his arm, ignoring the protests from Vrasceids and Harry.

The man flinches away from me, and I try not to take it personally. But I keep a tight grip on Harry's arm as I access the prison garb's Status, bypassing the automated pain deployment, shutting down its alarm system, and deactivating the suit via my System Edit Skill.

"You shouldn't be doing that," Ali says disapprovingly. He can't see me using my System Edit Skill, it's locked from him, but he can sense the changes in my body.

Even as the Spirit speaks, Harry is breathing deeply as Mana floods back into him for the first time in a long while. His health climbs once more, as does his Mana regeneration.

"Am I... am I really free?" he says, his voice cracking.

"Yes."

I'm not even done speaking when Harry is peeling at the clothing, ripping it off his body and leaving furrows in his own skin. He hisses as he tears it off, portions of his skin coming free as embedded nanospikes tear open wounds, but he doesn't stop. Not even when he is bathed by healing spells that Vrasceids throws on him, forcing wounds to close just so that the reporter doesn't inadvertently kill himself.

It's only when he's down to his skivvies that Harry stops, holding the tattered remnants of the prison garb before him to ask hesitantly, "You didn't bring any clothing for me, did you?"

"Just grab it from your inventory," I say.

Harry winces, muttering. I only barely catch it. "They took it from me. Everything I ever stored."

My fists clench as I realize I didn't plan ahead for that. Thankfully, someone did. Vrasceids hands over an armored jumpsuit sized for the reporter. In short order, the rest of us exit the small cell to offer Harry some privacy as he gets dressed.

We step out in time for us to watch the political prisoner's swishing behind leave. And for Mikito to step out of another cell, holding the head of the Flayer. Behind her, one of her clan members stumbles out, clutching a missing third arm stump.

"Harry?" she asks, looking toward the cell. Her Blitz is gone, since most of the fighting is over, though she's still Hasted. She breaks into a wide smile as Harry walks out.

I turn just in time to see the reporter's jaw drop as he spots the head Mikito holds.

"Is that…?" Harry says, focused.

"Yes." She walks over and hands him the head, which he takes automatically. A moment later, she's put away Hitoshi to give Harry a hard hug. "Sorry."

"For what?" Harry says awkwardly as he juggles being hugged and holding a severed head. Luckily, Mikito doesn't care about being splashed with the blood. "And what am I supposed to do with this?"

"Whatever you want," I say. "But we should move. That's two."

My pronouncement robs Mikito of the momentary joy of reunion, as it does the fan club. They offer muttered assurances to Harry, and the minimap dots move in hurried but controlled haste. We all hustle, dragging Harry along after he rechristens his empty inventory with the severed head.

Somehow, this has gone much better than expected thus far. Which means things will go to hell some time soon. For now though, we have Harry and are on the way to the second part of our plan.

As we run, I cast Extra Hands again, drawing forth another friend to leave for Kasva to play with when he arrives.

Held in Vrasceid's arms, Harry wails as we drag him out of his prison. "Two what!?!"

Chapter 21

The slap cracks across my face, not budging my face but making Katherine shake her hand in pain after the strike. A moment later, she's nearly screaming into my face. "What the hell are you doing?"

"Getting Harry back. And tilting the odds," I reply calmly.

We're in the lower edges of the sewers, a hidden meeting area offered to us by the Lady of Shadows that she guarantees none will be watching. Except perhaps her. But I don't call her out on that.

See? I can learn when not to annoy my allies.

"Are you insane? Your Hands are causing widespread destruction throughout the city. You might have killed a couple of diplomats, but you've just earmarked Earth and humanity as deranged killers who have no respect for diplomatic norms!" Katherine shouts, utterly furious. "Why didn't you check with me or Rob?"

"I didn't have time. And I also knew you wouldn't agree to this," I say. "But this is necessary."

"Rob was right. You really are a loose cannon." Katherine shakes her head with disgust. "Even if we win this vote, we won't win the next one. Did you consider that?"

A part of me wants to quail under the disgust she exhibits. I push it aside, reminding myself of my goals. The point of what I intended to do today. "I did. And we don't have a lot of time before the vote. So I'm going to be blunt."

Katherine braces herself, casting her gaze toward Mikito, who stands guard a short distance away, and Harry, who is being brought up to speed by Ruvuds in the corner.

I flick my fingers, bringing Katherine's attention back to me. "I need you to give me your proxy."

"*What!?!*"

"Your voting proxy," I say. "Give it to me."

"No! Why would I do that?"

"Because if you don't, you'll die?" I say, cocking an eyebrow. "As you said, you're persona non grata. Earth and humanity. If you try to show up, they'll kill you."

"I'm protected."

"I'm pretty sure they don't care anymore." I gesture around, taking in the world around and all the hell that has gone on. "Or do you think it's worth the risk?"

"How about you? You're even more wanted than me," Katherine says. "Wait, were you planning to force my hand?"

"No." Then, reluctantly, I add. "Not exactly. I have other reasons for what I did, but forcing you to give me the proxy is a lucky coincidence of sorts. More like a… conjunction of interest?"

My search for the right terms makes Katherine hiss again before she stalks away. I watch as she strides around in a circle, windmilling her hands. Her lips move, uttering breathless imprecations as she forces herself to calm.

Eventually, she returns to me. We do need to try to adjust the vote, no matter what she thinks. "How do you intend to survive going to the chambers?"

"Can't say." When Katherine's eyes narrow, I point upward. "They might be listening. But trust me, they might try to end me. But you might have realized, I'm really hard to kill."

"He'll be there."

"Kasva?" I nod. "Maybe. I can take him." The look she gives me is full of doubt, making me chuckle darkly. "Don't worry. I have a plan."

"Like the last one? Do you know how much chaos our information release caused on the Galactic scene? They don't know, but many suspect it was us who released that information." Katherine's eyes go distant, dark as a cloud of grief shadows her face. "The number of deaths among the powers that be have increased fourfold. A half dozen wars started in the last week alone. When they finally learn who caused this, there will be hell to pay."

"But it improved our odds, no?" Her silence is answer enough for me. "It has to be done. And trust me, I have a plan. Now, the proxy, Katherine. I need it."

"And if I say no?" she says.

"Don't."

"And if I say no?"

I meet her stubborn gaze, wondering what it is with damn obstinate, bull-headed women in my life. I look over my shoulder at Mikito, who gives me a small nod, acknowledging I've tried.

I clench my fist and whisper, "Don't make me take it."

"You can't..." She stares at my eyes and breathes out slowly. "You can, can't you?"

I nod.

"What have you done?"

"Just found a few answers," I say. "The proxy?"

Katherine searches my eyes. I let her, curious what it is that she's looking for. Or if what she seeks is still there. The man who left Earth with her was many years and even more lives shed ago. Sometimes, I'm not sure there's much of that man left.

"Promise me something," she says.

"What?"

"That you'll not harm Earth. Whatever you do with the proxy, make sure it's for the best for Earth."

I offer her a nod, and when it's not enough, I speak the promise out loud. I know she's using a Skill, verifying the truth of what I say. Just another Diplomat Skill.

When she's assured of my intentions, Katherine presses an arm upon my chest. Light glows for a second, and a new notification appears.

Earth Voting Proxy given to John Lee, Redeemer of the Dead (Galactic Paladin Level 12)

"Thank you," I say, bowing my head. I know how much that cost Katherine, and there's a look in her eyes, a pained look of broken trust that tells me I might have burnt my bridges here. "And I'm sorry."

I look at Mikito, who's sneaked up behind Katherine. The Diplomat's eyes widen, just briefly, before Mikito hits her, striking so fast and hard it bypasses her safeguards and knocks her out.

"How long?" I say, laying down the unconscious woman I caught.

"Long enough."

Harry, who just watched us knock out our friend, raises his voice, his voice shaking between outrage and fear. "What the hell is going on?"

***

We explain the plan to Harry as we hurry off, leaving Katherine to sleep off the attack. At least, enough that he stops hyperventilating and agrees to carry out his part. He's kind of important. Not linchpin, but close enough that if he disagrees, it'd make our job more difficult.

Maintenance tunnels carry us deep into the first circle of Irvina. Security clearances provided to us by the Lady of Shadows help get us through the security checkpoints. I leave just enough of a trail with System Edit that when people come and look later, it'll seem I Edited my way through.

We keep moving, the original trio of fan club members the only ones left with Harry, Mikito, and me. The others have dispersed, headed out of the city, off the planet, and preferably out of the sector. Many have plans to go to Earth, offered refugee status and a chance to Level and soak up Japanese culture.

I'm a little annoyed that Mikito's got all the fans, but I can see which one of us is a better ambassador for humanity's culture. Not to say Harry or Katherine don't have their own fans, but in a world filled with violence like this, it's no surprise that the ass-kickers are the major draws.

There are others of course, individuals who have made it out to the Galactic universe. Some of them have taken on public personas, promoting themselves and Earth. The singer who brings our pop culture to the galaxy. Matisse Bien, who vacillates between taking part in virtual movies and joining teams as a pinch-hitter, acting out his role when necessary. Of course, it's not as good as having an actual healer or ranged attack or crowd control member, but method acting gives him close enough approximation of Skills and abilities that teams desperately in need of a specific role make do.

There's the XI Legion, who'd been camped in the middle of France during the initiation, reenacting their little Roman wars. Clad in full combat armor, they'd been one of the more powerful group forces in Western Europe for a time. Of course, they also hired themselves out to the Movana, but we won't discuss that portion of their betrayal. In the end, they shipped off Earth long before I did, taking part in clan wars and dungeon clearances where a Legion of Adventurers were required.

There were others: the Hoodoo Doctor, the Operator, the Gurkha. Individuals who've gained notoriety on the Galactic circuit, just like us, and so have gained fans both at home and in the wider Galactic sphere. Still more humans move through Galactic society without creating a major ripple, affecting only individuals.

Just as most galactics do in the end.

That's the thing about celebrity, about fame. It strikes once and you might burn bright for a time, but it'll fade just as easily in a series of accusations, of bad decisions. It eludes those who desire it and is gifted to those who seek it not.

Knowing that, I realize there's no real point in being jealous of Mikito. It is what it is, and I've got bigger fish to fry.

"Is this route going to bring us to the Galactic Council building?" Harry asks as he cranes his head around, staring at the underground tunnels. "I thought the main entrance is above ground."

Ali answers, floating over to Harry. "No. The Council building has multiple entrances set up just for cases like us."

"Us?"

"Individuals who are in trouble with multiple groups." Ali smirks. "The right to vote is quite sacrosanct among them all."

"Doesn't that mean that they're probably waiting for us here?" Harry says, frowning. It's the obvious conclusion after all.

"Probably," Ali says, making Harry blanch.

In the corner of the minimap, I see we're getting somewhat close to the building. In a couple hundred meters, give or take a few crossings and turns, our particular path will intercept the main routes. Idly, I wonder how many other diplomats are making use of the underground tunnels today.

"Well!?!" Harry says, waving his hands around. "We're just going to walk straight into a trap?"

"Not exactly." Mikito looks at me and I shrug, so she continues. "We all have enchantments to make us look different. Security clearances should also get us past the automated sentries."

"And their Skills?" Harry says.

"We've got that covered too," I say.

Or at least I think so. Of course, the reporter isn't letting it lie just like that, but it's not as if I'm that interested in answering his questions, so we keep walking. Mikito and Ali are happy to do their best to reassure Harry, providing him the various pieces of enchanted equipment we've acquired for this. It mollifies him a bit, but not all the way. More importantly, we keep him guessing and irritated, drip-feeding him information.

It's not that we want to torture him, but we can all sense Harry's a little on the fragile side, the torture and interrogation having driven him past what should normally be his breaking point. He's still holding it together, but only by sheer willpower.

Making him irritated, making him angry, gives him something to focus on while we forge ahead. And more importantly, if he knew the plan, I'm not sure he'd agree to it. Even though it's mostly safe. I feel a little guilt at what I'm doing, but there's no time to placate him, make him see the reasoning. The need. So I'm going with trickery.

As we finally reach the end of the corridor, we take the first left at the T-branch. Ahead, voices can be heard—grumbling voices and one rather annoyingly high-pitched one. The group turns and stares at me. The kid who we've been trying to get an Advanced Class for stands in the middle.

"Redeemer." His father, the Cafire Representative, is the one who speaks, his voice low. "Are you sure this will work?"

The Cafire's group are similar in looks, creatures that look like the devils of Earth's Christian mythology. Red skin, black horns, a long, pointed tail. The full works. Unlike the other one we once met, they don't speak in iambic pentameter.

"Of course." I walk forward while Ali grows in size, tugging Harry along behind.

"You said that the last time," Yorera, the father, says.

"That's right. You keep saying you'll get it, but you keep failing," Xirera, the kid, says. "And we can't fight in here. Not without drawing attention."

"You don't need to." I reach sideways, extracting a set of manacles from my inventory. These came from the Weaver, delivered to Mikito while I was trapped. Runic engravings cover the manacles, and even to my Mana sense, which I've tuned down, they glow in the shielded passageway. "Just put these on us."

"John…" Harry raises his voice, eyes widening. Fear erupts from his voice, panic threatening to take him.

"You best start with him," I say, gesturing to Harry.

"*No!*" Harry struggles, trying to pull away from Ali.

Before Harry can make off, Agr'us casts a spell, one that she's been prepping for a bit. Harry ceases struggling, entering a dazed status.

"Trouble with your friends?" Yorera says.

"Nothing you have to worry about," I say coldly. "Just get it done. Him first, then the rest of us."

The kid with his scrawny appearance and flushed red skin takes the manacles off my hands and starts with Harry as requested. By the time Harry is able to pay attention, he's manacled and his Mana is suppressed. Unlike the previous time though, he has a full Mana bar. He just isn't able to activate any Skills.

"I can't do this, John. Please don't make me do this," Harry says, his voice pleading now.

"It's okay." Mikito bumps him with her shoulder, offering him a half-smile. She has her hands out, waiting to be cuffed too. "We got this."

"No, you don't get it. We can't, we don't have any Skills. They'll hurt us. Hurt me…" Harry's beginning to hyperventilate.

I shoot a glance at Agr'us. She hits Harry with another spell, this one meant to calm his emotions rather than put him in a dazed Status. Harry stabilizes a bit, and while he's stabilizing, Agr'us offers him a ring.

"What?" Harry says.

"Ring of Calm Emotions," I say. "It'll help. It only suppresses what you're feeling, but it'll help you get through this."

It's not the best option. In fact, there's quite a bit of literature that shows things like that ring end up doing more damage in the long run than they help in the short term. But in specific circumstances, their use has been recommended. And in our case, we need it.

Manacles slide over wrists, one after the other. Each time, the kid hesitates as he waits for a notification, then he moves on, not getting one. By the time he gets to me, he's looking less than enthused. When the heavy clunk of metal closing on my wrists echoes through the chambers, I reach into the System.

And find the notification that blossoms, telling me of my captured nature. I follow the Mana strand back, finding the node it arrived from, then down the strands that reach the kid. The manacles might block others, might stop most my other Skills, but System Edit isn't blocked. We tested it, verified it before committing to this.

The child's lips are turning down into a frown, disappointment crossing his flushed face, those glowing black and red eyes. He's turning to complain to his father.

In the stretched moment that contains us both and the System Mana flooding into me, connecting us, I find the information that marks his actions, the collaring, and the multiple strands of information that verify his actions against Title acquisitions. I find the Title requirements, the little tick and check mark it searches for for the one we're looking to get.

In that frozen moment, I make a few quick edits to his Status and the Title data. The System bucks as I manipulate it, hating what I do. It floods me back with error notifications, tickets and protests. In turn, I make adjustments further down the line, altering the kid's fate a little to appease the System.

And then, I'm done.

I take a few extra seconds to make sure the alteration to the Title is locked to the kid, that it doesn't cascade through the System, before pulling back. As time resumes its normal flow, the kid freezes. His eyes widen with surprise.

"Redeemer. Your promises are—" Yorera's already gesturing for his guards to grab us, his tail lashing in anger.

Xirera cuts him off with a whoop. "I got it! I got it!"

"You did?" Yorera's jaw drops, but he doesn't stop the guards from gripping us as he pulls his son around. "Show me!"

The kid does, adjusting his notifications so his father can see it. None of us get to see it of course, but I don't need to. I amended it myself, so I know what it says.

Title: Killer of Achilles

You've done what many would consider impossible. You've fought and beaten a Heroic while in your Basic Class. Such an act of heroism, fortitude, and foolhardiness will forever be marked upon your Status.

Effect 1: Access to certain Rare Classes. Increase in Reputation among certain factions. Decrease in Reputation among others.

Effect 2: +25% damage against those one Rank higher than you. +15% damage to those two Ranks higher than you. +10% damage to those three Ranks higher than you. +5 damage to those four Ranks higher than you.

Effect 3: +20% damage resistance

"The System's beneficence. This is better than we expected," Yorera says, reading the notification in detail. "You'll definitely get a good Class now."

Xirera can only bob his body in acknowledgement, vibrating with excitement. I keep silent, knowing his future, knowing the kind of Classes he'll get. The ones I trimmed out so that I could make this work. A small part of me feels guilty, but I push it away knowing that he's still bought one heck of an advantage. Just not the kind he thinks.

"Well, I guess I should make sure to carry out my side," Yorera says, grinning and clapping me on the shoulder. And if there's a little malice, a little greed in his eyes, well, it's to be expected.

After all, he's an Ambassador too.

"Come. We do not want to miss your vote."

With those words and a few gestures, Yorera has his guards drag us to the Council building. Behind us, we leave Xirera, who is still vibrating with excitement and rereading his new Title, almost glowing with happiness.

***

We're frog-marched through the corridors, our presence gaining more than a few raised eyebrows. There are questions asked, but we've put away our permits, passing by under Yorera's security clearance now. He doesn't stop, answering shouted questions with pleasant but useless nonsensical answers that give away nothing.

At our first major security checkpoint, we're pulled aside and scanned for weaponry. The few that we carry outside of our inventory have already been taken by Yorera's guards, held in their own inventory as a matter of course. The Council security check's our faces and Statuses, pursing their lips as they find nothing in their database.

Which is by design. The enchantments that change our looks are boosted by the Lady to ensure we're hidden. Of course, the lack of data engenders another round of questioning, but we stay silent while Yorera deflects the questions under the guise of Diplomatic Immunity.

As for the guards, they spend more time checking our manacles, only to mutter pleasant surprise when they read their details. I completely understand why, considering their quality.

Enchanted Manacles of Imprisonment (Master Class)

The problem of System-enabled individuals have long been considered and solved with the development of the Manacles of Imprisonment. Each set of manacles is as unique as its crafter, but they all suppress the usage of Skills while worn. Mana flow is inhibited, while Mana regeneration is directed into empowering the manacles themselves.

Effects: Skill Suppression, Spell: Powerful Suggestions, Spell: Lightning Grasp (Inactive), Spell: Sleep (Inactive)

Durability: 2300/2300

Satisfied that we're well secured as prisoners, we're passed through the security cordons with minimal fuss. As we journey deeper through the silver-covered hallways, they grow wider and wider as more diplomats and their bodyguards join the main thoroughfare.

Even if the session has already started—for quite a while now—being fashionably late and skipping out on the early morning, unimportant discussions is a time-honored tradition. But now, the Diplomats and Ambassadors are arriving for the afternoon session where actual bills of import are voted upon. And while only a portion of them might be coming in via the underground passages, when you're looking at a portion of the over ten thousand plus worlds, it's still a large number.

Of course, the actual Galactic Council isn't just made up of ten thousand planets. There are a lot more. Between the hegemons, empires, and serf contracts, many planets either have no seat on the Council itself or have permanently handed over their voting rights. Leaving us with this mixture of planets that have their own seats by being independent, stubborn, vassal planets that refuse to give up their presence—even if they vote as directed—and multiple minor and major empires.

All in all, it's a mess of a government system. Made more of a mess when the vast majority of the bills and other matters that are voted upon are ignored by non-signatories. It's kind of like the UN, but with a lot less bite if you can imagine that.

Except when the Inner Council acts, of course. That's when matters escalate, as the entire force of the Council and its bureaucracy take action. And for all its inadequacies, the empowerment of the System ensures that the occasional System-wide pronouncement and bill that do manage to pass can cause true havoc.

Like the creation of a Dungeon World.

As we pass and get side-eyed by the crowd, Harry grows increasingly paranoid and twitchy. Even the ring—a simple Advanced Class enchantment—is being overwhelmed by his growing panic.

I drop back, bumping him with my shoulder as I lower my voice. "Hold it together, old man."

"We're being frog-marched to our deaths as prisoners!" Harry hisses back.

"Well, at least there won't be any more torture," I say glibly. When humor doesn't calm the reporter, I murmur, "It's fine. I've got a plan."

"Really? Does it take into account the fact that he's going to betray us?" Harry says softly.

I grin at the reporter and he rolls his eyes. I don't even mind the fact that Yorera looks back at us, his eyes narrowing. My grin is as much a warning for him as it is to assure Harry. That neither side seem reassured does make me a little sad, but it is what it is.

"You see, Harry, the problem is when someone is a devious, backstabbing bastard all the time, it becomes very predictable. Then it's just a matter of figuring how you're about to get backstabbed when you deal with them." I pitch my voice relatively high, letting the guards around us hear me.

The really smart ones, the ones who are tasked with containing us if things go bad, look worried. Some of the guards shoot Yorera concerned glances, searching for a reaction from him. The alien continues to stride along confidently, playing as if he's not heard a single word I said.

Truth be told, there are two major ways this could go. The first—if he keeps his promise—makes things a lot simpler. The second—if he does betray us—will make things much more complicated.

The first time this might happen is when we enter the main building, when security intensifies once more. Where there were a half dozen semi-bored guards going through the procedures at the other post, here there are over two score, each of them glaring at Diplomats and Ambassadors without a care. There's even a change in their Classes.

Mook 1 (Loyal Council Guard Level 17) (A)

Mook 2 (Loyal Council Investigator Level 24) (A)

...

...

Mook 33 (Dedicated Council Lieutenant Level 27) (M)

Unsurprisingly, more than a dozen of the guards surround us the moment we make an appearance.

"Halt, Diplomat Yorera." Mook 33 holds his hands down by his sides and up and sideways, barring the way. He can do that, what with having ten limbs—four legs and six hands, all crystalline outgrowth from his sea-foam-green and pink cystal body. "You have unauthorized prisoners with you. Judgment of Galactic Criminals are on the sixth configuration of the moons. It is only the twenty-third configuration currently."

I feel Mana twitch as Skills trigger, putting us and the nearby guards under a privacy dome. It's a powerful one that also blocks most access to the System. At least for us.

"These are special prisoners. The Council will be grateful to see them," Yorera says. "I am invoking my right as a Diplomat under Treaty Clause 2567-891-53-c(ii)."

Mook 33's eyes glaze over a little as he accesses the relevant section, before his lips press in disdain. "A once-a-decade option? Unusual."

"These are unusual times," Yorera says.

Before Mook 33 can say anything further, a guard—a shivering blob of pink and green slime—glops closer and burbles at the lieutenant. "They are under powerful disguise enchantments."

The Skills the Slime-Mook uses cut through our physical disguises with ease. I'm not super surprised. They wouldn't be guards here if they couldn't do that much.

"Of course they are," Yorera says, not even missing a beat. "Do you think I want my surprise spoiled?" He glares at the Slime-Mook, his voice lowering. "If not for the privacy screen, I would have your head for your indiscretion!"

"These people, they seem familiar," Slime-Mook says.

A few of the other guards nod, and the lieutenant's crystal body trembles. He cocks his head, waiting for one of his subordinates to say something.

Harry's breathing speeds up, sweat dotting his skin, glistening like diamonds on obsidian sand. Mikito looks around as if she's entirely unafraid, but I see the way she's lowered her weight, angled her body ever so slightly. As for me? I just glare at everyone. And hope.

Famous as we might be, the Lady's Skills are in play. She warps memory, databases, and the eleven senses of sapient creatures. Yes, eleven—because we're talking about aliens and everything from tremor-sense, sonar, psychic, and aura senses come into play. And while most Skills affect some—

but not all—of these senses, this is the Galactic Council's headquarters. And guards with the full complement of sensing abilities and Skills are in play.

Without her, there'd be no way to sneak in. No way to get past them. Once more, we gamble everything on her Legendary Skill. And come out the winner. Because it is a Legendary Skill. And pointed in one direction, against a single planet? There's nothing that can be done.

"Restricted," Slime Mook finally speaks up.

The other guards nod, making the lieutenant's eyes narrow. He gestures and the group close in on us. Yorera tries to protest, but it doesn't matter, as the Cystalline Mook Lieutenant drags us all in the privacy bubble to a secure room.

Once we're within, the Council Mooks move to the corners of the room, keeping an eye on us. Yorera's guards stay in closer, hands on their weapons, smirking at us. Harry's literally hyperventilating now, while Mikito is standing utterly still, waiting for her chance. The three musketeers keep themselves next to Harry. Their job is to keep him safe.

As for me, I watch Yorera, who has a calculating look in his eyes. Our chance of sneaking in has been broken by an obstinate guard, so I'm curious what Yorera will do.

The Crystal Lieutenant speaks first, eyes fixed upon Yorera. "I am invoking Council Security Protocol 158, section 83. All information in this room will be locked and safeguarded under Council Secrecy Protocols and will not be revealed for a thousand years. Now. Speak."

Yorera shoots a look at me, visibly considering. Red skin flushes darker, turning almost deep scarlet red as his tail waves. Then he shrugs. "My apologies, Redeemer. This is not going to work."

I watch as the Mooks freeze, surprise showing on their faces. Yorera's guards are less surprised, instead pulling out weapons as the Samurai shift in position.

"You are saying this is the Redeemer of the Dead? The human we have been tasked at locating?" Crystal Mook grates out, his voice ever so careful. He waves one of his many hands, gesturing for the guards to close in on us.

Slime-Mook and the others close, weapons pulled.

"Yes." Yorera glares at me. "This was not my plan. I wanted to be deeper within, where my people are waiting. But this will do. This is the Redeemer of the Dead. The human you are searching for." His grin widens, sharp carnivore teeth flashing pearly white as he gloats. "Did you think I would risk my life, my child's life for a simple Title? You are facing the Council itself! And the rewards offered. Why, what I'll get—"

I never hear what he was going to get.

The Lieutenant Mook moves first. He thrusts his hand through Yorera's neck, catching him in the back of the spine, his crystal arm erupting from Yorera's neck then growing, engulfing his head in crystal. Yorera struggles, his guards moving to help him. The Slime-Mook rears up, engulfing a trio of guards near it—both Yorera's devils and another Council guard.

Beam attacks fire while Mikito kicks and beats another while her hands are still chained. The three musketeers bear down another pair of guards while Harry falls flat onto the ground, covering his head as best as he can.

As for me? I slip out of the manacles, my Skill Edit making the damn manacles fall away. Then I trigger Judgment of All on the enemies within. And there are more of them than I'd like. It seems only the Slime and the Crystal Lieutenant are on our side as they battle valiantly.

Unfortunate for our enemies, Judgment of All doesn't care where they are so long as I can sense them, see them. The spell erupts, tearing at them through their connection to the System, raw Mana flooding their bodies. Their screams, their struggles are brief. But not without cost.

We find the Slime a bubbled mess, his body eaten away by the poisons, the necrotic attacks used by Yorera's guards. The feedback attack from Yorera himself, as an Ambassador, has shattered the crystal light within the Mook Lieutenant. He lies dying, his body cracked. Even healing spells do little for him.

"Never mind me, Redeemer. My crystal is shattered. But the formation will grow," the Crystal Mook speaks, it's body twisting and shuddering one last time before it collapses in on itself.

In the silence, I look around. The musketeers did well, keeping Harry alive. Agr'us is the most injured, half of her hair burnt off, clutching at the stump of her arm. The remainder of her arm is lying a short distance away, bubbling as poison eats it.

"Lord Sato, are you well?" Ruvuuds is by Mikito, looking her over with his cat-eyes.

Mikito grimaces as the poisons threaten to eat away her leg. A brief foray over and a System Edit fixes the issue, allowing her to heal.

Harry is on the floor, trying to recover his bearings, his state of mind. Vrasceids is helping him, speaking softly as he strokes the reporter's back, offering comfort by presence and touch.

I don't have time for that. Instead, I move quickly, picking up the bodies of the guards and moving them into my Altered Storage before cleansing the space.

After that, we pull out the Lady's security clearances once more before I hack our way out of the security room. This time around, we use a secondary exit, one that leads us directly into the council building itself, bypassing other security stations.

As we move, I can't help but think we got off light.

***

Of course, eventually, Harry recovers enough to ask the questions. *"Why'd they help us? Were they more of your Questors?"*

I answer him, using the Party Chat, keeping our answers to the silence of the System. I lock it down with System Edit, though I know it isn't perfect. But if anyone is looking that close, we're screwed anyway.

"No. It was a trade," I say. *"Those attacks that Katherine was complaining about? They were distractions, but also payments. To certain factions with the Fist, kingdoms who wanted revenge. In turn, they'd help us out here."*

"Dangerous. They're defying the Council directly," Harry says. *"Don't they fear retaliation?"*

"Of course they do. Which is why the help will be limited. The moment Crystal and Slime-Mook helped us out, they were dead. Cutouts that can't offer further information."

Even if someone pulled information backward, searched for how they were told, I'm sure it was hidden. Coded words, additional cutouts. Ways of saying things without saying it.

"He has a name, you know."

"I do." But I carry enough names, enough grief with me already. His death, his sacrifice, is not one I take on. Even though I fear both are indelibly stuck in my memory anyway, that he'll come to me in the middle of the night like so many others. Accusing me, berating me.

The help I've acquired, the people I paid off and locked with my System Edit Skill are numerous. But my plans, my options are wide too. And so in each spot, our potential help is thin. And there's only so far they're willing to aid us. Getting us into the Council chambers to create havoc? Sure.

Directly killing others? No.

As with so many things, we're on our own for the majority. We hurry through the security corridors, our changed clothing and the firm stride we move with allowing us to pass without issue. Safeguarded by the Legendary's Skill and the knowledge that we can't be here.

In these safe, secure corridors of their security personnel.

Chapter 22

The journey to the Council chambers takes forever. Each diplomatic retinue has its own specific location within the building, one that's protected by the same rules and regulations of diplomatic immunity that pervade the building itself. The Galactic Council building is not owned or controlled by any single individual, instead guarded by the Council and their guards.

Within each diplomatic sector are the institutions that own their voting boxes, their own safe zones. Of course, there are limits to that self-governance within the building itself, but it does offer some level of security once we arrive.

Soon enough, we pass the external security perimeter. Inside the building itself, security is looser. We pop out then, stepping into the main thoroughfares. A simple privacy bubble created by a Skill from Harry keeps the majority of people from speaking with us.

Even those diplomats and guards who see through the bubble only glance at our group before turning away. Custom and manners means that the vast majority do not attempt to interact with us.

That is, until we're stopped by a familiar coral-eared, pale-skinned set of figures. The Erethrans that stop our team are not people I recognize automatically, even though I've seen images of the Vice-Ambassador that stands before us. Hands crossed behind his back, clad in the latest fashion, which in this case seems to include very little clothing—I wonder when that changed—the Erethran Ambassador shifts when we do.

I find myself coming to a stop and letting him enter the privacy bubble. I growl a little, annoyance in my voice. "Vice Ambassador Ramanner, what is the meaning of this?"

"Just a small thing. We're hoping to speak with you before the upcoming vote," the Vice Ambassador says. "If you don't mind, we will escort you the rest of the way to your demesne."

"And if I say no?" I ask, fist flexing.

"Why, I'd accept your request with good grace. And then go on to my next one, with the Movana." His grin widens even as his eyes stay cold.

I do my best to keep my face unmoving, giving away nothing. Unfortunately, people like Harry—who is off his game—and the three musketeers do. The Erethran Ambassador grins, deliberately shifting his gaze to those who gave up the goose before turning back to me. Revealing our presence, our location to our enemies would be bad. Really bad.

"Shall we continue your walk? I wouldn't want to hold you up too long." Rammaner steps aside slightly, letting us move forward if we wish.

I growl but accept the fact he's got us cornered. I can't afford to start a fight here, and his threat—while subtle—is clear enough.

We walk, the Ambassador and his companions content to stroll alongside me in silence. I take a few moments to call up their Status information as I consider what they want. The two other Erethrans are boring, an Assistant and a Bodyguard, or the Erethran equivalent with fancy titles to denote their Advanced Class Status. The Bodyguard is right on the border of crossing into Master Class, and a quick dip into the System shows he's stuck, unable to progress as he hasn't chosen to fulfill his Class Quest.

The Ambassador, on the other hand, is much more interesting. I stare at his Status screen and poke at it mentally, seeing what I can call forth.

Zimalin Ramanner, Platinum Tongued, Famed Courtier, Beloved of the System, Master of Ceremonies at the 5S0-8, Slayer of Goblins, Manticores, Sphinxes, ... (Senior Erethran Ambassador Level 3) (M)

HP: 2130/2130

MP: 2130/2130

Conditions: Diplomatic Immunity, Two are One, Secured Shield, State Secrets, Aura of the Empire's Voice, State Security Protocols

"That name..." I frown. "*I should know that name, right? It's not Catrin's, right?*"

"*Seriously. How did you ever keep a girl? You had a multi-month relationship. And her name was right above her head the entire time!*" Ali sends back.

"*I remember her name, just you know, not her last name. I didn't need to remember it, and it was always right there,*" I mentally rebut Ali. "*It's like remembering phone numbers. You don't need to, because your smartphone always has it. Or birthdays. Or the name of your Skills.*"

"*Separating molecules, you humans are so lazy.*" Ali sends an image of himself rolling his eyes.

I snigger, but I'm grateful that since the latest Level-up, his banishment doesn't mean he can't communicate with me. At least, so long as it's a voluntary one. We haven't tested an involuntary banishment as yet.

"*Ramanner. The ex-Chief of Staff. The one you Shackled.*"

"Right! He never mentioned he was related to the Vice Ambassador." I frown. His presence here, the lack of information. I smell a conspiracy. On the other hand, he is the Vice Ambassador, the guy second in charge. Maybe Ramanner didn't think it was necessary?

Ali's dire chuckle makes me grimace, only to see Mikito interrogating me again with an eyebrow. This time, I can only offer a shrug.

We march on, the Erethran Vice Ambassador breaking the silence to chat about inconsequential things. The latest play, the places to eat. He fills the silence with practiced ease, and his presence makes the other guards and the other diplomats glance at us and away.

Each step, each sideways glance by a diplomat, a courier or assistant as we walk makes me tense internally even as I offer monosyllabic replies to Rammaner. My stomach clenches, my fingers press together under the cuffs of my sleeves, and I find myself wishing I had some chocolate to eat.

Harry doesn't do much better, his fears warring against the enchantments on him and winning out. I see the occasional flashes of panic, of concern that run through him. I hate it. I hate pushing him so hard. But I don't have a choice, I don't think.

Mikito handles the walk the best, keeping an eye out for problems without looking more suspicious than any security guard would. It's still not perfect, it's still not great, and I can tell that the liquid grace she moves across the floor with is her fighting stance. Her body, her awareness is ramped up to its peak level.

All this tension, all this wariness will force a crash that'll really suck later. Until then, we watch, we breathe, and we function.

Finally, finally, we reach the hallway that leads to humanity's secure room. Our secure location, the one that only members of humanity can enter. Guards watch us as we move through the hallways, but none dare stop us. Not with the Erethran with us. And since the hallways lead to many places, they only glance at us before letting their eyes move on.

I'm just glad that traditions—and Council paranoia—dictate that security personnel are pulled back and out of hallways. You can't stay standing in a hallway for too long, no matter what. Which means there are, of course, roving groups of security and paid diplomatic couriers, but no stationary guards. In this way, with a little bit of luck and planning, you can slip into a rival's room, make a deal, and leave with no one the wiser.

"And here we come, to the end at last. Really, coming here is dangerous. One might almost call it insane. No one in their right-thinking mind, when pursued by the full power of the Council, would think to come to the very heart of their power," Ramanner says. "Which is why we knew you'd be here."

"We?" I say.

"The Empress Apparent sends her greetings." Ramanner gives a small salute, hand to his chest before he continues. "Also, and these are her words, 'Tell that fool this is the most I can do and that, if he survives, he should visit.'"

I blink while behind me, Mikito lets out a muffled snort of amusement.

"And what, exactly, did you do? Or is she offering?" Harry says. Something in his voice makes me turn around, slowing down our pace. His hands are clenched around one another. His fingers are pale, almost white around the edges.

The Ambassador sweeps his gaze up and down Harry, his lips tightening in disapproval. He hesitates before giving his head the slightest shake and turning away from the reporter.

"I do want to know the answer to that question too," I mutter to the Vice Ambassador.

"Ah. A simple matter of extraction." Ramanner shifts and holds out four stylized pins.

I frown, picking one up from his hand and scanning it to see what the System has to say.

Stylized Pin

Material: Gold

Of course, that's not enough for me. I dig in, checking the information provided, and my lips curl up. Because it might be a simple pin according to the description, but the bundle of Mana it's wrapped around is dense. I push, sliding past the data bundle, and find myself staring at another, more honest notification.

Manop Galactic Positioning System Pin (M)

When you absolutely must keep track of something, Manop's GPS Pins are guaranteed to work or your Credits back three times over! That's right, our lifetime triple warranty has never failed, even against Heroic Level Class Skills.

Effects: Provides your location to holder of the master-piece to this slaved pin. May be used in conjunction with master-piece to target spells and Skills.

"Really. You expect us to wear this?" I say.

Ramanner smiles. "I am hoping you do not." At the incredulous look, I give him, he shrugs. "I follow orders, but I must also express my displeasure at her actions. The Empress Apparent is placing the Empire in danger with the aid she offers you. So no, I would prefer if you didn't use this."

I turn the pin over in my hand before speaking slowly. "You know that kind of statement could almost be seen a rather direct method of manipulation."

Ramanner's smile widens as if he's enjoying me squirm. My fist clenches around the pin. If it was just a "simple pin," it'd be crushed.

"What I want to know is why there are only four pins," Mikito says softly, plucking a pair from Ramanner as she walks past us on her way to Harry.

When both of them put the pins on, I frown even more. "You trust him?"

"He could have had us thrown into jail already," she says. "And I trust Catrin."

While I mull the trust my friend puts in my ex-lover, she raises an eyebrow.

He shrugs, gesturing vaguely at the three musketeers. "We had not planned for them. I'd recommend they leave. Before... well. You know."

I frown, considering his words. They were useful to get us in. Most alerts will be looking for two or three people, which is why a group of six helps with camouflage. But Ramanner has a point. We don't need them here, and they'd slow us down when we run.

"Go," I say to the three.

Of course, they look at Mikito, who speaks directly to the Vice Ambassador. "Will you see them out?"

Ramanner frowns, then looks at me then at the three. Eventually, he nods, gesturing to the Bodyguard. "They will be shown out." Mikito opens her mouth to protest and is overridden by Ramanner immediately. "Do not push my largesse."

She shuts her mouth, chastised. At the door, I look between the group as she steps toward the three, whispering to them. I hear words of thanks and further, coded orders before they step away.

"Good eve to you. And I hope that whatever you choose to do, the fallout will be minimal," Ramanner says, his voice cold. "Or at least contained."

I can only offer him a grin, still turning the pin over in my hand. He glances at it, then at the ones on both Mikito and Harry before gesturing, bringing the three members of Mikito's fan club with him. They offer me respectful nods, then bows to Mikito before we finally turn to the door.

Humanity's abode. The only place where we can be safe for the short period that we need before the rest of the plan is put into play. I smile, placing my hand on the plate and willing it open. The System recognizes me, recognizes my authority, and slides the door open. I cast one last glance back to where the Erethrans and the three musketeers leave.

A part of me wonders how much danger I've put them in. How likely retribution will be for him, for Catrin, for the Empire and the fan club. In the end, I dismiss my concern for them. There's a point where care and concern for others becomes nothing more than a self-mutilating burden, when you have to accept that others are adults and able to accept the risks they take upon themselves.

There's a point where you have to let go and let them fall. And hope that you've held them up long enough that they've grown their wings enough to fly.

***

I step into the quarters, idly noting the security systems Katherine has bought. As I walk forward, further notifications bloom with information about Earth's embassy within the Council building.

The complex itself is relatively small, nothing bigger than a penthouse condo in size with floor-to-ceiling two-story tall windows straight ahead of us overlooking the voting chambers. There's a small floating orb in front of the windows where we will be able to cast our vote. And to our right, a staircase leads to a second floor where the offices lie. The main floor is fully open for simple gatherings and parties.

You Have Entered the Embassy of the Galactic Planet—Earth. This is a subsidiary Diplomatic Zone of Earth.

All laws, regulations, and planet-wide effects are in place. Current domain effects include:

- *Planetary Dimension Locked (Disruptive Interference Tier I)*
- *Sensor Net*
- *Past Mistakes Teach Best (+0.04% XP Gain)*
- *Dodgy Accounting (+4.2% Voting Mana Regeneration)*
- *... (more)*

I push outward and tap into the Sensor Net. Sense nothing, see nothing. The expected welcoming party is missing. No Kasva, which is somewhat of a surprise. I expected him to be here. To meet him at the end, to fight a drawn-out battle.

But maybe Ramanner was right. Only the insane would expect us to be here, to dare them in the lions' den.

This Diplomatic Space currently includes:

- *2 Secure Meetings*
- *3 Secure Office Spaces (1 Reinforced)*
- *1 Refreshment & Dining Room with integrated Kitchen*
- *Voting Sphere—Main & slaved voting sphere (in Reinforced Secure Office)*
- *Tier II Security System*

I barely pay attention to this notification since there's another one right after it.

You are the Earth Proxy.

Would you like to modify the current Diplomatic Space?

I assent to the request and make a quick purchase—a small study with a library within. Another purchase of a series of books fills the library. Hardcover editions of a series of readings, all useful, all important. It's a little gift for Katherine. Though she—Earth—is the one paying for it. I'd pay for it, but that's not the way the System works.

We spread out, Mikito moving with Harry to one of the nearby lounging chairs to relax. Now that we're in a safe spot, we need to do so. Since we'll be doing something else, something a lot more dangerous soon enough.

Alone, I flex my will, calling forth Ali. He takes a few seconds to form, passing through the membrane between worlds, his body pulling together much like the Mana doppelgangers. I give him a second to finish up before I walk the rest of the way in.

Something, something pushes at the edges of my senses. Maybe it's my Luck, maybe it's my augmented Perception. Maybe it's just because I've seen him before, saw how he camouflaged his body. I look up.

He's invisible, almost entirely blended into the ceiling. As I stare at him, I see his Status information is once again blank. The damn ghost spider-creature offers nothing. But luckily for me, the Lady had happily provided that information, at least as she knew it. Ali combines it all together for me, giving me his rather interesting Status.

Wex (Anasi Martial Glutton Level 38/ Senior Administrator Level 17) (H/?)

HP: 2430/2430

MP: 4380/4380

Conditions: Webbed Intuition, Threads of the Nest, Stored Reserves, You Are What You Eat, Body of the Dead

"Senior Administrator Wex. I have to admit, I'm surprised you're here," I say, calling to him.

"Expecting someone else?"

"Yes. Your champion." I watch as my friend scrambles, weapons coming out as she stares at the spot in the ceiling I look at. Harry doesn't notice Wex, but Mikito does. She has Hitoshi out, the Legacy weapon glowing scarlet as she points at the spider. "I actually prepared for him."

"I had a bet. I believed that you would dare this. You're always presumptuous, foolhardy in your decisions. Choosing to attack rather than retreat. What is your plan? To stare down at the Ambassadors and Diplomats below and use your Skill? Kill them all?" Wex asks, shifting a little.

Harry gasps, spotting him at last. Now that Wex is moving, I realize its not just sitting there talking to me but holds another bundle in its hand, a spider-thread-wrapped bundle that it'd been snacking upon. Martial Glutton indeed.

"That would solve some of our problems, wouldn't it?" I say, offering it a wide grin.

Harry shoots me a horrified look while Mikito begins the process of buffing herself.

"So you guessed right," I say. "But why's your buddy not here?"

"We are verifying multiple angles." Wex clicks, making the bundle disappear. "Unlike you, we do not like to gamble upon a single winning outcome."

I growl, even if he is somewhat correct in his assumptions. All too often, I've been forced to take one risk after the other without backup plans. Or few enough backup plans to matter. Calling forth a dragon, choosing the Heir I wanted, even the vote for the planetary governance.

"Maybe, but I'm not the idiot standing before a group of very enthusiastic killers by itself." Once more, I eye its Status, grateful for the information I have now. The understanding that came about after spending so much time Leveling in the Administrative Center.

Wex isn't a Legendary. It's a much weaker than normal Heroic—at least in terms of its "fake" Class. That was confirmed both by the Lady and my own experiences Leveling up. Even as a late-stage Heroic, it doesn't have the same level of Skills, the kind of ability to do damage that a real Heroic would. That's because most of its Skill Points have been dedicated toward the System Edit Skill—just like my last few ones.

Of course, it's made up by the fact that it can buy Heroic Skills, just as I would have to if I had progressed normally. Add the fact that we need to Level up both Classes at the same time, because we're forced to gain experience in two different formats, and its Combat Class just isn't that powerful.

Oh sure, it could go out and fight to level its fake Class, but without Class Skill points to dedicate toward combat Skills, Wex must rely on its purchased Skills to make up the difference and hide its lack of Skills. And with our responsibilities and the need to split our time, I bet it was not as easy as just jaunting off.

In the end, that probably means that an Administrator is weak in a direct confrontation like this. Or at least, theoretically. If you discount the use of the System Edit Skill in combat itself.

I have a feeling I'm going to get a lesson on its uses in a second...

"Maybe." Wex cleans its front legs again, rubbing them together.

For a second, I look into the fractured kaleidoscope of its eyes, the fractured vision of its almost invisible body.

And then we dance.

Chapter 23

It's not me who starts the fight but Mikito. She uses Makoto, her long-range strike, swinging Hitoshi in a short, chopping motion that makes the explosion of energy from the tip of the legacy weapon arc out in an ever-growing curve of energy.

Wex throws itself out of the way, swinging on an invisible thread attached to the ceiling and dodging the strike. It avoids Mikito's initial attack with ease, but as it lands on invisible threads, Wex doesn't take into account the living-flames Hitoshi provides.

They catch onto its threads, jumping from connection to connection, burning their way to Wex as they destroy its delicate web. The flames are hungry, seeking blood and flesh, and the spider lets out a squeaky exclamation of surprise as it slashes and parts its own web, forcing it to fall away.

In the distraction, I act.

First step, I throw up my Penetration Evolved Skill. It'll keep me alive longer than not. Domain and my Aura switch on, followed by Eye of the Storm as I figure my team could use the boost and distraction. Then I trigger the rest of the defenses in the building itself. Weapon turrets drop from the ceiling only to get stuck, caught in webs. Drones attempt to roll out of their resting spots, only to burst apart as explosive threads ignite, sending molten shrapnel into space. The defenses that Katherine paid for are rendered useless just like that.

"Fine," I snarl and raise my fist, clenching it.

Judgment of All doesn't require me to hit the Administrator, just for me to see it. And Wex might be mildly camouflaged, but it is moving too much. There are too many flames above it now to hide it completely.

Judgment of All starts up, and Mana floods out of me. And keeps flooding. My eyes widen as I sense Wex tearing at my Skill using its System Edit Skill. I try to block it, but I'm too late.

Notifications arrive, telling me what it was doing, all too late.

Judgment of All Activate

Administrative Override: Mana Cost Tripled

Duration Reduced: 6.5 seconds

Even so, my plunge into my Skill is enough to make the damn Administrator stop. Its mental intrusion scurries off just before it nerfs my damage too.

I feel, more than sense, the rush of Mana that hammers into the floating point of its body. To meet an obstruction. The Mana burns, tearing away at Wex—but not. I frown, digging into the discrepancy with my System Edit Skill even as I conjure swords and throw them at the damn spider, letting my floating weapons create problems for the scurrying spider.

Stored Reserves (Level 10) (Administrator Modified)

The Anasi Martial Glutton's premier Skill, it allows the Anasi to consume health and Mana stores from its victims and store them for later use. Stored reserves replenish health and Mana of the user at an increased rate.

Effect 1: Store up to 11,000 HP and Mana from consumed victims at a ratio of 1:100

Effect 2: Increased Regeneration of Health and Mana of user at need by 11%. Each addition unit regenerated decreases stored HP and Mana respectively.

Administration Modification: Stored reserves of HP and Mana take damage first. User resistances are still in effect.

"Son of a bitch! It's got a reserve for health," I shout to the group even as it bounces away from one of Mikito's attacks.

She's on her ghost horse now, riding on air as she charges it. Wex is fast, but she's good and the ever-changing size of the energy blade on Hitoshi keeps it guessing.

"I know," the Samurai snaps at me. Another cut, this one bouncing off the sudden silvery body of the spider. A second later, it's back to normal as the Administrator swaps around the traits of its physical body with Body of the Dead. "Stop standing around and help!"

"I am doing something. Didn't you see that... I guess you didn't..." I mutter.

Of course she wouldn't. Judgment of All, even now finished ticking down, never had an external effect because it soaked all that damage up in its health bank. Even nastier, its Resistances—including its Administrator Resistances—soaked up much of that damage. Which wouldn't have been that high otherwise, it being pure Mana damage.

"I got it!" Ali shouts.

The Spirit flies straight up, the conjured ball of plasma in his hand about to be lobbed at the Administrator. Only for Ali to suddenly stop as he hits a series of invisible threads. Even with my higher Perception, I can barely sense the way they shifted to catch it, forcing Ali to hold. A second later, they burn the caught Spirit, attacking him on the immaterial plane as well as the material plane.

The Spirit holds it together long enough to release the plasma containment in the general direction of Wex, catching the Administrator in the backblast. It isn't a direct hit, but it does destroy even more of its threads. Threads which keep growing back.

I debate flying up, but I'm not Mikito. I lack her Skills to avoid and dodge the damn web. And getting caught is a bad idea. Instead, I fall back on an old standby—using Blade Strike to cut at the spider above.

While I do that, while I let my physical instincts take over, I step into the other side of the fight, extending my System Edit Skill. For I can see how it's tearing at Mikito's Skills, knocking them down, aborting their start, increasing cost and otherwise hampering her.

Blitzed is put on cooldown. Isoide—her haste—increases in cost by ten times. Shatter is lowered in percentage, making it almost useless. Even Gi, her unblockable, undodgable attack, is nerfed as she's forced to expend multiple times her Mana to make use of it.

It's going after me too, but only occasionally. Domain only barely reaches them as they dart around the inside of the building. Eye of the Storm taunt effects aren't affecting it at all, its mental resistances more than sufficient. The damage effect is nice, since it adds to my Skills, but it isn't burning the threads as I hoped. And my Aura doesn't affect it directly. As for my Blade Strikes, it's easier to dodge or tank than to actually bother Editing.

I dive in, fighting Wex with my System Edit Skill. I cancel its Skills, block further Skill uses, attempt to delve into its Status Screen. We're fighting on a half dozen fronts virtually, and in a short period, I go entirely on the defensive.

It's many times more experienced than I am, multiple times stronger and smarter. I can barely keep up with the changes it makes on Mikito's Skills, and I barely pay attention to when it nerfs my own, destroying Penetration's duration, reducing the damage done on my own Blade Strikes.

But it's also hampered. Firstly, by the System itself. Like when I changed the Title for Yorera's son, the System doesn't like us making localized alterations like this. It fights back, wanting to revert to normal. On top of that, it's also hampered by the penalty the System placed upon it when it attacked me the first time we met. I sense the hitch in its Skill uses, the way it has to expand Mana in a surge each time it switches to a new line of attack.

And all the while, while we fight in the virtual, Mikito takes it on in the physical. She's cutting at it, bleeding its body even as she dodges around combat drones, slips past threads of flame and electricity, and avoids the occasional swing of Skill-powered blows.

Ali breaks free and, angry at its entrapment, fights back against the Anasi's threads. He's burning them, detaching them from the walls with his affinity, sending arcs of electricity down others to shock the spider.

And occasionally, occasionally, one of my Blade Strikes hits, cutting into the damn spider. It still looks pristine, undamaged, but I know its health bank is dropping, draining with each strike.

And we're fine. Mostly.

"Keep at it! We're winning," Ali crows. "Useless Administrator!"

Of course, that's when Wex stops playing with us.

***

The first thing it does is release a cloud of gas. I don't even need the green and purple nature of it to tell me it's a bad idea to be anywhere near the cloud—especially when it expels it from its behind. Mikito, maneuvering around its back, receives the full blast of it.

Of course, her ghost armor has a protection against direct breath attacks. But such poison Skills bypass the sensibility of pure breathing, using aura and physical contact to push its effects upon its victims. Mikito reels back, forced to pull away for a moment as she's assaulted by the poison.

Below, I pull out the Hod and trigger its dressing aspect, cursing myself for paying too much attention to its System Edit Skill and not taking the time to armor myself. "Ugh…"

My pity party is cut short when I look to the side and spot a forgotten member of the party. Harry, curled up on the floor, is thrashing as the damn area effect poison hits him. I snarl, and rather than risk it, I use Sanctum. It forms faster than ever, covering the reporter. I can only hope he's able to survive. Too late, the Hod finishes closing in around me. I feel the Status effects from the poison flare to life as the poison seeps into me.

You have been poisoned by an Anasi Internal Brewed Poison Cloud (Modified)

Effects partially resisted

Health and Mana Regeneration reduced by 38%

You are (mildly) intoxicated. Negative Perception and Agility bonuses applied.

You are receiving 14 HP damage per minute

The damage-over-time effect is negligible for me with my regeneration in play. The Health and Mana regeneration effects are more concerning, especially since this is after my resistances.

But Wex isn't done just yet.

"Look out!"

Ali's shout makes me look up to see a rain of white packages falling down around me. Some fall straight, some arc through the air, and many, many of them bounce off invisible spider threads, their final destination impossible to gauge.

Still, I try to dodge, especially when a few hit the razor thread and part. The damn corpses explode when they fall, engulfing the very air in flames and burning poison. My aura trembles, the Hod hissing as acid-coated rain and poisonous flames assault it. Soul Shield and the Hod's defensive shields sparkle, light chasing across the edges of the protection as I search for a safe place on the ground.

And realize there is nothing.

I take to the air, throwing Blade Strikes ahead of me, calling back my sword as I begin another spell. Beacon of the Angels, targeted to start within the demesne itself.

I swear when my Skill is cut short, the Administrator sliding in and brute-forcing the attack. My body shudders a little as the Mana that was meant to power the Skill flows back into me with nowhere to go. But I climb out of the explosion of body parts and flames, of poison and toxins below into the—relatively—clear air of the second floor. I cut again and again, letting my swords swing in preset patterns, destroying the threads that threaten to take me.

The remnant flames from the explosions pop the Hod's shield. Poison air eats away at my Soul Shield, but I ignore it, searching.

I spot Mikito first. Her horse is treading on bare air, its armored mane ragged, its ghostly body rotting. Its rider is lolling on the back, head hanging over the edge of the horse's neck, Hitoshi pointed at the ground. At least the Legacy weapon seems to be doing well, as a small whirlpool forms around its head as it absorbs the poisons.

Wex I miss until it's too late. It rises up from below me, using threads that I was certain were cut. Hopping through the sky for its fangs to close in on me from below. Dark energies, gravity, and other forms of magic are embedded in its fangs and along the edges of its mouth. Its jaw closes with a snap, popping my Soul Shield without issue. I struggle, attempting to escape and fail.

Rather than fight a losing battle, I trigger Blink Step. I sense it moving to shut it down, and I use my own Skill to block it. But it's sort of like a teenager trying to stop a professional linebacker. The sheer volume of Mana it can wield compared to me is an entire tier apart. The backlash of the direct conflict causes more damage than the grinding, necrotic bite itself.

I shudder, coughing as Blink Step is forcibly shut down and put on cooldown. Its Mana invades my Status, my body, and the essence of what I am within the System, changing, altering things. It hits my escape and defense Skills first, tearing its way through Portal, through Soul Shield and Sanctum. It even turns off Domain, which is hurting it more than Eye of the Storm.

That's okay though, since I'm leaning toward bringing the pain rather than worrying about damage. I force Mana into the System, activating Judgment of All and feeling it snap off. I don't try to stop it though, because I've already got Grand Cross rolling. It slams it shut, but I see the constant Mana use, the way System Edit is burning it up.

Of course, I'm not doing well. Penetration's Shield is powerful, but it requires me to do damage. And it's stopping me from doing it all too often, shutting down whatever it wants with impunity. It's not even trying to edit around restrictions, slamming full stops on me. The System is punishing it, fighting it, but it's taking it to finish this fight. And without damage, my Penetration Shielding is falling, the necrotic, toxic, and elemental damage on its fangs burning through the shield.

I have to finish fast. Good thing I still remember the lesson from our first fight. While it's busy dealing with the System, I conjure lightning. It's easy. There's so much energy being shed—from disrupted Mana, from my shield's sparking, from the escaped radiation and electrons of its energy attacks. I just borrow it, lowering resistances, increasing attraction. Making lightning itself come alive all around us.

It bounces from it to me, to the threads around us, and back again. Lightning, jumping and arcing, connected to one another. The System registers the damage, but it doesn't give it to my shielding, ignoring my Elemental Affinity as it stands outside of the System.

Wex tries to shut it down, of course, but it's an Affinity. There's no System finagling here. It records, it displays, but it doesn't control. But it can mitigate. The damn spider pulls me close, holding me tight with its legs, mouth still clamped onto me, as it absorbs the damage. Its body shimmers, shifting to something darker, something more rubbery. My grasp on its body, on the connection to it, slip as it adjusts to my attack.

"Idiot boy-o." Ali shoots over to me, having freed himself.

He slams a container of plasma into Wex's back, burrowing in as deep as he can before releasing the containment. Electricity tries to jump to the Spirit, but he's mostly immaterial. Beyond charring the Spirit a little at the edges—disrupting Ali's material plane connection—he's fine.

So's Wex, to my horror. The damn creature's resistances and bank of life is taking Ali's attack with aplomb. Things go from bad to worse as I reel from another System Edit assault that floods my body with Mana, turning my Judgment of All Skill on me. I batter the Edit attack aside, shoving will and my own Skill against it, but not before my Penetration Skill pops and my life plummets.

My body is on fire, the Hod is smoking and screaming as the power armor is melted, and my flesh decays as necrotic energy invades me. I liquify and burn, and my tender grasp on the lightning falls aside.

A last ditch maneuever. I haven't tried it before, but theoretically, if I let the bonds between my molecules slip far enough, I can fall. Right through its grip. I try for it, feeling myself and the Hod shudder.

And stop, for electromagnetic force is only one of the prime forces in the universe. And the damn Administrator is wielding gravity spheres in its mouth, pulling me toward its fangs.

"Wake up, Mikito!" Ali shouts. Its olive face is scrunched up in concentration as it pours plasma into Wex's torso, trying to push it through the body to hit something important. It must hurt, but the Administrator doesn't care.

A snap, a tear, and the Hod's outer armor around an arm falls away as the damage from the elements, from the lightning, from the fires that burn below and the toxins that drip take its toll. It falls—and so does the arm beneath it, as liquified and crisped skin offers no grip. The armor falls for only a second before swinging up, smacking Wex in the face as gravity spheres pull it up.

I'm held in place not by its mouth but the gravity it wields, attacked on all sides. The lightning is gone, only occasional sparks still bursting into life as excess energy keeps firing. I'm semi-immaterial, floating in space, smoke and toxins entering and mixing within my body, leaving a burnt, rotten smell in my throat, in my lungs.

Blood drips and falls, and even my defensive Skills fail. Peasant's Fury is working overtime to increase regeneration, but I'm taking more damage than it can keep up with. Elastic Skin and Harden help, as do my resistances, but poisons and toxins bypass a lot of the defenses. Wex's abilities are perfect for dealing with me.

The gravity spheres hold on to me and my mind spins, time and Intelligence stretching out for a few brief seconds. Gravity spheres work in one of two ways. It compresses and increases the mass in a location—making it denser and thus increasing the force of attraction. Or it increases G—the gravitational force itself. My Affinity doesn't change my mass, and releasing it leaves me still hanging in space. The Administrator isn't strong enough, physically, to handle an increase in mass, so the spell must increase the gravitational force itself.

Which means…

I trigger a Skill and pull at my sword. It lets me, not caring about the extra swords I conjure. They can cut, but they aren't that powerful, not with me thrashing in mid-air. But I release my soulbound weapon, letting it fall. And it shoots upward, just like my arm.

To strike Wex in the face. It plunges deep, point first. And then, behind it, the conjured weapons it let me have follow, just as they're scripted to. The attack isn't enough to kill it, but having multiple blades plunged into one's body from below and attempt to come out one's face is distracting as all hell. Never mind the plasma torch Ali wields.

Wex's concentration falters for a second, the gravitic spheres blinking off. Anger takes over the Administrator and it twists the spell with its System Edit. Rather than drawing, it repulses. Ali, the swords, myself are launched away at speed.

The floor rushes up to me, shattering my newly renewed Penetration shield. The mixed-metal and stone floor cracks beneath my body, webs of kinetic energy dispersed. Flames from burning corpses gutter, as dust and air billow out from the impact point, before reasserting themselves with vigor.

My head rings, my body shattered. I feel bones grind, a lung pierced, organs ruptured. Frenzy threatens to activate, before it is slapped down by the Administrator. It holds itself in the air, Ali and Mikito caught in its webs as it lowers itself toward me.

I wonder when it caught Ali. Maybe in the half-second when I fell, when it turned its full attention on the Spirit.

A glance at its Health bank, as my Skill tells me we did well. We took out nearly all of it. Just a little more and we would be tearing into its real health. We could win.

I just have to move.

But I can't. The Hod is broken, my body not much better.

Wex lowers itself, thread spooling from its behind as it speaks. "A good attempt, but futile…"

Wex begins to monologue.

And it freezes when I grin.

***

The golden book comes slamming down at an angle, which is a good thing. I'm too broken to dodge, even if I wanted to. And if I did move beforehand, it'd give Wex time to dodge. As it stands, the damn Administrator manages to get a bunch of threads in the way and its body scurrying to the side.

But the book is huge and it's moving as fast as a bullet. The amount of time Wex has to dodge is counted in milliseconds. The book keeps moving, crushing the spider into the wall and pushing, turning the Administrator into so much paste. I spot a single leg, uncovered at the side of the wall, twitching. Before the flood of blood and guts push out from the edges of the book itself.

"Squish," I breathe and let my head flop backward.

Pain, pain that threatened to take me, floods over my consciousness. I ride it out, floating in the sea of agony as the System battles the poisons and toxins still in my body, as it deals with the flames. A refreshing wave of energy flows over me, healing some of the damage. Another wave and my body bubbles and twists, toxins and poisons exploding from my skin. A noxious green, yellow, and black paste bubbles from my body, mixing with the red of my blood.

Above, screams resound from Mikito as the same happens to the Samurai. She's shocked awake by the cleansing, dropping to the ground a moment later when she releases her steed. The normally calm and unshakeable Samurai blanches when she spots the state I'm in. Not that she looks much better. Her hair's almost all fallen out and patches of flesh peek out from the damaged clothing she wears, raw and open as the System keeps healing it.

"I… I failed," Mikito whispers, bowing to me.

"Pish-tosh," Ali says, floating down. "It caught you unawares with that sleepy poison. Overrode any of the defenses you had by cheating."

"I should have anticipated. Planned better," Mikito says, shaking her head. "I could have bought other Skills."

"Which the Administrator would have likely rendered useless." The voice that cuts in is thick Glaswegian, barely understandable. Totally at odds with the thin black tie, charcoal-grey-suited figure that floats over to us. Except, you know, the extra long limbs and fingers and the grey and pallid skin with oversized eyes on a famine-shaped body. "It was only when it felt secure that we were assured of its death."

"Pride before fall. And then, squish." I lever myself up, laughing a little in pain and sardonic humor. It might be a little hysterical, as my mind and the System try to compartmentalize the memories of burning and rotting alive. Simultaneously.

"Yes. I received your message," Feh'ral says. His eyes flicker sideways, up to the library and the books I purchased. The signal to it, the locator beacon that allowed it to step across time and space to our side. With a little help. "The Lord is less than pleased with us both. I do not think he will help us further. But he is delighted that the Council is no longer probing his defenses."

"Wasn't his entire schtick being left alone?" Ali says. "The entire false Forbidden Zone and everything."

"He might exaggerate the level of his neutrality," Feh'ral says, fingers back in front of his body and tented. He turns, his entire body floating around to stare at his golden book. A moment later, the book shrinks and flies back into his hand. "If he did not, did you think I would have sent you to him? The Lord has always had conflicts with both the Council and what we now know to be the Administrators."

"Why...? Oh. The Forbidden Zones." I nod. "They have no control in there, do they?"

Feh'ral inclines his head and I snort, pushing myself the rest of the way to my feet. I idly tap a few things and send off the Hod, watching as it pulls itself into a shattered cube before blipping away, sent off for fixing. I just hope they can get it sorted before I need it again.

Who am I kidding? They won't.

"Is Harry okay?" Mikito asks, looking at the still-present bubble of the Sanctum.

I turn my head to follow her gaze, then glance at the party interface. "He's alive."

"But silent."

I have nothing to add to that. I hope he's fine, but the silence is less than promising. It's possible that he's unconscious as well, but his status effects don't show that. Which might mean he's catatonic in an entirely, non-System way.

Unable to do anything about that for now, I turn to Feh'ral. "I'm glad to see you."

As my body continues to patch itself together, I breathe slowly, wishing I had the Mana to cast a Cleanse. I reek of the toxins and poisons from the corpses and Wex's bile, all mixed with the remnants of my flesh and organs.

Non-combat Class or not, the gods damned Administrator really showed me what the System Edit Skill could do in a fight. I need to learn how to do the things he did—and how to protect myself and my friends.

Thankfully, the vast majority of the things he Edited are being fixed by the System as it reverts me to its baselines stats, dealing with the problematic issues the Administrator created. Anything the System doesn't get around to, I'll handle. Once I stop hurting.

"I take it that the Questors have voted," I say when Feh'ral doesn't answer. "It's good to have you guys on board."

"No," Feh'ral says.

"What?" I shout.

Feh'ral inclines his head, as if my expression of emotion is something wrong. "The Questors have decided that your information is good. They commend you. They offer you this..."

Congratulations! Title Granted: Innovative Questor

You have contributed a significant piece of information to the Questor library. You have been hereby granted a new Title. Your word and research data will be given more weight during the System Quest studies.

Effect: Reputation increased with all Questors. Reputation decreased with other factions.

I scroll through the notification quickly, then dismiss it with an angry wave. "I don't want a consolation prize. I want to know why you all aren't helping."

"The information was good, but insufficient. The information provided increased a number of Quest completion rates. But it was insufficient to provide a marked and universal increase." Feh'ral's hands open wide, as if to say what can you do. "The information has been banked. It will be dispersed. It will not be lost. The sacrifice has been noted."

I find myself shouting, "That's it? That's all you're going to do? Because you guys didn't get enough of a completion rate, you just pat us on the head and let my world, let us, die? Just because you can't fulfill enough of your damn Quest?" I'm angry, and if my chest, my body burns with anger—and lingering damage—it also helps me avoid the thought that I have done much the same before. Chosen the Quest over others, over the individual good.

Feh'ral nods impassively.

"If that's the case, what the hell are you doing here?" I snap.

Mikito watches us calmly, though I note her hand has dropped low, in the position she uses for calling forth her weapon. The motion which would allow to swing it up and bisect Feh'ral if needed. Ali, on the other hand, is looking… well, conflicted. Between being amused at my reaction and horror at the implications.

Feh'ral grins, and I find myself shivering. That damn #creepylibrarian still makes me shudder. "I disagreed with the majority. As did a few others. We believe you can lead us to more, to the completion of our most sought-after desire. And, I believe, where you go is where I must too."

I growl, ignoring the rather obvious conversational bait. "So you're here by yourself."

I shut my eyes, forcing some calm over myself. A hand presses something into my hands and I look at it, spotting a chunk of chocolate. Ali gives me one of his shit-eating grins even as I debate throwing the hunk of liquid sunshine at him.

"Hey, at least we got a Legendary on our side," Ali says.

I let out another groan but decide against the blasphemy and pop the chocolate into my mouth. He is right. We do have a new dangerous and creepy ally. It's not what I wanted, but he came when we needed him. When we would have fallen.

As I stare around the shattered, broken domain, I shake my head. In the distance, the windows—thankfully one-way—showcase the voting hall. All of this, all this fighting, and we're not done yet.

For there's still what we came here to do. The final piece of my plan. And after that... well.

Perhaps the Questors are right to abandon us.

Chapter 24

We walk forward as the System strains to clean and put the domain back into place. Thankfully, System-chicanery means that no one noticed the fight within. Or if they did, they ignored it.

It's still weird, shifting from a life-and-death struggle to just silence, to boredom and a moment of relaxation. Or as relaxed as you can get, knowing that you might have enemy fighters running in at any time to end you. It's a weird mixture of boredom and tension, of breathless waiting and shuddering, tension-escaping moments.

The calm after a hurricane hits, after the earthquake has come and gone, while you're waiting to see if there are aftershocks. When you have to get on with life, but you're unsure if your world is about to come apart once more.

Before the windows, I come to a stop. For the first time, I can look properly at the chamber for the Galactic Council. The center of power for the System supposedly, the place where the galaxy revolves. Except we know that for the lie it is.

Seats abound, all facing a giant stage. The council chamber looks too big and too small at the same time. Too small to contain the entire galaxy's places of power and too big, for it extends on and on, the farthest windows no larger than half the size of my hand. On the sloping ground, along a trio of open air mezzanine locations, are benches and tables for those with less power or who desire to be closer to the action.

From speaking with Katherine, I know each chamber's windows shift, optimizing the view of occupied locations. Unoccupied chambers are shifted back by more System chicanery.

The whole room is shaded steel grey, illuminated by purple and blue lighting, with minor variations in lighting depending on the section. I absently note small force bubbles in certain areas, set up so that individuals with noncarbon-based, nonoxygen-breathing genetics are able to interact and exist. Some of those bubbles contain water, liquid nitrogen, liquid carbon, magma, and in one case—well separated from everyone else—plasma. The wide variety of aliens that make up the System can be seen in both the kinds of environments they require and the caution taken by others interacting with them.

And interact they do, speaking, gambling, and in a few cases, even fighting. But the poor spike of vegetation on the stage, wobbling and trembling while speaking in Galactic with all its heart—if it has a heart—no one's truly paying attention to. It only takes me a few minutes to grasp what it's asking for—a plea for help as they are being invaded and conquered by another opposing nation. I, like everyone else, dismiss it from my mind. As much as I might feel for them, I have my own problems.

And isn't that the condemnation and a pure example of the living condition? We all have our own problems, our own burdens, all of it pressing down upon us. And for us, no matter how big, no matter how terrible another's problems might be—objectively and subjectively—ours will always matter more. It takes courage, bravery, and empathy to step outside of our own minds, our own hearts and concerns to aid another. Especially when that aid has no ulterior motives, when there is no hope of gratitude or payment. When it is done because it's the right thing to do.

There are some, people who martyr themselves on the altar of charity, sacrificing their own lives, their own self or well-being for others. Too many of them, we find out later, aren't as self-sacrifical or pure as we think. Mother Theresa let people writhe in pain, denying them painkillers and medicine, in some crazy belief about the cleansing power of pain. JFK was a womanizing, charming son of a bitch whose record might have been indelibly stained by the Bay of Pigs if he had not performed well once during the Cuban Missile Crisis.

At the end of the day, charity when you can afford it, when you yourself are stable, is the most real-life form. And yet… and yet, how sad is it that we should only offer help, that we will only offer help, when it's convenient for us?

What a world we live in. Sadly, knowing all that, I still tune out the Kapre-variant and focus on the council. So many, thousands of them, all of them negotiating and socializing, each of them ready to sell out the other for an advantage for their civilization. Some nothing more than vassal states, others stubbornly independent, and still others wholly controlled by the big empires.

Turning on Society's Web, I spot the cluster that makes up the Movana and the Truinnar, the main Ambassadors gone but their second-in-commands holding court. They stand in the central flow of the group, standing where others may watch them cluster, while their sycophants surround them in vassal groups.

Those planets sucking up for protection hover at the edges. Sometimes, one or another planetary ambassador breaks off to chat to these orbiting ambassadors as another deal, another agreement is worked out. But the center of these empires hold still as the worlds revolves around them.

The Erethrans have their own section, though it's smaller, quieter. They're standing and sitting around, focused and watching, their guard up. None of them bother to interact much, and the few who approach are rebuffed. Even in terms of volume, the Erethrans are smaller, but unlike the Movana or Truinnar, the Erethran Empire is more homogenous. Fewer planets need to have a seat here, passing their votes up the chain. Of course, the standoff nature of the Empire is getting more than a few side-eyes.

Especially by their ostentatious allies like the Fist or the Expansionists, all of whom have their own loose clumps. The political factions, unlike the Empires and Kingdom-based powers, are less clustered, more organic in their movements. But under Society's Web, their secrets, their alliances, the flow of power is all an open book to me.

In the end, the vote is called for the poor vegetable-creature. A sphere, a giant shimmering globe, appears. Not that it ever left, just hidden from sight until now so as not to distract others.

The globe shifts in size, shrinking as the request is small, just a motion to restrict trade. He barely needs a tenth of the people to vote for his request to pass. If his request passes, it has to be paid for somehow, and the System enforces such payment on the planets and governments of the Council itself. To make a change, there has to be sacrifice. In this case, of System Mana to empower the choices that are being made.

It's an interesting system, one that favors Dungeon Worlds like ours with our overabundance of Mana and thus an overabundance of weight to our potential actions. Of course, on a galactic scale, a single Dungeon Planet is worth only a few dozen other planets—less if one is lacking in System infrastructure, as is Earth. But it can still matter, especially if one is able to gain a significant number of Dungeon Worlds.

The voting sphere fills with pure System Mana in bursts and dribbles, as those who decide to support its cause pour in their efforts. Unfortunately, another aspect of the voting is that a vote, once cast—once System is dedicated—can never be taken back. A failed vote is just a waste, like the one below.

The Kapre-varient trundles off in failure, another speaker soon taking his place. The globe disappears, the Mana gone.

I watch, taking it all in, tracing the votes, the reactions of those below, their deals. With Ali's help, I mark the votes, the voters, and the expected results of our own vote, tapping into my Neural Link to do the math, display the graphs. Watch as the numbers flow and bump, adding or subtracting as I mentally adjust the calculated percentages.

Trying to decide how close we are to succeeding. Trying to work out if we can hope to win.

***

Behind me, Harry comes out of the Sanctum. He looks… worse for wear. He's holding on by the tips of his fingers to some form of sanity, some form of calm. He stumbles over to a chair near the windows and sits, staring at the assemblage below, his hands shaking. I jerk my head to Ali and the little Spirit floats over to have a quiet chat with the reporter, soon followed by Mikito.

Feh'ral stands, watching beside me. His eyes dart strangely at first, before I realize he's reading unseen notification screens. Taking in information, though he declines to explain what kind when I ask. In fact, he seems disinclined to speak at all, even when I probe him for further information on the Questors.

The silence from within the domain stretches while the buzz of conversations and votes being made below permeate the room. Occasionally, I notice that the system puts in a vote for Earth, obviously a preset voting system. I leave it alone, choosing not to interfere.

Watching the votes pass by me, I can't help but shake my head at many of them.

Condemnation of the destruction of the Dawn Will Guild

Registration of the boundary lines between the Kingdom of Ius and the Republic of Qx13

Application for Galactic Quest (localized) for destruction of the Tier II dungeons in PK-space

Budget Approval for the 248,815th Expedition to non-System space

Deployment request for Galactic Troops to the xv-138 region to reduce planetary dungeon overflows

And on and on. The hours grind past, and even when it seems there's supposed to be an order to the votes, somehow, other motions, other bills and clauses and requests sneak their way in. It's a bewildering array of bureaucratic magic, where planets trade voting rights or hand over speaking opportunities or offer to bring up a slate of previous issues, all to get their own areas voted upon.

A couple of times, sapients get a little too aggressive. Someone calls forth a rock, crushing an opponent. He in turn gets impaled on a rock spike and has to extract his mangled body from it by himself. Another pair, screaming at one another, find themselves suddenly unable to speak, the flesh of their mouths sealed shut, stitched over. Someone tries to interrupt for a third time when it's not their turn. They're teleported out of the Council chamber entirely and a penalty added to their planet's Mana total, deducted immediately.

All of that is overseen by a wizened, twisted knot of string and hair. The Secretariat of the Council runs the Galactic Council with complete impartiality, holding to only one thing and that is the laws of the Council. Nothing, and no one, tells him how to run the hall.

Not even the Inner Council.

Of course, that he's actually the puppet of the Weaver is a not-so-hidden secret. One that the powers that be—people like the Erethrans and, thus, me—know and the smaller players don't. It's why no one in the Inner Council objects when he runs roughshod over their own powerplays. So long as they play within the stated rules, they know he won't interfere.

In a corner of my mind, I watch it all, absently noting that every single one of my Hands have now expired. I make sure to call them up, now that we're here. Now that we have time. One wanders off to cook and eat, another to the study to read, and the last sits in a corner, brooding. I'd protest at the caricatures of my behavior if it wasn't so damn accurate.

In time, I ignore them. I watch the proceedings below with interest in the beginning, before boredom takes me and I turn away. Harry watches and records, muttering explanations to himself and his viewers—eventual viewers—doing his best to provide commentary. He throws himself into his work, though I note the way his foot never stops bouncing, the occasional stuttered pause.

More than once, I note Harry cursing or muttering in bewilderment as a political maneuver catches him by surprise. A lot of the time, he mutters things about needing more research.

I leave him to it, glad that work has the reporter absorbed, and walk over to find Mikito seated in lotus position, hands clasped before her, and meditating. I sit across from her, only for the Samurai to crack an eye open.

"You should try it. It'll calm your mind and center you."

"Calm might not be the best option. They've killed all my doppelgangers. They must be wondering where we are by now." I drop my voice lower, leaning in and adding, "And I don't know how long the others will stay distracted."

Mikito sighs, exhaling roughly before she fixes me with both eyes. "Will worrying change things?"

"No."

"Then as you like to say, what is, is. There is nothing more that we can do. So eat some chocolate, meditate, and stop bothering me."

She shuts her eyes and I find myself alone once more. Forced to stew in my own thoughts. With nothing better to do, I focus within, playing with not the System but my Elemental Affinity, gently sensing the flow of bonds, the force of attraction and repulsion that makes up the Affinity. I consider the weakness shown, my lack of ability. And I explore new concepts, new ways of interacting with the system—gently.

Time passes slowly, inching forward as votes and new clauses and constitutions are put into play. We're forced to wait, until finally, finally, Harry speaks.

"It's time," Harry says, gesturing down below.

"You sure?" I say.

"Yes. This bill needs to be voted upon. Afterward, it will be yours, with no others set to speak."

I look at Ali, who shrugs and nods at the same time, as if to say he's as sure as he can be.

When I dither for a second more, Feh'ral speaks up. "Go."

I stand, looking around at the group. A part of me wonders if this is the right thing to do. The right course of action. But I've gone this far. Sacrificed too much.

I close my eyes, then nod. "Fine. Let's go save Earth."

Chapter 25

The votes go as expected. The numbers climb fast then slow down, as those who hesitate, who are compromised by Earth or me hover between opposing or abstaining. The simple sphere fills with liquid blue Mana for each positive vote, sloshing around the sphere as some hesitate. The sphere itself is large, many times larger than the Kapre-variant's and most other votes'. This is a long-term vote, one meant to enforce itself across the entire Galactic System, and is subsequently large.

The votes come, and while I wait for those who hesitate, I look upon the notification that hangs above the sphere. The one that holds all the hopes of Earth.

Motion to restrict Dungeon Planets from the Galactic Council
Requires 2398Q Unites of System Mana.
Effect: Strips Dungeon Planets of the Planetary System Network, foregoing voting rights on the Galactic Council and all System-enabled Planetary Upgrades.
Prior purchased System-enabled planetary networks will be refunded and/or modified to suit new restricted framework.

Eventually, the Mana stops entering, leaving a clear amount of space for liquid to enter. There's a small demarcation line and the liquid filled is below that by a few hundred thousand Mana points. I'm surprised that we made it that far. That the abstainers have held out for so long, that the pressure and horse trading has done so well that the liquid sloshes near the edge of completion but does not cross it.

Yet.

The Erethrans, the Duchess, a few of our other allies hold the line. Refusing to throw their votes for the motion. Direct vassal states follow their lead in most cases, though I note a few quick glances, a couple of surprises that are revealed. Ramanner, amongst his people, gestures more than once to a few hard-eyed compatriots who look with glinting malice upon the ones who have betrayed them.

The liquid trembles on the edge of crossing. I watch as those who abstained are turned on or toward. The vultures and the grifters, the deal makers and the Negotiators arrive, ready to sway. I know some hold off for the better deal.

I wonder if I'll make more enemies by what I do next. Cutting their deals short, making all their hard work and plans just so much wastepaper.

Then I grin. Because it doesn't matter. I never gave a damn anyway.

***

My voice cuts through the hubbub, and the aliens' attention is drawn to my figure on the stage. The hair-and-string-ball of the Secretariat allowed the speech as per my right as one of the affected parties. The only affected party with a seat. It's a little unusual to speak while the voting is happening, but not impossible.

As the Council stares at my figure, my words keep coming. Keeps pouring out, as if a dam is unleashed.

"I invoke my right, as proxy holder for the Dungeon Planet *Earth,* to speak about the motion."

The Secretariat of the Council spins tendrils of hair and flesh together then pulls it apart creating a minor thunderclap. It silences the hall, the entire Council no longer able to make themselves heard to one another. A simple Skill.

"Thank you."

The Secretariat doesn't care, impassive eyes shifting to the timer that has appeared, indicating how much time I have to speak. Fifteen minutes. More than sufficient.

"You know, a decade or so ago, I was a barbarian with a stick in the middle of nowhere, watching the sunset on a beautiful lake. A nobody to the great and powerful personages before me. And then, you and your System came along. Rather than give us a chance to integrate peacefully, normally, you made us a Dungeon World."

In the pause, in the silence, the aliens shift. I feel the information flow, the data passing and bouncing between Ambassadors and Diplomats and Bodyguards, as my presence is located. As they get ready to take me down when my time is up. Favors are called in and confirmed, bounties marked as pending collection. All this information flows, and attached to all that data streaming out of the Galactic Council, I sense the familiar touch of a friend's Skill.

"You killed us. Billions of us humans. Transformed even more animals, some who might have become something more in a few tens of thousands of years. Altered the path of our destiny." Exhale. Wry tone, almost amused. "Some of the survivors these days, some of them are grateful. Because when you made us a Dungeon World, you gave some of us strength. Power. Perks.

"You gave us a leg up, and some of us have taken it all the way to the stars. We've got Heroics now, and soon, we'll have some of them in truth. Not a cheaty bastard like me, but people who earned it the hard way, wading through streets filled with blood, tearing through dungeons, and making it all the way through."

I can see the speech is losing them. Some of them are shifting, turning away, getting bored. They're wondering when I'll get to the point, and I get it. I wonder about that too.

"We even did things you didn't expect. United a Dungeon World before you realized it was possible. Made it our own and took our seat here. And then…" I gesture upward. "You try to take it away. Because we got too uppity, because we threatened your local cliques."

A pause. A dramatic pause. Then, laughter, harsh and filled with bitter humor. It catches their wandering attention, brings their focus back to that small figure on the stage. The one taunting them, lecturing them.

"At least that was what you were told. Fed little lies, as if you were children, and satisfied with those little lies, thinking you were adults, you ran around with the sharp scissors of vindication and tore into us. Thinking that what you learnt is the truth."

The Secretariat shifts, hair and tendrils twitching. But it makes no move to stop me. And so long as he doesn't, no one else can, even if there are guards pounding at the shield surrounding the stage, trying to get in. Covert and not-so-covert attempts at breaching the shield are blocked with lazy ease. Some of the too obvious ones even die for their presumption.

"But it was easy to feed you those lies. Because all of you, coming light years across the galaxy to fight for scraps of power, for a chance to get ahead of everyone else, are too blind to see. You, who are meant to serve those who voted you in or those who you rule could not find the monster from the forest when you were too busy looking out for your own desires.

"And all the while, out there, people cry and die, struggling for some form of normalcy. Entire solar systems, billions of lives lost because you are all looking out for number one. Forget peace or social responsibility or justice.

"You people disgust me."

I watch as the Counselors try to shout me down and fail. They're all muted, but the looks I'm given tell me that my grandstanding is less than loved. I don't care.

"Justice shouldn't just be for those who can pay for it. For those who can spend the time and expertise to get it. You shouldn't have to be willing to sacrifice everything to find it. It certainly shouldn't be coming at the hands of an unhinged lunatic without any safeguards behind it."

A slight dig there at myself. At Classes and Levels and the entire concept of might is right. Because sadly, that seems to be the only way the System works. At least, not without deep sacrifice.

"Justice is meant to be for everyone, at any place. And if the universe doesn't work that way, well, what's new? It's never worked that way. But that's your job in this chamber. To fix the wrongs an uncaring System creates, to offer a vestige of fairness that the slavering jaws of monsters do not.

"That's what you chose to do. To make the galaxy a little fairer, a little brighter. A little more just. And you all failed. Because you're so damn desperate for power."

Voice, lower. The next words are said almost at a whisper. "But that's all right. If you want power, if you want to know the truth, I'll give it to you."

More people are moving, some trying to approach the platform only to be rebuffed by the Secretariat's shield. Others are leaving, as if they sense the danger of what is to come. More send out messages while others have never stopped recording what I'm saying, alerting their people, the guards.

"But first, let's get this over with."

I will my answer to the System and watch as the sphere hanging above the chamber darkens. As my vote for Earth floods in. Liquid System Mana pours into the globe, pushing the vote over the edge. There are gasps, shouts.

More than a few of my allies look shocked as I finish what my enemies started.

I betray Katherine and Rob and Earth before the Council itself, taking away Earth's seat.

In the shocked silence, I find myself grinning savagely. I watch as the galactic ensemble scrambles, as they work out the implications of what I've done. A small notification appears in the corner of my eyes, informing me that we no longer have the room, the embassies within seven days.

My allies are shocked. Some are barking orders to others, all of them closing ranks as they wonder what is happening.

"You think this matters? It doesn't. You think Earth is that easy to take? Then try it. But you won't find me there. You all seem to think it matters to me, so I figured I'd show you. Remind you.

"There are further secrets to be found. More power to acquire. Truths more important than some stupid, useless planet of uplifted apes."

Above my all-too-cocky body, the timer shifts and reduces while the sphere pulses. Some others throw in their votes now, fulfilling vows and promises. Many others hold off, confusion warring with avarice.

And still, my voice drones on. "Real power. Not this sham." A hand waves over the surrounding seats, taking them all in. "Because you've been lied to all your life. For millennia, you've been spoon-fed a lie, as if your broken, warped seats matter.

"But this is the truth."

I push my Status Screen outward. Fighting the Title, making it turn off. There's a block, a System Administrator-level block against what I'm trying to do. I pitch myself against it, feel the security responses from the administrative block flood into my body, tearing at it. I burn, body twisting and nerves flooding with Mana. My knees give way, my nose bleeds, my eyes squeeze shut. Pain racks my body as the Administrators' security systems attempt to stop what I'm doing.

I pitch myself against their defenses and find myself failing. Failing—until something deeper, something hard-coded into the very bonds of the System itself takes action. It comes like a tsunami wave of System Mana that takes no prisoners, that cares not for the swimmers on the beach. My health drops precipitously again as it "helps."

My body glows blue, green, white as directed System Mana floods into me from outside, healing my body. My friends aid my efforts, keeping me alive as the System and I battle the Administrators, changing the code.

Finally, the barrier, the permissions that were blocking me from showing this to the vast public give way.

John Lee, Redeemer of the Dead, Monster's Bane, Redeemer of the Dead, Duelist, Explorer, Apprentice Questor, Galactic Silver Bounty Hunter,…, (Junior System Administrator Level 16)
HP: 4138/6300
MP: 8674/6350

My voice, speaking to them all. I'm being carried away, hands gripping me, pulling me aside as regeneration kicks in, patching me together even as the overabundance of System Mana slowly flows away, slowly breaks down.

"A lie. Because you are but pawns in a world you've never seen and yet still insist is real. If you want answers, ask your Inner Council. Ask them why they've hidden this secret from you. Ask them about the shadows behind the throne, the ones who manipulate everything you believe in, that change the very fabric of the System. Ask them why the System is theirs to manipulate—and not yours."

Voices rise, shouting, screaming, asking questions and demanding answers. The voices are as diverse as the audience, and fights have begun. So much so that even the shield around the stage is failing as the massed volume of the Council take action.

"Ask them how many lies they've really told and how many Classes they've rendered useless. What they've hidden from you by hiding away this Class." A pause. "And what it means that the System itself fights them."

A small timer in the corner of my eyes ticks over.

Time's up.

Explosions of Mana. Skills and spells thrown at one another, at the stage. An assault and retaliation, and the council chambers devolve into pure chaos. Some, the more opportunistic, lash out at rivals. The Secretariat disappears, leaving the Council to deal with itself.

Spells and Skills wash over the figure on the stage, taking down its Soul Shield within seconds, consuming its health. That it laughs, as though the destruction is but a small matter. I feel the snap of the doppelganger's death, the flood of knowledge as information returns to me.

Information, long suppressed, breaks free. And like any dark truth, any secret long held close, its revelation leaves chaos and hurt behind. There are some secrets, some knowledge that can only ever bring pain and tragedy.

And I've just revealed the galactic-sized version of one.

THE END

*John and his team are on the run, from former friends and new enemies. There's only one place of safety for them now. Only one option. To finish the System Quest in **the***

***Forbidden Zone (Book 11 of the System Apocalypse)**.*

Epilogue

We run.

After dropping the bombshell and setting the entire Council chamber alight with speculation and recrimination, we run.

There's no going back for us now, no home to return to. I've betrayed not just the Council and the Administrators, but Earth too. It's all for a good cause—to take the target off Earth's back and place it firmly on mine. The betrayal probably stings just as much even if they realize that truth.

I've completed my commitments, even if it's not the way they expected it. Perhaps the Duchess and the Lady are happy. Most likely not.

In either case, there's no turning back now. We have to find the answer or die.

So we run. Attempting to escape the death trap that is the Council Hall and Irvina itself. To locate a single Administrative Center in the middle of the Forbidden Zone, where perhaps…

Perhaps there are answers.

We run, with the hounds baying at our feet, ritual glyphs forming over our heads and Skills flying. Toward hope, toward danger, toward an end.

Finally.

Author's Note

Broken Council starts the final arc of the System Apocalypse series. Having drawn the ire of the Galactic Council, and revealed one of their greatest secrets, there is nowhere left for him to run. John's only hope, only goal now is the System Quest. In finding the answer, he might find a solution.

This book was rather complex to write. I had to fit multiple plot threads in, close off some and work in some character arcs that I've wanted to do in a while. Trying to make sure it all made sense while giving a satisfying conclusion was tough, especially figuring out where the end of this book was meant to be.

As always, I'm grateful for everyone who has followed me on this long journey. I've received more support for this little story in my head than I could ever expect. I truly do hope that you've enjoyed the journey thus far.

If you enjoyed reading the book, please do leave a review and rating. Reviews are the lifeblood of authors and help others choose to continue with the series or not.

In addition, please check out my other series, Adventures on Brad (a more traditional LitRPG fantasy), Hidden Wishes (an urban fantasy GameLit series), and A Thousand Li (a cultivation series inspired by Chinese wuxia and xianxia novels).

To support me directly, please go to my Patreon account:
- https://www.patreon.com/taowong

For more great information about LitRPG series, check out the Facebook groups:

- LitRPG Society

  https://www.facebook.com/groups/LitRPGsociety/

- LitRPG Books

https://www.facebook.com/groups/LitRPG.books/

About the Author

Tao Wong is an avid fantasy and sci-fi reader who spends his time working and writing in the North of Canada. He's spent way too many years doing martial arts of many forms, and having broken himself too often, he now spends his time writing about fantasy worlds.

For updates on the series and other books written by Tao Wong (and special one-shot stories), please visit the author's website:

http://www.mylifemytao.com

Subscribers to Tao's mailing list will receive exclusive access to short stories in the Thousand Li and System Apocalypse universes:

https://www.subscribepage.com/taowong

Or visit his Facebook Page: https://www.facebook.com/taowongauthor/

About the Publisher

Starlit Publishing is wholly owned and operated by Tao Wong. It is a science fiction and fantasy publisher focused on the LitRPG & cultivation genres. Their focus is on promoting new, upcoming authors in the genre whose writing challenges the existing stereotypes while giving a rip-roaring good read.

For more information on Starlit Publishing, visit their website:

https://www.starlitpublishing.com/

You can also join Starlit Publishing's mailing list to learn of new, exciting authors and book releases.

https://starlitpublishing.com/newsletter-signup/

Glossary

Erethran Honor Guard Skill Tree

John's Erethran Honor Guard Skills

Mana Imbue (Level 5)

Soulbound weapon now permanently imbued with Mana to deal more damage on each hit. +30 Base Damage (Mana). Will ignore armor and resistances. Mana regeneration reduced by 25 Mana per minute permanently.

Blade Strike (Level 5)

By projecting additional Mana and stamina into a strike, the Erethran Honor Guard's Soulbound weapon may project a strike up to 50 feet away.

Cost: 50 Stamina + 50 Mana

Thousand Steps (Level 1)

Movement speed for the Honor Guard and allies are increased by 5% while skill is active. This ability is stackable with other movement-related skills.

Cost: 20 Stamina + 20 Mana per minute

Altered Space (Level 2)

The Honor Guard now has access to an extra-dimensional storage location of 30 cubic meters. Items stored must be touched to be willed in and may not include living creatures or items currently affected by auras that are not the Honor Guard's. Mana regeneration reduced by 10 Mana per minute permanently.

Two are One (Level 1)

Effect: Transfer 10% of all damage from Target to Self

Cost: 5 Mana per second

The Body's Resolve (Level 3)

Effect: Increase natural health regeneration by 35%. Ongoing health status effects reduced by 33%. Honor Guard may now regenerate lost limbs. Mana regeneration reduced by 15 Mana per minute permanently.

Greater Detection (Level 1)

Effect: User may now detect System creatures up to 1 kilometer away. General information about strength level is provided on detection. Stealth skills, Class skills, and ambient Mana density will influence the effectiveness of this skill. Mana regeneration reduced by 5 Mana per minute permanently.

A Thousand Blades (Level 4)

Creates five duplicate copies of the user's designated weapon. Duplicate copies deal base damage of copied items. May be combined with Mana Imbue and Shield Transference. Mana Cost: 3 Mana per second

Soul Shield (Level 8)

Effect: Creates a manipulable shield to cover the caster's or target's body. Shield has 2,750 Hit Points.

Cost: 250 Mana

Blink Step (Level 2)

Effect: Instantaneous teleportation via line-of-sight. May include Spirit's line of sight. Maximum range—500 meters.

Cost: 100 Mana

Portal (Level 5)

Effect: Creates a 5-meter by 5-meter portal which can connect to a previously traveled location by user. May be used by others. Maximum distance range of portals is 10,000 kilometers.

Cost: 250 Mana + 100 Mana per minute (minimum cost 350 Mana)

Army of One (Level 4)

The Honor Guard's feared penultimate combat ability, Army of One builds upon previous Skills, allowing the user to unleash an awe-inspiring attack to deal with their enemies. Attack may now be guided around minor obstacles.

Effect: Army of One allows the projection of (Number of Thousand Blades conjured weapons * 3) Blade Strike attacks up to 500 meters away from user. Each attack deals 5 * Blade Strike Level damage (inclusive of Mana Imbue and Soulbound weapon bonus)

Cost: 750 Mana

Sanctum (Level 2)

An Erethran Honor Guard's ultimate trump card in safeguarding their target, Sanctum creates a flexible shield that blocks all incoming attacks, hostile teleportations and Skills. At this Level of Skill, the user must specify dimensions of the Sanctum upon use of the Skill. The Sanctum cannot be moved while the Skill is activated.

Dimensions: Maximum 15 cubic meters.

Cost: 1,000 Mana

Duration: 2 minute and 7 seconds

Paladin of Erethra Skill Tree

John's Paladin of Erethra Skills

Penetration (Level 9—Evolved)

Few can face the judgment of a Paladin in direct combat, their ability to bypass even the toughest of defenses a frightening prospect. Reduces Mana Regeneration by 45 permanently.

Effect: Ignore all armor and defensive Skills and spells by 90%. Increases damage done to shields and structural supports by 175%.

Secondary Effect: Damage that is resisted by spells, armor, Skills and Resistances is transferred to an Evolved Skill shield at a ratio of 1 to 1.

Duration: 85 minutes

Aura of Chivalry (Level 1)

A Paladin's very presence can quail weak-hearted enemies and bolster the confidence of allies, whether on the battlefield or in court. The Aura of Chivalry is a double-edged sword however, focusing attention on the Paladin—potentially to their detriment. Increases success rate of Perception checks against Paladin by 10% and reduces stealth and related skills by 10% while active. Reduces Mana Regeneration by 5 Permanently.

Effect: All enemies must make a Willpower check against intimidation against user's Charisma. Failure to pass the check will cow enemies. All allies gain a 50% boost in morale for all Willpower checks and a 10% boost in confidence and probability of succeeding in relevant actions.

Note: Aura may be activated or left-off at will.

Beacon of the Angels (Level 2)

User calls down an atmospheric strike from the heavens, dealing damage over a wide area to all enemies within the beacon. The attack takes time to form, but once activated need not be concentrated upon for completion.

Effect: 1000 Mana Damage done to all enemies, structures and vehicles within the maximum 25-meter column of attack

Mana Cost: 500 Mana

Eyes of Insight (Level 1)

Under the eyes of a Paladin, all untruth and deceptions fall away. Only when the Paladin can see with clarity may he be able to judge effectively. Reduces Mana Regeneration by 5.

Effect: All Skills, Spells and abilities of a lower grade that obfuscate, hinder or deceive the Paladin are reduced in effectiveness. Level of reduction proportionate to degree of difference in grade and Skill Level.

Eye of the Storm (Level 1)

In the middle of the battlefield, the Paladin stands, seeking justice and offering judgment on all enemies. The winds of war will seek to draw both enemies and allies to you, their cruel flurries robbing enemies of their lives and bolstering the health and Mana of allies.

Effect: Eye of the Storm is an area effect buff and taunt. Psychic winds taunt enemies, forcing a Mental Resistance check to avoid attacking user. Enemies also receive 5 points of damage per second while within the influence of the Skill, with damage decreasing from the epicenter of the Skill. Allies receive a 5% increase in Mana and Health regeneration, decrease in effectiveness from Skill center. Eye of the Storm affects an area of 50 meters around the user.

Cost: 500 Mana + 20 Mana per second

Vanguard of the Apocalypse (Level 2)

Where others flee, the Paladin strides forward. Where the brave dare not advance, the Paladin charges. While the world burns, the Paladin still fights. The Paladin with this Skill is the vanguard of any fight, leading the charge against all of Erethra's enemies.

Effect: +45 to all Physical attributes, increases speed by 55% and recovery rates by 35%. This Skill is stackable on top of other attribute and speed boosting Skills or spells.

Cost: 500 Mana + 10 Stamina per second

Society's Web (Level 1)

Where the Eye of Insight provides the Paladin an understanding of the lies and mistruths told, Society's Web shows the Paladin the intricate webs that tie individuals to one another. No alliance, no betrayal, no tangled web of lies will be hidden as each interaction weaves one another closer. While the Skill provides no detailed information, a skilled Paladin can infer much from the Web.

Effect: Upon activation, the Paladin will see all threads that tie each individual to one another and automatically understand the details of each thread when focused upon.

Cost: 400 Mana + 200 Mana per minute

Immovable Object / Unstoppable Force (Level 1)

A Paladin cannot be stopped. A Paladin cannot be moved. A Paladin is a force of the Erethran Empire on the battlefield. This Skill exemplifies this simple concept. Let all who doubt the strength of the Paladin tremble!

Use: User must select to be an Immovable Object or Unstoppable Force. Effect varies depending on choice. Skill combines with Aura of Chivalry to provide a smaller (10% of base effect) bonus to all friendlies within range.

Effect 1 (Immovable Object): Constitution, Health and Damage Resistance (All) increased by 200% of User's current total. All knockback effects are mitigated (including environmental knockback effects).

Effect 2 (Unstoppable Force): Agility, Movement Speed, Momentum and Damage Calculations based off Momentum increased by 200% of User's current total. Damage from other attacks increased by 100%. Only active while user is moving.

Cost: 5 Mana per second

Domain (Level 1)

With chains that bind, and threads that extend from one to another, a Paladin is the center of events. In his Domain, enemies will break and allies will bend knee. Let the enemies of the Empire tremble before a Paladin with his Domain.

Effect 1: All enemy combatants receive -10% attribute decreases, a +10% increase in Mana cost and lose 25 HP per second while within range of the Domain.

Effect 2: All allies receive a +10% increase in health regeneration, a 10% increase in attributes, and a reduction of -10% in Mana cost (semi-stackable).

Range: 10 Meters

Cost: 500 Mana + 5 Mana per Second

Judgment of All (Level 6)

An Emperor might sit in judgment of those that defy them, but a Paladin sits in judgment of all who fall before his gaze. Desire bends and debases itself. Duty shatters under the weight of ever greater burdens. Morality shifts under the winds of circumstance. In the eyes of those he serves, a Paladin's judgment must be impeccable. Under his gaze, those underserving will fall. So long as his honor holds true, judgment will follow.

Effect: Skill inflicts (Erethran Reputation*\$HonSysCal*1.5 = 442) points of on-going Mana damage to all judged unworthy within perception range of user.

Duration: 65 seconds

Cost: 1000 MP

Grand Paladin Skills

Grand Cross   Extra Hands   Burden of the   Defense of the
Worthy   Fallen

Final Judgment   Combined Arms   Bonds of the
People

Grand Cross (Level 2)

The burden of existence weighs heavily on the Paladin. This Skill allows the Paladin to allow another to share in the burden. Under the light of and benediction of the Grand Paladin, under the weight of true understanding wayward children may be brought back to the fold.

Effect: Damage done equals to (Willpower * 2.2) per square meter over radius of (1/10th of Perception^2) meters. Damage may be increased by reducing radius of the Grand Cross. Does additional (Willpower) points of damage per second for 11 seconds.

Cost: 2000 MP

Extra Hands (Level 1)

A Paladin can never be everywhere he needs to be. But with this Skill, the Grand Paladin can certainly be in more places. Mana Regeneration reduced by 5 permanently.

Cost: 5000 Mana per duplicate.

Upkeep cost: 5000 Mana per day per duplicate. Must be paid by original Skill user.

Effect: Creates maximum two duplicates of the user. Duplicates have 90% of all (unboosted) Attributes, gain no effects from Titles and may not equip Soulbound weapons but has access to all (non-purchased)

Skills of user. Each duplicate has their own Mana pool but regenerate at 50% of normal regeneration levels. Mana levels take the place of health points for duplicates.

Original Skill user has a telepathic connection to duplicates at all times and will receive a download of duplicate memories upon their destruction or cessation of upkeep costs.

Note: This Skill cannot be used by duplicates

Junior Administrator Skills

System Edit

A core Skill for System Administrators.

Effect: Make trivial to minor amendments to System processes

Cost: Variable (HP & MP)

Other Class Skills

Frenzy (Level 1)

Effect: When activated, pain is reduced by 80%, damage increased by 30%, stamina regeneration rate increased by 20%. Mana regeneration rate decreased by 10%

Frenzy will not deactivate until all enemies have been slain. User may not retreat while Frenzy is active.

Cleave (Level 2)

Effect: Physical attacks deal 60% more base damage. Effect may be combined with other Class Skills.

Cost: 25 Mana

Elemental Strike (Level 1—Ice)

Effect: Used to imbue a weapon with freezing damage. Adds +5 Base Damage to attacks and a 10% chance of reducing speed by 5% upon contact. Lasts for 30 seconds.

Cost: 50 Mana

Instantaneous Inventory (Maxed)

Allows user to place or remove any System-recognized item from Inventory if space allows. Includes the automatic arrangement of space in the inventory. User must be touching item.

Cost: 5 Mana per item

Shrunken Footsteps (Level 1)

Reduces System presence of user, increasing the chance of the user evading detection of System-assisted sensing Skills and equipment. Also increases cost of information purchased about user. Reduces Mana Regeneration by 5 permanently.

Tech Link (Level 2)

Effect: Tech Link allows user to increase their skill level in using a technological item, increasing input and versatility in usage of said items. Effects vary depending on item. General increase in efficiency of 10%. Mana regeneration rate decreased by 10%

Designated Technological Items: Neural Link, Hodo's Triple Forged Armor

Analyze (Level 2)

Allows user to scan individuals, monsters, and System-registered objects to gather information registered with the System. Detail and level of accuracy of information is dependent on Level and any Skills or Spells in conflict with the ability. Reduces Mana regeneration by 10 permanently.

Harden (Level 2)

This Skill reinforces targeted defenses and actively weakens incoming attacks to reduce their penetrating power. A staple Skill of the Turtle Knights of Kiumma, the Harden Skill has frustrated opponents for millennia.

Effect: Reduces penetrative effects of attacks by 30% on targeted defense.

Cost: 3 Mana per second

Quantum Lock (Level 3)

A staple Skill of the M453-X Mecani-assistants, Quantum Lock blocks stealth attacks and decreases the tactical options of their enemies. While active, the Quantum Lock of the Mecani-assistants excites quantum strings in the affected area for all individuals and Skills.

Effect: All teleportation, portal, and dimensional Skills and Spells are disrupted while Quantum Lock is in effect. Forceable use of Skills and Spells while Skill is in effect will result in (Used Skill Mana Cost * 4) health in damage. Users may pay a variable amount of additional Mana when activating the Skill to decrease effect of Quantum Lock and decrease damage taken.

Requirements: 200 Willpower, 200 Intelligence

Area of Effect: 100 meter radius around user

Cost: 250 + 50 Mana per Minute

Elastic Skin (Level 3)

Elastic Skin is a permanent alteration, allowing the user to receive and absorb a small portion of damage. Damage taken reduced by 7% with 7% of damage absorbed converted to Mana. Mana Regeneration reduced by 15 permanently.

Disengage Safeties (Level 2)

All technological weapons have safeties built in. Users of this Skill recklessly disregard the mandatory safeties, deciding that they know better than the crafters, engineers, and government personnel who built and regulate the production of these technological pieces.

Effects: Increase power output from 2.5-25% depending on the weapon and its level of sophistication. Increase durability losses from use by 25-250%.

Cost: 200 Mana + 25 Mana per minute

Temporary Forced Link (Level 1)

Most Class Skills can't be linked with another's. The instability formed between the mixing of the aura from multiple Mana sources often results in spectacular—and explosive—scenarios. For the 02m8 Symbiotes though, the need to survive within their host bodies and use their Skills has resulted in this unique Skill, allowing the Symbiote to lend their Mana and Skills. (For more persistent effects, see Mana Graft)

Effect: Skill and Skill effects are forcibly combined. Final effect results will vary depending on level of compatibility of Skills.

Cost: 250 Mana + 10 Mana per minute (plus original Skill cost)

Hyperspace Nitro Boost (Level 1)

When you've got to win the race, there's nothing like a hyperspace boost. This Skill links the user with his craft's hyperspace engine, providing a direct boost to its efficiency. Unlike normal speed increases for hyperspace engines, the Nitro Boost is a variable boost and runs a risk of damaging the engine.

Effect: 15% increase in hyperspace engine efficiency + variable % increase in efficiency at 1% per surplus Mana. Each additional 1% over base raises chance of catastrophic engine failure by 0.01%

Cost: 250 Mana + (surplus variable amount; minimum 200 Mana increments) per minute

On the Edge (Level 1)

Shuttle racers live their lives on the edge, cutting corners by feet and dodging monsters by inches. There's only one way to drive a ship with that level of precision, and no matter what those military Pilots tell you, it's with On the Edge.

Effect: +10% boost in ship handling and maneuverability. +10% passive increase in all piloting skills. +1% increase per increment of surplus Mana

Cost: 100 Mana per level + (surplus variable amount; minimum 100 Mana increments) per minute

Fate's Thread (Level 2)

The Akashi'so believe that we are all but weavings in the great thread of life. Connected to one another by the great Weaver, there is not one but multiple threads between us all, woven from our interactions and histories. Fate's Thread is but a Skill expression of this belief. This Skill cannot be dodged but may be blocked. After all, all things are bound together.

Effect: Fate Thread allows the user to bind individuals together by making what is already there apparent. Thread is made physical and may be used to pull, tie and bind.

Duration: 2 minutes

Cost: 60 Mana

Peasant's Fury (Level 1)

No one knows loss more than the powerless. The Downtrodden Peasant has taken the fury of the powerless and made it his own, gifting them the strength to go on so long as they Manage to make others feel the same loss that they did. -5 Mana Regeneration per Second

Effect: User receives a 0.1% regeneration effect of damage dealt for each 1% of health loss.

Spells

Improved Minor Healing (IV)

Effect: Heals 40 Health per casting. Target must be in contact during healing. Cooldown 60 seconds.

Cost: 20 Mana

Improved Mana Missile (IV)

Effect: Creates four missiles out of pure Mana, which can be directed to damage a target. Each dart does 30 damage. Cooldown 10 seconds

Cost: 35 Mana

Enhanced Lightning Strike

Effect: Call forth the power of the gods, casting lightning. Lightning strike may affect additional targets depending on proximity, charge and other conductive materials on-hand. Does 100 points of electrical damage.

Lightning Strike may be continuously channeled to increase damage for 10 additional damage per second.

Cost: 75 Mana.

Continuous cast cost: 5 Mana / second

Lightning Strike may be enhanced by using the Elemental Affinity of Electromagnetic Force. Damage increased by 20% per level of affinity

Greater Regeneration (II)

Effect: Increases natural health regeneration of target by 6%. Only single use of spell effective on a target at a time.

Duration: 10 minutes

Cost: 100 Mana

Firestorm

Effect: Create a firestorm with a radius of 5 meters. Deals 250 points of fire damage to those caught within. Cooldown 60 seconds.

Cost: 200 Mana

Polar Zone

Effect: Create a thirty-meter diameter blizzard that freezes all targets within one. Does 10 points of freezing damage per minute plus reduces effected individuals speed by 5%. Cooldown 60 seconds.

Cost: 200 Mana

Greater Healing (II)

Effect: Heals 100 Health per casting. Target does not require contact during healing. Cooldown 60 seconds per target.

Cost: 75 Mana

Mana Drip (II)

Effect: Increases natural health regeneration of target by 6%. Only single use of spell effective on a target at a time.

Duration: 10 minutes

Cost: 100 Mana

Freezing Blade

Effect: Enchants weapon with a slowing effect. A 5% slowing effect is applied on a successful strike. This effect is cumulative and lasts for 1 minute. Cooldown 3 minutes

Spell Duration: 1 minute.

Cost: 150 Mana

Improved Inferno Strike (II)

A beam of heat raised to the levels of an inferno, able to melt steel and earth on contact! The perfect spell for those looking to do a lot of damage in a short period of time.

Effect: Does 200 Points of Heat Damage

Cost: 150 Mana

Mud Walls

Unlike its more common counterpart Earthen Walls, Mud Walls focus is more on dealing slow, suffocating damage and restricting movement on the battlefield.

Effect: Does 20 Points of Suffocating Damage. -30% Movement Speed

Duration: 2 Minutes

Cost: 75 Mana

Create Water

Pulls water from the elemental plane of water. Water is pure and the highest form of water available. Conjures 1 liter of water. Cooldown: 1 minute

Cost: 50 Mana

Scry

Allows caster to view a location up to 1.7 kilometers away. Range may be extended through use of additional Mana. Caster will be stationary during this period. It is recommended caster focuses on the scry unless caster has a high level of Intelligence and Perception so as to avoid accidents. Scry may be blocked by equivalent or higher tier spells and Skills. Individuals with high perception in region of Scry may be alerted that the Skill is in use. Cooldown: 1 hour.

Cost: 25 Mana per minute.

Scrying Ward

Blocks scrying spells and their equivalent within 5 meters of caster. Higher level spells may not be blocked, but caster may be alerted about scrying attempts. Cooldown: 10 minutes

Cost: 50 Mana per minute

Improved Invisibility

Hides target's System information, aura, scent, and visual appearance. Effectiveness of spell is dependent upon Intelligence of caster and any Skills or Spells in conflict with the target.

Cost: 100 + 50 Mana per minute

Improved Mana Cage

While physically weaker than other elemental-based capture spells, Mana Cage has the advantage of being able to restrict all creatures, including semi-solid Spirits, conjured elementals, shadow beasts, and Skill users. Cooldown: 1 minute

Cost: 200 Mana + 75 Mana per minute

Improved Flight

(Fly birdie, fly!—Ali) This spell allows the user to defy gravity, using controlled bursts of Mana to combat gravity and allow the user to fly in even the most challenging of situations. The improved version of this spell allows flight even in zero gravity situations and a higher level of maneuverability. Cooldown: 1 minute

Cost: 250 Mana + 100 Mana per minute

Equipment

Hod's Triple Fused Armor

The product of multiple workings by the Master Blacksmith and Crafter Hodiliphious 'Hod' Yalding, the Triple Fused Armor was hand-forged from rare, System-generated material, hand refined and reworked trice over with multiple patented and rare alloys and materials. The final product is considered barely passable by Hod—though it would make a lesser craftsman cry.

Core: Class I Hallow Physics Mana Engine

CPU: Class B Wote Core CPU

Armor Rating: Tier I (Enhanced)

Hard Points: 9 (6 Used—Jungian Flight System, Talpidae Abyssal Horns, Luione Hard Light Projectors, Diarus Poison Stingers, Ares Type I Shield Generator, Greater Troll Cell Injectors)

Soft Points 4 (3 Used—Neural Link, Ynir HUD Imaging, Airmed Body Monitor)

Battery Capacity: 380/380

Active Skills: Abyssal Chains, Mirror Shade, Poison Grip

Attribute Bonuses: +93 Strength, +78 Agility, +51 Constitution, +44 Perception, +287 Stamina and Health Regeneration per minute

Note: Hod's Triple Fused Armor is currently under limited warranty. Armor may be teleported to Hod's workshop for repairs once a week. All cost of repairs will be deducted from user's account.

Skills in Hod's Armor:

Abyssal Chains

Calling upon the material connection to the shadow plane, chains from the abyss erupt, binding a target in place.

Effect: Target is bound by shadow chains. Chains deal 10 points of damage per second. To break free, target must win a contested Strength test. Abyssal Chains have a Strength of 120.

Uses: 3/3

Recharge rate: 1 per hour

Mirror Shade

Mirror Shade creates a semi-solid doppelganger using hard light technology and Mana.

Effect: Mirror Shade create a semi-solid doppelganger of the user for a period of ten minutes. Maximum range of doppelganger from user is fifty meters. Doppelganger has 18% physical fidelity.

Use: 1/1

Recharge Rate: 1 per 4 hours

Silversmith Jeupa VII Anti-Personnel Cannon (Modified & Upgraded)

This quad-barrelled anti-personnel weapon has been handcrafted by Advanced Weaponsmiths to provide the highest integration possible for an energy weapon. This particular weapon has been modified to include additional range-finding and sighting options and upgraded to increase short-term damage output at the cost of long-term durability. Barrels may be fired individually or linked.

Base Damage: 787 per barrel

Battery Capacity: 4 per barrel (16 total)

Recharge Rate: 0.25 per hour per GMU

Ares Platinum Class Tier II Armored Jumpsuit

Ares's signature Platinum Class line of armored daily wear combines the company's latest technological advancement in nanotech fiber design and the pinnacle work of an Advanced Craftsman's Skill to provide unrivalled protection for the discerning Adventurer.

Effect: +218 Defense, +14% Resistance to Kinetic and Energy Attacks. +19% Resistance against Temperature changes. Self-Cleanse, Self-Mend, Autofit Enchantments also included.

Silversmith Mark VIII Beam Pistol (Upgradeable)

Base Damage: 88

Battery Capacity: 13/13

Recharge Rate: 3 per hour per GMU

Tier IV Neural Link

Neural link may support up to 5 connections.

Current connections: Hod's Triple Fused Armor

Software Installed: Rich'lki Firewall Class IV, Omnitron III Class IV Controller

Ferlix Type I Twinned-Beam Rifle (Modified)

Base Damage: 39

Battery Capacity: 41/41

Recharge rate: 1 per hour per GMU

Tier II Sword (Soulbound Personal Weapon of an Erethran Honor Guard)

Base Damage: 397

Durability: N/A (Personal Weapon)

Special Abilities: +20 Mana Damage, Blade Strike

Kryl Ring of Regeneration

Often used as betrothal bands, Kyrl rings are highly sought after and must be ordered months in advance.

Health Regeneration: +30

Stamina Regeneration: +15

Mana Regeneration: +5

Tier III Bracer of Mana Storage

A custom work by an unknown maker, this bracer acts a storage battery for personal Mana. Useful for Mages and other Classes that rely on Mana. Mana storage ratio is 50 to 1.

Mana Capacity: 350/350

Fey-steel Dagger

Fey-steel is not actual steel but an unknown alloy. Normally reserved only for the Sidhe nobility, a small—by Galactic standards—amount of Fey-steel is released for sale each year. Fey-steel takes enchantments extremely well.

Base Damage: 28

Durability: 110/100

Special Abilities: None

Enchanted, Reinforced Toothy Throwing Knives (5)

First handcrafted from the rare drop of a Level 140 Awakened Beast by the Redeemer of the Dead, John Lee, these knives have been further processed by the Master Craftsmen I-24-988L and reinforced with orichalcum and fey-steel. The final blades have been further enchanted with Mana and piercing damage as well as a return enchantment.

Base Damage: 238

Enchantments: Return, Mana Blade (+28 Damage), Pierce (-7% defense)

Brumwell Necklace of Shadow Intent

The Brumwell necklace of shadow intent is the hallmark item of the Brumwell Clan. Enchanted by a Master Crafter, this necklace layers shadowy intents over your actions, ensuring that information about your actions is more difficult to ascertain. Ownership of such an item is both a necessity and a mark of prestige among settlement owners and other individuals of power.

Effect: Persistent effect of Shadow Intent (Level 4) results in significantly increased cost of purchasing information from the System about wearer. Effect is persistent for all actions taken while necklace is worn.

Ring of Greater Shielding

Creates a greater shield that will absorb approximately 1000 points of damage. This shield will ignore all damage that does not exceed its threshold amount of 50 points of damage while still functioning.

Max Duration: 7 Minutes

Charges: 1

Simalax Hover Boots (Tier II)

A combination of hand-crafted materials and mass-produced components, the Simalax Hover Boots are the journeyman work of Magi-Technician Lok of Irvina. Enchantments and technology mesh together in the Simalax Hover Boots, offering its wearer the ability to tread on air briefly and defy gravity and sense.

Effects: User reduces gravitational effects by 0.218 SIG. User may, on activation, hover and skate during normal and mildly turbulent atmospheric conditions. User may also use the Simalax Hover Boots to triple jump in the air, engaging the anti-gravity and hover aspects at the same time.

Duration: 1.98 SI Hours.

F'Merc Nanoswarm Mana Grenades (Tier II)

The F'Merc Nanoswarm Grenades are guaranteed to disrupt the collection of Mana in a battlefield, reducing Mana Regeneration rates for those caught in the swarm. Recommended by the I'um military, the Torra Special Forces and the No.1 Most Popular Mana Grenade as voted by the public on Boom, Boom, Boom! Magazine.

Effect: Reduces Mana Regeneration rates and spell formation in affected area by 37% ((higher effects in enclosed areas)

Radius: 10m x 10m

Daghtree's Legendary Ring of Deception (Tier I)

A musician, poet and artist, Daghtree's fame rose not from his sub-standard works of 'art' but his array of seduction Skills from his Heartthrob Artist Class. Due to his increasing infamy, Daghtree commissioned this Legendary ring to change his appearance and continue Leveling. In the end, it is rumored that his indiscretions caught up with the infamous artist and he disappeared from Galactic sources in GCD 9,275

Effect: Creates a powerful disguise that covers the wearer. The ring comes with six pre-loaded disguises and additional disguises may be added through expansion of charges

Duration: 1 day per charge

Charges: 3

Recharge via ambient Mana: 1 charge per Galactic Standard Unit per week

F'Merc Ghostlight Mana Dispersal Grenades (Tier I)

The F'Merc Ghostlight Mana Dispersal Grenades not only disperse Mana in the battlefield, the Ghostlight Dispersal Grenades degrade all Mana Skills and spells within its field of effectiveness. Used by Krolash the Destroyer, the Erethran Champion Isma (prior version) and Anblanca Special Forces. Five times Winner of the Most Annoying Utility Item on the Battlefield.

Effect: Reduces Mana Regeneration rates, Skill and spell formation use in affected area by 67% ((higher effects in enclosed areas)

Radius: 15m³

Evernight Darkness Orbs

When the world goes light, the Evernight Darkness Orbs will bring back blessed darkness. If you need darkness, you need Evernight!

Effect: Removes al visible light and mute infrared and ultraviolet wavelengths by 30%

Radius: 50m³

Seven Heavenly Spire Wards

Quick to set-up, the Seven Heavenly Spire Wards were crafted by the Thrice Loved Bachelor's Temple of the Sinking Domain as their main export. Using the total prayer and faith of the temple, they produce a set of wards every month.

Effect: Set's up a 30' by 30' defensive ward; protects against both magical and technological attacks and entry

Fumikara Mobile Teleport Circles

These one-off use mobile teleport circles allow connection to existing and open teleport networks.

Effect: Connect to open teleport networks within a 5,000 kim radius of the teleport circles. Allows teleportation of individuals to the networked teleport centers

PoenJoe Goleminised-Mana Generator Mark 18

The latest Mana Generator by the infamous PoenJoe, the Mark 18 is guaranteed* to not blow up on you in optimal conditions. This partially sentient Mana Generator can extract up to 98% of a Mana Crystal's saved energy in 0.003 seconds. Currently loaded in an Adult Kirin Mana Core.

Effect: It's a Power Generator. Guaranteed to provide up to $98 \times 10^{*}99$ Standard Galactic Mana Units

*Not actually guaranteed. In fact, we're 100% certain that containment failure will occur.

Payload (Level 2) (Embedded in Anklet of Dispersed Damage)

Sometimes, you need to get your Skills inside a location. Payload allows you to imbue an individual or item with a Skill at a reduced strength.

Effect: 71% effectiveness of Skill imbued.

Secondary Effect: Skill may be now triggered on a timed basis (max 2:07 minutes)

Uses: 22

Recharge: 10.7 charges per day in SGE

Made in the USA
Las Vegas, NV
18 December 2021

38555475R00267